DEADLY DAY TRADING

Andres Kabel

DEADLY DAY TRADING

ISBN 978-0-6483068-3-2

PROLOGUE

There's no such thing as a bad trading day, Irene Skews, day trader magnifico, reminded herself, her hand poised over the keyboard, index finger lifted. Click! Her copious bangles pealed against the desk. Her order—the sale of a thousand Solution 6 shares at $18.10—vanished, to be rewarded with the computerized chime of a trade consummated.

Two sleeps until Christmas, in the year of 1999, and Irene wished only that the day after tomorrow could be a trading day. For here amongst the buccaneers of Tech Power Trading, she counted herself happy.

In front of her, overlapping windows on the screen scrolled with share prices, order queues, market indices, and one-line news items—endless hieroglyphics in reds and greens and whites. She inhaled the aroma of the trading room: coffee, McDonald's fries, sweat, the sour smell she called adrenaline rather than fear. The public address system cooed: "All Ords 3,121, down 20." She heard responding groans, and a choked obscenity.

She blew a kiss into the air and wheeled her office chair back from the screen to survey the two rows of shoulder-height cubicles, bookmarked by huge television screens at both ends.

A prickle traversed the back of her neck.

Mostly the traders were doing what they paid TPT for, feverishly buying and selling shares. But by the coffee table halfway down the aisle, a handful of fellow traders chatted. Len Maguire stroked his beard. The sweetie-pie Singaporean, Lawrence Lim, jiggled a teabag. Gil Oldfield had his handsome head lowered. What was awry?

Perhaps her qualms were merely the inevitable sense of dislocation upon returning to the physical world. Immersed chaos was Irene's way, absorption in the never-ending flow of stock market data, newspapers, emails, newsletters, and loudspeaker announcements. She lived and breathed that babble of information.

Last night Irene had spent hours on HotCopper, the online chat site for like-minded investment enthusiasts. She had devoured the stunning news of opportunity: Nasdaq, American home to the booming dot-coms, had risen—again!—26 points to 3,937. But in the morning, as she digested the ten o'clock opening trades on the Australian Stock Exchange, instead of rushing into the stocks hyped overnight, she had paid heed to the info babble.

Over the first half-hour of trading, she'd concentrated on exiting every one of her positions. Pat-on-the-back time, she now breathed, for the All Ords index had tumbled, all arrows down, all colors red.

Tech Power Trading's twig of a receptionist was slanting the banks of venetian blinds facing the sunshine pouring in from Collins Street.

Irene said, "You're a wonder, dear." She liked Robyn, even if the poor girl looked permanently stunned. "Glare simply has to be a trader's worst enemy."

Robyn gave a hesitant smile.

Irene couldn't shake her edginess. She rose, straightened her jacket, and made for the coffee area.

"...that is the key, I believe." Lawrence Lim's soft accented English was barely audible above the noise. "I do believe watching the market can help. Signs of sustained strength or weakness, that's what I look for."

Gil Oldfield wasn't paying attention. His tanned face, with its customary early shadow, was directed at a television interview. Formerly a "real" share trading professional, Gil sneered at TPT's day traders, Irene especially.

Something flickered at the edge of Irene's mind.

"Dears, wasn't that a ride and a half this morning?" she said. "I knew it, simply knew it, in the very first minute. So what if Nasdaq had a wonderful day, so what? Where's the good news in Australia, that's what I want to know."

A brusque bark halted her words and she ceased stirring sugar into her tea. She looked up at the inflamed cheeks of Len Maguire. Santa, the traders called him, because of his large gut and bushy gingery-white beard.

Len, here at the coffee spot...

There it was.

Len never, *never ever*, left his screen in the first two hours. His system, he'd once told her while wiping greasy fingers on his beard, that's when the volatility peaks.

Today Len wore a jacket, a bulky leather affair, over new jeans and his trademark Harley Davidson T-shirt. A heavy jacket, on a mild day forecast at twenty-three degrees…

Irene gasped.

Len jerked and looked directly at her. Behind smeared glasses his eyes blazed. A weird beatific smile lit his face. Then his hands sprouted squat metal extensions.

"Listen up!" Len roared.

Lawrence stumbled back into Gil. Heads appeared over cubicles. Irene lurched away from the guns.

"You call this a tough trading day," bellowed Len. "Invest in some of this, you bastards!"

Before Irene could react, Len shoved both guns into Lawrence's cheeks. Two retorts shattered the hush. Lawrence's head exploded in a spray of red.

Irene wailed, stumbled backward. Screams whizzed around her head. A man ran past, only to cry out and fall at another shot.

Len screamed, "This is for the shorts."

Gil had become pinned under Lawrence's body and was clawing at the bloodied weight.

To Irene's horror, Len chuckled. "Here's to the bloody pro…fessionals."

He shouted something else, aimed, and fired once, then again. Gil's twitching ceased.

"No," moaned Irene.

All she could think of was home, her cats. Down the aisle, toward the rear of the office, between abandoned screens still scrolling in kaleidoscopic colors, she tottered backward on high heels, those darned rickety heels.

Her nostrils stung with an acrid reek. Len was shooting

steadily at traders rushing for the entrance. Bodies lay in the aisle like discarded mannequins.

Her ankle turned on a high heel. She shook the shoe off. The screams had ceased, replaced by Len's guttural raves and victims' wet moans.

She turned and ran, a limping gait with one shoe missing. Under the desk of the last cubicle, she glimpsed a face. Then she was past the television screen, around the corner, blubbering.

"Irene!"

Just fifty meters away, at the door of the training room, moonfaced Gus Youde signaled frantically.

"Run!" Gus shouted.

Irene staggered toward him. She risked a look over a shoulder.

Len! He'd followed, was peering into the final cubicle. Shrill cackling filled her ears. A shot rang out.

Irene lost her footing and plummeted onto carpet. Pain stabbed an elbow. She scrambled on hands and knees over the prickly surface toward manic voices.

A quick backward glance froze her. Len had emerged from the cubicle. He was muttering and his beard was spotted with blood. He'd discarded one gun, now he raised the other. The mad eyes caught hers.

Len began to run full tilt, every stride bringing him closer.

Terror lent Irene wings. Somehow she was in the training room and Gus was piling tables against the door. Others were there, Robyn among them, but Irene barely noticed. She cowered in a corner, listening to her jewelry chime in time with her shakes.

She heard shots, Len's roar. Then later, much later it seemed, a universe away, sirens wailed.

CHAPTER 1

On the threshold of Draconi's Bar & Grill, Peter Gentle paused to bask. His scalp tingled, heated from the daily constitutional, north this morning, almost as far as the Zoo.

The soothing semi-light, the aromas of java and garlic and something human, the clatter of cutlery, the scrape of wooden chairs on wooden floor, best of all the enfolding hubbub of voices…

He sighed.

A gruff voice more familiar than his father's interrupted his reverie. "I should have recorded that."

The voice belonged to Hector Lowe, Draconi's owner and manager and seemingly round-the-clock maître d'. Peter smiled at the walrus face a foot below his eyes.

"Come on, Hec. No way."

"Loud enough to bottle."

Hector shooed Peter through the maze of people squeezed about tiny round tables, to the imposing central bar fronting the kitchen.

Peter blinked to clear the cobwebs around his cortex. Eight

o'clock on a Wednesday morning was decidedly suboptimal, especially after a night shortened by a million gnawing tasks. Two AM had found him emailing off a progress report on the Yarra Building Society fraud job. Then his current online game of Diplomacy had snared his mind. An hour later he'd barely had the energy to wheel his chair back from the computer and shuffle to bed. As always these days, sleep had come instantly.

Unlike Mick's sleep, Peter thought. Last week, during one of their annoyingly rare get-togethers, Mick, his so-called partner in Tusk & Gentle, Private Investigators, had confided over a wine that he suffered from insomnia. Chronically. Had done so ever since his retrenchment eighteen months ago. Who would have thought? The hulk always seemed coiled with energy.

Peter grabbed an Australian Financial Review from the rack and perched on a stool. He spied bacon and eggs sizzling over flames.

"One of those, Hec. Make it a big one."

"Not long to go, is there? A month?" Hector lifted one foot onto the rail around the foot of the bar. "Until your license comes through."

"Something like that."

Gloom gripped Peter's forehead. To think that "the world's brainiest brain," as Mick had branded him, would end up urinating into soft drink cans during all-night surveillance… Why not admit everything is going sour, he thought. Life's a crock. Who to talk to? Mick's Baltic face surfaced in his mind. Mick might understand.

"I've got something that might interest you." Hector gestured across the bar to the barista, employing sign language that Peter hoped would yield him a coffee. "Are you up on computer security?"

"Of course," Peter lied.

His coffee arrived with a clatter and he dunked his nose in the long black's rich steam. So I need your crumbs now, he thought. Not that he blamed Hec. All his friends were similarly solicitous, as if such a lowbrow occupation spurred images from World Vision. In fact, right now he was more than fully occupied, racking up poorly paid hours on this surveillance assignment for an insurance agent he knew from his Rock Mutual days. The salesman, married but besotted with a twenty-year-old Crown Casino employee, was being driven mad by the suspicion that the buxom croupier slept around. And via Harvey Jopling, Draconi's other near-permanent patron, a half-interesting fraud job had arrived, something else to squeeze in on the eighth day of the week.

"Do you know Jim Van Kressel?" Hector asked.

Peter's shrug was a twitch.

"Jim popped in this morning." Hector's dolorous eyes were intense. "Carrying the weight of the world on his shoulders. I mentioned you. He owns and runs Tech Power Trading, that share trading place up Collins, you know, the one—"

"The massacre!" Peter's eyes widened. "I knew I'd heard the name. Jesus. Surely the place closed down?"

Who could forget the slaughter the papers had tagged "the Share Spree," the "Massacre On Collins"? On the blue-blood finance street of Melbourne, just before Christmas…

Peter suffered a brief shiver. Violence troubled him, and even now, four months after the man—what was his name?—ran amok, Peter remembered that day. He had exited 120 Collins, the tower in which Harvey Jopling worked, to confront police sirens and swirling chaos. The very thought of carnage in a financial institution, nine dead… as someone in the Skulk Club had said, this was only meant to happen in America.

Hector scooped up Peter's empty cup. "If you knew Jim, you'd understand why he's persevered. Anyway—"

"Hacking?" Despite all logic, a cog engaged in Peter's head.

"Just let me finish, m'boy. Apparently there's been a possible hacking incident at the firm and Jim can't tolerate any publicity. He's a good man, Peter."

Aren't they all? Peter began to drum fingers on the polished bar, one of those habits that lately seemed to get on his girlfriend Mandy's nerves. "Perhaps I'll ring him."

"That's the spirit." Hector grabbed Peter's napkin and scribbled a number from recall. "Comb your hair before you go."

A retort faded from Peter's lips. Hector rushed off. Peter stood and leaned sideways to catch his reflection in a gap in the bottles blocking the bar's mirror. Jesus, Hec was right. The lick of black hair across his forehead rose like a rooster's comb. Disgusted, he sat down to tug the locks into a semblance of order.

He couldn't help recalling how deep in their sockets the eyes in the mirror had been.

Peter gazed at the power breakfast groups around the cramped tables, the late commuters at the window benches. The cognoscenti had scoffed five years ago when the freshly retired judge bought the venerable Block Arcade and then gutted four of the ground floor cafes and shops to create his dream. But Peter had fallen in love with Draconi's the moment he set foot in it, and now came daily, if not more often. He'd even taken a tiny office in the warren of high-ceilinged rooms upstairs. And Draconi's was where, together with Harvey, he ran the Skulk Club.

His steaming dish of bacon, eggs, and field mushrooms arrived. Attacking it, he mused about taking on a hacking investigation. How interesting, he thought, and what's more, just what the doctor ordered—a corporate job with a corporate price tag.

But wouldn't it be an illogical act, lunacy really, to take on such unfamiliar work?

Not that he was wholly ignorant about hackers. Two of the Skulk Club members—the Skulkers as they called themselves— worked in the computer industry, and at recent meetings Peter had been drawn into heated debates about security on the Internet, about law and order versus social control.

Peter finished his breakfast, clenched his teeth. Hang the logic.

He found the phone number on the egg-smeared napkin and rang Tech Power Trading. It took a mere minute for a low female voice to arrange a ten o'clock meeting with Jim Van Kressel. Only afterward did Peter realize the implication. He grimaced and phoned Mandy.

After he begged off from their arranged lunch, Mandy's husky voice couldn't disguise her irritation. "So when, Peter, when?"

Peter envisaged her long fingers cupping her bony jaw. "Tomorrow?"

Her voice softened. "Okay. Look after yourself."

On the way out, Peter ignored Hector's raised shaggy

eyebrows. His shoes clicked across the intricate mosaic tiles of Block Arcade.

After an hour in the office, he ventured into Collins Street. Though the morning fog had lifted, the sky remained cloud-locked. On a slow tram up the hill, he worked on his pitch: Peter Gentle, hacker-investigator extraordinaire.

They'd taught him the value of a pitch in his years at consultants Thompson White. Jesus, he thought, it's coming up, the two-year anniversary of my sacking. Next Monday, the 17th of April in this new millennium year.

The top end of Collins Street, presided over by the stately pillars of the Treasury Building, was as familiar to Peter as his childhood home in Box Hill. After all, he'd slaved for five years in 101 Collins, just back over Exhibition Street. Harvey and Mandy worked at 120 Collins and Peter's apartment was mere blocks away. Once dubbed Melbourne's "Paris end," it now had the air of an elegant woman hovering on the edge of neglect.

The warm sun flared through a gap in the clouds just as Peter alighted at Spring Street. He walked under the stirring leaves of the plane trees, back to the construction of metal and glass that housed Tech Power Trading. He shaded his eyes to peer at the firm's name on a building-wide banner fluttering under the second-floor windows. 28 Collins Street had to be the ugliest building in the precinct. External air conditioners, grafted on willy-nilly, gave it the appearance of a slum apartment block. The gaudy presence of McDonald's at street level didn't help, nor did the contrast with its neighbors—stately stone buildings bearing names directly from the gold boom of the 1850s.

He stood rooted. On that horrific December day, he'd seen

ambulances arrive, body bags wheeled out. Up there is where it happened, Peter thought. Jesus, Jesus, Jesus.

"Wimp," he said.

A woman wielding a bulky mop watched him from the McDonald's entranceway. She pointed upwards and crossed herself. He shuddered and strode into the narrow lobby.

The newspaper accounts had made much of the fact that the TPT office had only one entrance for the entire floor, with the fire escape outside this entrance. Only the killer's waywardness—Maguire, Len Maguire, that was his name—had prevented many more traders being trapped. On the second floor, Peter was nonplussed to find the layout unchanged, a single solid door behind a plush reception area. A smooth-skinned receptionist, still in her teens, ushered him through the door.

Peter had been in stockbrokers' trading rooms a number of times, but TPT had a vastly different ambience. He followed the receptionist down an aisle between multicolored cubicles occupied by amateur traders, if that's what they were. No one gave him a glance. Oversize TV screens at either end of the aisle broadcast a business channel. The traders' computer screens were full-page size and tiled with windows of rolling text and numbers. The day traders he could see were a mixed lot, only one wearing a suit, some downright scruffy. The hall-sized area stank of takeaway food and cheap coffee. All resoundingly ordinary, except for yellow cardboard models of mini-skips and garden bins hanging from the ceiling.

What had Peter expected? Bloodstains on the carpet and bullet holes in the walls? Ludicrous, he chided himself. But the carpet did look pristine, and the maroons and deep greens coloring the walls and partitions seemed fresh. The room at the head of the aisle had a similar color scheme.

"Hold my calls, Robyn."

Jim Van Kressel was also a surprise packet, no taller than Hector and portly, bordering on fat. A red-and-gray cravat festooned his tailored shirt. Wavy black hair was rendered distinctive by a band of silver. Peter's nostrils filled with the tart scent of aftershave.

"Come in, come in." A pudgy hand shook Peter's. The CEO gestured at a small round table by the window. "Squeeze in."

An unexpectedly intriguing facet of being a private investigator was the need to analyze and categorize human beings. Sometimes Peter wondered if he'd even noticed people in his previous thirty-four years. Offices, for example, revealed so much.

Van Kressel's office was packed to the gills with tall filing cabinets, a wall of shelves holding reports and folders, and a dark wooden desk a quantum neater than Peter's work and home desks. A stainless steel affair on wheels housed one computer, another sat on the desk. The rear wall was covered from ceiling to floor with ad campaigns, tombstones commemorating acquisitions and financings, and framed photos of Van Kressel with politicians and other luminaries. Proud, obsessive, and ultra-organized, Peter thought.

Peter said, "Mr. Van Kressel—"

"Call me Jim. And let's not muck about." Dimples, carved out of rosy red cheeks, dominated Jim's oval face. "There's not enough hours in the day right now, so we'll skip the prelims. I've never hired a snoop before. Wasn't even on my mind when Hec suggested it. But any bad PR now will end up slapped on the front page, and I need that like a hole in the head."

Peter glanced out the window. Not much to see, tree branches, the greenery-lined driveway to the Hotel Sofitel. It occurred to him that he'd never been senior enough to have a direct view of Collins Street.

Jim, referring to his pad, said, "Let's see if I can wrap up a life, you can blame Hec if I balls it up. Peter Gentle, mid-thirties. Son of a retired policeman, Assistant Commissioner in fact. One of those mathematician types, an actuary, worked for a life insurer, then a consulting firm. Packaged off a couple of years back. A private eye for one year, specializing in corporates, fraud and the like. Hec said you were in the thick of that investment company scandal last year." His smile was an easy action that crinkled the direct brown eyes. "How am I doing, Pete?"

Peter hated being called Pete. "Spot on, Mr. ...Jim."

"So tell me, Pete. How can you help me with my little hacking problem?"

Peter hesitated, consulted his mantra. Data, analysis, conclusions—his principles, principles suitable for any project. Maybe even for life itself, he frequently joked to himself, although the older he became, the less a joke it seemed. Quickly he stepped through the logic.

Data: after he and Mick stumbled upon a high-profile murder case a year ago, Peter had had the bright idea to launch a new career as a corporate investigator. The law required him to apprentice under a licensed investigator for a year. Mick, because of his police service, had wrangled an immediate license, and in theory was Peter's mentor. But Mick's wife, Dana, inexplicably refused to let him near the job, and the eleven months since had been a day-to-day struggle. Instead of garnering a clientele of companies seeking someone bright and trustworthy to peer into murky cracks, all Peter had managed was peripheral work from dodgy small-fry corporates who haggled over peanut-sized invoices. Plus brain-dead, bottom-trawling surveillance or missing person's work. And strive as he had, the money was running out.

Analysis: unless he cracked a few jobs at the top end of town, he was history. But jobs in corporate Melbourne don't come without referrals. Catch-22.

Conclusion: Jim Van Kressel was a godsend.

"Look, I have to be straight." Peter blinked with surprise to hear himself jettison the pitch. Say a prayer for me, Mick, he thought. "I'm no hacking guru."

Jim leaned back, arms folded on his potbelly. "That bullshitter Hec."

"I can get techo help. What I do bring to the table is a unique ability to get to the heart of it all quickly. I work with logic, Jim. I gather facts, analyze them, and come up with conclusions. You'd be surprised how often I get it right."

"Hec said you're a polymath."

He did? "Well, as you'd know in your business, geeks rule now. But me, I solve real-life problems."

"What's the last movie you saw?"

In the last year Peter had pitched for over fifty mandates, but none had resembled this interview. "Why?"

"Call it my theory."

Peter thanked his lucky stars Mandy had dragged him to a

cinema at Easter. "*American Beauty*. Wasn't Spacey brilliant?"

Jim nodded without indicating if *American Beauty* was a plus or not.

Peter held his breath. The voice of logic whispered that now was the time to ask questions, but he quelled it.

After what seemed like minutes, Jim heaved his frame up from his chair. His chest jiggled. He slapped Peter on an arm.

"You've sold me, Pete." Jim pulled his chair around the table, close to Peter, and sat down again. "Here's the brief. Time to take notes."

Peter felt a surge of joy. "No need." He tapped the side of his head. "It all goes in here."

A chuckle. "Fair enough. Now listen up. What we do here at TPT is give the ordinary man or woman a leg-up to compete with the pros in buying and selling shares. It looks complex out there on the floor, but it's not." Jim spoke rapidly. This was his pitch. "For a fee and a tiny commission per trade, we hook our day traders up with systems as fast, well-informed, and professional as any stockbroker in town. They pay by the hour or by the month. Nearly all our fifty seats are taken up by monthlies. Our punters arrive in the morning, trade like crazy, go home. That's it, period."

Jim drew small squares on his pad and linked them with arcs to a larger square he labeled "TPT network."

"Our computer system is a self-contained network," he said. "I've spent a fortune bulletproofing it. All traffic to and from the outside world is via the network."

"Bulletproofing?"

The plump face darkened for an instant. "God, what am I

saying? Now here's the rub. Quite deliberately, I haven't given our traders any home access to the network. You want to trade at home, hop onto CommSec or E-Trade. I force our hotshots to come into the office, that's the entire point. At home all they get is notification emails from us, most of them system-generated portfolio summaries and the like."

Peter was imagining informing the Skulkers of this juicy catch. A sudden blaring over the speakerphone made him start. He recognized Robyn the receptionist. "Jim?"

Crimson flared on Jim's cheeks. "What?"

"Alison. Again."

The fervor sagged from Jim's face. "God save me. Tell her I'm out."

The phone fell silent. Who was Alison? Up close Peter could see purple filaments down the sides of Jim's nose. Alcohol?

Jim drew a circle at the edge of the page, labeled it "Crazy Oleg."

"Crazy Oleg came to me yesterday arvo. He's our top day trader, you might have seen him on *60 Minutes*, cleared half a mil last year. A real character but very important to us. Charismatic, as you'll see. Oleg complained about emails he's been getting from us, from a TPT researcher, name of Kurt Diamond. Oleg tried a couple of his stock picks, lost some money, then emailed him to piss off. Very direct, is our Oleg."

The door opened to admit a woman with brown curly hair, an ultra-slim laptop nestled under an arm. She carried her slender frame with assured erectness. She looked familiar.

Behind wide spectacles, blue eyes narrowed at the sight of Peter. "Sorry, Jim. I didn't know you had company."

Jim's smile contained wattage sufficient to light a room. "No, no, I wanted you to meet Pete. Peter Gentle, our chairperson, Finola Vines."

Peter cursed himself for not having conducted background research. Of course, he thought, the E-com Queen, as one newspaper wag had dubbed her. Peter had even seen her speak once, at some lunch Harvey had invited him to. Every movement needs its proselytizers, and Finola was one of the pundits feeding the dot-com sharemarket boom.

"My pleasure." Finola's handshake and face said otherwise. She was smartly dressed in a white jacket and gray pants, and Peter tagged her as late forties. The stony reception brought him down from the clouds. I can walk out now, he thought, only morons gamble like this.

He said, "Jim's asked me to help out."

Finola's voice was flat. "Help out."

Jim said, "That problem with Oleg. Pete's a private eye."

"Really?" Finola leaned against the door, arms crossed over the laptop, foot tapping. Her fine-boned face, neither plain nor pretty, possessed the restless energy Peter had come to recognize in fellow workaholics.

Jim grinned. "Don't be so conservative, Fi." He turned to Peter. "Fi is the reason I'm here at all. But the grubbiness of business still throws her."

Peter decided to push ahead. "When did these emails start?"

"A week ago. We're only talking a handful of them. But Oleg is grumpy and wants action against Kurt Diamond."

"What does this have to do with hacking?"

Jim's eyes flicked to the figure at the door. He leaned across the table to seize Peter's arm. "We don't employ anyone by that name. The emails are fake."

"Fake?" The familiar tug of fascination snaked through Peter's bowels.

"This Kurt Diamond mongrel. Find him. Or her."

Peter risked a look at Finola. Her eyes were slits. Now wasn't the time to discuss contracts and minimum fees.

He rose. Wait till Harvey and the Skulkers hear of this, he thought. "Leave it to me, Jim."

Jim stood to extend a hand. "Urgent, Pete. Nail the bastard."

CHAPTER 2

The neglected vegetable patch, that's what decided him.

Mick Tusk switched off his rust bucket's engine, cutting off Paul Rodgers in the middle of a belter from *Electric*, the new album. Hard to believe, the singer of "All Right Now" in pristine voice at bald-headed fifty.

Gil Oldfield lived in the posh section of Tecoma, near the southeast corner of the Dandenong Ranges National Park. Three minutes' drive from Tusk's house in Belgrave, but worlds away in all aspects.

Ditto Oldfield himself. These days Tusk often saw him outside Belgrave Primary, dropping off or picking up six-year-old Katie, in the same class as Yolanda Tusk. These days Oldfield shied away from contact. No conversationalist himself, that suited Tusk just fine—until recently.

They'd first run into each other at school events last year. Toward the end of the 1999 winter, Olivia Oldfield, whom Dana had befriended, had invited the Tusks home for dinner. Such a huge cream brick place, pool and industrial-sized barbeque out back. The four of them ate pumpkin risotto and drank expensive red. Though Tusk had recently met up again with geeky Gentle, he hadn't yet been converted from beer to wine, so he drank little.

When the women had headed off to chat in the kitchen, Tusk had wondered what the hell he could say to the intense yuppie. Oldfield wore a white cotton shirt over black pants. He had distinctive looks, short wavy hair greased back, a hawkish face shaved so close the skin almost sparkled. Uncharitably, Tusk noted how readily the face would age, turning fleshy and accentuating acne scars.

Oldfield crapped on about shares. He spoke in lightning spurts, waving his hands, calling Tusk "pal" every second sentence. Tusk tuned out. The host must have noticed, for he took Tusk into his study, a wallpapered room decked out with shelves and computers and, of more interest, top-line hi-fi gear next to a cabinet of CDs. Typical rich wanker, the CD jewel cases looked untouched, not scuffed like Tusk's.

Oldfield put on a chugging song overlaid by a deep voice, vaguely familiar.

"Eddie Vedder." The banker's head oscillated fast, taking Tusk back to childhood memories of the Noddy books. "Pearl Jam, pal. Awesome, isn't it?"

Awesome indeed. Tusk's heart thawed. Never mind that the gap between them—generational, socioeconomic, philosophical—was a gulf, the man rocked.

Tusk's contribution to the night, after spotting the preponderance of '90s metal in Oldfield's collection, was to recommend Black Sabbath's *Paranoid*, the album that kicked off the whole heavy metal thing. "Check out the source, Gil. Sounds a bit dated but feel the power."

The next couple of times they met, they exchanged music views. Tusk began to collect Pearl Jam. Then Christmas came and went.

Silence from the vast house…

Over the last few days, Tusk had pieced together a more complete dossier. Gil Oldfield, age twenty-eight. Super smart, workaholic. A bigwig at an investment bank Tusk had never heard of, made a fortune too bloody young. Jumped off the treadmill in '99, became a share trader at that place in the city. Holiday home in Apollo Bay. Married to his childhood sweetheart, a nurse at Knox Hospital. One daughter.

Tusk's best source had proved to be Dana, who still saw Olivia on a school committee. Since Christmas, the picture of Oldfield was dire. Screaming nightmares. Turfed out of the B-grade basketball team for temper. Hardly ate, not even his fave, Olivia's pepper steak. Functional, it seemed, but barely.

"He has a lovely voice, he used to sing at Saint Mary's," Dana had said. "Now he doesn't even go to church."

She hadn't queried Tusk's sudden interest. He hadn't told her of the conversation he'd had with Yolanda.

"Daddy?" Yolanda's face had screwed up the way it did when the world troubled her. "Why can't everyone be happy?"

Now one glance at the prick's veggie patch pushed Tusk off the emotional fence he'd sat on ever since.

Dana grew cauliflowers, tomatoes, beans. Tusk sometimes held a hose. Their efforts were puny compared to Oldfield's four-feet-deep creation along the fence. Pumpkin, corn, onions, carrots, sweet potatoes—a bloody greengrocer shop. Now it all rotted unattended, just shriveled plants, knee-high weeds. Tusk couldn't help recalling from his youth the tomatoes dying in their pots whenever his father Arne binged. In Brunswick, no one noticed. Here in Middle-Class-ville, the sight shocked.

He jiggled his neck to ease tension, took the curved path to the front door. Drawn blinds. Thudding bass, loud.

The doorbell chimed. 4:04 by his watch. His mind was clear as a mountain lake.

The door inched open. Katie Oldfield, with her father's face, all knife-edged angles, and her mother's brown-blonde hair. A nice kid, a fine friend to Yolanda.

"Katie, your dad in?"

How bizarre. He recognized the high voice of Ozzy Osbourne, the sputtering riff of Tony Iommi. "War Pigs," the intro track of *Paranoid*, up loud. Headbanger loud. Rage loud.

Katie's brown eyes held maturity Yolanda's blue eyes gave no hint of. Tusk's fists clenched. She stared a moment, then ran off. He cracked knuckles. Christ, he thought, not even Sabbath should be that loud.

When he came to the door, Oldfield's appearance stunned Tusk. All the movie star features had collapsed into jowls and a gray pallor. Black hair an oily mess. Jeans and a rumpled T-shirt. The eyes, as Tusk's police mentor Cap had always lectured, told the full story. Sunken and inflamed, they seemed barely human.

"G'day." Oldfield's morning shave had missed a swathe under the left ear.

"Got a minute, Gil?"

"Not today, okay?" No "pal" this time. Oldfield was breathing hard, almost panting. "Busy."

The door began to swing shut. Tusk stepped forward and

23

bumped it back off an arm. With the door fully open the music was a roar.

He advanced close enough to catch a sour unwashed stench. No alcohol, thank Christ, but what antidepressants had the quacks prescribed? "We need to talk."

"Talk?" Oldfield's voice shrilled. "Talk?"

The yuppie raised his left arm and jammed the elbow up to Tusk's face. Tusk recoiled. A livid scar ran from elbow to wrist.

"Calm down," Tusk said. "I understand. It's hell to be shot."

"Oh, is that it? An empathic ex-policeman, come to counsel me." The sneer belied Oldfield's swimming eyes. "Stuff you."

The music stopped. The house was dark. But for the sunlight through the door, Tusk would have been hard pressed to see. Where was Katie? Black Sabbath started again, had to be on Repeat.

"You're right," Tusk said. "I've never faced a man like that."

A lie of course. The near-invisible scar around Tusk's neck pulsed.

"Faced?" Oldfield's voice cracked. "Let me tell you, pal, I didn't face anything. He just blew Larry's brains out all over me. Then stood over me. He was God, pal, God. The bastard laughed."

A miracle, *The Age* had called it. Spree killer Maguire had shot Oldfield twice, point blank, but maybe because of the corpse sprawled over Oldfield, or maybe because Maguire was keen to move on, the bullets had merely gouged a furrow in an arm and nicked a knee. Little more than flesh wounds. But Tusk's experience told him that inner wounds were the worst.

"You come to counsel me?" Oldfield's face twisted into a

grotesque grin. Iommi began his guitar solo and Oldfield bobbed his head in time. Droplets flew off his cheeks. "Eh, counselor?"

Fucked-up goods for sure. Tusk was reminded of a movie he saw years ago. Jeremy Irons in *Damage*. Dana had hated the incest revelation but Tusk had nodded. Homicide work told you the same thing. Damaged souls never resurfaced. All you could hope was to prevent the infection of others.

He moved without thought, shoved Oldfield sprawling into the living room. One hand on Oldfield's belt, the other bunched in his T-shirt, he lifted the body and crashed it against a framed wedding photo on the wall. The CD skipped, momentary respite before the sonic bludgeoning resumed.

Tusk brought his face up to Oldfield's eyes, fist hard up under the arsehole's Adam's apple.

"Gil," he whispered, barely able to form words through clenched teeth.

Oldfield gurgled.

With an effort, Tusk eased the pressure. "Listen, pal. Hit Katie again, pal, and I'll make Maguire look like Gandhi. Right, pal?"

"I didn't. It was just—"

Furnace red flared across Tusk's eyes. His hand lashed. Blood gushed from the rabbit's nose.

"Daddy!"

Katie stood across the room.

"Christ." Tusk let go.

Oldfield slumped onto the floor.

Katie rushed to her father, her eyes scorching Tusk. Couldn't she see what he was trying to achieve? Tusk pressed the CD player's eject button. The tray sprang open. Oldfield's moans punctuated the abrupt quiet.

Judgment, that's what Katie's unrelenting gaze pronounced. Weariness seized Tusk's chest. For some reason, he pictured Gentle's intent face. Genius, he thought, save me.

CHAPTER 3

During his tour of TPT, Peter Gentle's regard for Jim Van Kressel grew. Jim hailed every trader by name and received at least a hurried greeting from each one. Several yelled "Papa!" A man with a Woody Allen face startled Peter by leaping up to high-five the delighted CEO.

"An hour of trading to go, folks," intoned a smooth voice. "All Ords at 3,099."

"That's Murray on the blower." Jim paused to heft up his trousers by the belt, as he did every few meters. "Made so much money trading last year that he quit. Now he's one of the three announcers we employ on rotation. That's a major feature of my business model, a really small permanent staff. Just about everything we need is supplied by contractors."

Jesus, Peter thought, what a different world. The variety of traders! Most were young, twenties or early thirties, nearly all male, some decked out in all-black sloppy gear, some in daggy jeans and jumpers, even one man in a purple velvet jacket. Peter spotted pink hair, dreadlocks. Then there were the gray-hairs, more self-contained, more women in this group. Some seemed apologetic to find themselves there. Others, like one middle-aged man dressed like a garbo in singlet and shorts, were patently odd. A fifty-something woman in an ill-fitting stylish outfit blew Jim a kiss with a flourish that reminded Peter of his mother.

The equipment, the hunched backs, the flurry of fingers, the whoops and curses, all these belonged in a professional trading room. But something about the atmosphere—perhaps the diversity, perhaps the emotions on display, perhaps the way some traders glued their eyeballs inches from their screens—reminded Peter more of the Crown Casino's rows of poker machines.

Jim explained that trading applicants were firstly evaluated for gross instability and then had to complete a two-week intensive course that cost them a fortune. "That way we weed out the worst risks."

Weapons inspection would help, thought Peter.

They passed a table with a coffee percolator, teabags, and foam cups. Peter stilled a shudder. This is where Maguire began shooting, he recalled.

Jim went on. "Even the trainers come from outside, there are thousands of laid-off middle managers out there. But we also make use of our superstar traders like Oleg. They enjoy the limelight, and of course the punters lap it up."

He loves this business, Peter thought.

"We're particularly short-staffed at the moment. Owen, our computer op, is in Fiji, so you'll find Camilla run off her feet."

Leased telecom lines gave the traders near-instantaneous access to SEATS, the stock exchange's automated trading system. Nearly all the programs cluttering the traders' screens, from the trading software to charting packages, were licensed from third parties. "You can buy them for your home PC if you want. But we've customized the ticker, the program that displays prices and buy/sell queues. It's the most advanced interface in Australia."

Peter hunched his shoulders. "I get it. Anybody can register at home with an online trading firm and have automated, no-human-hands trading with the Stock Exchange. What you get at TPT is extra speed and reliability."

It didn't seem very much to hang a business off of.

"No, no." Jim beamed. "We also bundle up the very best software at wholesale prices. Our data feeds are the most comprehensive in the industry. With us you get initial and ongoing training. You get camaraderie and peer group support. You get a hothouse trading environment that motivates commitment. But best of all, our commissions are a fraction of what the online brokers levy."

Jim halted at the other end of the aisle. "If you want to make one or two trades daily, go ahead, do it in the comfort of your home. That's share investing, not trading. But if you want to mix it with the big boys and trade actively, which is where the money is, this is it. And we're the only day trading show in town."

From a business perspective, it still sounded risky to Peter. All that hardware to amortize, all those subcontracted costs. The monthly and hourly fees Jim outlined were hefty but, a quick mental sum suggested, not nearly hefty enough. Then he saw the logic. Although the commission per trade was tiny, TPT encouraged the traders to make hundreds of trades daily, jumping in and out with trends or taking advantage of price anomalies.

Jim's was the only office at the north end of the second floor.

Around the south corner were two modest offices, a couple of desks outside them. Finola Vines was on the phone in one office. A tanned man stared at Peter from the other.

Jim asked, "You trade shares, Pete?"

"Now and then."

And just as well. Peter's handful of share investments, mostly in-and-out punts on dot-com floats, all on the strength of tips from Skulkers, were the one bright spot on the financial front.

Twelve months ago his money situation had been catastrophic. The severance payout was close to exhausted, forcing him to lease out his city apartment and move back to Box Hill, with all the attendant stresses of putting up with his parents. Then, out of the blue, he and Mick had swapped unemployment for involvement in that murder case, a case that turned sour and terrifying.

That job's $80,000 check had enabled him to move back into the city, to buy his canary yellow Volkswagen, to resume life as he treasured it. But now…

Peter gestured at the eccentric paraphernalia everywhere, models of large open-topped waste containers hanging from the ceiling, dozens of colored bins, and shredders tucked next to partitions.

Jim chuckled. "My last company, Australian Waste Management. I built it up, was lucky enough to sell it at the peak. Imagine it, me, a boy from Moonee Ponds, the big success story of garbage."

No explanation at all, really. Peter was beginning to discern the brash Van Kressel way.

Tucked away in the most remote section of the floor were a

tiny computer room and a long training room. In one corner of the training room, a thin-faced man with mousy hair sat at a desk by a trading screen and a small television, speaking into a microphone. He waved at Jim.

"Seats forty at a pinch," Jim said. "Full data feeds, complete capability. Our traders can simulate on that big screen, they can even trade live. You should see Oleg in full flight here."

Peter inspected the door he'd just walked through. "This is where Maguire tried to shoot his way in."

Jim grabbed his elbow. "No. Rule number one. Don't talk about that mongrel in earshot. Okay? Back in my office, quiz me all you like. But I don't want the punters spooked."

Peter felt reckless. "I thought it would shut you down."

The look that blanked Jim's face, for an instant, said it all. "So did I, Pete, so did I and every bastard in town. I knew each one of those poor devils personally. Thank God for Fi, she never wavered. You know the oddest thing? Our monthly half-day marketing seminars have been full ever since. There's a ghoulish element, no doubt, but the PR also brings in genuine customers. We're running a waiting list for the first time. Fi is working flat out to open a second office up the other end of Collins."

Sweat glistened on Jim's brow. "This business will fly, Pete, just watch. You just stamp out this Diamond nonsense."

***

Left sitting in the training room to wait for Crazy Oleg, Peter regrouped mentally, mapping out the data collection phase. Jim was setting up an initial round of interviews for the afternoon, introducing Peter as a consultant, not an investigator. High priority had to be a call to Alexa Shevchenko, she'd know a hacking expert or two.

TPT's star trader materialized with catlike suddenness. Tall, slim, and staggeringly young, Oleg wore a long-sleeved white shirt with clerical collar, black trousers, and Reeboks. Spiky pink hair contrasted with a chalk-white pallor. He gulped from a can of Coke.

When they shook hands, Peter felt callused fingertips.

Peter said, "Jim asked me to check on this Kurt Diamond."

"I am in middle of trading." Oleg's bulbous nose, and red spots on the high cheekbones, spoiled any pretension to handsomeness, but the man stood out, and Peter was certain he knew it. "Costs money, you understand?"

"It's important, Oleg."

Oleg's green eyes sized Peter up. Something must have made sense, for he slouched into the adjoining seat. The Slavic accent disappeared as he recounted the facts. Twice last week Diamond emailed him at home, after which Oleg issued a one-liner ("Not wanted—go away"). Two nights ago another email landed.

Oleg tossed his empty can over a shoulder. "I complained the official way to the help desk, to that Gusty. Of course no response, so I escalated to Papa."

"Gusty?"

"Ha! Gus Youde."

From a pocket, Oleg pulled folded print versions of the emails and handed them to Peter. The only interesting thing about the bland stock-picking emails was Oleg's surname, Kilpatrick. An Irish-Russian?

"Is good?" The mock accent was back. "Papa sacks this man, yes?"

No wonder he's done well here, Peter thought. He decided to play along. "What's your secret, champ?"

Oleg's thin lips squeezed out a hint of a smile. "Mario, Sonic, Doom. Lessons one, two, three."

From entry to exit took six minutes.

***

Any hopes Peter had of a smooth passage through TPT were scuttled by the network manager, Camilla Brown.

"Typical," she said. They sat at Camilla's cluttered desk outside the computer room. "Another example of the Fuehrer's faith in his team, I don't suppose."

Camilla had a plain face given life by large searching eyes. Her hair was piled up in light brown curls. A double string of pearls hung over a black turtleneck sweater with sleeves rolled up to the elbows.

"He blamed me, didn't he?" she said.

Peter shook his head, tried to disarm with a smile. "Just said it's urgent."

"Urgent," she muttered. "Everything is urgent except those who built up this company."

Something must have shown in Peter's face, for she sighed. "You've caught me at a bad time. I was sitting here, you know, when I heard the shots. I hid back there." She pointed into the warren of computer boxes, monitors, racks, and wires. "I heard him shooting at that door. He was maybe three meters from me."

Jesus, Peter thought.

She raised her hands. They wavered. "I've got an eight-year-old boy, a six-year-old girl, an ex who won't pay his alimony, I wake up drenched in sweat, I've been here since day one, and his highness won't support me for a disability claim. And he expects loyalty."

"Tell me about the network."

She peered at him. "Right. Sorry. I assume you're au fait with NT networks."

Her presentation, neatly sketched with a chewed pen, proved highly professional. Peter didn't understand most of the networking symbols, but to his surprise, the protection of TPT's computer system was conceptually simple enough. He pictured the myriad computers on the office floor all linked to a handful of central computers that Camilla referred to as "servers." Security came down to the servers' interfaces to the external world. The high-speed dedicated data line connecting TPT to the Stock Exchange was, according to Camilla, "unhackable, period." Access to the Internet and email was zealously guarded by rings of hardware devices called firewalls, buttressed by the latest "intrusion detection software."

"Every six months we get a security company to try to hack in." Camilla's lips puckered in distaste. "In early 1999, they got in, but we adjusted the config and now we get a clean sheet every time. And look at this."

Camilla pointed to the email address—KurtDiamond@ techpowertrading.com.au—on the printed copies from Oleg. "If these had really come from this network, we'd see them in the stored directory of sent emails." She brandished a sheaf of output. "I've been through this month's emails, sorted by address. No Kurt Diamond. It's a spoof."

Peter's stomach rumbled. Pleasure of pleasures, tonight was

the monthly meeting of the Skulk Club. He swallowed, could almost taste the vino, hopefully a bold Pinot to suit his mood.

"Right," he said. "A spoof."

Suspicion creased Camilla's brow. "You know, an email with the source address altered. It's easy enough to do."

"So it was sent to Oleg's home from some unknown machine, with the header forged?"

"Bingo. But, as I've already told Jim—" a jab of her pencil onto her desk snapped the lead "—once the email is on its way it travels via unpredictable physical nodes, and those physical addresses are stored in the data packet. How could anyone tamper with those? If I could grab the email files off Oleg's computer, I bet I could trace the forger as easy as pie."

Peter steepled his hands over his mouth, thumbs hooked under his chin. "But—"

"I know, I know. We can't do that without alerting Oleg about the forgery. You've met him. It would be in the press in an hour."

Peter saw them everywhere, these professionals who couldn't be faulted in what they did, but who took such a circumscribed view that their work proved ineffectual. "Hang on. Even if you could trace the email, it might be from one of those anonymous emailing sites."

Petulance returned to Camilla's features. "I guess so. But does it matter? Now we know it's a spoof, it's not a TPT responsibility. It's Oleg's baby. Who knows, it could be a prank, one of those big-titted foxes he keeps boasting about."

Hardly, Peter thought.

"Did Mein Fuehrer tell you about the flamer?" Camilla asked.

Flamer? Peter shook his head. Tiredness, that pervasive leadenness across his chest, returned.

Apparently last Friday someone using anonymous email addresses had flooded TPT's email server. Thousands of emails clogged up the system for hours. Camilla had been in all day Saturday cleaning it up. So far the attack had been a one-off affair.

"You can tell it's the same person sending all the emails," Camilla said. "There are five different abusive messages cycled through the different source addresses."

Peter took hard copies of a dozen emails, wondered why Jim hadn't revealed this data. The messages were crude and emotive: "Bottom feeders of the finance pond," "Die, greedy scum" and the like. Was this "flamer" the same person who sent emails to Crazy Oleg?

He felt pride at coping with Camilla's briefing. Once finished at TPT, he could buy a couple of networking primers, get to grips with the technical details of emailing.

Camilla prattled on and Peter let her. He asked for the network logs on a floppy and reassured her that he'd keep her informed. He left her with his card.

Progress deserving of a drink, he thought—an evil notion at 3:55. He considered ringing Mick, but if the meter was on, he'd be lucky to receive a grunt.

Already he had some understanding of how Oleg had been misled. And that was the only issue Camilla was interested in, because her theory, a hacker working outside the company network, absolved her of blame.

Peter's goal was who. For that, he needed more data on why.

**

36

Oleg's comments about the help desk prompted Peter's next stop at the desk near Finola Vines' office.

Gus Youde was a flustered bear of a young man, with one of those moon-shaped faces that shrieked nerd. Behind monstrous broad glasses, his eyes drifted away from direct contact. Long blonde hair rose and fell from a central part. He wore a blue open-neck shirt. Dandruff dusted the windbreaker hung on his seat.

They shook and then listened as the announcer signaled the close of the day's trading. The index ended 22 points down, at 4,133. Voices sprang into conversation around the corner.

"Another bad day for most," Gus said. "A few of them, those who specialize in the finance sector, will have done well. The others…"

"Is the rumor true?" Peter indicated a faded Lord of the Rings print, one of a dozen fantasy fiction posters covering the two filing cabinets at either end of the desk. An intricate model of a Star Wars Death Star twisted on a string from the ceiling. "Are they going to film Tolkien?"

"No way," Gus said. "They'd never be able to satisfy us fans."

SF fan, fine, nerdy was fine too. The question was: could Gus help? Luckily, he turned out to be less obtuse than his appearance suggested. On his screen he showed Peter the help desk calls Oleg had made over the last month. Three times Oleg had rung with software queries, easily handled.

"The traders don't bother to teach themselves the software properly, especially the charting program." Gus' voice, soft and deep, was his distinguishing feature. "They just have a go and then ring me when they get stuck."

The fourth and last call was logged yesterday. Gus' comment had been "complaint about Kurt Diamond (who?)" and the response was marked as "no action."

Peter pointed. "Why no action?"

Gus wrung his pale, freckled hands. "It sounded crazy. I just assumed Oleg had made a mistake."

Quite understandable, Peter thought.

Kurt Diamond? Gus had never heard of him.

***

Mick was forever lecturing Peter to "follow the frigging money." TPT's Chief Financial Officer worked in the office adjacent to Finola's. When Peter headed in that direction from Gus' desk, the tall occupant of the second desk rose to proffer a hand.

"Adam," he said in a confident voice. "Adam Menadue."

Peter shook the meaty hand. If Gus Youde was the company geek, Adam was its footy player. In his early twenties at a guess, he had tight black curls, the broad shoulders and easy movements of an athlete, and the face of a rugged actor. From the MYOB accounting system manuals on a raised shelf, Peter surmised he was an accountant or bookkeeper.

Peter introduced himself and pointed at a stone beside Adam's in-tray. The shape and size of an egg, it was dark gray with light streaks.

"Your hobby?" he said

"Sure is. Go on, feel it."

Peter ran fingers over the stone. The surface was slick as graphite.

"Lovely," he lied. He despised ornamental hobbies.

"And here." Adam unbuttoned his shirt, under his red-and-blue tie, to pull out a tear-shaped gem, the color of crows' feathers, loose on a thin string.

"I guess my father started it," Adam said. "He used to travel a lot to Russia and he'd bring back these exotic stones. Now it's an obsession. Tumblers, rock cutters, a workbench, the lot. Relaxes me after this shit here."

Adam had a life insurance salesman's smile. "Better get back to the grindstone, eh?"

At least someone in the company besides Jim is friendly, Peter thought. He tapped on Brad Funder's door frame.

Funder's eyes, cold behind black-rimmed glasses, lifted to scrutinize Peter.

"Yes?" Funder's jutting chin rose with the question. He had thick eyebrows and a squat nose. Cropped salt-and-pepper hair came to a point on his wide brow.

When Jim had told him the accountant's surname, Peter had laughed. Now he wondered if Funder had overheard. "Jim asked me to talk to you."

Funder lowered his silver pen. A cufflink glinted. "Not today, thank you very much."

"Pardon?" Peter heard a shrill edge in his voice. "But Jim—"

"Can I possibly be more explicit?" A slight British accent. "Come back tomorrow."

Funder's gaze lowered back to his work. He hitched his shoulders and began to write.

Peter's mouth worked open and shut, open and shut. He turned to see Adam Menadue and Gus Youde watching from their desks. A ringing phone distracted Gus. Adam shrugged.

CHAPTER 4

5:31 on the VCR, maybe a couple of minutes fast. The family room floor solid against his back. Trees in the backyard growing hazier.

Mick Tusk was hoisting the squirming, giggling form of Nelson higher, avoiding lashing feet, when the phone rang.

Not a word from Dana, just the phone thrust at him. The message on her face echoed the words from a week ago: "Mikey, why on earth do you still have anything to do with him?"

Tusk felt facial muscles relax for the first time since the Oldfield incident. "G'day, genius, how they hanging?"

"Big guy," came the rushed voice. "I've won another corporate. Hacking, of all things."

Tusk's first thought was of the anti-smoking ads. "The Quit campaign office?"

"Funny, ha ha."

No disguising Gentle's pleasure in the call. Tell the truth, Tusk was just as chuffed.

"Well done," he said.

What made the wife-genius rift so bloody hard to take was

that he couldn't blame Dana. She'd endured so much shit during his final dark days on the Force. It took his breath away to recall how she'd fought to build them a new life out here in the sticks, far from the scumbags and strife. And last May, when Gentle had sucked him into a whirlpool of violence, Tusk had witnessed her heart damn near break.

Gentle's voice rose in pitch. Tusk let the spewing computer jargon wash over him. He watched Dana's lush black curls jiggle as she sliced a zucchini on the wooden board the kids had given her for Christmas. Nelson tugged at his jeans. Bully whined and scratched at the back door.

Tusk caught something interesting in the flow and interrupted. "Did you say Tech Power Trading? Isn't that the place Maguire shot up?"

"I tell you, it felt weird going in there. Why do you ask?"

Tusk pictured Oldfield's scar, the daughter's eyes. "Nothing, no reason."

Gentle's voice dropped. "Any chance of tonight?"

Tusk watched Dana's hands stop still.

The Skulk Club. They're laughing at you, Dana argued. It wasn't that simple. No, he didn't belong. But he enjoyed the artless, powered-up company of Gentle's high-flyer mates.

Last June Harvey Jopling had taken Tusk to dinner, that Flower Drum place in Little Bourke Street, to invite him into the Club. The investment wanker's grin had been infectious. "Mick, there are only two requirements of a Skulker. No slagging off at meetings. And attend, attend, attend."

Eyes on Dana, Tusk now said, "Maybe next month. What the hell do you know about hacking?"

"At least I've got a computer."

"Ha. How does playing that war game of yours help with computer crooks? What happens if you fail?"

Gentle put on a pompous voice. "Failure is not in my vocabulary."

Tusk almost smiled.

The call wound up. Tusk struggled to identify his tangle of emotions. Righteousness at his decision, for sure. See, he loved Dana as strongly as the first time he saw her across the sweaty ballroom floor. No complaints about his health either, his body had never felt this good. The kids, the air, the very life… he loved it all. Paradise, no doubt about it.

Yet every time Gentle rang the tug was so strong. The tug toward what? Buggered if he knew.

Dana's face wore the determination he reckoned Greeks were born with, the wildness he'd seen on tennis star Philippoussis' face on TV.

He owed it to himself to try. "I could leave early—"

"No and no and no."

Yolanda's face swiveled from her homework amidst dinner cutlery. Tusk looked away. Would Katie Oldfield tell her friend about the afternoon's rumble?

"We agreed," Dana said. "And you promised."

Tusk stepped out the back door. He focused on the orange glow over the top of the fence. Bully's front paws rose up onto his thighs.

Thank Christ for dogs.

CHAPTER 5

"Man, this is so Melbourne," Renni Maisel was saying in the Californian drawl she still cultivated. "Try it in Sydney and see what happens."

Cocooned within clamor and friendship, Peter Gentle felt balmy with pleasure. "Harvey reckons it's because Melburnians know we're at the arse end of the universe. We need to huddle together."

Renni laughed and drained her glass. A Melbourne University friend of Peter, she now aspired to partnership at Merriwether Lang, one of the major legal firms. She personified the Skulk Club's boisterous side and never missed a meeting.

A near-full house tonight, twelve of the thirteen members enmeshed in conversation. As always, Hector had allocated them a long corner table upstairs, separate from the regular Draconi's diners. The youngest Skulker, stockbroker Paddy O'Loughlin, had chosen this month's wine.

Peter swirled the Piper's Brook Pinot Noir in his bulbous glass, then inhaled before sipping. Moderation, he told himself for the tenth time. He scanned the assembled Skulkers. Standing at the other end of the table, Hector, for once out of his trademark black apron, had lined up Harvey Jopling for an ear bashing. The two were hard at it, politics no doubt. Arnold Ng roared with laughter; they'd have to send him home in a taxi. Giuseppe Marino, an accountant with the Australian Taxation Office, was writing something on a napkin for Alexa Shevchenko, who caught Peter's eye and waved.

Alexa, the head of an Internet startup, was in full flight. "Giuseppe, just remember what Scott McNealy from Sun Microsystems said: 'You have zero privacy anyway. Get over it.' In my opinion, that's spot on. Modern operating systems have… hey, let's put it plainly, Windows has bugger-all security built into it."

Peter was reminded to ask her about hacking experts.

Several attendees had asked after Mick. Nothing warmed Peter's heart more than the inexplicable ease with which the ex-policeman had entered the Skulk Club world. To think the hulk had once blasted them as "cream-skimming yuppie wankers"!

Peter undid the top button of his shirt under his tie. He turned to his other neighbor, Carlo Fonti, dear friend and once actuarial colleague. "What do you think of this day trading?"

He'd updated most of his Skulker friends about his new assignment, had glowed inside at Harvey's smile, the biggest he'd witnessed in ages. But Carlo's opinion was always the one he sought most.

Carlo took his regulation twenty seconds to mull over the question. He seemed to have less hair than ever. "I call it unlicensed gambling. Have you asked what the trading life of these amateurs is?"

Peter shook his head. He knew Carlo well enough to guess where he was going.

"I bet it's only a few months. Every bull run brings out the taxi drivers, the secretaries who bet their mortgages on the latest float. In the trade they call it the Greater Fool Theory. I saw the best exposition on the web last week, on Suck.com, a guy pointing out how everyone knows that fools drive the stock market, but everyone bets there are even greater fools who'll pick up the tab when the bull run collapses."

"Spot on." Paddy, flashy in a blue-striped shirt, had come up to lean over Peter's shoulder. "Plain as the nose on your face, it's happening now. Can you believe how jumpy the market is?"

For some reason Peter felt the need to defend Jim Van Kressel. "It's not as if TPT's traders aren't warned."

Carlo's eyes smiled. "Are they? Take a look at the marketing, Skull. Sure they make it look like all the cautions are there. But check out the emotional pitch. Check out the verbal sales jobs."

"Some of them make a heap of money."

"Luck. Bull run luck."

Peter sighed, unable to contemplate describing Crazy Oleg to his friends.

His mobile vibrated: a message. As he moved away from the rabble to check it out, Harvey waved and tapped on his watch, signaling that the meeting was about to start. Peter gave a thumbs up.

He loved how these evenings consumed his mind and all his senses. Mandy, who typed up the minutes for Harvey, often mocked that the official proceedings rarely took half an hour. But that didn't mean the club was, as Mandy implied, just an excuse for wining and dining. Peter and Harvey tried to add depth with movie nights, gallery viewings, occasional informal speakers, even book recommendations. Anything except bloody sports events, Peter thought while attending to his mobile.

Two messages awaited him.

"Mr. Gentle, I've got something to tell you." Peter couldn't identify the man's voice, low and inviting. "It's… it's about that Oleg business. I've rung Jim but he's also offline. Is there any chance you could come and see me, I think we should discuss it face to face. Thanks, I mean…"

The next message clarified and set Peter's pulse racing. "Oh, I should have left my address. It's 10 Amess Street… oh this is Gus, Gus Youde in case you didn't realize. 10 Amess Street. Carlton. I'd greatly appreciate…"

Peter gulped down his wine. The request made no sense. Nothing during the afternoon's chat suggested Gus had anything to contribute. But the message was too explicit to ignore.

Harvey's face tightened with annoyance when Peter promised he'd return within the hour. Tomasina Symons accosted him with slurred ravings about the $5 billion Hong Kong deal Telstra had announced during the day, and Carlo waved, but no one else noticed his exit. People were always rushing in and out of Skulk Club meetings.

Outbound traffic was still fierce. By the time Peter chugged up Rathdowne Street, past the housing commission flats, it was nearly eight o'clock. He turned left instead of right, corrected, and then struggled to find a parking spot further up Amess Street, near a boarded-up pub.

Number 10 was the neatest terrace house amongst its

neighbors. A sanded-down park bench sat on the narrow porch. The flowerbed behind the iron fence bloomed and potted plants hung from the wrought-iron latticework. The windows and door had been recently painted a gleaming green.

Peter marched through the open gate. He was daydreaming, imagining presenting a fait accompli to Jim Van Kressel in the morning. The business prospects this would present…

When he knocked, the door eased open. He could hear tinny music, as if from a transistor radio.

"Gus?" he called.

There was no response. He pushed the door ajar enough to make out a hallway brightly lit by suspended spherical lamps. The walls were swirling scenes of warriors and damsels on hills and in snow, accompanied by dwarfs and ogres. A genuine fantasy nut, Peter thought.

"Gus?"

When he stepped in, the smell hit. Acrid and sweet at the same time, he recognized it immediately. Goosebumps brushed his scalp, feathered his neck and spine. No, he begged. The last time had been just like this, a hall acting as tunnel into a hell he'd never asked for. Only last time Mick had been with him, Mick had gone ahead, Mick had looked after him.

The notion of leaving and calling the police rose and disappeared.

There was no logic to his next move, no logic at all. Step by step he conquered the hall, barely wide enough for two to pass without banging shoulders. Past three rooms, clearly bedrooms. The reek surrounded him, filled him. His footsteps resounded on bare boards. A horrid taste of wine and coffee rose up his throat.

The living room was empty.

At least it had been a living room once. Now one wall was lined with mismatched tables housing a jumble of computers and printers. A screensaver swirled on one computer. A bell-like folk singer's voice issued from computer speakers. On the opposite wall, overflowing bookcases and shelves jostled for space in front of peeling wallpaper. Beneath the sole window, an ancient television gathered dust.

"Gus?" Peter whispered, a formality.

His heart threatened to heave out of his chest. It's a crazy world, he thought, you do learn to live with this. For he remembered what Mick told him last time: touch nothing.

One step into the renovated kitchen and he doubled up to spasm his guts.

The fridge door had swung all the way back on its hinges and lying smashed into the bottom section of the fridge was a body. Peter recognized Gus' jacket. He might not have placed the face-down head, resting on a cracked plastic shelf, for it was a visceral horror. An impossible chunk had been gouged out, exposing bloody, congealing, glistening flesh. Blonde hair matted with black trailed over the vegetable tray. Blood lay everywhere, still oozing across the floor, splattered and streaked inside the fridge, spotting the nearby walls and floral tablecloth. Only Gus' left ear was pristine, shockingly pale and vulnerable. Mercifully, Peter couldn't see the face.

Gus had had his head almost blown off. Peter was slap-bang inside a nightmare. He turned, slipping on his own vomit, nearly going down to join the poor man.

Only then did rational thought intrude. The killer could still be in the house. The back door was open! Revulsion became terror.

"Mick," he pleaded, as if his partner would materialize out of thin air.

Somehow he was stumbling down the hall, careening from wall to wall. Somehow he made the open front door. Sobbing, his nose running, he gripped the door frame with both hands. His stomach launched again. He turned his face up to blink through tears at stars over television aerials, two wondrous stars. He leaned into the cool air.

When he stepped out onto the porch, a blow landed over his left ear. A cry and he was down on concrete.

"Mick," he moaned. Waves of agony split his head.

"Who you calling, prick? Eh, prick?" An odd voice with an odd accent.

Peter struggled to rise but a weight on his back squeezed air from his lungs.

The confusion was too much. His universe was a jumble of sensations—his snuffling breath, panting sounds above, gravel under a nostril, pain everywhere, a drifting cloud in his head like the edge of sleep.

Someone breathed hotly into his ear. "Last warning. Clear off."

Peter was reminded of some actor's voice but it was all moot. The world switched off.

CHAPTER 6

What exactly was he doing?

Mick Tusk tensed stomach muscles, curled up off his back. A forlorn 11:04.

Off with the headphones. The CD tray purred open. Goodbye ancient Cheap Trick CD, hello Semisonic, the *Feeling Strangely Fine* gem he'd stumbled upon at Basement Discs, the music fan's mecca across the lane from Draconi's Bar & Grill. In that other world, the big bad city.

He knelt to program a single track. "Closing Time" was cliché rock with teen lyrics but he found himself drawn to it again and again.

The night had burned quietly. Once the gyrations of getting the kids to bed were done with, he and Dana sat in the family room. *Blue Heelers* came and went. Dana switched on the standing lamp to read *Captain Corelli's Mandolin*. Tusk dipped into a Holocaust history while allowing himself to be distracted by the bravura jokes on *The Panel*.

No need to even imagine the existence of a dipstick dining club in an obscure lane under the cold, cold towers.

Later, when Dana's breathing had settled into sleep, Tusk had lifted her arm off his stomach and eased out of bed. As Talking Heads had put it back in 1980: same as it ever was.

Lately he'd begun to ask why. Insomnia was the label, but why? Was it physiological? Did their hand-to-mouth existence register as hidden stress?

Sometimes these hours felt like waiting.

Luckily the headphones were still off when the phone rang. He got to it before the second ring.

Gentle was half sobbing, half panting. "Mick, he's... shit, he's dead." A long moan. "I shouldn't have..."

Waiting's over, Tusk thought. "You okay?"

"No. Oh Jesus... Look, nothing serious, but Gus..."

"Get a grip. Where are you?"

Tusk heard out the unbelievable news: house, body, attack. His first rational thought: fuck, my fault.

"Don't move," he told Gentle. "I'll be there in thirty. Expect the coppers."

In the Teledex he found the mobile number of Senior Constable Deirdre Lasker.

"Lasker." Her voice cool, she knew what a mobile call meant. Dinner table laughter in the background. Tusk remembered her boyfriend, the super-cool lawyer.

"Dee, it's Tusk."

"Perfect timing for a catch-up call."

"10 Amess Street, Carlton. Gentle is down. Says there's a gunshot victim inside."

"God, what's he done this time?"

A yawn, byproduct of sudden tension, filled Tusk's chest.

"Not him, someone else. I'll see you there."

He was fumbling his jeans on in the bedroom when Dana's lamp startled him.

She said, "It can't be."

Tusk's urgency evaporated. A chasm expanded inside. Christ, he could even identify the feeling, the powerlessness of a kid, lying in bed listening to Arne berate his mum.

He kept his eyes off her. "Someone pummeled the shit out of him." No need to mention the body. "Someone rough."

He zipped up. Dana clambered out of bed. When he grabbed a jacket, she yanked it out of his hand.

"You promised, you promised, you promised."

He looked at her then. Loose curls dangled over her sleep-creased face. Brown eyes so bleak. Even at this moment he could admire her breasts as they rose and fell.

She clenched her fists. Christ, he thought, if she hits me…

They'd never been to this point before. Any further and he might as well slit his wrists. He raised his hands. Surrender.

"I won't go." Breath whistled in his nose as he regained control. "It's okay."

An image: Gentle bawling on cobblestones, scared to the point of witlessness, that night long ago.

"Come here, honey," he said.

She began to sob the moment her arms wrapped around him. "Oh, Mikey, I'm so scared."

"Me too, Dana. Me too."

She gripped his arms, looked up with wet eyes. "I know he's your friend. I really do know that, Mikey. But it's not what you want to do that terrifies me. It's…"

The intensity of her feelings brought a catch into his chest. He clamped it down. He drew her back into his arms, inhaled the wonder of her hair. "Shh."

Reading psychology had helped Tusk. Dana wouldn't be blunt enough to call it "generalized rage at the world coupled with poor anger management," but the police psychiatrist hadn't hesitated. Reading psychology helped. The fuck it did.

No reply when he rang Gentle from the family room. He left a poor excuse of a message.

In bed Dana was all over him. Or maybe he was all over her, a desperate grab at the closeness screwing can bring. And for a moment it did.

But an hour later, when he was certain Dana was dead asleep again, Tusk crept back into the family room. He changed the CD, donned headphones. Doctor, he thought, a double dose of insomnia tonight.

After he switched off the lamp and lay down on his back by the stereo cabinet, the pent-up energy in his arms and legs tortured him. He reached up through the welcome darkness and found the volume control.

"Genius," he whispered. "Fuck it, I'm sorry."

He turned Deep Purple up loud enough to hurt.

CHAPTER 7

Lazy blue light strobed into Peter Gentle's ruined head.

The police had cordoned off Gus' terrace house, out beyond the gutter. Cameras flashed. Keep out of the papers, he heard Mick lecturing, publicity is the death of the PI. Right now Peter couldn't give a damn. The wooziness came and went, the aches in his shoulder, hand, and hip were tolerable, but his head alarmed. Spasms gripped the top of his skull like a migraine gone ballistic.

"He was here, then. Like this?" Detective Inspector Conomy, hand raised in simulation, hugged the wall between the porch bench and the doorway.

The tall policeman in the stylish suit carried himself casually, with the grace of a panther. In his younger days he'd have looked boyish, with his pixie face and windswept hair, but the hair had turned white and he now sported a double chin. Peter had trusted the ready grin at first sight. Talk about contrast, he thought, nothing like the police aggro in last year's case.

He nodded, setting off another attack that doubled him over. Where was Mick?

"Take it easy, mate." Conomy grabbed Peter under the arms. "No idea what he hit you with?"

"No."

The Skulkers, back in the paradise of Draconi's, would find the name amusing. "Call me Rich," the Homicide detective had said. Did his colleagues dub him Rich Economy? Refreshed by the dumb humor, Peter breathed deeply. Not brain-damaged after all, he thought.

Senior Constable Deirdre Lasker emerged from the house, notebook and pen in hand. Another plus that Deirdre was here. Uncharacteristically she wore makeup, and a cream jacket softened the blockiness of her frame.

"We'd better get you to Casualty," she said. Whenever Peter marveled that someone with such a young face could be a policewoman, her no-nonsense voice dispelled his doubts.

"No, no." Peter straightened, felt sick, retained the posture. Sweating at the effort, he leveled steady eyes on her. "I'm fine."

Deirdre threw a glance at her superior, who nodded.

"One shot?" Peter pointed back into the bowels of the house, where a crime scene team was at work. The body bag had passed him ten minutes ago.

"Come on, mate." Conomy tugged his arm.

Peter shrugged off the helping hand and stiffly followed Conomy into the living-cum-computer room. They sat on rickety office chairs.

"They'll do the autopsy overnight," Conomy said. "But it's straightforward enough. One shot to the back of the head, from close. Real close. Massively bad karma, no possibility of an accident. We're talking rage or extreme fear."

"Karma," Peter said.

Conomy nodded. "Karma. The good and the bad, mate, that's how the world is split. Pure and simple. And this perpetrator is bad, pure bad."

Amazing deduction, Columbo, Peter thought.

Conomy continued. "The killer could have stood behind the cupboard and surprised the victim. Or the victim knew the killer."

Peter tried to concentrate. Although he felt marginally improved, a raging thirst had begun.

"Mate, there's one puzzling aspect." Conomy's thin eyes squinted. "The open back door, no sign of forced entry. The back gate also wide open. If Youde knew the killer, wouldn't he or she have come in the front door? If Youde was ambushed, wouldn't the killer have shut the back door? Either way, that suggests it was opened afterward, to escape. Then why run around the block to ambush you by the front door?"

"The front door opened at my touch." Peter frowned, his pounding head refusing to buckle down to logical analysis. "Surely he must have let the killer in."

All he wanted was to get home, to collapse into his sweet bed. But Conomy's musings elicited thought. Why on earth was Gus killed? Peter couldn't imagine anyone more ineffectual. Had he stumbled on the hacker at work? But Jesus, the hack was so trivial, almost harmless. Surely an insider could have wreaked more damage in a million other ways? It all sounded so illogical. And nothing taunted Peter more than the notion that something on this earth couldn't be explained.

"I called Sam Vinci, as you suggested." Conomy's eyebrows

arched. "Can I be frank?"

Peter pictured slick-suited Inspector Vinci, swearing at him on a similarly apocalyptic night. "Sure."

"Sam said you're a babe in the woods. But he told me you helped him solve the quant fund murders. Good lateral thinking, he called it. And he vouched for your honesty."

Peter nearly spluttered. Helped Vinci? Peter had solved it all himself. As for lateral, his analysis had been logical. At least as a result of the referral, Conomy hadn't asked about his license.

He grunted. "Well, let me vouch for Inspector Vinci's ambitions."

Conomy crossed his arms and stared for a moment. "Anyway, tell me, Peter. What are you doing here, mate?"

Of course, the iron fist in the velvet glove. What the heck, Peter thought, realizing at that instant that he no longer had a case anyway. A misdemeanor had escalated into murder, Jim could no longer avoid the press, and TPT would have no need for the services of Peter Gentle, Private Investigator.

It was nice while it lasted, he thought bitterly. As succinctly as he could, he recounted the day's proceedings. Conomy took notes and listened without interruption.

At the end Conomy asked, "And the victim's mental state this afternoon?"

"He did seem fretful but I assumed that was just him. He struck me as nervy."

"Could Youde have been this hacker?"

Peter shrugged. Anything was conceivable. Where was Mick?

"How did he and this—" Conomy consulted his notes "— this Oleg Kilpatrick get on?"

"I can't be certain. Oleg seemed contemptuous toward him. Gus? He just seemed friendly, full stop."

Conomy rose. "Right. I'd better say hooroo, check out the troops. Constable Lasker took your details?"

A shriek rang out. "Oh my God."

A woman in her early thirties, her reddish hair done up in a bun, stood with knuckles in her mouth, staring at the police in the kitchen. A swarthy man had her by the shoulders. Gus' housemates, Peter surmised. How many people lived here and in what relationship?

It was no longer his business. His head had taken a turn for the worse. He said a few words to Deirdre in the hallway. When he emerged, the crowd had nearly disappeared. The black sky showed unbroken cloud. Had he imagined the stars earlier? Down the street his VW awaited, a haven.

While he buckled up his seat belt, it came to him, the reason for the murderer's weird voice. Of course it had been manufactured, with fake pitch and fake accent. And it had been modeled on one of the most distinctive actors Hollywood had ever seen. How many times had his father made Peter watch *The Maltese Falcon?* Peter Lorre, that's who the assailant had mimicked.

So what? All Peter desired was the security of his apartment.

The dashboard clock read 1:31. A vice tightened deep inside his head. Without ceremony, he retched bile over the steering wheel.

***

One breakfast during Peter's first summer school holidays after entering Mont Albert Grammar, aged twelve, his father handed him a hardcover book without a dust jacket. The spine was beginning to crack, loose pages stuck out, and it smelled like his grandparents' bookshelf.

He hadn't even been aware that Dad read books. The policeman was the busiest father amongst all his friends, forever out of the house, on the job.

At first Peter found the book, bundling up a famous public letter, heavy going. He'd never heard of the author Emile Zola, but read in a foreword that he was a French writer from the turn of the century, which explained the archaic style. But as Peter read, something about the letter gripped him.

The underlying story itself was exciting, a tale of the anti-Semitic incarceration of Alfred Dreyfus, imprisoned on Devil's Island upon being wrongfully accused of spying. Zola, a distinguished man of letters, took up the case. In Zola's letter's rousing finale, his passionate cry for justice, "J'accuse," echoed through the French courts and freed Dreyfus.

Peter read outside, sheltering from the summer sun under their gnarled apple tree. He skipped lunch and read through the afternoon on his bed. His mother insisted he eat dinner, but afterward he threw himself back on the bed. When he finally snapped the book shut, sending dust up his nostrils, his mind and heart beat as one.

After his mother tucked him into bed, he lay awake for hours. Way past midnight he heard his father's car pull into the driveway. He ran down the hall, book in hand.

He hugged the tired man. "Thanks, Dad."

"What's it saying, Peter?"

"Justice."

The word rolled across his tongue like heavy surf.

***

He woke fully clothed on his bed. He stank. The curtains were open and the white chink of sky visible past the adjoining building signaled daytime.

The dreamed memory flooded back. He still had the Zola book somewhere. Did Gus Youde read as a kid? Tolkien maybe? From such books lives are formed, he thought.

An image of the raw meat of Gus' skull made him gulp. Why on earth didn't Mick show up?

Not my concern, he thought. He sat up stiffly. The bedside clock showed 8:10.

Amazingly his headache was only mild. When probing fingers found a massive lump, he winced. His right hip spasmed upon standing and bruises made their presence felt all over, but he would live. The attack was some kind of mistake, that was the only explanation.

There was a tear in his stinking suit pants. Jim Van Kressel could pay for a new suit. Peter tried to picture Jim's face when he heard the news about his help desk staffer. Had Jim liked Gus? Jesus, it didn't seem fair that one business copped so much bad luck.

And Jim's bad luck was also Peter Gentle's. Bleakly, Peter wondered if he would receive a "bashed on the job" bonus.

The hot shower made him gasp. He lathered and scrubbed but still the smell remained. He tossed the ruined suit into the bin and found another one, a relic from his consulting days. The fridge didn't even contain orange juice.

A terse email from Harvey: "Trick Dacy, you left me in the soup."

He replied: "Tom Yum soup, I hope. Fill you in later."

He had reports to write, a dozen more emails to process, a Diplomacy game to check out online. Or should he head back out to the Richmond fraud investigation? After dithering, he emailed Jim Van Kressel a brief report, decided to ring TPT in the afternoon, once the news had been absorbed.

Indecisive, he paced the living room. Four years ago the estate agent had categorized the apartment as cozy, and cozy it was. A bedroom spacious enough for a long desk by the queen size bed, a small kitchen with all mod cons, a large living area, that was just about it. Not even a spare bedroom, but who needed one?

Inner-city prices were rocketing due to the CBD residential boom and he could have sold and moved out, but that wasn't the point. The very first day he'd caught a train from Box Hill to the city, as an eighteen-year-old heading to enroll at Melbourne University, he'd known he was born to live in the throngs.

The lingering smell in Peter's nostrils persuaded him. He slammed the door on his way out. Only when the elevator arrived did he miss his mobile. You'd forget your head, he could hear Dad say. Back in the apartment it took him five minutes to locate the phone in the bin, with the suit.

Three messages. The briefest of queries from Harvey late last night ("Guess you got caught up, ring. Forgot to say congrats, this TPT mandate sounds a ripper"), then one from Mick at 11:25 PM.

His partner sounded strained. "Look, it's not going to happen. Dee will look after you. Ring in the morning."

The last message was Mick again, an hour ago. "Hope you're not too pissed at me. Ring."

Peter had persuaded Mick to invest in a mobile but it rang through. He didn't leave a message. Maybe Mick was at home...

..."Dana Tusk."

A surge of anger jolted Peter. "Am I permitted to speak to him?"

He heard her pause, pictured her hostile eyes.

"Listen," she said. "Don't get the wrong idea. He's not like you, he has responsibilities."

Peter could hear one such responsibility, the hyperactive boy, whining at the other end of the line.

Dana's voice softened. "Are you okay? Mikey will want to know."

"Oh, sure he will." Peter jabbed the phone.

Childish, he thought on the walk down Bourke Street Mall. He waved to the Taiwanese guitar busker setting up his amplifier. The post office tower clock chimed nine. Ordinarily, he might have dropped in at Darrell Lea for a pick-me-up chocolate, but yesterday's doldrums had settled back in. What's the point, was the question that kept swirling around in his head. Everyone spoke of admiring his offbeat career move but what they really meant was, how long will it take to fail?

Block Place was as quiet as it ever got. A few tourists sat at the tiny outdoor cafe tables and consulted maps. Pigeons descended from the high windowsills to fossick for crumbs. From Dinkum's, the place next to Draconi's, the aroma of cooking pies set Peter's stomach grumbling.

Inside Draconi's, he could see no one familiar, not even Hector. It was hours too late to catch Harvey.

The first coffee was a gift from heaven, banishing the phantom stink from Carlton. Although he'd predicted it, the sight of Jim Van Kressel on the front page of *The Age*, underneath a shallow beat-up of the Telstra deal and the never-ending saga of South African cricket crook Hanse Cronje, jarred him. "Day Trading Firm Struck by Murder Again" was the headline. The article said little about Gus Youde's death and focused on last December's massacre.

He was shaking his head when Paddy O'Loughlin slid onto a neighboring stool and signaled for a waiter.

"Ah, Skull, isn't that a rum thing." Paddy pointed at the article. "I go to a party now and everyone is telling stockbroker jokes."

Paddy, a curly-haired live wire whose handsome face was beginning to show the ravages of a wild bachelor life, had recently started at J.B. Were.

"Isn't TPT a competitor?" Peter recalled Paddy fulminating one night against the online brokerages springing up, "conning mums and dads into a cheap nasty service without advice."

"Don't misunderstand," Paddy said. "I'd sooner see TPT bite the dust than sink a Guinness, but not like this, Skull, not like this."

Peter's mobile blared. It was Jim Van Kressel, terse. "How quickly can you get in here?"

"Look, I appreciate the call," Peter said. "You don't need to apologize. I'm sorry that—"

"Pete, just listen. Can I expect you in ten?"

Peter looked at the sublime carbonara just arriving. "Fifteen."

He scoffed down the pasta and another cup of brew. *The Age* referred to London's FT-SE 100 index dropping 154 points overnight, but Paddy's late-breaking news, that New York's Nasdaq tanked 7%, its sixth-largest fall ever, was a bigger revelation. Jesus, Peter thought, this will stir up TPT's traders, enough to give Jim the heart attack he looks ready for.

He half-listened to Paddy's spirited chat on the tram trip up Collins Street. Nerves tingled in his bruised body. No doubt Jim simply wanted to pay him off. But why had he sounded so adamant?

CHAPTER 8

Wakey-wakey. 6:14, a hint of light through branches. Somehow Mick Tusk had ended up on the couch. He sat up, identified the sound that woke him, Bully's panting. He watched the nutcase dog tear around the backyard.

He yawned. Thank Christ for such a heavy sleep.

Ring Gentle? No point for another hour or two. Tusk pictured his old stomping grounds in the Police Complex, the homely chaos of Homicide. Could Boy Wonder still be there?

Even as a kid, flailing against the world, he'd loved the solitary promise of dawn. He skipped his stretching routines to join Bully outside and retrieve his sweat-encrusted running clothes from the line. As he changed, dark cool air blessed his naked skin. A tail slapped his shins.

Man and dog headed west rather than the customary east, at first a slow shuffle to warm stiff muscles. He took in the ancient smell of gum trees, the thudding of his footfalls, the lightening of the sky. Bully, darting under trees to sniff and piss, covered twice as much ground as he did.

The very definition of heaven, but Tusk couldn't dredge up a smile.

After breakfast of grapefruit and plain toast, he snuck up behind Dana, dressed in her blue skirt for work, and hugged her hard. Her hesitant smile held relief but also fear.

On his way out, he left Gentle another message, an apology of sorts.

Yolanda didn't stop yakking on the short drive to school.

"Can we get another dog, Daddy?" Her smile was impish.

"As if."

Tusk was relieved Katie Oldfield was nowhere to be seen.

The hour-long drive to Footscray was always a drag, especially at this time of day. For Christmas he'd received, at his own instigation, The Clash box set, three hours' worth now copied onto cassettes. Such pleasure, even while idling in fumes, to lose himself in the incendiary riffs, the strident vocals of Joe Strummer.

Uncle Mart was hosing down a yellow cab, the oldest of the three, when Tusk drove up. They stood outside Mart's tiny weatherboard, deep in the hodgepodge blue-collar heartland, southwest of the Market. Dana kept suggesting he find a taxi owner nearer home. Sensible idea, but habit sent Tusk back to the man who'd sheltered him, on and off, during the downtime teen years.

Forty years in Footscray, no kids, no pets, Auntie Eve dead now four years, Tusk sometimes wondered what life meant to his uncle. Not that he wondered long. The short barrel-chested man with rounded shoulders and silver hair rarely smiled, but he didn't gripe either. Although his red-cheeked Scandinavian face was uncannily similar to that of Arne, Tusk's father, Uncle Mart had never hit Tusk. Therein lay the difference.

***

A decade ago Arne had retired after thirty years' service with the tramways. As far as Tusk could figure, his old man never enjoyed a single day at the helm of the clunky vehicles that spanned Melbourne. But when he slammed on the air brakes for the last time, for some reason Arne decided to be melancholy. He threw a farewell party at his rickety place in Brunswick.

They'd both begun to recover from the wars of Tusk's youth and were talking again. Not often, but enough for Tusk to accept the invitation.

The day of the party, he worked a long shift in the squad car. He'd been a policeman for three years, loving every minute, working as hard as shit to make up for his late entry age. At nine o'clock he stepped into the smell of pickled herrings, dumplings, beer, and vodka. Cigarette smoke swirled toward open windows.

His father slapped his back. In the living room, thirty balding trammies drank and shouted. They called his father Arnie, a distortion of his Estonian name Arne, or just as often he was "the fucking Balt." Tusk's mother periodically brought out plates of food from the kitchen. Tusk didn't speak to her.

He drank beer and pictured Mercy, the woman he was seeing at the time. The image of her hot body sent him edging toward the door, just before the pumpkin hour.

"See you, Arne," Tusk said.

Sour vodka breath. "Eh, where you think you're goin'? This is my party."

"Got someone to meet."

"You screw around too much."

Tusk opened the sagging screen door, held out his hand. "Congrats, Arne. Free as a bird now."

A stiff finger poked Tusk in the chest. "You can't fool me, Mihkel. I seen the way you look at my mates. You think you're too fuckin' good for us."

The house had fallen silent. Next door a cat wailed. Tusk inspected the finger digging into him. An electric current buzzed in his arms.

"You weren't so high 'n mighty when you lived on the streets." Arne's eyes burned. "Then you were happy to see your father's money when you came begging. Now you're a copper, you think we're dirt. Right, boy?"

To respond would have prompted their first fight since the big one all those years earlier. And Tusk was in uniform. He drove off to find Mercy.

The next day he told Cap, his best mate and mentor. Cap had his limp by then, was pretending to count down toward retirement.

Cap said, "I thought I told you to keep clear of him."

"What, forever?"

Tusk never forgot the ferocity that engulfed the battle-lined face.

"Fuck you, Mick, haven't you got it by now? We're talking conflict of interest now."

"Pig's arse."

"Look." Cap seized the tip of Tusk's chin and squeezed. "That bastard... I told you, you were a victim then. Now you're the protector, mate, you've got no time to play victim. Got it?"

Tusk didn't visit his father for months.

***

"Is going to rain," Mart said in his raspy voice.

Tusk shrugged. No point in indicating the white clouds above. "Gassed up?"

"Plenty, plenty."

That was the extent of it. Tusk drove off after logging on to the computerized queue. Almost right away he scored a chatty fare from Williamstown to the airport. Too bloody chatty really, but the tip handed to him outside the Qantas terminal more than made up for it.

On a whim, he stayed off the meter, zoomed down the exit ramp. Off the freeway at Brunswick Road, through back streets just blocks from the childhood shithole. What would Arne be doing now? Maybe sleeping off a hangover or going for one of his marathon walks down Sydney Road. In theory Tusk and his old man were reconciled. Maybe so, but their last get-together had been at Christmas and the next one might well be next Christmas.

Remnants of police tape fluttered across the gate of 10 Amess. Tusk double-parked two doors down. He stood by his open car door, hands on hips, squinting in the sunlight.

Carlton was one of the few inner-city suburbs Tusk admired. He liked the wide streets of terrace houses, its quietness, its mix of residents. For every parasitic suit hoping for zooming property prices, there was an Italian putting up a family home, or a gaggle of uni students in semi-squalor.

Why the hell was he here? A sop to his conscience, better late than never? Or was he vicariously imagining combing the place with Conomy and Dee?

He'd been pleased to see Rich Conomy's name in the morning paper. One of the good guys of the Force, a pleasure to work with. Tusk pictured the deceptive loping gait, the soft smile. *The Age* quoted DI Conomy: "We have classified this as a homicide." A busy night for the squad, this murder plus a multiple knifing in Sydenham plus who knew what else.

How tempting to knock on the green front door. He tried to imagine the attack on Gentle, but the geek had told him so little. The newspaper account hadn't helped an iota, had even omitted Gentle's name. Just as well, Tusk thought.

"Hey, mister. Want to buy somethin' belongs to the killer?"

A kid no older than twelve, dark eyes, thin bare arms.

"Why aren't you at school?" Tusk asked.

The boy sneered. "Ten bucks. I saw the killer drop it."

Brand new Nike cross trainers, Tusk saw. An entrepreneur. Thank Christ his boy wouldn't grow up around here.

"Crap," he said.

A shrug, perfectly executed to titillate. Tusk wondered how the little prick knew he'd be interested. Why hadn't he surrendered this item, whatever it was, to the police?

Tusk sighed inside, kept his face still. "Show me."

"Ten bucks."

"Three."

"You a wrestler?"

Tusk fought an urge to laugh. "Only with my dog."

"I've got a dog." The boy flashed a toothy smile. "Rover. One of those blue-and-white cattle dogs."

The lie hung between them. Suddenly thankful for a ray of lightness in his day, Tusk found a five-dollar note, held it out.

With a snap, it disappeared. In Tusk's palm sat a smoothed irregular hunk of glass the size of the tom bowler marbles he hoarded as a kid. No, not glass, but highly polished stone, a deep hue of shell white streaked with brown veins.

A bloody waste of money and hope.

The boy must have seen something in Tusk's face. He pointed to the gutter directly opposite Number 10. "There. I found it there."

"You said you saw the killer."

"Is your dog big?"

Tusk contemplated lunging but the sound of voices turned both their heads. A policewoman was emerging from the terrace house, talking to a woman with red hair and a pale face. The policewoman bent to open the gate, spotted Tusk. She straightened, wary.

Tusk pretended to consult a note in his hand, shook his head in mock bafflement. Turned back to the taxi.

The boy was gone.

With a dull click, the shiny junk landed amongst the change in his pocket.

CHAPTER 9

As expected, Peter Gentle found TPT on edge. Robyn, the receptionist, barely spoke as she ushered him onto the trading floor. Although he drew a few glances from traders, not even the murder of a staffer could distract them from the market. No chitchat today, the televisions muted, just the silence of unrelenting labor broken by sporadic muttering. Today's announcer's voice was heavy with gloom. The All Ords was already down thirty points and the tech news sounded bad.

Peter poked his head into Oleg's cubicle but the jackhammering fingers never paused.

To his surprise Jim's office was full. Finola Vines, elegant in green top and white skirt, perched on the edge of the table. Peter fancied he saw venom in her nod. Inspector Conomy leaned against the whiteboard and next to him blinked a curly-headed man in a plain suit and disastrous orange tie.

Jim shut the door.

Peter took a spot just inside the doorway. His head lump painfully nudged a shelf behind him. His body had stiffened up again and ached in a dozen places. Through the window he spotted the begrimed antlers of a tram go by.

"Best to assemble everyone," Jim said. He wore a black pinstripe suit, jacket on despite sweat beading his brow. He strode behind his desk and Peter heard the sigh from his high-backed chair.

"Hello, Pete. Our illustrious inspector tells me you were whacked on the head." Only hollowness around Jim's eyes betrayed any stress. "A nasty hammering, he reckons. And in the line of duty, for which I'm most grateful. You look okay, I must say."

"I'm fine." Just don't ask me to go back to Carlton, Peter thought. He knew now that this was no check handover ceremony.

"I've just finished briefing the staff," Jim said. "It's safe to say they're in shock. Bloody hell, I'm in shock. Gus was…"

For a moment Jim lowered his head. Finola's mouth opened as if to speak.

Jim's head rose, his face stony, "Gus was special. Pete, the trading seats out there are full but by this arvo this murder will have the punters fretting. I'll have to be out amongst them for a few hours. In the meantime I need bloody answers."

The point of logic, Peter thought, is that it's logical. Why hadn't he heeded yesterday's analysis? Why was he here at all?

"I wasn't a hundred percent honest with you yesterday, Pete," Jim said. "About this Crazy Oleg business. You see, Len Maguire went off his head but I always found him to be very precise. So I've always been puzzled by some of the things he shouted out there… back then."

The executive, stilled once more by memories, massaged his

cheeks. Peter glanced at Conomy, who winked.

Finola said, "Jim, are you okay?"

"Never ceases to amaze me," Jim said, "how the whole thing just won't distance itself. The thing is, Pete, Irene Skews heard Maguire clearly, just before he shot poor old Vern. He yelled, 'This one's for the Jewboy, this one's for the bitch, this one's for Diamond.' The first is me—for some reason Len always referred to me as Jewish. The second is probably Fi. The police assumed the last referred to a ring he gave his wife a month earlier."

Peter's brain buzzed. "You think he received emails from this Kurt Diamond?"

"It's a nightmare possibility. Pete, will you help?"

Data: a beating and a body, after stupidly taking on a job with nothing to offer. Analysis: the murder makes everything much worse. Conclusion: run!

"I don't see how," Peter said.

"I want you to interview everyone here. Get out and talk to Gus' friends. Assume the worst regarding Len's words. Your brief is expanded—the hack, dear Gus' murder, everything."

"But—"

Jim's voice grew sharper. "And Inspector Conomy has been gracious enough to support this initiative."

Conomy straightened from his slump against the whiteboard. "The more hands on deck, the better. Close cooperation, of course. Peter, you'll need to talk to Nick here."

Finola had risen. "Jim, aren't you listening?"

Jim looked at her, then directed a dark stare at Peter. "You saw him, his body. Gus… Gus wouldn't have hurt a fly. God, I haven't even viewed the body, don't think I will. But what I do know is someone killed my friend. Someone invaded my company." He pounded the desk. "Somebody's got to figure this out. You're not going to walk away from that, are you?"

Peter glanced away. New data: fascination—how could spree killer Maguire be connected? Of course, beyond the patently real emotions, Jim was deliberately playing on his curiosity.

He pictured another time, standing on Princes Bridge, yelling to Mick, "Justice, that's what we're on about here. The right of every human being." Jesus, he felt like a weak reed.

"I'll see what I can do," he said.

Finola shook her head. Jim nodded gravely, an oddly moving gesture from such a remonstrative man.

The new policeman was crossing the room, hand extended. His curls topped his square head like a judge's wig.

"Nick Tagliaferro," he said.

Peter noticed one of Tagliaferro's thumbnails was a deep purple-black and his fingernails were dirty. With his Mediterranean skin he could have exuded a rough charm, but the face held permanent sourness.

Conomy said, "Nick's from our Computer Crime Squad. I only called him an hour ago, so don't ask him any tough questions yet. Another five minutes, fair enough."

Tagliaferro smiled, transforming his face from dumb and glum to plain dumb.

Jim was up and ushering them toward the door. "Pete, we'll talk money later. I need this to be your top priority. I'll issue an email, let everyone know your role, no beating around the bush this time. I'm going to actively coordinate this whole investigation, which means I'll hound you blokes. I'm on call, too, so ring whenever. Now get to it."

For a moment Peter felt panicky. Then he saw Finola's unyielding gaze and he stiffened with resolve.

Outside Jim's office, he was thrust back into the world of day trading. The announcer's drone was unbroken, signaling market volatility. The aisle was still empty, no time for coffee. Someone wailed, "Give me a break."

Finola swept off.

Conomy said, "You didn't tell me you're Horace Gentle's boy."

Spare me, Peter thought, is that why you're letting me in on this? "He rang?"

Conomy nodded. "Saw me interviewed on TV. Don't be hard on him, all he said is that you're hardworking."

"He'd know."

"Constable Lasker has begun interviewing. Peter, feel free to crisscross with her, but of course I expect frequent liaison." Conomy gripped the arms of both Peter and Tagliaferro. "It's a given that you two hacking experts will work well together, right?"

Tagliaferro's blink was that of a rude waiter. Peter hoped his own nod gave Conomy more encouragement.

Conomy released them. "Nick, what's your game plan?"

Tagliaferro referred to a notebook. "I'll get a couple of uniforms to go out and grab Kilpatrick's computer, also Youde's computer. I need to spend bulk time with the network manager here. I'll see what we can do to track down that flamer, too. I'll talk to Constable Lasker, see how we can find Maguire's computer."

Not a hint of joint work, Peter thought. Having now made the decision, it occurred to him he no longer had to explain to Harvey and the others how his plum new job had vanished in twelve hours.

"A full plate," Conomy said to Tagliaferro. He handed Peter a sheaf of papers. "Interviews with the victim's housemates. Two of them. I've been to see Youde's parents, they haven't spoken to him for years."

"Can I have the spree killing files?" Peter asked.

Conomy chuckled. "You'd need a truck, mate. See what I can do."

He ambled down the aisle, leaving Peter stuck with the sourpuss policeman. He noticed a Bombers lapel pin on Tagliaferro's jacket. Should he talk football? Another professional flaw, he thought, lack of footy knowledge.

"So you're an expert on hacking," Tagliaferro said.

Peter elected for flattery. "Not as much as you. Actually, I was hoping to look at Oleg's machine myself."

The policeman handed Peter a card. "All taken care of."

And he was gone, also heading toward the other offices.

Peter tapped a foot, wished he had a Panadol for the hip bruise. One of the traders, the woman he'd seen yesterday, was staring at him over a partition. She was younger than he'd first judged, perhaps in her forties. Her outfit, a cream affair with padded shoulders, looked two sizes too big.

Where should he start? No conceptual framework for the data gathering, no conceivable way to draw lines connecting Gus Youde and Crazy Oleg and... a shudder hit him at his front-page memory of madman Maguire. No doubt they'd find that Gus was killed by a friend or even a random burglar. But Conomy was correct—why assault Peter after the event? Why threaten him?

The logical starting point was Gus' job as help desk. In such a small company, he'd spot things.

Peter hurried past the watchful eyes of the woman in cream. Around the corner, Tagliaferro was poring over printouts at Camilla Brown's desk. Camilla herself was emerging from the training room with Conomy and Deirdre. Peter waved at Deirdre but she seemed too intent on watching Camilla, who was clearly shaken.

Peter knocked on the CFO's door. Receiving no response and cursing his own deference, he opened the door and peered in.

The same pugnacious face rose from what looked like the same work.

"Yes?" Brad Funder gave no indication he'd ever met Peter before.

"Mr. Funder, can we talk now?"

"Sorry, no."

Peter stepped in, cheeks hot. "Look, I appreciate—"

"Appreciate all you like." Funder enunciated each word. "We've had a murder overnight, in case you didn't notice. The police told us we'll all be interviewed, and I'll talk to them, but not, repeat not, to an amateurish investigator. It's pointless, another of the idiocies perpetrated in this company. And you can quote me."

"I'll—"

"Go ahead, run to Van Kressel. He can't make me talk to you."

The shaking in Peter's arms reminded him of the arguments with his father, years ago. He took another step forward.

Funder half rose. Hands planted on the desk, hot eyes fixed over glasses halfway down his nose, he glowered within spitting distance.

Peter's fury sagged from him.

CHAPTER 10

The morning air of the city smelled different from Mick Tusk's memory. At the same time infinitely familiar.

10:46 standing at traffic lights, across from the pigeon-shit steps of the State Library. Skin oiled after the walk from his distant parking spot.

He inhaled. Over fumes and dust, he could pick out a bleak aroma, like two stones rubbed together. Or when a tram slides to an emergency stop, burning sand.

Fuck you, Tusk directed at the careless power of the skyscrapers.

But his gait across Swanston Street felt purposeful.

The Library's security guard gave him the once-over. In the dark of the microfiche room he wound the spool until he reached December 24th. Christ, such a jolt to see the headlines. On through the pages to Christmas Day and finally Boxing Day, the 26th.

Tusk summed up Mr. Leonard Charles Maguire. A salesman—insurance, dental goods, pharmaceuticals—nearly all his life. Long-time community member out in Eltham, well enough liked but with an odd streak. Suspicious circumstances with his first wife's death in 1990. In mid-1998, aged forty-one, gave up selling, started up at Tech Power Trading. The traders nicknamed him Santa, reckoned him jolly but a bit barmy.

A boaster, claiming huge winnings, in actuality a loser. Blew his stake by early '99, snuck into his wife's account, blew that. Conned CEO Van Kressel into a margin facility. By December well under water.

The newspapers offered no clue as to why Maguire cracked when he did. Why he came to TPT with two loaded guns and a brace of ammo. He asked after Van Kressel and Finola Vines, luckily for them out inspecting office space. He chatted with other traders for a few minutes. Then went crazy. Walked the office killing. Somehow slipped out of a police cordon. Shot down twelve hours later in a parking lot in the east.

And then the most chilling discovery. His eleven-year-old son beaten unconscious with a hammer, then drowned, dried, dressed in his Sunday best and lovingly laid out in his bed. A tender love note on the dresser. Crumpled in the garbage bin, similar love letters to his other son, thirteen years old, and his second wife. Both of whom presumably escaped death when their second-hand Toyota Camry broke down overnight in Whittlesea.

Clear enough prognosis in the end: borderline evil, unstable, bankrupt, tipped into monstrousness.

Outside, the day had unfurled into classic autumn. Tusk paused at the top of the steps, gazed at the Daimaru glass cone under a sunny blue sky.

The only lack of closure remained his. Why the hell was he here?

***

His strides echoed through recollections of his early years on the beat. He flowed past the old Queen Victoria Hospital site, now swarming with kids skinning knees on skateboard ramps. Past country tourists circling a loud busker in the Mall. Along the el cheapo strip of Swanston Street. Under the watchful Town Hall. Up the hill to the posh end of Collins.

Half the Skulk Club worked around here, Gentle had told him once.

His ears were taking time to acclimatize. Arms crossed, he stood outside 28 Collins, eyes up at the Tech Power Trading banner, listening. A motorbike easing into the gutter. A tram whining up to speed before the plunge into the Swanston Street gully. A cigarette lighter flaring. The throb of air conditioning over at the Sofitel Hotel.

So this was where it happened. An ordinary office building. The golden arches of Maccas beckoning the likes of Nelson and Yolanda. After the maniac shot up the second floor, he must have emerged right here.

Tusk shook his head. How the hell did Maguire simply walk through the crowds and arriving cops?

The whole thing had shaken him at the time. He'd been out on the road all day, arrived home to catch the six o'clock news. Dana said later she spotted how it screwed him up. Nine innocent lives snuffed out, tales of bleeding wounded. The late news clip of the Kmart parking lot in Burwood, a dark stain spreading from under the rug tossed over Maguire's corpse.

The curse of memory. Tusk's exact recall of thought number one: that's it, that's evil right there. And thought number two: I should be there, should be there.

Dana had reacted by shoving him into Christmas preparations. It was their turn to host Christmas Day, and her overflowing clan needed to be presented a tidy house and garden, needed to be fed. So he didn't really track the aftermath of the spree. Just let it hover at the perimeter of his mind.

Until now.

Tusk watched two secretaries, surely still in their teens, chatting on a green bench. They rose, flicked ciggies away, crossed the street to disappear into Number One Collins set back behind National Trust storefronts. Seconds later a stringy guy in bleached jeans swooped on the butts.

Tusk couldn't shake the image of Gil Oldfield's feverish face. He pictured the sorry bastard cowering up there in Number 28, pictured Maguire aiming, shooting him point blank. The public was never given the full wrap about evil, how it claimed the lives of survivors more completely than if they'd died.

Those images blurred with the one of Gentle's stricken face after violence. Lucky that a pro like Conomy was now in charge, Boy Wonder had to be well out of it.

The city made Tusk hungry. He trotted across Collins to a green newsstand and eyed the chocolate bars lined up behind magazines. In his early days on the Force, he'd eaten crap like this—Cherry Ripes, Aeros, Violet Crumbles—by the ton.

"You going to drool there all day?" said the man.

Tusk shook his head and moved away. A tram passed. He was beginning to see how Maguire, Oldfield, and TPT meshed in his mind.

Fourteen years ago Tusk drew a line and stepped across it. Cunts like Maguire descended in the opposite direction.

Someone had to stop them, and once upon a time Tusk had been the one.

He rolled bunched shoulder muscles.

CHAPTER 11

"I never saw it, the real part," Robyn Fox was saying softly.

No one at TPT had time for Peter Gentle, it seemed. Camilla Brown was ensconced at her desk with Sergeant Tagliaferro, Deirdre had the young man Adam in the training room, and Conomy was nodding his head sagely in Finola Vines' office. Even Jim Van Kressel's door was shut. So, his heart still pounding from the failed confrontation with Funder, Peter leaned on the marble benchtop in the reception area and interviewed Robyn.

He wasn't sure why, but Peter had begun by asking about the massacre.

"I didn't notice anything different about Mr. Maguire." Robyn's voice was high, with the slight huskiness of a smoker. She wore white pants and a black top that flattered her slight figure and featured her tanned gym shoulders. A large silver cross hung on a chain around her neck. "Not that he ever said boo to me. I was putting letters in Finola's in-tray. And then I heard bangs, then the screams..." She had large hands and Peter saw red fingernails tremble on her computer mouse. "Mr. Funder took me into the training room. Murray and Gus were there, and

Irene came running. The men piled desks and chairs against the door. We heard swearing, banging. He fired into the door. It seemed like hours before he went away. It was terrifying."

Peter could never understand how anyone tolerated brain-dead jobs like Robyn's, isolated out here, functioning as a pretty face and pleasant voice. He pointed to her large calendar mat, to a corner covered with dozens of tally marks arranged in groups of five.

"What are you counting?"

Her docile brown eyes, swimming in makeup, showed interest for the first time. "Oh, those. Jim's always saying how important it is for me to make a good impression on the traders. Make them feel welcome, you know? Well, I count every time they're rude to me."

"Rude?" Peter nearly laughed, estimated two hundred marks.

"To see if I'm improving."

Looking at Robyn's clear-skinned face, lovely enough yet somehow too long, too artificial, Peter felt pity. How many of those tally marks represented indifference rather than rudeness, he wondered.

He only half-listened to her answers to his perfunctory questions. Instead he wondered what Mick would have done with the Funder situation. No doubt the big brute would have overreacted, threatened the arrogant bean counter. The fantasy felt delicious.

What Robyn told him added little to his sum of knowledge. She'd worked at TPT since last June, after moving from Sydney, and hadn't yet made good friends at the company. Except for Jim, of course, she told Peter, she had nothing but praise for him.

As well as receptionist duties, she did word processing for Jim and sometimes for Finola, although her tone suggested she was glad to minimize the latter.

No, she didn't know Gus well, wasn't the news terrible? He'd always been nice to her, indeed seemed to get along with everyone, though some of the men, Adam particularly, spoke ill of him behind his back. No, she didn't know of any enemies of Gus, and yes, he got on well with his boss Brad Funder. She didn't know when Gus left yesterday, she'd left early herself.

Peter had expected no more from her. "Do you trade yourself?"

"Uh, no. I don't even own a computer."

While she answered a couple of calls, an orange-brown paperweight caught his eye.

"That?" Robyn said. "Oh, Adam gave me that. He gives them to everyone. The girls, that is."

One hour till lunch, Peter was thinking. He couldn't wait to tell Mandy about the new assignment. But first he needed to improve on his meager pickings so far.

"Can I help you?" Robyn's voice, directed toward the front door, was nervous.

A deep voice filled the reception area. "Yeah. Seen a geek anywhere?"

Mick!

Peter whirled. He grinned at the leviathan, imposing in black jeans and blue short-sleeved shirt. Mick's answering smile was hesitant.

"Big guy," Peter asked, "what are you doing here?"

"Fucked if I know." Mick came forward to Robyn, hand outstretched. "Sorry about the language, miss. He does that to me."

CHAPTER 12

Through a door and into the inner barn of Tech Power Trading. Under a silent TV screen big enough for a cinema, Mick Tusk stopped to stare.

Gentle hadn't stopped grinning. "Isn't it something?"

"Something all right," Tusk said.

Another world, more like it. Atonal computer bleeps issued from cubicles lined up in rows like racehorse stalls. Dozens of people—the newspapers had called them day traders—faced computer screens twice as large as the ones Tusk recalled from Homicide.

Noisy: a buzz of chatter, mobiles playing tunes, someone swearing bitterly, an intercom spouting gobbledygook.

"Neutron bomb time," Tusk said. "Hey, why the hell didn't you drop this bloody case?"

Before Gentle could respond, a pale-faced skateboard reject with pink hair bounded from the nearest cubicle. He'd risen from a green rubber ball, some kind of ergonomic device.

The man's cubicle contained two—count them!—computer screens filled with multiple colors. Chocolate bar wrappers, empty Coke bottles strewn over the floor. Discman and cordless headphones on the desk—what kind of music?—and nothing else. Not a scrap of paper.

So this is modern fucking capitalism, Tusk thought.

The man looked Tusk up and down. "They say they take my computers."

"We need to check the soft copies of the Diamond emails." Gentle looked okay for someone who'd had the shit thumped out of him. No scratches or bruises visible on his botched Jagger face, nothing in the patented, hands-deep-in-pockets slouch to suggest pain. His sunken eyes spelled burnout but then they always did. "Oleg, meet Mick."

Oleg rubbed his back with one hand, waved at Tusk with the other. "If I have a friend like this," he deadpanned to Gentle, "I enter race-fixing business."

Tusk said nothing, resolved to keep quiet until he could extract Gentle. The place spooked him.

At the point of stepping from the elevator, he'd almost balked. So irrational, but the images of Maguire and his victims—shit, make it personal, his image of wild-eyed Oldfield and his solemn daughter—the images had intensified the closer he came.

Gentle asked Oleg, "Jim's told you there is no Kurt Diamond?"

A nod. "It is so dumb. Why such silly deception? You know, I told the policeman I complain about Gusty. But I say I never get angry with him."

"Could Gus have been this Diamond character?"

Oleg barked laughter, slapped Gentle on the arm. "Come on,

Peter. You did meet him, no? Gusty? All he cared about was his stupid games."

"But you're a gamer," Gentle said.

"Real games, my friend. Not these games anybody can play, all this role-playing crap. He was just boy-chick. You know, the police ask me for my movements. Ask my girlfriend, I say."

The faint smell that defeated the aircon reminded Tusk of nothing less than prison, too many people under pressure in an enclosed space. Where were Conomy and Dee, surely sniffing around? And Van Kressel—he was curious to meet the bigwig.

Tusk couldn't help himself. "Oleg, were you present at the massacre?"

Oleg's face curled up in disdain. "Ha! Everyone run. Bang bang, he shoot them. Me, I slip under desk and pull chair in behind." He gave a theatrical sigh. "So much blood. So much."

One of Oleg's computers chimed. Without any farewell, the arcade kid whirled and returned to his rubber ball. Fingers pounded the keyboards.

"Mr. Gentle?"

Tusk turned to see a clunky woman in a cream outfit. Too much jewelry, a wave of perfume.

"I'm Irene Skews." She thrust her rectangular face up close to Gentle's. "But of course you can call me Irene. And I'll call you Peter, can I, dear? I'm devastated, simply devastated, by Jim's tragic news. Can I help you?"

"Um, yes." Gentle sidled by. "In a moment."

To Tusk's astonishment, Gentle rushed off. Tusk followed him to a water cooler at the end of the huge room.

"Phew, that was close." Gentle sipped water. "Mick, don't get me wrong, it's fabulous you're here, but what on earth are you doing here? Did Dee ask you to mother me?"

"You big-noting yourself again? An impulse, that's all."

"But Dana…"

"Yeah yeah. You finished drinking the well dry?"

Around the corner, in a small office area, were the cops. An Italian plainclothes Tusk didn't recognize was harassing a woman outside an equipment room. He spotted Conomy's messy white hair, the Inspector in an office with his back to Tusk, talking with a severe-looking woman. Before Tusk could pop in on his ex-colleague, a young man rose to greet them.

"The boss man told us to help you." A crinkly smile. "So here I am. First the men in blue, now the specialists, eh?"

"Adam Menadue," said Gentle, "meet Mick Tusk."

"My pleasure." An easy handshake with some power. Black curls, athletic frame. "Let's talk in the training room."

The three of them set up chairs in a circle. At the other end of the training room, a porky man spoke into a mike while shaking his head at a computer screen.

"Tell me about Gus," Gentle said.

"Right." Menadue sat at ease, hands clasped. "Poor old Gusty, who'd have thought?"

Years back, Tusk had arrested a Menadue, a young buck, for drunk and disorderly. The ensuing fuss to make it stick had taught him just what a name meant in Melbourne.

Gentle said, "Why does everyone call him Gusty?"

"You met him. He'd sigh and sigh, it was like listening to the wind. Look, I don't want to speak ill of the dead, but we weren't exactly friends. We got on but only just. He took a dislike to me from the first time we met. He had this way of sneering, did you spot it?"

Tusk tried to picture the victim, couldn't. A photo, that's what he needed.

"Did he bear grudges?" Gentle said.

"Nah." Another smile, fine lines radiating from the corners of the eyes. "I can't imagine why anyone had it in for him. I mean, he was so useless."

Gentle kept glancing at the clock on the wall. Nearly noon. "At work, you mean?"

"Yeah, well." Menadue leaned back in his chair and Tusk observed watchfulness beneath the geniality. "I'm not saying anything but people talked, you know. He didn't exactly set the world on fire with his help desk, now did he?"

The man's easy contempt was beginning to get Tusk's goat. Gentle's too perhaps, for he straightened up. "Adam, something else please. I'd like the detailed MYOB management report for the nine months to the end of March."

Tusk hadn't a clue what an MYOB was, but liked what he saw, the silver-spoon arsehole's eyebrows rising, the eyes hardening. "What's the accounts got to do with Gusty and computers?"

"We'll see. Can I have that this afternoon?"

"Dunno." Tightened lips. "I'll need to ask my manager."

"I think not. Would you like me to fetch Mr. Van Kressel?"

"Take it easy. Look, I'll see what I can do."

Gentle stood and extended a hand. "I'll come back this afternoon."

"Listen." The easygoing pal of a minute earlier was gone.

Menadue rose, stroked his stubble. "I saw what happened before with Funder. Anyone told you about lunch yesterday?"

"Maybe."

"Funder is a head-in-the-clouds wanker." All loyalty for his boss had deserted Menadue. "Wouldn't know up from down. But he was always at Gusty. We had this work lunch yesterday at The European and Funder started to complain about this new software Gus had been installing. A big upgrade, and Funder whinged about how it isn't functional. 'That's not good enough,' he said when Gusty gave all these reasons. 'Your trouble is you don't have enough company ethos.' He speaks like that, he really does. Well, Gusty looked like he was about to cry. He sort of blurted, 'You can talk.' And you should have seen Funder's face. I've never seen it go red before. Didn't open his trap again, right through lunch."

A blabbing schoolboy, Tusk thought.

"Anyone else hear this exchange?" Gentle said.

"Not sure. It wasn't a big deal to me, I was just trying to get through lunch without dying of boredom."

Gentle looked positively balmy. "Do you know what Gus was talking about?"

"No idea." Menadue too had relaxed. "Whatever it was, Funder didn't like it, not one bit. Trust me, he was ropable."

Once they'd parted from Menadue, Gentle half-ran back to the water cooler. Frantic fingers dialed.

Has to be Mandy, Tusk thought. He gazed down on Collins Street, pitied the office drones heading to lunch. He listened to Gentle's urgent tones. "Can we make it half an hour later? One o'clock?... So what if Harvey's got a two o'clocker?... Hey, what about the time...?"

When Gentle finished, the knuckles of the hand gripping the phone were white.

"Yoo-hoo, Mr. Gentle," called the Skews woman.

She stood by a coffee table with a middle-aged man wearing a brown skivvy, maybe Fletcher Jones trousers. Nothing like a share trader, more a superannuant on a rare trip to the city. Face stretched out like a dachshund's, alert eyes darting behind conservative specs.

"Call me Peter." Gentle sighed. "This is Mick."

"Well, Peter, Saul has something remarkable to tell you." Skews elbowed the man in the side. "Haven't you, Saul?"

"God save us from blathery women." The man shook Gentle's hand dismissively, ignored Tusk. "Saul Phillips. I can't stay chatting. Unlike Irene here, I have some trading to do. The day's been a disaster so far. But what I did tell her is… well, this morning we received an email from Papa Van Kressel instructing us to ignore some chap, Kurt Diamond. Well, in fact I got two emails from this bloke months ago."

Tusk couldn't believe their luck. "You're sure?"

"Oh yes." Phillips bared his teeth as if trying to smile. "I always remember names. Faces, no, names, yes. I've been trying to remember when this was. It must have been last July or August. This Diamond gave me some stock advice that seemed loony. What's this all about?"

"He's a fake," Gentle said. "We're wondering if there's any connection with Gus' death."

"Oh my!" Skews raised hands to her cheeks.

An extended groan cut through the surrounding din. Good to hear people having fun, Tusk thought.

Phillips said, "I can't be much help, I'm afraid. I ignored the emails and that was that."

"Would you have stored the emails?" Gentle asked.

"No. I clean out my computer every month or so." An announcement, something about Sausage Software, turned Phillips' head. "Say, I'd better get back to the grindstone. A heck of a day, I can tell you. You too, Irene, you should spend more time on it, girl."

Phillips headed to a cubicle further back along the aisle. Gentle wore his gotcha look, the one that gave Tusk the shits back in high school. Tusk felt an absurd echo in his own mind. Somehow the priority to get Gentle off the case had disappeared. For better or worse, he knew the geek was in it for good.

"The macho men don't like the way I trade," Skews said to Gentle. "But let me tell you, dear, I've done better than most of them."

Saul Phillips, macho? Tusk took serious note of Irene Skews for the first time. She cut a beefy, clumsy figure. Blonde hair trimmed mannishly short, makeup caked in the way of an altogether older generation. Animal hairs on her outfit. But even as she fiddled with her amassed bracelets and necklaces, the pale green eyes remained still and sharp.

Gentle said, "Irene, there is something you can help me with. I'd like to hear in detail what Len Maguire shouted."

Tusk watched her blanch, felt a prickly shiver himself.

"Come on, dear, let's get out of the way. If you must, I'll tell you all about it."

Skews tugged Gentle to her cubicle. In contrast to Oleg's desk, hers was a mess of piled reports and printouts. The riot of paper spread to the floor, stacks of material piled up against the partitions.

She caught Tusk's stare, chuckled. "Mick dear, don't judge the book by its cover, is all I can say to you. You talk to any of the traders here, we're all different. We all use individualized trading methods, we all specialize in different sectors or stocks." When her fingers weren't at her jewelry, they prodded Gentle excitedly. "As you can see, I don't trade flat out, I'm a value investor, and to find value I read The Flow. That's my pet name for all the data."

Tusk almost laughed. The words could have come from Gentle's mouth.

Interest replaced thinly disguised weariness on Gentle's face. "The data?"

"Ah, Peter, how can I explain it? I read and listen and discuss, and absorb all this"—she pointed at the chaos of her cubicle—"and then tap into the wealth of numbers, facts, and pure fancy on the Internet. And then I just let The Flow swirl around my head. I tell you, dear, the right answer always comes."

They heard out her entire life story, of a spinsterish librarian who had become the great love of a household-name actor twenty years older. A rich widow now, obsessed with day trading. She knew everyone at TPT, spoke adoringly about Van Kressel ("Isn't he just a sweetie, what he's been through..."), sympathized with someone else called Camilla ("Imagine, a single mother and the trauma she went through with that Len"), and even had a kind word to say about receptionist Robyn ("Now there's a sweetie, she needs a man, doesn't she?"). About Gus Youde, Irene was effusive ("Such a sweet, sweet man, so unprepared for the world"). She'd never heard of Kurt Diamond before.

After a while Tusk tuned out. He pictured Dana, heard Uncle Mart whine, "A parked cab, bloody bad business." Guilt mingled with adrenaline.

Gentle was interrupting. "What, Gus was in love?"

Skews beamed. "So you *are* listening. Yes, just a month ago, I saw him going to lunch and he just said, 'Irene, I'm in love.' He had these big droopy eyes, he looked so sad. I said, 'Why, Gus dear, that's brilliant news.' He just shrugged. 'But does she really love me?' he said. Since then I've been at him, to find out who she is, but he never told me. Whoever she is, imagine her sorrow now."

"Irene," Gentle said, "I have to dash. Can we talk later?"

"Of course, dear, of course. But I didn't tell you what Len said, may God rot his soul."

"Oh."

A visible shudder brought Skews even closer to Gentle. In a choked voice she quoted Maguire's vitriol about Jewboy, bitch, and Diamond. Tusk listened spellbound as she described the nightmare. He pictured trembling Oldfield, the ordeal the man had faced. Skews recounted how Maguire, gun in hand, chased her, how she'd made it to the training room. How "the brave, brave men" somehow barricaded the door against the madman's fury.

For the first time in half an hour, the odd, razor-sharp woman fell silent. Her eyes were blank, stranded far away.

CHAPTER 13

As soon as he rushed into Draconi's, Peter Gentle spied Mandy at a table by the Block Arcade window. Lately she had begun wearing her bewitching black hair in a bob. The restaurant was packed. She turned to look at him with those big eyes he could sink into.

His mouth twisted into the grin reserved for her alone. "Sorry I'm late."

Her dress was one of his favorites, a blue affair that scooped down over her bust and exposed her vulnerable collarbone.

"Hi." She smiled, something odd in her expression.

Peter felt on fire. Life was happening. He grinned again at Mandy, consulted his Palm Pilot and tried Inspector Conomy's number. To his surprise, the policeman answered on the first ring. Peter filled him in on Saul Phillips' encounter with Kurt Diamond, and on Funder's lunchtime quarrel with Gus.

"I forgot to ask Phillips about Gus," he said. "If there was any connection or quarrel between them."

"Mmm," was Conomy's only response.

Another call came in just as Conomy signed off, this time Jim

Van Kressel requesting a briefing. Van Kressel swore when he heard about the Funder discovery.

Triumphant, Peter leaned back to survey Mandy, her full-on bony face so easily animated, the engulfing eyes. God, she looked beautiful.

Mandy shook her head and dropped a half-eaten herb bread onto her plate. "That's part of the problem."

What problem? Peter's joy was punched from his chest.

"You're so preoccupied," she said. "I know it's not deliberate, but how many times in the last month have you canceled or mucked me up? And every time we're out, you interrupt to yell on that bloody phone."

Hector had materialized by their table to take their order. Peter felt paralyzed. What on earth was Mandy talking about?

"Gnocchi Matriciana," he croaked. He reached across the table to touch Mandy's immobile fingers. "What about you, Mandy?"

Mandy pulled her hand away. Her lips were bloodless. "Nothing thanks, Hec."

"Nothing?" Peter looked up but Hector was gone.

"What's going on?" he asked.

She heaved a sigh. "I know your heart is good, Peter, but…"

"What's going on?"

"I've enjoyed our time, Peter, you know I have. You can be so sweet when you're not drinking. And I appreciate how hard you've tried to follow all my crazy passions."

Peter's arms were logs, heavy on the tablecloth.

"But my life is so frantic," Mandy said in a quiet voice, her accent reverting to the outback patois he'd observed when they first met. "What with Elle and all. And I know you don't mean to, but it's always you, you, you. I didn't walk out on Wal and come to Melbourne just to end up an appendage to Peter Gentle, Australian of the Year."

Peter's cheeks had turned to ice. He stared at her, willing the nightmare to cease.

"I... I..."

He'd been too late the moment he arrived, he realized. Mandy was rising. At that instant he remembered her wiry limbs, the slope of her breasts, her hot breath panting into his neck.

"I think we should try some distance." Already, it seemed, she was a presence through a fog. "Maybe..."

"But, Mandy, it's..."

The voice drifted across a windswept desert. "I'm sorry, Peter, I really am. Maybe in a few weeks..."

Wetness pricked the corners of Peter's eyes. He looked up, ready to beseech. But Mandy had already vanished into the maelstrom of Draconi's.

He blinked, blinked again and again, tried to marshal rational thought. The blanket of voices, normally so soothing, grated, and for the first time in hours, the lump on his head pulsed.

Idly he reached across for Mandy's herb bread. Should he have seen this coming? Bitterness coiled in his guts. It's always the same, came some long-forgotten loner's mantra.

A chair scraped. Hector sat in Mandy's spot. The restaurateur pushed Peter's gnocchi across the table and tucked a crimson napkin into his own collar before shoveling fettuccine under his mustache.

"M'boy, m'boy," Hector said after a couple of mouthfuls.

Peter straightened. He wasn't going to give Hector the

satisfaction. "It's not what you think."

"Here." Hector flicked a business card through the air.

Peter inhaled until his lungs could hold no more. Printed on the card in plain black letters were a name and a mobile number. Or was it even a name? Unforgiven, it read.

"What's this, Hec?" Peter knew his voice was shrill, but could neither help it nor care less. "Have you been saved?"

"You need help, Peter. This fellow is a hacker."

Peter swallowed. Mandy walks out on him and the ex-judge volunteers a hacker?

"I know, it's a bit weird." Hector's eyes, nestled within bushy eyebrows and folds of wrinkles, were kind. "But I meet all types. And this young man is exemplary at his craft."

Peter inhaled the steam of bacon and chili aromas. His stomach bridled. An impulse to throw the card into Hector's face, and then storm out, passed. All of life felt estranged.

He closed his eyes, heard Hector's chair being pushed back. He let the tumult of Draconi's wash over him.

***

The first time they made love he brought her back to the apartment for a pre-movie drink.

He sat down at the computer. "Look."

He could smell her, perfume and indefinable sweetness, over his shoulder.

"What? A game? You're showing me a computer game?"

"Don't laugh. Didn't you ever play Diplomacy when you were a kid? It's a board game put out by Hasbro, they're the Scrabble people."

Her hands rested lightly on his shoulders. "Honestly, Peter, your romanticism knows no bounds. Maybe I remember the name, but there weren't too many board games in my youth. Country folk stick to Monopoly and Scrabble. Oh and Squatter of course."

So he explained how the board game had spawned an email version that preoccupied thousands. How in each game seven players competed for world domination by allying and betraying, exactly as in global realpolitik. How Diplomacy perfectly suited his intellect, his passion for practical outcomes. That he was ranked in the top hundred worldwide and was in training for the 2002 World Diplomacy Convention to be held in Australia.

"The rules are so simple," he said breathlessly, "I could teach you in five minutes."

"Peter…"

"But like chess, the game is infinitely complex."

"Peter."

Her tone made him swivel in his chair. She stood naked save for red shoes. Her lips were parted, her chest rose and fell.

His mouth went dry.

***

"Genius. You okay?"

Peter opened his eyes. Mick, cup of tea cradled in a big paw, stood over the table. Jesus, was everyone going to see him in this state?

His mobile saved him. A female voice, bell-like and nothing to do with Mandy, said, "Mr. Gentle?"

"Peter Gentle speaking."

"Well…" In the background, Peter could hear reports that reminded him of the cap pistol he used to fire with his brother Anthony. "My father gave me your number. I wonder if I could talk to you."

The last thing Peter needed was another case, especially from someone so imperious. "I'm not sure, Mrs. …"

"I'm sorry, I'm being rude. Belinda Van Kressel is my name."

Jim's daughter!

She said, "I badly need to talk to someone and Pa said you're a good listener. He said you'd know what to do."

"Look, right now—"

"It's about Gus." Sobs exploded down the line.

Peter came to his senses. What a day for weird connections. "Of course, Ms. Van Kressel. Where can we meet?"

He heard her regain control. Though part of him ached to echo her weeping, another part came to sluggish life. Belinda gave him an address in Springvale, southeast of the city.

"It's a shooting range," she said.

Weirder and weirder. "I'm leaving now, Ms. Van Kressel. I'll be there in half an hour."

He signed off, gulped a forkful of gnocchi and rose. "This case is going ballistic now."

"Tell me about it," Mick said. "Just had a buzz from Dee. Said thanks, you done good. That accountant, the one I haven't met, his fingerprints match a partial on the victim's door."

"Why didn't Dee ring me?"

"That I don't know."

The phone trilled again.

Peter answered, "Mandy?"

Silence at the other end told Peter he'd misjudged.

"Sorry," he said. "Peter Gentle here."

"Ah, Peter Gentle," a singsong voice echoed.

Peter nearly dropped the phone. Chilly tendrils reached inside his head. "Who are you?"

Mick craned forward to listen.

It was the voice from last night, the voice still in his head, the voice of pain and concrete hard up against his cheek.

Peter Lorre's ghost spoke slowly. "You failed to listen. Now I'm coming for you, worm."

"No!" Peter shouted into the phone, by now silent.

The sudden hush radiating from around his table spoke louder than a scream.

CHAPTER 14

Sporting Shooters Association of Australia, the sign read. A low, red brick building across the double divide of Dandenong Road from Sandown Park Racecourse. Separated from mammoth Springvale Cemetery by the Visy Recycling Centre, a compound of row upon row of stacked cubes of mottled tan garbage. Three flagpoles, an Australian flag limp on the central one.

Hardly the place for a chick, Tusk thought, then rebuked himself for political incorrectness. He pulled in beside Gentle's yellow travesty.

3:02 PM and only one fare for the day.

"Looks like the kind of place you get your rocks off on." Gentle grinned, exposing the gap in his front teeth. He seemed to have bounced back from the Mandy bust-up.

"You'd make a good target," Tusk said.

"Ha."

Truth was, Tusk enjoyed working with Gentle, had done so from the word go. He often puzzled over why. He'd grown up a hard case, was now transforming into a SNAG, but neither incarnation meshed with this intense boffin. At age fifteen the two of them had found an unlikely chemistry that vanished by age sixteen, until two decades later a chance encounter brought their orbits together. Maybe he liked the nerd simply because Gentle never disguised enjoying his company.

"I just can't figure it," Gentle said. "The daughter of a CEO. Here."

"Sounds sexist."

"I've got so much to tell you about this case." Gentle began his agitated cycle of hand motions and foot tapping. "Not a single thing makes sense."

"Later." The threatening phone call troubled Tusk. Why the hell draw attention by issuing threats?

He led the way inside. Through a carpeted area displaying club notices, past a deserted rifle range, through a door into an open-air fifty-meter range set up for eight shooters. Cordite reek, the crack of shots.

Gentle had lost his grin, twitched with every shot. Tusk felt for him. Only recently had Gentle bothered to explain, turned out his cop father had been in a shootout with eight-year-old Peter as pawn. No bloody wonder he bolted at violence.

Tusk's edginess grew.

Only two patrons. Down one end, a fool in a suit with an automatic pistol, at the other end a stunner with flowing black hair, dressed in jeans and blue checkered top, shooting a .357 Magnum. Her smooth-skinned face was sodden with unchecked tears. She lifted, fired, lifted, fired. A good shot, a damn sight better than Tusk himself.

She didn't stop shooting until Gentle was almost upon her. When she turned, she was heaving, her blue eyes a ruin of grief.

Trembling arms told Tusk she'd fired way too many rounds.

"I loved him," she said. "Ma says what's the point in going public now, but if I just hide like some kind of… some kind of dog, what would Gus think?"

Tusk waited. Luckily Gentle also kept stumm.

A sob, then Tusk watched the woman gather strength. She was young, early twenties if that, slim with all the curves. Narrow nose, full lips, no makeup or jewelry, not that she needed any. Leg-hugging tan boots worth as much as Tusk's entire footwear collection.

She led them outside, to seats in front of the closed bar. She removed protective glasses and earplugs.

"Belinda Van Kressel." A Melbourne private school accent.

"I'm Peter Gentle and this is my partner Mick Tusk. We're happy to help in any way."

"It's a nightmare. I haven't even seen darling Gus' body." Belinda lit a cigarette with shaking hands. "But of course, you're the one who found him. Was it…?"

"How long did you know Gus?" Tusk asked. Time for some structure.

"Okay." She took a deep breath, then smoked while her words tumbled out. "We met at *Bladerunner*, a special showing of the Director's Cut. Pa's a buff, kind of. He takes people to movies, it's like he can't stand to be on his own. I was with a girlfriend and Pa invited Gus at the last minute. They often saw movies together. At the start I didn't think much of Gus, he wasn't my type. But over dinner with Pa, he made an impression on me."

"When was that?"

"Last year. November 11th. I remember the date, it was the start of my life, that day. I asked him out. He told me later he couldn't get up the nerve to do it himself. That's one of the sweet things about him. I've always gone with guys who want to rule the world. Gus, all he wanted was peace and some love."

She clamped her mouth shut for a moment. "We didn't tell anyone. I knew my parents would have a fit."

"Why?" Gentle asked.

"You've met my Pa. Well, he might have been okay about it, but my Ma, she kind of runs the family. I knew she'd throw a wobbly, she's always lecturing me about finding the right guy. Gus didn't want to sneak around but I knew I was right."

"But they did find out, didn't they?" Gentle said. "When, Belinda?"

"Tuesday night."

Twenty-four hours, give or take, before the murder. Tusk took out his notebook.

"I know this is difficult," he said. "But can we step forward from that point? In detail, please."

She had spunk, grant her that. Twisting her black curls, guided by their queries, she told them that after work on Tuesday her father took Gus to see *Erin Brockovich*. Over dinner ("Marchetti's Latin, Pa practically lives there") Gus asked for Belinda's hand. Apparently it was a shock to her old man, and at home her mother took the news even worse ("She slapped me when I said I loved him. I couldn't believe it"). Belinda locked herself in her room, the lovers conferred over the phone. High angst all 'round.

At work yesterday morning, Gus bailed up her father, who

promised a decision in twenty-four hours. Gus was optimistic.

"He said, 'Anyone who loves *Bladerunner* will honor love.' But Gus just doesn't… didn't know Ma. She was, like, wild, yelling at me, ringing Pa every hour."

The other shooter, face heated from his thrill for the week, passed their seats. Belinda paused at the clunk of a can from the dispenser. On his return, the man's shiny eyes dwelled. Tusk met the gaze and the shooter disappeared fast. In the silence Belinda continued.

"We met when Gus got off work. What time? Maybe 5:15. We met at RMIT, where my Business Admin course is. He looked so…" She broke off. "So cute. And so strong. Look."

She held up a finger bearing a thin plain gold ring. "You know what we pledged? If Pa said no—and it was Pa who counted, if he could stand up to Ma it would work out—if he rejected Gus, we were going to get married anyway. Quick, like maybe even today."

A crack in the distance, a different pistol.

Tusk said, "What happened after that, Belinda?"

"We parted about half past five. Gus said he had something he needed to do. I drove home, into another mother shitstorm. It was just the worst. In the end I holed up in my room. I couldn't take it anymore—rang Gus, around seven I think."

"This thing Gus needed to do." Gentle's tone was urgent. "What do you think it was?"

"I don't know. Do you think…?" Belinda blew cigarette smoke back over a shoulder. "That's all he said: 'There's something I need to do.' I thought it was some game he was scheduled to play. He loved his games, Gus did."

"The phone call. How long was it?"

"Oh, only thirty seconds. Just love you, love you, you know."

"And then?"

Belinda went still. "And then nothing. And then this. I lay awake all night. He promised to call. I keep wishing…"

Tusk said, "Take it easy, Belinda."

"You know I wish I'd kept talking to him forever. Maybe he'd be alive now."

Tusk took care with his next question. "Your parents. What did they do last night?"

"Pa had some dinner to go to. He came in late, after midnight. He sounded sloshed, I heard him stumbling, but he could have just been tired. Ma went out too, after banging on my door, like, for an hour. I heard her come home about eleven."

The singsong of a fancy mobile tone brought a gasp from Belinda. She fumbled in her jeans pocket, stabbed the phone, crying again. "Why can't she leave me alone?"

Witnessing grief had been part of Tusk's job before they shafted him. He'd never shied from it, had come to realize his responses were polarized. Either sadness, salted with fury, arose immediately. Or, like now, he was as detached as a video camera.

"Belinda, you'll need to talk to the police," he said. "I'll get you someone with a bit of understanding."

Swimming eyes blazed. "I'll tell them, the police. It's that animal Adam, I know it."

Gentle gasped. "Adam who?"

"Adam Menadue. We went out last year, for ages. Ma kept at me to stick with him, him being so well connected, but I broke it off in October. Not that he's ever admitted it."

Gentle's fingers drummed on his knees. "Did you and Adam meet at your father's work?"

"Through Finola of course. You don't know, do you?" A short disgusted laugh. "Oh my God, trust Pa to find me two idiots without a clue. Adam Menadue, son of Rory Menadue, moneybags himself. Husband of Finola Vines. Of course Ma would put me together with spunk Adam, she could hear the cash registers ringing."

Tusk pictured Adam Menadue's spoiled face. Gentle's mouth was flapping in astonishment.

"I wouldn't put it past him," Belinda said. "He was like so immature, not that you'd know it at first. I had a fat crush on him until I saw through it all. Always putting me down, hanging with that creep David. In your face with anyone who even looked at me. And the bastard rang last night."

"Adam?" Gentle was hunched forward so far, Tusk worried that he might burn himself on Belinda's cigarette, forgotten in suspension between her fingers.

"He was abusive. Called Gus names. I hung up as soon as he started."

"That was when?"

"If he killed Gus, I want him electrocuted. The bastard."

"Time, Belinda? What time?" Revelations—fresh data, Gentle called it—always hyped him up.

"A bit after Gus, maybe 7:15."

"These names he called Gus…"

"None of your business." For the first time, Tusk saw temper flash, not a pretty sight. "Oh, Gus. How could the bastard?"

Gentle said, "How did he know about you and Gus?"

"Oh, you do have a brain. I asked Pa that today. He'd told Finola yesterday afternoon."

Her head collapsed onto her arms on the table. Gunshots blended with her sobs.

Tusk restrained Gentle with a raised palm, asked, "Did Adam know Gus well?" Meaning—did Menadue have the victim's address?

No response from the quivering mass of curls.

"Belinda."

No reaction.

He took Gentle by the elbow, whispered, "All done now."

Out of earshot of Belinda, he rang Dee's mobile, left her a message. Fucking magnificent, he thought, that's how I feel.

Gentle's rush had abated. He was gazing blankly at three rifle shooters making fools of themselves on their stomachs. Mandy, Tusk guessed. He sighed. Worst thing was, because Mandy was the secretary of Jopling, all of Gentle's mates would know before long. A rule Tusk learned in his teens: never mix friends and sex.

He looked at Belinda, smoking with her face averted.

"You ready?" he said to Gentle.

Which was when Dee rang back, at her businesslike best. "On my way, Mick."

CHAPTER 15

Outside the shooting range, the flagpoles' shadows had lengthened.

"Belinda and Gus," Peter Gentle said. "I can't credit it. You never met him, big guy, talk about opposites."

Like Mandy and me, came an unwelcome thought. Somehow his ears still heard gunfire. He listened to bird calls from the direction of the cemetery, the traffic roar from Dandenong Road.

Mick pointed his key ring, and the taxi chirruped. "And no one bothered to inform you?"

Peter pictured Jim's pleasant face. "That thought did cross my mind." He hesitated. "I met Mandy in Harvey's office, you know."

Mick was leaning against the cab, stretching his calf muscles. "Yeah."

"She made fun of the Skulk Club minutes, she was typing them for Harvey. One look and I was, as they say, smitten."

"You told me."

"Mick, am I that selfish? How many hours have I spent in art galleries with her? What about picnics with her and Elle, don't they count? The movies I've had to watch…"

Mick was as inscrutable as ever. "But you like movies now."

Peter sniffed. "That's not the point. It's just… if I could just understand her logic, it might be okay."

A couple drove up to the recycling center and threw flattened cardboard into a skip. Peter kicked a Volkswagen tire. What was the point of this why-doesn't-Mandy-love-me nonsense? "This case, Mick—mind if I fill you in on the possibilities as I see them?"

"Yeah, I need a briefing. Like who is this Oleg freak?"

So Peter hunkered down mentally and reviewed the case in all its baffling glory. Since Mick had met some of those involved, the telling didn't take long.

A breeze blew up and a faint putrid stench joined the gunpowder smells assailing Peter's nostrils. The data imparted, he felt drained.

"What fraction of the story do you reckon you've got?" Mick said. "Half? A quarter?"

"At least now we've found a quality suspect."

Peter pictured Adam Menadue's hunky face. Even disguised, it was hard to equate Adam's easy drawl with his attacker's voice. Murder seemed even more out of the question. But, as Mick never tired of telling him, so many murders proved surreal.

But why would Adam impersonate a TPT analyst? It didn't fly. Better to move on, he thought, than dwell on lies or bloody Mandy. He fished out the card Hector had given him and dialed the number on it.

The voice that answered had the same clipped caution that Mick would use. "Yes?"

"Is this, er, Mr. Unforgiven?"

"Very funny. You are?"

"Peter Gentle."

"Ah, yes. Let's meet at Luxe Wine Bar, Inkerman Street, St Kilda. Does nine o'clock suit?"

A hacker with refined taste, Peter thought. He'd only been to Luxe once, had liked the industrial decor and the wines by the glass. "I was thinking right now, say 4:30."

"You were thinking."

Peter felt good about the man already. "It's what I do."

A grunt. "Love the modesty. Meet me at Jackie O's, Barkly Street across from Acland. We've just signed a confidentiality agreement, right?"

"On the dotted."

Peter terminated the call, watched a giant garbage truck rev into the recycling center.

Mick had his arms up above his head, hands joined. The rocky shoulder and neck muscles strained. Peter couldn't read the flat blue eyes. He remembered Dana's wild Greek face, remembered what Mick was risking. A true friend of Mick, he thought, would send him home.

"Hec referred me to a hacker," he said. "We're meeting in St Kilda. You know, Mick, I'm not happy with Adam Menadue as hacker and murderer."

"He's hiding something," Mick said. "You should be pleased, bloody good progress today."

"Thanks," Peter said. "I couldn't have done it without you. Can I get your help tonight, maybe even tomorrow?"

Mick looked away, gazed at the hangar-sized shed at the rear of the recycling center, where noisy clanking had begun.

Humor sometimes worked. Peter said, "It pains me to ask a football moron to assist, but… look, I know you reckon this is over my head. So why not give a hand?"

And what about my stalker, he thought. "Oh, I forgot, you're a basketball moron now, not footy."

"Sorry, no can do." Mick's eyes turned back to fix on him. "I'm playing hooky right now. Better go earn a crust."

"Please?" Peter's voice caught.

Mick took a massive breath. He walked a slow circle around the taxi. He put on his sunglasses, once more looking every inch the movie villain.

"I'm not forcing you," Peter said.

Mick slapped the cab's roof. "Yeah, okay. Just this one trip."

Peter deliberately stayed deadpan. Bugger Mandy, he thought. Bugger Dana and every illogical female in the world. His energy had returned, the chase was on, and Mick was with him.

"That's it?" Mick said. "How's about 'thanks, partner'?"

Peter laughed. He affected an American accent. "Thanks, pardner."

A smile graced the unyielding features. "Up yours, too."

***

Mick's taxi dogged Peter's passage on the drive to St Kilda. The news on the radio wasn't good. The All Ords had shed 1.6% to 3,100 by the four o'clock close, and tech stocks had taken a hammering. Contrasting images of Oleg Kilpatrick and Irene Skews sprang into Peter's head. He wished them luck.

While driving past Caulfield Racecourse, he received a call from Constable Tagliaferro.

The Computer Crime man's accent seemed stronger over the phone. "I heard about the daughter. And thanks about Phillips. They're out retrieving his computer now. Anything else new?"

He's fishing, Peter thought. "No, nothing. What does Adam Menadue say?"

"Too soon. The Inspector wants to quiz the daughter first. I'm at HQ with the Kilpatrick computer. We're gonna start on the flamer's emails in the next half-hour."

"Maguire's computer?"

"We had nothing in storage. The widow has moved down to the peninsula and a couple of Frankston boys are heading down to interview her."

Peter bottled up his impatience. "Anything on Oleg's machine?"

A moment of hesitation. "No trace. It's clean."

Peter sensed the policeman was lying. He gritted his teeth. If this was the cooperation he could expect, what hope was there of this Unforgiven character making any difference at all?

CHAPTER 16

Though developers had sunk claws into St Kilda, Mick Tusk admired the suburb for how it never lost a beat. Still bohemian, still a blur of nationalities. Occasionally on Sundays he and Dana brought the kids to sample the cake shops, stroll through the art market to the water.

The scabrous back streets he knew even better.

The bustle of Acland Street invigorated him. At the end, across Barkly Street, loomed the oversize pink fluorescent sign of Jackie O. What a name, like that punk band, Dead Kennedys. He hummed a few bars of "Holiday in Cambodia," the rabid single he'd taken a fancy to at age fourteen. Ah, those days of haunting weirdo record shops, emptying his pockets for vinyl at the expense of food.

He found Gentle waiting outside the restaurant. After relaying the news from Computer Crime, Gentle led the way in.

For most of his life Tusk had preferred the smoke and beer fumes of pubs to yuppie cafes. Another change, courtesy of Gentle, forcing him into Draconi's so many times, he'd grown to relish a few minutes each day in some cafe. Jackie O hit the spot. Pleasant light, big band jazz playing softly, a relaxed tableau of small square tables with wooden chairs. An Indian waitress laughing with the man behind the cramped bar. Aromas of roasted vegetables and coffee beans.

4:31. Four couples, mostly in black, one pair quarreling. An older man with a homburg. A weary woman with kids. No hackers, as if Tusk had any idea what a hacker looked like.

Gentle took a table by a green bas-relief wall. Tusk sat opposite. Only then did he spot the tall figure in the tiny office by the bar.

"Don't tell me we've been stood up." Gentle looked very St Kilda, the slouch, the creases still sharp on his suit.

Tusk waved to the watching man. "No such luck."

Time to be careful. He laid his sunglasses on the table, rose with hands alert.

He should have kept his sunnies on, for the bulky man who strolled over wore a pair as black and forbidding as his. The so-called cyber-crook cast an intimidating profile, his face surrounded by a triangular beard, connecting mustache, and brown hair spilling over his shoulders.

The man halted a meter away. A finger rose and pointed toward Gentle.

"You're Peter Gentle." Cadence from suburbia. "But you, sir"—looking at Tusk—"who are you?"

"My partner Mick. Mick Tusk." Gentle rose, seemingly not fazed at all. They shook hands. "What do we call you?"

"Unforgiven will do. Or some say U."

"Like, hey U?"

Unforgiven showed white teeth. "Like F U."

Unforgiven slid in next to Gentle, and Tusk relaxed back into his seat. Relaxed because the hacker's façade was just that, a façade. Up close, Unforgiven oozed the harmless aura of the Gentles of the world. Pallid complexion, brow shiny with sweat, a pimple on his top lip. Unhip cargo pants, a zippered top partly open. Tense shoulders, as if set to fly.

The waitress was all smiles. Tusk was pleased to find blackcurrant tea. Both geeks ordered short blacks.

Gentle said, "So you're a hacker."

"So you're a private investigator." Unforgiven's gaze turned to Tusk. "And you, sir, beat up gays on Saturday night."

"Hey—" Gentle began but Tusk laid a hand on his thin forearm.

"It's okay," Tusk said. He gazed directly into Unforgiven's shades, tapping his own sunglasses on the glass tabletop. "It really is."

Unforgiven hesitated, removed his sunglasses. His eyes slid away from Tusk's scrutiny. "My apologies, sir, you fit certain of my preconceptions. Tell me, what is this job we've assembled to discuss?"

"How do you charge?" Gentle asked.

"Like a Canberra lobbyist." Unforgiven ran fingers back through his silken mane. "Apologies, I should restrain the flippancy. Describe the situation and I'll offer a price."

Their beverages arrived. Tusk took notes this time. As always, Gentle summarized so well that Tusk wondered what sort of a policeman could have been made of him, if grabbed early enough to stamp out the bad habits.

The shape of the case was beginning to seep into Tusk. Like

Gentle said, too many disparate elements. A minor impersonation of officialdom, apparently the product of computer crime, connected by a gossamer-thin thread to a four-month-old massacre. Possibly linked to the execution of the boss' wannabe son-in-law. Maybe even linked to Gentle's very arrival at TPT.

When Gentle was done, Unforgiven's eyes, pale and of indeterminate color, flicked between the two partners. "Thank you. I can see why they say you're good at this."

Gentle beamed. Tusk suppressed a smile.

Unforgiven donned his sunglasses. "Gentlemen, let us talk on water."

The hacker rose, waved to the waitress on the way out. Gentle scrambled after.

Tusk paid the bill and caught up with them halfway along Acland Street. Unemployed kids basked in the autumn sun, just as he had all those years ago. The two intellects swung left at the tram terminus and walked in silence between the ugly Palais Theatre and ghostly Luna Park. The short jetty off the beach was empty apart from a family with a screeching toddler, two boys fishing with spools.

Unforgiven led them to a railing looking toward the marina. "First, let me say that I'll take the job."

Who's hiring who, Tusk thought.

"I find it most unusual and repugnant," said Unforgiven, "that this hacker has targeted individuals in this manner. Whilst not overtly damaging, this feels like a black hat hack."

A seagull landed on the railing. Tusk spoke for the second time since meeting the man. "Black hat?"

"Sir, it's a strange and wondrous world out there in cyberspace." Unforgiven fingered a red object on a string around his neck. "I liken it to the Wild West. The operating systems underpinning all our computers, the entire Internet, were built by developers who ignored security. Blame Microsoft above all. What that means is that hacking is easy, child's play."

Tusk listened to the rustling of the tiny breakers, glanced at Gentle. "Do I need a fucking lecture?"

"You do, sir. Everyone needs this lecture, fucking or not." Unforgiven crossed his arms. "The point is that most hackers are white hat hackers. They do it for the challenge, some to validate their own existence, others to show off to peers, a macho trip like a bullfighter. Some even for altruistic reasons, because they believe in some vision of an empowered future. And do you know how we can tell most hackers are white hat?"

Gentle's symphony of foot tapping was working through its first movement. "Because if they were mostly evil, we'd all be cactus."

"Coe-rrect." Unforgiven cocked a finger, pointed at Gentle. "It's an obsessive, weird community. Six degrees of separation is three in my world. Largely, we regulate our own. We even regulate the bumbling fat-cat corporations out there."

Tusk watched the gull edge closer to Gentle's elbow. He found this talk of evil cartoonish. Of the three, only he knew evil.

"Specifically," said the hacker, "it's bad form to pick on an individual unless you have a grudge, which of course is a possibility here. Corporates, yea, dimwits, nay. So yes, I'll track down this man."

"Man?" Tusk was fascinated despite his irritation.

"Yes, ninety percent of hackers are male. Make that ninety-nine percent for black hat hackers."

"Are you white or black hat?"

Unforgiven turned to gaze at St Kilda Pier further along the beach. "This doesn't sound like a difficult hack, although it has intriguing aspects. You ask the right question, Peter, why target day traders at home? Why a false identity, even if designed to lose them money? Why not attack the company? If individual hatreds are in play here, why not destroy their computers, or mess up their trading accounts?"

"Exactly," Gentle said.

"We've lost the physical computers for good," Unforgiven said. "Actually, that is one thing the pigs are good at, examining machines. Of course any hacker worth his salt could have cleaned up before now."

Tusk bristled yet again. He hadn't heard that word pig for years, and then only from bikers. But there was no malice in Unforgiven, only a jaded worldview that Tusk found in men much put upon. Like Cap, like himself maybe. How old was this guy?

"Let's hope the pigs relay their findings," Unforgiven said. "Can you make sure you get soft copy of any Diamond emails they find?"

Gentle noticed the seagull, flinched.

"Shoo," he said.

The bird flapped and wheeled away.

"I'll try," Gentle said. "This Tagliaferro is territorial."

Unforgiven grimaced. "He has a reputation. What else? I'll start scouting around, determine if anyone is claiming bragging rights to this exploit. Can I get email addresses of the traders and staff?"

Gentle fished out a sheaf of papers from his jacket pocket. "Here's what the network manager gave me. The logs, addresses, anything I could think of. Let me know what I missed."

"Nicely done. These will help me ferret around the servers."

"Camilla claims their network is secure. She talked about penetration tests."

Tusk said, "Now we're talking my lingo."

To his surprise Unforgiven grinned. "Yes, don't you love it? Those puerile marketers. I've even heard of covert and overt pen tests. Well, we shall see what TPT's defenses are made of."

Unforgiven's handshake was muscle-free. Tusk was glad to be finished, had felt exposed ever since they left the restaurant. Out here he and Unforgiven looked like drug dealers, Gentle a yuppie user. He gave Unforgiven a business card, as did Gentle.

"You were going to quote a price," Tusk said.

"No charge, sir."

"What?" Gentle said.

In Gentle's world, dollars were the only language. Not so in Tusk's. He tried to understand the contract on offer, tried to see beyond Unforgiven's image, the carapace all geeks constructed for the outside world.

"It's okay," he said firmly to Gentle.

"So this is a good turn?" Gentle grinned. "A U-turn?"

"Memorize my number," Unforgiven said. "Ditch the card. I don't like the physical aspect of this job."

Me neither, Tusk thought.

Unforgiven hesitated, as if about to change his mind. Then

the hacker was flowing away, archaic hair swaying.

Gulls bitched around them. A woman bent to scoop dog shit into a plastic bag. The two truants fishing off the end looked their way, conversed, laughed. The low sun glistened across the pancake surface of the gray-blue water.

Gentle was the one to shatter the calm. "Is that it then, Mick?"

"Afraid so."

Tusk made an effort to smile but his lips barely moved. He reached inside for a song. Up surged the jangly guitars and thick drums of an old Tom Petty number, from his Heartbreakers era, something about the waiting being the hardest part. True, how true. If he didn't believe this internal tug-of-war would be resolved, he'd fucking go mad.

The thought shook him. Could he do a Len Maguire?

They left the pier, walked through the early evening crowd. Before Tusk fanned off Acland toward his taxi, he cuffed Gentle lightly on the arm.

"Take care, genius," he said.

He was hoping to be hit with that unstoppable dumb optimism Gentle kept dredging up. But Gentle's eyes were moody.

At least the parting words offered solace.

"For sure, big guy. Most appreciated."

CHAPTER 17

From the window of Jim Van Kressel's office, the jagged skyline blurred in the dusk. The scent of aftershave was strong.

Peter Gentle restrained himself. "You're joking."

Despite the day's onslaught of bad news, the twinkle in Jim's eyes remained inexhaustible. Neat piles of work sat on his desk. Only blotchy cheeks and puffy eyelids betrayed the exhaustion he had to be feeling.

If anything, Finola appeared even fresher. Barely acknowledging Peter, she tossed a whiteboard marker in her fine-boned fingers. The whiteboard was covered with lists and flow diagrams. Peter couldn't discern the slightest resemblance between her and Adam.

"No joke, Pete," Jim said. "He said he visited Gus at home a month ago. Apparently there's an entry in his diary to match. I can't believe he'd do anything like that, anyway."

"No, not Brad," Finola said. "Not with his résumé. Where's the motive?"

Peter recalled Funder's efficient hostility. "He was most unhelpful to me."

Finola's eyebrows rose.

Jim took an iced donut from a half-full box on the desk and glanced at Finola. "Pete, to be honest, I hired a hotshot CFO too early. It's hard for us to keep a guy like that occupied."

Scoffing the donut, Jim ran through his notes of a call, twenty minutes ago, from Inspector Conomy. There wasn't much positive to report. The autopsy merely confirmed a close-up shooting from behind. Gus' house was overflowing with fingerprints and forensic material but apparently Gus' friends, all of them in a club of role-playing gamers, frequently held gaming sessions there. Gus and the other two inhabitants had been close friends, nothing more, and alibis existed. A neighbor two doors down heard the shot but ignored it. No trace of the murder weapon had been found. They'd begun interviewing Belinda.

Most interesting to Peter was the news that not only was Crazy Oleg's computer "clean," as Tagliaferro had told him, but someone, presumably the hacker, had wiped all data off the hard disk. Tagliaferro hadn't lied but had withheld.

"The inspector blasted me," said Jim.

"But Jim," Finola said, "surely he can't expect you to expose your entire family to the press."

"No, he was right to tick me off." Jim grabbed another donut. "You too, Pete, I should have filled you in on Belinda and Gus. But I've felt constrained. Thanks for talking to her."

Peter found it odd that neither Jim nor Finola mentioned Adam. "A pleasure."

"I doubt it. She rang me from the police station, called you a few choice names. But then she yelled at me too, didn't she? Now, how about you update us on your day."

Peter zoomed through his Thursday, omitting any mention of Unforgiven or Belinda's accusations against Adam.

"Bloody great work, Pete." None of it could have been new to Jim, but a smile lit the dimpled face. "Eh, Fi? Didn't I say?"

Finola's eyes bored into Peter. "That is impressive, I must say. Maybe I should eat humble pie."

Peter's hip bruise ached from all the standing. He yawned. "No point in getting carried away, Mr. Van Kress—Jim. The data is too limited for optimism. And I've made no headway with the hack."

"A donut, that's what you need." Jim chuckled. "Here, a chocolate one. I announced a donut hour this arvo, Robyn bought ten boxes. God knows we needed something to lift the punters' spirits."

On his way to find Camilla Brown, Peter devoured the sticky donut. Too sweet, he thought, pining for a glass of red. A row of desk lamps provided the only light in the dark trading area; evidently Jim was too stingy to leave the lights on. Peter passed Oleg, hunched over what looked like a game of Doom II, and another trader peering at his screen with a book on his lap. Irene's desk lamp was on, but she wasn't in her cubicle.

Waiting, waiting, he thought. All the data was in someone else's court. Or was it? Was Belinda's mother a suspect? Come to think of it, the data couldn't be complete without checking Jim's alibi, although how? What about Finola? She'd certainly been antagonistic from the start.

Rounding the corner, he was taken aback to find Adam Menadue rising from his desk.

"Here's your reports." A disarming smile. "I bet the police

appreciated the skinny on good old Funder."

Peter took the proffered sheets. Adam's smug expression triggered rashness.

"I know about you and Belinda." He glared into Adam's stunned eyes. "Where were you last night?"

Adam reared. "Are you insane? I've done nothing but help you out." He was shaking, whether from rage or fear Peter couldn't tell. "In case it makes any difference, I was home last night. With Father."

Cross at himself for playing his card early, Peter stepped back.

Adam slung his jacket over a shoulder. His voice was harsh. "Having stayed late to help you out, mate, I'll be off. And I'll forget what you just said. Fair enough?"

"Fair enough. But the question still stands."

Adam gulped. "Man, you've got some nerve."

Peter watched Adam's back recede. He sat on the edge of the bookkeeper's desk to skim the report. Just as he'd expected, it was useless, too macro.

He found Camilla squinting over a narrow keyboard in the computer room. Grimy glasses imparted an academic look.

"If it's not one thing it's another," she said to his request, but she whipped off her glasses and took him to Gus' desk, where she showed him how to log on and access the MYOB accounting system. A litany of woes accompanied the demonstration. Peter could see flecks of white in the corners of her mouth.

Already the desk had been stripped of any trace of Gus. Peter found it spooky and he told her so.

Camilla's voice trembled at the edge of tears. "Oh, I know. I keep wanting to cross myself every time I go past. And I thought

I'd left all that Catholic mumbo jumbo behind. What about you, Peter, you saw the… the body. How can you stay so calm?"

A good question. "He was a good-hearted man, wasn't he?"

An undefined expression flickered on her face. "One of the best."

Peter took the opportunity to ask if Adam could hack.

"Adam?" Camilla curled a lip. "He can hardly log on to his own machine."

She seemed impressed when Peter memorized the access codes with a glance. He told her the hacker news from Tagliaferro but didn't mention Unforgiven. She knew even less than he did and mainly seemed pleased that the hack hadn't hit the press.

Finally, she excused herself. "I said I'd pick Oscar up from Little League and I need a drink on the way."

"Thanks," said Peter. He meant it.

"Interested in joining me?"

Peter blushed. "Better not. Plenty to do yet."

It was her turn to avert her gaze.

When he made his way to the front five minutes later, after practicing MYOB access, he felt bedraggled. Hard to view Camilla as a suspect, he thought.

The trading area was pitch black. Oleg and Irene hovered around the door of Jim's lit office.

"In case you two didn't notice," Peter said, "closing was three hours ago."

Jim was on the phone, hand pressed against his forehead. The donut box was empty.

"Yes…" Peter could just hear Jim say. "Yes… yes, Alison, I

heard you. Look, someone at my door. No darl, not Fi. Why do you always…?"

Oleg grunted. "No computer at home. Remember?"

Irene crowded up close to Peter. "I've been catching up on reading. Peter dear, you look like you could do with a good night's sleep. Jim won't tell me, do you know why Brad left so early?"

The Jim Van Kressel who charged from the office, hefting a bulging briefcase, was nothing like the slumped figure Peter had just glimpsed.

"Oleg," Jim cried. "You ready for that seminar tomorrow?"

"Sure, Papa." Oleg grinned and winked at Peter. "I wave my arms, do some magic on the screen, they all go ooh, aah, and Papa is one more step to fortune number two. Right?"

Jim chortled. "Who's the one making a fortune? Irene, any progress with Motley?"

"Oh, Jim." Irene beamed. "The poor dear is just so ill."

Oleg said to Peter, "Cats. Me, I prefer women. If I treat them like you treat your animals, Irene, I have a harem."

Before Irene departed, Peter was forced to endure a photo of her in fur stole and feathered hat, ringed by four cats on stools ("Freddie, he's the one from when Fred was alive, Mandarin's the old tabby, that's Motley, and E-cat is the Burmese"). Oleg left with her.

"You wouldn't know Crazy Oleg dropped a bundle today, would you?" Jim said. "Most of them did. Let's hope tomorrow is brighter, I wouldn't want any of them to go under right now."

Jim flicked switches. Behind them the floor became a ghostly arena lit faintly by the globes strung on the Collins Street trees.

"Got anything on tonight?" Jim asked in the reception area.

Peter longed to get home and doodle on a pad, a bottle of red at his side. Mull over the data. Give Harvey a call. Maybe even find the courage to ring Mandy.

"Nothing overpoweringly urgent," he said.

"Good. You can join us."

"Join you?"

Jim's smile would have enticed mice into a trap. "Finola's fiftieth. You can meet Rory, her better half. Have an in-depth with her stepson."

Adam was stepson, not son? At that instant Peter knew, although none of his data was a guide, that he had to be at this function. And that this case was murkier than he, or anyone else, had imagined.

"Why not?" he said.

With a flourish, Jim locked the front door and set the alarms.

"Don't let them tell you otherwise." Papa Van Kressel's face was drawn but wore a wolfish grin, different to his stock standard smile. "Owning a business is the thrill, Pete. Turning the lights on and off, making the world go around, that's what I'll do till the day I die."

CHAPTER 18

Shit happens.

By the time Mick Tusk eased into his uncle's driveway, the dangerous fuzziness before sunset had settled in. The afternoon westward migration of traffic growled under an orange horizon.

6:29. Way past the changeover time. Uncle Mart came up the path with Dom the night driver.

"Sorry I'm late," Tusk said.

"No problem," said Uncle Mart. His face spoke otherwise. His leathery hand shook Tusk's.

Tusk nodded at Dom.

Uncle Mart slid into the cab. When he emerged seconds later, his face was a stranger's. Veins pulsed under pinched eyes.

"Hey, Mihkel, what is this? Bloody fifty-six dollars."

Tusk had rehearsed excuses. "Sorry, uncle."

Dom smirked.

"What you been doing? Are you drinking again?"

Uncle Mart jabbed a finger into Tusk's chest. Tusk caught his sour smell.

"Sorry."

"Sorry, sorry. I let you drive my taxi, you come back with this bloody poofter meter."

The tableau—wizened Estonian, Greek dickhead, ex-policeman—slowed for Tusk. His mind ranged over the day. Thought: every step I took, had to be taken.

Uncle Mart was winding up. "You're a bloody no-hoper. Arne, he's maybe right. Always too bloody big for your bloody boots."

He shouldn't have mentioned the old man.

Tusk rammed his rigid face to within an inch of his uncle's eyes.

"Fuck you," he said.

He whirled and screeched off in the Peugeot.

All Tusk's life, action had been king. But for the blood tie, the history, he'd have thumped the arsehole.

Window down, cool air.

Music. His fingers found a cracked cassette case. Save me, Paul Rodgers, he thought. The rolling, riffing hymn to desire and regret, Free's "Wishing Well," filled the car, filled his head.

CHAPTER 19

"I can't stress how much I need this bloody mess cleaned up pronto," Jim Van Kressel said when he arrived with the first round of drinks.

Peter Gentle's bruised body screamed for a seat. Instead, the two of them stood at a bench in P.J. O'Brien's within the bowels of Southgate. Peter was miffed. Here he was in the company of a self-declared bon vivant, on the blessed riverbank, and the millionaire insisted on a fake Irish tavern possessing neither windows nor decent wine by the glass.

A sip of crap red emboldened him. "How can I clean anything up, if you never tell me the whole story? You know as well as I do that Adam is a prime suspect."

Jim had used the pub's restroom to change into formal wear retrieved from his car, a black tuxedo with a satin lapel and a spotted green bow tie. A frilly pleated shirt expertly disguised his bulk.

"Why does every good turn bite you on the bum?" If Jim was troubled by the accusation, he didn't show it. "Fi asked me to take Adam on, at the end of '98. He takes after his father, what more can I say? Would I hire him now? Nope. Does he do a good enough job? Yep. Would he kill Gus because of Belinda? Too bloody serious for him, I'd say."

Peter had to bite his tongue. This man was his ticket to salvation, had treated him well, yet every encounter increased Peter's suspicion that he was being manipulated.

"Here's to Gus," Jim said. "Salt of the earth."

Peter tapped his wine glass against Jim's schooner. Twenty-four hours since the horror of the body… "Your wife really wanted Belinda to stick with Adam."

"Aha, I hear my daughter talking. Look, until now Alison and Belinda have always been close. Too close, if you ask me. Now Belinda's stretching her wings, so you need to take what she says with a pinch of salt."

"The police are going to quiz Alison, you know."

"Ridiculous. Anyway, she was home last night."

Oh sure, Peter thought. "What did Finola think of Belinda and Adam? Or Belinda and Gus?"

"You'll have to ask her, Pete. Fi doesn't talk much about her home life. A rocky road with her stepson, I know that much, but it's been none of my business."

P.J. O'Brien's Tavern was a maze of wooden booths and alcoves. In a nearby grotto, ringed by blue curtains and labeled The Pen Corner, a man waved fingers in greeting as he joined a group of office workers. He was hefty with spiky gelled hair. Peter read his T-shirt: Built Tougher Than Your Momma's Meatballs.

Over pints of Guinness, Jim's words flowed, and Peter discovered that the executive was a store of fascinating data.

Take Crazy Oleg. Oleg's widowed mother had brought him from Russia as a teen, then married an Irishman who owned a chain of inner suburban laundromats. With outstanding Year 12 results, Oleg could have been a lawyer or doctor. Instead he persuaded his stepfather to let him run the laundromat business. Five years later, at the ripe old age of twenty-three, he sold it for enough to springboard a trading career.

Or take Gil Oldfield, another star trader. Wounded during Maguire's rampage, he'd retained his seat at TPT but was spooked, wouldn't come into the office or touch his portfolio.

"A tragedy," Jim said. "The poor son of a bitch won't even talk to me on the phone."

But evidently Jim's real aim was to convince Peter that Finola Vines was a saint. Finola's life story turned out to be much as Belinda had venomously summed up. Fifteen years ago, Finola married widower Rory Menadue, a descendant of the retail pioneer. Rory, five years younger, came with a teenage son. Finola was already commencing a stellar career as a stock analyst, one of the first Aussie tech analysts, Jim claimed. A midlife crisis in 1995 led her to jump ship, to become a freelance champion of the new and techno.

"Best thing that ever happened to me, meeting her back in the early '90s. Everyone calls TPT my baby, but Fi had the idea, latched on to the explosion of online broking in the States. When she rang me in '97, she found me ripe for an adventure. And I can honestly say I've never regretted a minute of working with her. You married, Pete?"

"Ah, no." Peter pictured his silent father and loquacious mother, awkwardly juxtaposed in Christmas party photos. Of his siblings, Julia's marriage was icy, Anthony had divorced years ago, and young Sam seemed blissfully single. And look at Mick and Dana...

Jim's eyes were fierce. "My advice, don't. Fi's marriage is no bed of roses, I reckon. You'll meet Rory tonight. One of those... you know, one of those people who casts himself as an expert without being one."

Cackles broke out from an adjacent group of businessmen. A man in a red shirt, white jumper draped over his shoulders, roared with laughter.

"A dilettante?" Peter said.

"That's it. He's interesting but would I hire him? Not in a pink fit. But at least Fi's only married once and stuck with it. Not like yours truly, with two wreckages behind me." Jim sniffed. "Alimony, two bitter kids who keep putting the bite on me. This one's third time lucky, lasted twenty years. Not easy, by any means. Alison is younger... a handful."

Besides Belinda, Jim and Alison had an older son studying in California.

Smoke seemed to hang in clouds below the low fake-scuffed brown ceiling. Drowsy, Peter forced himself to concentrate. There was no stopping Jim now.

"I made Fi my chairman, these days chairperson I guess, gave her fifteen percent of the stock. She's also on a government advisory and chairs a B2B software company. Gives heaps of talks, next week a keynote in Perth. She's running this year's fundraiser for the Gallery. Bet you saw last year she was a nominee for Businesswoman of the Year. Crikey, Pete, with someone like Fi and with my background, how can TPT fail?"

Is he in love with Finola, Peter wondered.

"We're real yin and yang, Pete. I'm a hard nut, she's the dreamer. Votes Labor, for God's sake. Doesn't drink, practices all this yoga nonsense. She's even president of some fan club, this '60s singer. But no one works harder for TPT. Since Maguire, I reckon she's been in the office four days out of five. You know what the big news is, Pete? She's networking to line up capital for an expansion to Sydney."

"You could have done better with some of the other staff."

Jim peered at him, as if deciding how to take the insult, then chuckled and slapped the bench. "Fi reckons I can't recruit and you know what, maybe she's right. Certainly looks like we'll go through an overhaul in the next few weeks. Funder was a mistake. Brown is also turning out badly, she's been against me since the shooting."

Priceless, this drunken candor, although Peter had no illusions. If salesman Jim wanted to conceal anything, he'd have no compunctions or difficulties.

Next to Finola, Jim cast his own life as dull, though to Peter it seemed anything but. Born to a Dutch-descended father and a Catholic mother toward the end of World War II, Jim had no memory of his father, killed in action. Jim and his older sister were raised by their mother.

"My Ma taught me the value of hard work. I'll never forget one morning. The day before, I'd broken a finger at school, the doctor bandaged it, told me to rest. But no, Ma switched on the light at 4:45, yelled at me, get up, we need the money, am I a boy or a girl? So there I was, finger screaming with bloody pain, delivering papers in the rain. That kind of experience sticks, I have to admit."

After the proverbial stinting childhood in Moonee Ponds, Jim did it hard in university, working to support himself while gaining an engineering degree. After a couple of years in Mount Isa, he became a power plant salesman back in Melbourne, and in 1978 joined a tiny waste management and treatment firm. Appointed CEO in 1989, he hocked his house and bought into the firm, which he then rapidly expanded. When it was acquired by an American company in 1993, he exited two years later with "a cool ten mil."

By that time he was fifty-one and Alison urged him to retire. Soon realizing retirement bored him, he sought investment opportunities. Eventually, he and Finola launched Tech Power Trading in April of 1998.

Peter managed to resist much quizzing about his own life. He did find himself drawn into an overview of the high-profile case that had inadvertently launched this new career. The computerized fund, the murdered genius, the bodies, the crime boss, the mansion in Toorak… he sketched them all.

It wasn't something he often discussed, though in his mind he frequently revisited the case. Such a terrifying experience, yet somehow enriching. Weirdly, his most frequent memory was of waking in a Knox Hospital bed, jaw broken, groggy, to see Mick gazing down on him… the rising horror as he registered Mick's neck encased by a purple ring, aftermath of the near-strangulation. Even now, in certain light, Peter could make out the imperfections in the skin grafts, how they delineated the barbaric halo.

And then Dana had entered, yelling blue murder. She'd blamed Peter for the entire episode, never mind that Mick was a free agent far better equipped than Peter to handle the job. Her lack of logic rankled still.

Jim's speech had begun to slur. "Well, TPT sounds mild compared to that."

"I wouldn't call Maguire mild."

Jim fell silent. In the ensuing gap, Peter remembered to ask what Rory Menadue thought of his son and Belinda being together.

"Ha! He's been crawling all over Belinda," Jim said. "Me as well. Kept hinting at marriage. Thank God she broke it off. Believe me, the last few years I've learned to smell money-grubbers."

"But he's a Menadue heir."

"That's what he'll tell you. Everyone believes he's loaded, but Finola told me he's only a grandson and all he gets is an allowance from a trust. Doesn't work, fritters his cash away. Fi's the one who supports the three of them. You know what I reckon he is?"

"A dilettante?"

"Ha. A frigging freeloader is what I think. A nice guy though. I'll be interested in what you think of him."

Peter yawned. His head lump felt tender. Was Jim's fingering of Rory a smokescreen?

At last Jim sat down. Around an upended beer keg, surrounded by raucous German tourists, the conversation swung to movies. As Belinda had also said, Jim was crazy about them, all kinds, but especially comedies and thrillers. He "caught a flick" two or three times a week, either in town or at the Brighton Bay near home, knew all the ratings, even maintained his own database. In his new house he'd installed a home theater.

They pushed through the fire-engine-red swinging doors into Southgate's ground floor arcade.

"Pete, Pete, Pete." Jim's voice was mushy. "Next week, when you've sorted out this mess, and this baby's back on the road, lemme take you out. Bite to eat, drop of grog, catch a flick, eh? *Mission to Mars*? Sound good, Pete?"

CHAPTER 20

School concert. Mick Tusk clapped whenever his wife clapped. Afterwards, he carried sleeping Nelson to his car seat, Yolanda's high-octane account like sparrows twittering in a tree.

Later, at home, he stood staring at the late news.

Dana laid a hand on his shoulder. "Mikey."

She wrapped arms around him. Major news item: the murder of Gus Youde. The parasites focused on TPT as if a curse lay on it. Images of December. Full-screen shot of avuncular Len Maguire. Inspector Rich Conomy tight-lipped at a press conference.

In bed they screwed.

"Sorry," he said after five minutes.

"Oh, Mikey." She wiped a wet cheek on his chest. "I love you."

In the family room at 12:02, for no reason at all, he rang Detective Inspector Balthazar Candle of the Organised Crime unit.

"Ivory, it's late, mate." Candle had stuck with Tusk after the guillotine fell. Rarely a month went by without one calling the other to say not much.

"Since when." Tusk could hear loud TV laughter.

"I heard your gonzo mate is in on this massacre site."

News traveled fast. "Not my idea."

"Listen." The lower tone said banter was switching to tradeable info. "Rich Conomy."

"Yeah, I know. Good old Rich."

"Good old Rich fuck. He's one of the seniors who rolled you."

Tusk breathed, quelling memories. A day smashed by rain, a summons to the top floor. Sacking by committee, all scripted jollies. He could recall the choice that opened up before him: clam up and do his best for family and future, or bust their smug fucking faces. Docile was the choice, and how many times had he regretted it since? Now, phone in hand, he felt ill. Police ranks had closed after him, he'd never really understood why he'd been sacked when even harder cases survived. Or more to the point, by whom.

"Nah," Tusk said.

"Better believe it. It's that Buddhist shit. He hates violence for its own sake. My source tells me, when he saw the Burbank report, he went spare."

"Water under the bridge. I'm a taxi driver, Candle. Weekend masseur. Rich's opinion is his."

Candle chuckled. "Yeah, yeah. Just tell Mr. Gentle to watch his back."

"Owe you one."

"One?"

Nineteen minutes later his mobile interrupted R.E.M.'s "Orange Crush."

"Sir, may I ask where your partner is?"

Nestled hard against Tusk's leg, Bully lifted his head, sensing something in his owner. "Unforgiven?"

The hacker's snicker sounded more relaxed than any moment of their bizarre afternoon session. "One of you needs to come down and look at this."

"Now?"

"It's cyber-time here."

Tusk's fog lifted. No sound of Dana. "I'll be there. One condition."

"Condition?"

"Cut the sir crap."

"Yes, sir."

CHAPTER 21

Would Finola Vines permit gatecrashing of her fiftieth? On the escalator up to the restaurant on Southgate's second floor, Peter Gentle's apprehension grew.

He needn't have worried. As soon as they arrived at Walter's Wine Bar, Jim guided him through the milling crowd and thrust him, almost proudly it seemed, at a tall woman in a low-cut business jacket and dark skirt.

"Darl, this is Pete." In the space of five steps, Jim had transformed from striding executive to supplicant. "The private investigator I told you about."

"How nice, Jim."

Based on the most circumstantial of data, Peter had expected a dumpy shrew, but Alison Van Kressel was as striking as her daughter, if not more so. Her deep black hair was thick and straight, and her narrow face featured a model's high cheekbones and dainty chin. Flawless skin, full lips, and wide, almost oriental eyes of a vivid blue were a magnet, and she knew it.

Her sardonic smile took pleasure in Peter's reaction. Next to her, an older man fingered his bow tie and a balding man watched with interested, gray eyes.

"Nice to meet you." Alison's voice was scratchy. Peter decided her only flaw was her nose, long and sharp, but even that conveyed ruthlessness. "Now if you'll excuse me."

She nodded at the two other men and brushed past Peter. She paused to whisper in Jim's ear. Then she was moving through the throng, thrusting out her breasts and calling, slim arms outstretched, to a party arriving at the door. Peter saw Adam, resplendent in gray tux, at the head of the group.

Jim shook hands with the balding man. "Pete, let me introduce Rory, the luminary I told you about."

"Nothing too true, I trust," said Adam's father in a buttery voice.

In another world, Rory Menadue would have been a hairy butcher. As if to compensate for the bald swathe over his skull, he'd grown his brown hair around his ears. Wide sideburns connected with a cropped beard covering chin and lower face. A crescent mustache completed a hirsute appearance that somehow, improbably, was imbued with elegance.

Peter experienced ebullience. The only male in the room not wearing black tie, he should have felt his customary sense of isolation outside his own crowd. Instead, the instant he'd heard Alison hissing, "I'm not happy, Jim, I'm not happy," the puzzle solver in him had come to life. This wasn't a social occasion, it was a hunt, and he was the hunter.

"My pleasure, Mr. Menadue," he said with a smile. "Adam tells me you visit Russia often."

People jostled around them. Jim was gone. The air was full of heady perfume, and laughter sparked over the burble of voices and chink of plates. Rory glided in close to Peter, one hand in pocket, the other holding a flute of bubbly.

"Yes well, Adam rarely gets facts quite right," Rory said. "Many years ago, I was indeed considered one of the top Russian cultural experts in Australia. But now my focus is China."

"China?" Peter said. "How fascinating. The closest I've been is an assignment in Hong Kong."

First impressions of suspects are the second most important, Mick had told Peter once. Second to what? Mick's eyes had grown fervent: "Second impressions. Put the hard word, genius. Then check your preliminary reaction. Compare. Most times you'll know, one way or the other."

Easier said than done. Peter's first impression of Rory was no help: polished, academic, self-contained. He tried the test on Alison, almost smiling at the prejudices he recognized in the verdict: shallow, rapacious, and stupid.

"Pete, I can't tell you how reassuring it is to see such interest." Shorter than Peter, trim with rounded shoulders, Rory wore a long-tailed tuxedo and crimson cummerbund. "For most Australians, China holds no more interest than, well, Russia."

"If you don't mind, it's Peter, not Pete."

"Father, may I?" It was Adam, blithely inserting his party into their space. Clearly the police hadn't caught up with him yet. "Peter, meet Kylie. And David O'Shaughnessy, a friend of mine, and Sal. Folks, this is Peter Gentle. He's doing some work at TPT."

Peter shook hands around the group. Adam was animated and Peter found himself discussing the South African cricket scandal. They were a suave bunch for their age, Kylie a clear-skinned brunette, Sal a platinum blonde whose breasts strained at her white dress, and David, a short, quiet man with a disconcerting habit of pursing his lips, as if whistling under his breath.

"Fi! Birthday girl!" Jim's voice cut through the hubbub. Jesus, Peter thought, is he ever plastered.

Adam was whispering to his father, their eyes on Peter.

Finola swept in, seizing hands, working the packed room. She wore a stunning green dress and a string of pearls around her neck. When she pecked her stepson on the cheek, Peter caught the briefest flash of contempt pass from Adam to David.

"Happy birthday," Peter said when Finola reached him.

"You're everywhere," she said.

Before he could tell if she was annoyed, she was off. Peter watched her hug Rory, saw caution in their smiles.

Finola's arrival was the signal for everyone to be seated.

The birthday party took up three long tables by the windows. To his surprise Peter was placed on the head table, between Rory Menadue and David O'Shaughnessy. He was embarrassed to spot Jim on the second table, head bowed to Alison's intense whispers.

His elevated mood had more than a little to do with the venue. Walter's Wine Bar, his kind of noshery, looked out over the Yarra River. Opposite loomed the middle and western stretches of Collins Street. He never tired of feasting on the towers—insurance companies, banks, hotels—rising above the warm ochre walls of the Flinders Street Station clock towers. Black water glinted under the glow of humanity. Spindly branches of riverbank trees swayed.

And the restaurant itself, subtly lit under a low ceiling, exuded elegance. Mahogany chairs squeaked on polished boards. Behind the central bar, lined with opened bottles and trays piled with baguettes and biscotti, chefs rushed around the open kitchen. Waiters and waitresses in burgundy aprons combined solicitousness with steely efficiency. Peter even loved the tables, with their white linen tablecloths covered with paper, the hefty cutlery, the stylish salt and pepper shakers, the linen napkins.

The best wine list in Melbourne, Hector had told him once. Swirling Gevrey-Chambertin burgundy in his balloon glass, Peter told himself this was the life.

Rory was an urbane companion and Peter warmed to his enthusiasm for "the cradle of civilization." A student of the language, a collector of calligraphy and antiques, an expert on classical texts, Rory was all of those.

"Sometimes I feel a greater kinship with China than Australia," he said. "I lead friendship tours there once or twice a year."

"No enemies allowed?"

Rory chuckled. "It's all about building bridges, you know. I take people who ought to understand the reality of China. I show them the sights, arrange discussions with senior people." His hands etched enthusiasm in the air. "I formed the Australia-China Cooperative Society five years ago, you might have heard of it."

Adam, arm around Kylie's shoulders, smiled from across the table. "Ah, but what Father neglects to say is that his society no longer wants him."

Rory smiled back. "Adam's right, and that's one of the most

interesting aspects of my work. Trying to form effective cross-cultural organizations is devilishly hard. A few troublemakers and all is lost. Here, if you're interested, Peter, you should come to the inaugural meeting of my new attempt."

The card read: "Rory Menadue, President, Australia-China Open Arms Society." A Collins Street address, near King Street, Peter judged.

David O'Shaughnessy nudged him. "Having a good time, Mr. Investigator?"

Peter's father would have called David "sharp." He had a small-boy face, tousled brown hair, diminutive ears, and a large freckle beside his left nostril. He and Adam continually exchanged looks, and Peter corrected his first impression that David deferred to his more boisterous friend.

"You know what interests me," David said. Distinctive eyebrows formed a horizontal line above watchful eyes. "Adam and I check out the races now and then. I'm always asking him what the difference is between the horseflesh addicts laying bets with the bookies, and the guys trading at TPT. He tells me there's a world of difference, but bugger me, I can't spot it."

"Are you a share trader yourself?" Peter often came up against similar questions, in his old job or at Skulk Club meetings, albeit in a more sophisticated form. But now he was keen to return to the Menadue heir, to quiz him about Belinda and Gus.

"No, I sell computers, but I saw an ABC documentary on the 1997 Asia crisis." David's tan was so uniform Peter wondered if it came from a solarium. "You know that no one picked the market collapse here? That got me thinking, it sounds awfully like the hundred-to-one bolter at Flemington."

A tap of knife on glass hushed the gathering and signaled the start of formalities. While a silver-haired stranger welcomed them all, Peter strained to keep an eye on the Van Kressels and Menadues. Rory rose to deliver a witty anecdote about Finola's fortieth birthday party, a decade ago. Then Finola herself stood up, glass in hand, and at that point, Peter was lucky enough to have his eyes on Alison Van Kressel's aquiline face. The momentary undisguised hatred was disturbing.

What a pity Finola doesn't like me, Peter thought while he listened, for the forceful woman turned out to be an energized orator. She spoke of the challenges of turning fifty, of her dream of online empowerment of investors, of the joys of starting TPT. If the speech seemed altogether too serious for a drunken party, Peter enjoyed it nonetheless.

The only discord in his eyes was a spirited attack on Melbourne.

"Have I grown to love my second city?" Finola's expression said she was only half-joking. "I wish I could say yes. But as any Sydneysider will tell you, Melbourne remains a backwater."

Rory shook his head.

"Hear, hear," Peter heard David murmur.

"More entrepreneurial, wild business is what Melbourne needs," declaimed Finola. "But sadly we see so little of it."

Predictably, she then offered TPT as a prime example of the entrepreneurial and wild. This speech isn't for us, Peter thought, it's for herself.

She closed with an odd reference. "Like Van Morrison says, it's a brand new day. Thank you, my dear friends."

When she sat down to scattered applause, Peter noticed Rory

purse his lips. Finola had given her husband a warm acknowledgment, but it had paled next to her endorsement of Jim, "the epitome of the new generation of Melbourne business."

Adam, who hadn't received a mention in the speech, was nuzzling Kylie's neck. His whisper carried. "Now that the evil stepmother has finished selling herself, we can get to Henry's."

Kylie giggled. Peter saw David nod.

Peter, his hip aching, felt like leaving himself. But the arrival of dessert, a trio of chocolate creations, intervened. Over the next half-hour, Peter divided his time between Rory, David, and occasionally Adam. Periodically he heard Jim's raucous laugh. Once, sipping Sauternes, he wondered how Mandy was spending their first evening asunder.

His mind drifted. The soothing prospect of being home, deep into a Diplomacy session, beckoned. A couple of nights ago, France, his long-time ally, had stabbed him in the back and he hadn't yet analyzed a proper response. Should he now ally with the crippled Austria?

Exhaustion eventually forced him to rise. All done, he thought, I've checked out the TPT founders' spouses, taken another look at Adam, gathered what data I could.

At the head of the table, Finola, relaxed and in charge, nodded when Peter excused himself. Rory Menadue suggested they chat about China over lunch, Adam's fake grin bloomed when they shook hands, David whistled at the edge of Peter's hearing. Peter looked for Jim to say farewell but his client, red cheeks inflamed, was busy grandstanding. Across the room, Alison Van Kressel laughed.

Peter's hip jarred painfully on the walk down the spiral

staircase to the riverbank. He hummed a tune, something unfamiliar but poppy, felt cheated to realize he was echoing David's whistling.

His fresh data added two additional suspects. Alison: super bitch whose anger at Gus would have been something to run from, who was "out" at the time of the murder. Rory: just as keen for a hunk-spunk union, nibbling at Jim's garbage fortune, with a dubious alibi from dubious Adam.

Two lovers nestled down on the jetty. Peter took in the oily flicker of the Yarra as he climbed up onto Princes Bridge. He plodded across the river, a humming tram his beacon. Groups of young people, bare arms defying the autumn chill, hurried past.

It was only 10:30, but Peter took the necessary detour to his Block Arcade office with reluctance. No more than five minutes, he promised, then home and Diplomacy heaven. He glanced down Block Place, thronged with packed tables outside the cafes. A singer whined over a thrashing acoustic guitar. The outside of Draconi's was quiet. He rested his head against the steel wall of the elevator on the way up to the second floor.

His office was an aberrant cranny between lawyers' chambers. Barely room for a desk and a filing cabinet, but Hector leased it to him for a pittance. And it was thirty-seven seconds away from Draconi's.

He leaned his sluggish head on the door, hunted in his pocket for the key, heard the scuffing sound of footsteps on the carpet. Sometimes the solicitors' articled clerks slaved all night, so he straightened to say hello.

This was no clerk. A dark figure charged down the corridor.

CHAPTER 22

The electric thrill of the bad, bad boy. That's what coursed through Mick Tusk on the drive to St Kilda. Music up loud, the Zep-tinged somber metal of The Tea Party. No response from Gentle's mobile.

Unforgiven lived in up-market Canterbury Road, the other side of the parklands of Albert Park Lake. Hideously painted townhouses on the lake side, Edwardian mansions, flats, and terrace houses on the opposite side. Unforgiven's was the smallest single-fronted terrace Tusk could see. Tiny really, though neat and recently painted cream and red. Tusk wondered about Unforgiven's day job.

Unforgiven wore a shapeless tracksuit and his face was pasty. His hair hung free and wild, like Meat Loaf's. He glanced over Tusk's shoulder, led him into a small front room.

Christ, Tusk thought. Bare walls, thick curtains. An unholy mess of computer shit on and under perimeter tables: keyboards, weird boxes, printers, thick manuals, scattered CDs. Two office chairs, plastic antistatic mats on gray carpet. Fluorescent standing lamps supplementing decorative ceiling fixtures.

Crappy chill-out music emerging from glass-enclosed cubes.

A grunge Tomorrowland, Tusk thought.

"Progress has been made," said Unforgiven.

1:16. Tusk flipped open his notebook. "Remember, I'm a cretin, okay?"

"No big words, I promise. And please, no notes."

Tusk stowed the notebook. At least the geek hadn't called him "sir." Around them machines hummed.

Unforgiven proved almost as good as Gentle at summarizing. Somehow, the hacker had checked out the computers of most of TPT's day traders and staff, "barring a handful switched off." None was hacker or victim.

"Peter is correct." On his home turf, Unforgiven looked relaxed and confident. "TPT is well secured. This script kiddie would never break in."

"What the fuck's a script kiddie?"

"A derogatory term. Teenagers find hacking tools on websites and run them, but there's no intelligence behind it."

The air in the room was stale and warm. "How do you know our perp is one of these kiddies?"

Unforgiven shrugged. "A feeling. Now, take a look at this."

Tusk pulled his chair closer to the three live screens in front of them. Unforgiven pointed to the middle one, crammed with lines of gibberish.

"Shit, what's this?"

Unforgiven's grin told Tusk he was young, mid-twenties max. "TPT's server."

Tusk thought, what's a server? "You said—"

"I'm no script kiddie. Where there's a will there's a way, in my world. It's a matter of honing your craft. Observe, here's that flamer. For the attack on TPT, he used this handle."

An overlong fingernail tapped on a name—Justiceordie.

"Justice or die." Tusk grunted. "Pissed off, you reckon?"

"But this isn't what I rang you about. Tagliaferro has this as well. What I've done is fossick around the traps. Lo and behold, there is in fact a newbie going by that handle. An amateur. Flush with downloaded vanilla tools."

"That easy?"

"No, nothing is ever that easy. He's used a Web-based email facility, which accords him substantial anonymity. Luckily it's one we have access to, and I have managed to find his original email address. Better still, he's with ZapNet, one of the smaller ISPs. Another place within our reach."

One track of electronic joke music faded to a close, another began, this time Gregorian chants plus mellotron and electronic bleeps.

The jargon had left Tusk behind. He pondered Unforgiven's use of "we." Was the hacker part of a gang? Was he crooked?

Unforgiven leaned back, clasped hands behind his head, under the hair. "I have an address for you. A real-life address, bricks and mortar."

"No joke?" Tusk's neck crawled with long-absent goosebumps of wonderment.

"Box Hill." Unforgiven held up a tiny slip of paper inscribed with a name and a Station Street address.

"How long till that Tagliaferro joker finds this?"

"Ten years?" Unforgiven shredded the address slip into a plastic bin. "I do believe this calls for a celebration. Wait here, could you?"

Wait here so I can't spot ID clues, Tusk guessed. He prowled the small floor space, looked for the music volume control, didn't know where to begin. Christ, he thought, who'd work in this bolthole?

He expected Unforgiven to return with glasses for a piss-up. Instead, the hacker bore two bowls with spoons.

"Don't be concerned." Unforgiven was back to his apprehensive best. "It's only chocolate mousse. I made it myself."

"Thought I'd seen it all," said Tusk.

But the mousse was superb, creamy with a bitter kick. Still standing, Tusk polished it off with rare speed.

Unforgiven was watching him, his own mousse barely touched. "Satisfactory?"

"Beaut."

"You're just saying that."

"No, no. Best mousse I've tasted in yonks."

"Look, you don't have to be polite."

"Christ," Tusk said. "Tastes like dog shit, U, is that what you wanted to know?"

Unforgiven smiled, a shadow that vanished. "Just as expected. Now, you'd better let me get back to work."

"Only too happy. You're a champ, U."

Eastbound drivers late at night were easy pickings for the traffic boys, so Tusk drove carefully. In Carnegie a chilling thought made him pull over and switch off the cassette player.

Unforgiven answered after three rings. "Yes?"

"Could Gentle's computer be a target for this hacker?"

"Well well well. Quite right. Do you have his email address?"

"No."

"Never mind, I'll see what I can do. What about your computer?"

"Don't have one." Another bone of contention with Dana. A surge of guilt at the thought of her.

"The stats tell us there are folks like you. Well done, though."

At home, by the time Tusk quieted Bully outside his back door, it was 2:32.

A familiar lead weight had lodged in his chest. He stared out over the still garden, every tree and bush planted by Dana. Pinprick stars watched. He breathed the grassy air, recalled the fusty atmosphere in Unforgiven's universe.

Fuck it, he thought, I wasn't even with Gentle. No danger, no bother to anyone.

How could he keep going like this?

Inside, no sound of Dana or the kids. He slipped on headphones—Red Hot Chili Peppers' "Californication"—but fell asleep before the second chorus.

CHAPTER 23

Peter cried out and leaped away from his attacker. A blow glanced off his back. He scrambled around the corner.

Perhaps his pursuer expected him to flee straight onto the elevators. Instead, Peter flung himself to his left, down the stairs. He slammed into the landing wall, pivoted, took off again. Insensate, certain of death from behind, he jumped and jumped, miraculously not turning an ankle.

At the bottom of the twisting flights of stairs, he stumbled onto hands and knees on the mosaic tiles of Block Arcade. He was gibbering and shaking.

He stood up on tottering legs, willed himself to run. Rasping breaths tore at his lungs. But the arcade was deserted. The stairs were silent.

A wino shuffled past in Elizabeth Street. Peter's body rippled with shudders. The indicator told him the elevator was still on the second floor. I've lost him, he thought. Maybe.

He'd always equated Draconi's with heaven, flippantly. When he staggered through the solid front door, it was heaven. The front tables were empty, no one glanced his way. Mouth slack, he heaved.

He peered through a window. Nothing stirred outside.

"Skull!"

Harvey Jopling waved from a rear table.

Peter swallowed, took a deep breath, pushed back his shoulders. Sweat trickled down his back. Safe, he thought, safe, safe, safe.

Weak in the thighs, he walked over to join Harvey's party. Had he stumbled on something to spur the attack? No way was he going to ring the police. If he reported it, they'd wrap him up so tight, he'd never solve the case. And Mick? The thought of ringing the big man and listening to the inevitable apology was too cruel to contemplate.

Harvey snapped his red suspenders. "Come on, Skull, meet the head kickers from Western."

Peter was glad to join the wine-sodden group, four rowdy middle managers from Western Bank, all succumbing to Harvey's take-no-prisoners socializing. He mumbled hellos. Someone pulled over a chair for him and then he was left in peace.

He gulped a glass of wine and watched his friend, jacket and tie off, chin thrust out, lead a lively discussion on whether the E-com bubble had burst. Harvey lived and played as if every day were his last. Though only Peter's age, gray streaked his black hair, and his chiseled jawline had thickened over the last year. But he never seemed to sleep, clocked up staggering hours, and to Peter appeared unstoppable.

Then Peter remembered the figure bearing down on him and weakness seized his stomach. The man had been thinner rather than fatter, but whether he'd been tall or short, Peter couldn't recall. The ghoulish head must have been a balaclava. The attacker had certainly been quick. If he'd been able to hide any closer than around the corner, he would have nabbed Peter for sure. Saved by the luck of office layout, Peter thought. None of his thinking offered any comfort.

"Who gives a shit," he heard from one of the bankers, a broad-faced man with jutting ears. "They could kill all of them, wouldn't make any difference. I can't stand the press TPT is getting. Take a look at the market figures, mate, it's just a tin-pot operation."

Poor Gus, Peter thought, not only dead but now a weapon in a boozy tirade. He said nothing, was glad that Harvey, ever diplomatic, didn't reveal his involvement.

Peter drank on. By the time the party broke up with swearing and backslapping, his panic had abated. When he lurched to his feet, he could contemplate the unthinkable, that he'd cope. This was knowledge he'd acquired last May but hadn't tested since, the knowledge that fear wasn't incompatible with a measure of courage.

"Easy, Skull." Harvey's work done, his face was haggard. "Take my arm."

No one lurked outside. Swaying against Harvey, Peter took the most public route home, up Collins and along Lonsdale.

"No need, Harvey," he said when his friend accompanied him through the security doors of his apartment block. Thank God for Mick, he'd insisted Peter retain an unlisted phone number and keep his address confidential from clients. "She's apples."

But Harvey stuck with him until they stood at Peter's open door.

"Want to tell me about it, Skull?"

"Nah." Peter felt nauseous.

"Mandy told me this afternoon. I'm sorry."

Peter had forgotten all about Mandy. Momentary bitterness hit him. Just because she was Harvey's secretary, did she have to spill the beans? The entire Club would know soon.

"You want some news," Harvey said, "or should I wait till you're sober tomorrow?"

"Course I want news." News was data, data made the world go around. And the world was going around, spinning dangerously.

"Paddy gave me a tingle today. He's heard on the grapevine that one of TPT's execs has been negotiating under the table. Wants to go into competition."

"Funder? Brad Funder?"

"That's the name. It was all hush-hush. I gather it's all on hold now."

Is that what Gus cottoned onto? Peter remembered Funder's cold eyes. The bastard! "Thanks, Harvey."

Once the door swung shut, Peter found the restroom bowl, knelt over it. The world swam but his stomach held up. To his surprise, he found himself crawling to the bedside phone and ringing his father.

"You're drunk, Peter," said ex-Assistant Commissioner Horace Gentle. Peter could hear his mother's querulous voice in the background.

"Sorry, Dad. Sorry I haven't rung. Haven't been around, thorry 'bout that."

His father gave a dry chuckle. "Should I feel worried that it takes a binge to hear from you? Now that you're so sorry, come for Sunday lunch."

Peter's mouth was gluggy with thirst. "Sure, sure."

"A little bird tells me you're helping Rich Conomy out."

Peter groaned. "Dad, this is a social."

"I know, I know. Just thought you'd like to know I think the world of Rich. He'd get to the top if he was interested. You know his father was a copper? In Adelaide. Killed in a gang shootout, must be twenty years back. Rich is a policeman's policeman, Peter."

For years, merely talking to his father put Peter's teeth on edge. Now the lecturing tone brought a sense of peace.

"Say hi to Mum," he said.

He hung up. The room reeked of his sweat.

Overwhelmed brain and body gave way. He collapsed into sleep on the carpet.

CHAPTER 24

A hand on his shoulder brought Mick Tusk rearing from sleep. Upright on the sofa, fingers splayed.

"Sorry." Dana in her nightie.

Tusk blinked, impossibly confused. The family room light was on. Birds twittered outside, he recognized the special darkness before first light. Red numerals: 6:01.

"What's up?" How many years since Dana had risen this early, other than to see to the kids? Since she came jogging with him, one time only.

He saw she carried an apple. Her face, creased with sleep, was grave. Reddened eyes, for once unreadable.

She leaned over to kiss him on the mouth. Tusk shivered as curls tumbled onto his cheeks, his forehead. The lips dwelt.

She said, "You'll need to get moving, Mikey. Tuesday I want you back at your uncle's to apologize."

CHAPTER 25

Sonorous chimes woke him. The doorbell! For a moment Peter Gentle's heart hammered, then reason prevailed. He sat up and massaged his neck, stiff from sleeping on the floor. Outside, pink sky proclaimed sunrise.

When he bent to the peephole, his expectation was to see Inspector Conomy or Senior Constable Lasker. Or Harvey checking up on him.

"Mick!"

He unlatched the door. "What's going on?"

Mick wore ankle boots and his trusty brown leather jacket over a black T-shirt.

"No wonder you can't make a fist of this PI caper." Mick removed his sunglasses. His face was stern. "No fucking application. Look at you."

Just what I need, Peter thought, Dana's thrown him out, it's my fault. "Mick, tell me—"

"And talk about bloody hygiene. Get cleaned up. We're out of here in ten."

Peter theatrically pinched a cheek. "No, no dream."

And the big man grinned, the monster grin Peter saw so rarely that it faded from memory between sightings. "I'm as surprised as you. Dana's—" Mick grew still for a moment "—she's given me leave of absence for four days. To quote unquote babysit you."

Peter's smile flooded his heart. Never mind that four days didn't seem remotely long enough, never mind that his mouth was sour and parched.

He tried to picture Dana smiling, couldn't. "Why four?"

"Reckons it's as long as she can bear. She knew it all, Gentle, your wars, my cloak and dagger." He mock-punched the wall. "Let's move it. Gentle and Tusk ride again, eh?"

"Our cards say Tusk and Gentle."

"Ah, didn't want to bruise that ego."

Peter left Mick scribbling in his notebook. He downed three glasses of water. In the shower he saw that the hip bruise was already yellowing at the edges, and the lump on his head had subsided a little. He gargled mouthwash. No suit, he declared, and chose black chinos, a white collarless shirt, and a dark blue jacket. His body felt light, his head clear, as if he'd returned from a week on a beach.

While Peter shaved, Mick recounted his quarrel with his uncle and the midnight dash to Unforgiven's den.

"How could you go without me?" Peter said.

"He rang you first."

Peter's face fell with recollections of the previous night. He did his bit and sketched the birthday party, the attack, the Funder tidbit.

"Christ." Mick's face had reverted to stone. "You didn't ring me."

"No."

Peter brushed away the arising silence by brainstorming tactics. At first Mick insisted on dogging him all day, but the workload was demonstrably too high.

"Okay," Mick said, "but only while you're at TPT. And don't bloody argue."

Peter saluted.

Mick's task list read: check the flamer's address found by Unforgiven, visit Gus' household, follow up Oleg's alibi. Peter's: dig into the accounting system, organize to see Rory Menadue and Alison Van Kressel. For the planned meetings with Finola and Brad Funder ("Third time lucky," Peter said), he would wait for Mick. Lower priority were another session with Belinda Van Kressel, an expedition to Peter's office, and maybe a catch-up with Unforgiven.

They elected to keep quiet to Conomy about the Box Hill address. Unforgiven was a card Peter preferred to keep hidden.

Mick's growing impatience had them out of the apartment by seven. In the elevator, Peter quashed a fleeting image of Mandy. Too busy, he thought, just too busy.

An overcast sky greeted them. Blissful aromas wafted from a double-parked bread van. He spied a row of heavy-duty wheelie bins, emptied but waiting to be collected, their lids flipped back. Were they from Jim's former business?

Another day's walk missed, Peter thought. His daily city exploration—not exercise, exercise just ground down the joints—was an acquired habit. In 1996, before buying the apartment, he'd shared a place for a year with Thompson White workmate Carlo Fonti, and it was Carlo's habit to walk the streets, sometimes for hours. Somehow Peter found himself tagging along. Surprise, surprise, he'd become accustomed to the routine, had grown to enjoy it. And once he had the apartment, walking the precincts came as a natural accompaniment.

He was catholic with timing, walking whenever the urge arose, but mornings were best. He loved the sensation that the stirring metropolis belonged to him, that few others cared enough to patrol its blood vessels in the wee hours. Once he heard Carlo muse about the "poetry of walking feet." Peter dismissed the very notion of poetry, but he'd liked the sound of that phrase.

Walking beside Mick in a zigzag route through interconnecting lanes, amidst the commuters, Peter marveled at how secure he felt. The leviathan looked invincible.

Mick caught his gaze. "How's the head?"

"Dandy."

"Dandy. What kind of a word is that?"

"Mick, I have to say I'm not as confident as I should be. You know me, most times I don't get methodological doubts."

"Not confident of what?"

They were crossing Collins Street, heading toward the Centreway arcade, fronted by the Foreign Language Bookshop. A delivery man in baseball cap and tiny shorts trotted past, hefting a milk crate.

"Of solving this," Peter said. "There's something missing. Something I can't even grasp in order to ask the right questions."

Mick stopped in the arcade. An Indian man in suit and turban, loaded with briefcase and takeaway coffee, paused to watch. "Listen. They're just people, right? And your job is to solve this, not make friends, right?"

Peter nodded.

Mick held his left hand up at chest level, palm flat toward him. He drew back his right fist, like an archer cocked to fire.

The Indian businessman hurried off.

"Then let's stir the mix, Einstein," said Mick.

Fist smacked into palm.

CHAPTER 26

Fuel time, 7:12. Mick Tusk scanned suit heaven, aka Draconi's. His leg muscles twitched in time to the guitars of Guided By Voices, their gem "Surgical Focus." Such joy in him, he almost pounded fists on his chest.

"There." Gentle's fingers tugged at his jacket.

Hector was waving a napkin, down at the Block Place end. By the time they navigated the crush, the Lord of Draconi's had added a table to an existing one, occupied by a fat man and a straight-backed woman.

"Pete." The man's frown intensified at the sight of Tusk. "Sit down, we've got a pile of things to discuss."

Gentle beamed. "This is weird, meeting you here. Mick, meet Jim Van Kressel. Finola Vines. My partner Mick Tusk."

Tusk shook Van Kressel's flabby hand. So this was the TPT head honcho. Intelligent eyes, wavy black hair with a white streak, a drunk's nose. A shaving nick on his thick neck. Rundown brogues at odds with a creased expensive suit. After Gentle's rabid praise, Tusk had expected more.

As the woman rose to greet him, he heard Van Kressel mutter

to Gentle, "He's your partner?"

"I was attacked again," responded Gentle.

The Vines woman shook Tusk's hand. Thin hands with long fingers, narrow face halfway between good looking and ordinary. Curly brown hair, high-pressure eyes behind severe specs.

"Call me Finola," she said.

"Mick," Tusk said. "They tell me it's happy birthday."

"Hec, please, come join us," Van Kressel said to Tusk's surprise.

The restaurateur clicked his fingers for a waiter, pulled up a chair. He winked at Tusk. When they first met, Tusk had labeled the judge a fool. The label hadn't lasted an hour.

Tusk ordered raisin toast, garbage-guts Gentle chose bacon and eggs. Sections of *The Age* were scattered on the table. More cricket scandal news. Front-page headline: "Tech Stocks Dive as Bears Run Wild."

"I caught CNN." Van Kressel was plowing into a steaming plate of carbonara. "Not good, no good at all. Nasdaq dropped another two and a half percent, the Dow fell nearly two. Pete, what's this about an attack?"

Tusk met Van Kressel's appraising eyes while Gentle described the episode.

"Bloody hell," said Van Kressel.

Vines was picking at a bowl of muesli. "Jim, I'll be in the office all day." Her physique was slight but she struck Tusk as strong, with the inner mettle Dana possessed. "The priority is to keep the office calm, reassure the traders. And Jim, that PR meeting is now at eleven."

Van Kressel said, "God knows the troops need a semi-decent day today."

A familiar voice called out. "Skull! Not again?"

Gentle's mate Harvey Jopling, dapper as ever, strode up. Behind him came Carlo Fonti, laptop slung over his shoulder. Gentle introduced them to Van Kressel and Vines.

"Grace us with your presence next Skulk Club, Mick?" As usual, Jopling shook hands as if his life depended on it.

"Wouldn't miss it." Tusk meant it, had all the hope in the world after Dana's dawn kiss.

Their corner of the Draconi's madhouse revved up. Hector tacked on yet another table. Food arrived fast, heady aromas filled Tusk's senses. Jopling had them laughing at a send-up of ex-premier Jeff Kennett. Kennett was featured in the morning papers defending his autobiography, which had cost the state government a hundred grand. Hector mouthed off at some insurance execs reported as reaping fortunes after a takeover. As usual Fonti watched, silent unless prompted.

In the clamor, Tusk kept his eyes on the clients Van Kressel and Vines. Their body language nixed Gentle's conjecture that they were lovers, but why so despondent? Given the crises in the office, Tusk thought, anyone would be.

He hoped his street theater had woken Gentle up. Forget logic, he thought, people commit crimes. Somewhere in this maze of relationships—the victim, the newly hoity-toity Van Kressels, the old-money Menadues, the TPT staffers, the share punters—were linkages. Linkages formed by motives. Cap had put it best: "The seven deadly sins, Mick, just line 'em up, you'll solve every homicide they chuck at you."

But Len Maguire? Nobody liked him, he seemed connected to no one. Should Tusk ring Gil Oldfield and quiz him about the cunt?

Guilt surfaced. He'd probably made young Katie Oldfield's situation even more fraught. But what could society do? The answer sickened him. They'd wait till Oldfield stepped too far over the line. Only then would some flatfoot cop—a young Mick Tusk perhaps—arrive to lock him up.

While he finished his toast, he flicked through *The Age's* weekly entertainment mag, dwelling on the local rock concerts page. No time or money to catch gigs these days. But J. Mascis, the slacker genius guitarist behind Dinosaur Jr., was down to appear at the Corner Hotel next Monday. Maybe if this did wind up on Monday… he shook his head.

He drank an herbal tea. The Skulkers and Hector were listening to Finola boost some company Tusk had never heard of. He saw Van Kressel lean over to Gentle, heard the tycoon's low voice. "Belinda didn't come home last night."

"What happened?"

"She wasn't in when Alison and I arrived home from Fi's bash. I rang her mobile. She's at Gus' house, of all places. God, did she give me a serve."

"You?"

"For being weak with her mother, in a nutshell. Pete, you need to know…" Van Kressel leaned so close to Gentle that Tusk lost the rest. She'd seemed like a rich brat, but Tusk's heart went out to Belinda.

"More java, Hec," Gentle called.

Tusk elbowed him. "Enough caffeine. Time's short."

"Quite right." Vines smiled, revealing an incongruous overbite.

"Slave drivers," Van Kressel said.

Jopling laughed. "The markets beckon."

As the party broke up, Tusk took Gentle aside.

"This is a good chance," Tusk said. "You stick with the bigwigs back to the office, okay? I'll zip up to Carlton. I heard that about the daughter, I can catch her, check out the housemates at the same time. Then off to Box Hill."

Gentle nodded. "It's great to have you on board, big guy."

Van Kressel was using the table and chair to heave himself up. Jopling slapped Hector on the back.

"Yeah, well," Tusk said. "What was the whisper from Van Kressel?"

"It's hard to believe," Gentle said. "Jim quarreled with Alison last night. She scratched him. He's left her, Mick, can you believe it? He's staying at the Sheraton."

Tusk inspected Van Kressel with new eyes while shaking hands with Hector. No shaving nick that, but a wound. Even millionaires, he thought. He pictured Dana, arms around him at their front door. Van Kressel's gloomy eyes met his.

The Skulkers were farewelling. Fonti whispered something to Gentle about Mandy.

Jopling winked at Gentle. "You hear me? Take it easy, Skull."

Tusk held the abuse victim's eyes, gave a slow nod of solidarity.

CHAPTER 27

Early morning offices, Peter Gentle thought, were a recipe for depression. From Jim Van Kressel's room, TPT's empty cubicles and blank screens struck him as especially forlorn. He sighed at the memory of Harvey's concerned parting wink.

Jim was at the window, brooding down onto Collins Street.

Peter joined him. "You seemed upset at Mick."

Woolly clouds heralded showers. Two trams in tandem scraped around the corner from Spring Street. An orange-vested cleaner deftly manipulated a long pole to wash a high window. People milled around the news kiosk. The beauty of the ordinary, Peter thought.

"Well, he did give me a shock," Jim said. "Never would have picked him as your partner. But who knows, maybe we need some muscle around here. God knows everything is going to hell in a handbasket."

Jim's glumness rendered him barely recognizable. His cheeks drooped, smudges rimmed bloodshot eyes. No rampant aftershave today.

Peter curbed a tapping toe. "I split up with my girlfriend yesterday."

The chief executive hung up his jacket. "And that's meant to cheer me up?" Jim took a deep breath. "It's all for the best, anyway. I should have left her years ago. You should pray, Pete, that you never experience anything like last night." He fingered his neck scratch. "I was lucky to get out with my bloody wallet."

"Jim, I have to ask you this. Where were you on Wednesday night?"

Jim's eyes flared. "You're joking."

"You can see it's the way I work. The logic."

"Logic, is it? Excuse me, Pete, but you can come across as a bit weird."

"Maybe so."

"Okay, okay." The surge of irritation seemed to act as a tonic. "Just use your bloody logic to catch this bastard. The police have my alibi, Pete, if that's the word to describe what I was doing when a close friend—for God's sake, he was a movie buddy— when a buddy gets butchered. I attended an industry function, stayed on till eleven. I bet fifteen people can vouch for my every minute. Does that satisfy you?"

"Sorry, Jim."

Jim sank into his chair and pressed his phone's loudspeaker button. The dial tone filled the room, followed by the singing of number tones. "Listen to this."

A wave of nostalgia brushed Peter. How long since he'd experienced the communal joy of speakerphones, the pleasure of urgent voices crackling from across the globe?

"Yes?" Peter recognized Alison's huskiness.

"It's me," said Jim.

"Oh, Jim, come home. Please. I'm sorry, so so sorry."

Peter couldn't believe this was the woman he'd met twelve hours ago. He edged toward the door but an abrupt slash of Jim's hand stayed him. He shuffled with embarrassment at Alison's sob-laden litany, an endless sequence of entreaties and promises, all transparently bogus. When Alison asked after Belinda, Jim acted ignorant. But when she begged him to please, please, please meet with her, anywhere at all, please, Peter was staggered to hear a softening in Jim's voice.

"Maybe, baby." Jim's eyes were shut. "I need you to talk to my friend Pete Gentle. Will you be in the gallery today?"

Peter's disbelief remained while Jim settled for Alison to meet the investigators at noon and then brought the conversation to a close.

Jim handed over an address on a Post-it. "Here. Alison's gallery in Collingwood. Probably the straw that broke this camel's back, actually. God, when I think of the money she's thrown away."

Peter didn't know what to say, was glad when Jim dialed again over the speakerphone to ask Inspector Conomy for an update.

"Yep, a good time to catch up." Conomy's voice was mild as ever. "When is the private investigator coming in?"

Peter was pleased to hear a dose of the old vigor in Jim's voice. "Pete's talking to Fi now, Inspector."

"Don't let him leave, mate. I'll get there ASAP."

On his way out, Peter thanked Jim for arranging the interview.

"It's important, Pete," Jim said. "Just you check her out, satisfy your logic, okay? She's mad at me, has been for weeks, wish I understood why. But she's essentially a good person."

So much data, Peter thought on his way down the silent aisle, so little clarity. Jim's thawing troubled him. And why arrange for him to hear Alison out, unless Jim himself doubted her?

Finola's office was nothing like Jim's. The back wall was taken up by two old bookcases and a personal stereo on a bench. Photographic prints of sky and sea dominated the side wall pillars. On her desk, messy piles of papers surrounded a laptop in a docking station. Rather than the standard visitor's table, a green sofa and two easy chairs filled the entrance area.

Finola was swaying in time to soulful singing, vaguely familiar, issuing from the stereo.

"I've been churlish." She lowered the volume of the music. "You didn't look like my idea of a private investigator. And to tell the truth, I'm overprotective of TPT. But ever since Jim rang me today for breakfast—from a hotel room, for crying out loud—I've realized we need all the help we can get."

What a strange kettle of fish, Peter thought. Did her change of heart derive from her clear liking of Mick? "Jim's arranged for me to talk to Alison."

She sighed. "Can you see what's happening here? I bet he goes back to her. It breaks my heart, Peter. Jim's such a warm person, everyone loves him. But he falls for domineering women. I gather his first two wives were of the same ilk."

"You're not exactly a weakling." Stir the mix, Peter imagined Mick saying.

Although no one was about, Finola walked over to shut the door. She led Peter to the couch and sat beside him. He caught a rich, oily fragrance.

"Don't imagine I can't keep up with you, Mr. Peter Gentle." Her eyes bore into his. "Because believe me, I can. There's nothing between me and Jim, never would be. He's just my sweet, sweet friend. Is friendship something you believe in, Peter?"

Peter nodded.

"Well, I surround myself with friends. But I applaud your digging. Let me give you something else to dig into. Over breakfast, I told Jim his marriage wasn't the only one stuffed up."

Unbelievable, Peter thought.

"I told Adam last night I wanted him out of my house. Honestly, he's hated me ever since we met. Fifteen years is long enough to persevere, don't you think? This week it's all been coming to a head."

"How did he react?"

Finola gave a bitter chuckle. "Oh, the usual. Words, the slamming door."

"I'm sorry to hear that."

"Are you?" She sighed. "Forgive me. Maybe you are."

"Wednesday night, Finola." Stir, stir. "What were your movements?"

"I was wondering when you'd ask. Let me be exact. I left home about seven, drove to the Gallery to attend a committee meeting. At ten we closed the meeting and I had drinks with the chairman, that's Sir Leo, and our finance director. I arrived home just on midnight. My husband was home all evening. He tells me Adam came home after seven and they watched *The 7:30 Report* and *Blue Heelers*."

An analyst's precision, Peter thought, or maybe rehearsal.

"Finola, are you sure you believe Rory and Adam?"

Her chest rose and fell. "Rory's happy to lie whenever it suits him. I've tried so hard to make this marriage work. Oh, he's grand company, still good in bed, and he does love me in his fashion. But money's the issue. Money's always the issue."

She looked up at the ceiling. "He presented a demand last night. After my birthday, can you credit it? That's what he does, flatters me for weeks, then bang bang it's business. Told me his cash is tied up in some stock Adam recommended, said he's booked his latest useless trip to China. I informed him I was going to sort Adam out once and for all, and asked for his support. The look on his face was the clincher."

Peter waited. The bluesy male voice was singing something about being on a threshold and not wanting to wait anymore. Finola tilted her head to listen.

"I'm an idealist, Peter," she said, as if spurred by what she heard. "Always have been. My mind is made up. Adam goes, and if Rory won't back me, he goes as well. I've had too many years of dreaming my dreams, of supporting Rory and Adam for nothing in return."

"So…" Peter said.

"So I wouldn't believe Rory if he swore on a bible. Especially if he swore on a bible. But I can't believe Adam would shoot someone in the back of the head. How could he?"

How indeed, Peter thought.

"Listen." She took his left hand and gripped it hard. "Our stuffed-up lives aren't the issue. You're in deep now, Peter Gentle."

Peter flushed. "What—"

"Look at me," she said. "Do it. Solve this. Whatever it is, it's evil. Whatever happens now, I want TPT prospering again. You heard me last night, this is my dream. What's your dream, Peter?"

Something in Peter's face must have provided the answer. "No? More's the pity. Well, this is mine. And Jim's."

Peter hid a gulp and withdrew his hand. "I'll try, Finola."

"Do you have Rory's office address?"

"He gave me his card."

"Ah, he would. What time do you want to see him?"

Peter thought quickly. "One o'clock. But can you—"

"I'll make sure he's in his office then," Finola said. "Don't spare him, Peter. The truth, that's what we need."

Peter left Finola's office drained yet exhilarated. Mick, you don't know what you're missing, he thought.

He sat down at Gus' desk and logged on to MYOB. The computer's time display read 8:32. It only took a few minutes to orient himself with the accounts. From experience, he knew he'd be unlikely to spot fishiness in anything less than days, but that wasn't the plan.

"Another office, another dollar," he said to the quietness.

But cynicism seemed out of place. Since he'd first presented himself in a new suit to Rock Mutual's Assistant Actuary in 1987, he had loved offices. Designed for thinking, offices enclosed, made one feel at home. He'd always assumed he'd spend all his days under fluorescent lights.

But it was not to be. He could still recall the visceral shock of Felix White's monotone delivery of the retrenchment news. After four years of stellar performance, just because Thompson White was being absorbed by an American firm, Peter was flung, metaphorically at least, from the office world.

Brad Funder was first to arrive. He rushed past, closed his door, and inspected Peter through his window. 8:40. Peter ignored him.

Just before nine, Adam Menadue sauntered around the corner. He stopped short at the sight of Peter, then glanced about. His face was pale.

"Who said you could poke around?" he asked.

Peter kept his eyes on the screen. "You keep tidy accounts."

In the corner of his eye he saw Adam looming. Peter's ancient fear welled.

"Get out of there."

Peter looked up into an inflamed face. Adam held a briefcase in his left hand. His right fist was clenched.

"Excuse me?" Peter said.

"You've got no right."

Peter stood up. His arms trembled. "What are you hiding, Adam?"

"You bloody weed."

A female voice entered the fray. "Are you… are you okay, dear?"

Irene Skews wore a lacy black dress. Her eyes were wide.

"Piss off," Adam yelled.

Finola's voice thundered brutally. "Adam!"

Adam's briefcase crashed to the floor. He whirled.

Finola stood outside her office, hands on hips. "Time to talk. Come into my office. Now."

Adam's eyes blazed. Peter had rarely seen on a person's face such confusion, anger vying with fear.

At the same instant, a chattering trio rounded the corner. Out front loped Oleg in a long greatcoat, followed by Saul Phillips wearing a homburg, and a stranger in a windbreaker. They halted to stare.

Irene's voice shook. "Peter, I came to invite you to join us for brekkie, dear."

Adam snatched up his briefcase. His face was puce. "I don't need this."

He directed a look of pure hatred at Finola and stormed toward the bunched day traders.

"My, oh my," said Irene.

Saul grabbed Irene's arms and drew her aside a moment before Adam, shoulders hunched, charged through.

He marched straight into the extended hands of Inspector Rich Conomy.

CHAPTER 28

Under one of the Peugeot's wipers, a parking fine flapped in the freshening northerly. Client reimbursable, Mick Tusk thought.

He stood in the tugging wind and watched cars crawl along Russell Street. He recalled Van Kressel's eyes, the aloneness of the man. Maguire did that, he thought. His breakfast idea came back to him.

7:45, not too early to ring an old pal. He dialed a number memorized a week ago.

"Olivia and Gilbert Oldfield's residence." Oldfield sounded high.

"Tusk here. Mick Tusk."

"What do you want, pal?"

To apologize, Tusk thought. "A question. When Maguire shot you, did he say anything?"

A pause. "Anyone told you how sick you are?"

"I need it for something else."

"Oh, this was something else all right. He looked at me and leered through that shitty orange beard. Said, 'Here's to the bloody professionals. Here's to astrology, eh?'"

"Why?"

Oldfield's voice lowered into hoarse reverie. "I'd stirred the… stirred him about his use of astrology in trading."

Smoky exhaust from a laboring van swirled up Tusk's nose. "Which of the day traders was he closest to?"

"Maguire? Close? Go do your homework, pal."

"You sure?"

"Want me to make something up? Or you'll be around to fuck me up again?"

The cold hand of fury brushed Tusk's chest. "You been a good boy, Gil?"

A bitter laugh. "Good as gold, pal. Good as gold."

***

He trotted through the first cool raindrops to the Carlton terrace house. A dark-skinned man answered the door. Thin, hair on the backs of his hands, a suit with a missing button. Deep brown eyes sized Tusk up.

Tusk said, "Like to speak to Belinda, please."

"Can I ask who you are?"

Tusk handed over a card.

A voice came down the hall.

"Kosta?" Gus' other housemate, the doughy woman Tusk had glimpsed yesterday, wore a white T-shirt and jeans, no footwear. Blonde hair tinged with red, tied back tightly. A cigarette, clearly a permanent ornament, dangling from her mouth. A look of undisguised contempt.

"I don't think so," Kosta said.

The woman grabbed the card. "You've got a cheek."

Tusk said, "In fact, I'd appreciate a chance to talk to both of you as well."

Kosta tightened his grip on the doorknob. "The funeral is this afternoon. Maybe next week."

"Maybe never," muttered the woman.

Stir the mix, Tusk had said to Gentle. Did that mean rousting up these poor people?

He was saved from making a decision by a gorgeous head peering over the woman's shoulder.

"Mick!" Belinda Van Kressel pushed through the others. "It's okay, Kosta, Stella. He's the man who helped me yesterday. Come in, Mick. Have you locked up that animal?"

Tusk couldn't recall any special warmth at the shooting range. Now Belinda seemed best friends. I'm her link to revenge, he thought.

"They must be questioning him," he said. "You bearing up okay?"

"Oh, like peachy." Belinda's voice held an hysterical edge.

The house was pretty much as Gentle had described. Narrow hall, bedrooms. A living room converted into some kind of computer center—what would Unforgiven make of it?

A quick glance into the murder scene kitchen. Again no surprises, a mat covering the stain on the linoleum in front of the fridge.

They sat in the computer room, four office chairs in a circle. Stella had stubbed out her cigarette. No one offered Tusk refreshments.

"So what exactly do you want?" Kosta asked.

"You and Gus belonged to some kind of gaming society, didn't you?"

"We've told the police about it," Stella said.

"Oh, Stella," Belinda said.

It was Kosta who filled Tusk in. He and Stella and Gus were members of a loose group, twenty people or so, calling itself Elysium. They played role-playing games ("think dungeons and dragons but we're way past that") over the Internet, often combining as a team in "massive multi-user games," whatever they were. But Tusk saw that Elysium was much more than a collection of hobbyists. They used the Web to facilitate a close-knit community. For some, like Gus, it was their only social circle. Gus, Kosta, and Stella had decided four years ago to lease the house together.

Tusk turned to Belinda, sitting in a daze. "Belinda, since we talked last, have you remembered anything else Gus said? Any other clue as to who might have done this?"

Belinda's face was dangerously pale, her eyes barely visible behind puffy eyelids. "I told you. It was that loser Adam."

"So nothing else that might help us?"

Stella said, "She's already answered."

Belinda glanced at Stella, then shook her head at Tusk.

"Belinda, did Gus keep a journal?" he said.

Kosta looked to Stella, who stared resolutely at Belinda.

"Why, yes," Belinda said. "I never thought of that. Sometimes he'd tell me over the phone what he was writing." Her eyes flooded. "I must ask the police for it."

"No journal was found," Tusk said. "Kosta, any ideas?"

The man shifted in his seat.

Stella said, "Kosta."

"Do you Elysium folks believe in justice?" Tusk asked Kosta.

"Of course." Kosta, eyes on Stella, was breathing audibly through his mouth. "It's one of our central concepts. Justice and love."

Tusk edged his chair closer to the man. "There's someone out there hiding from what he or she did to Gus, right there in the kitchen."

"Please, Kosta," Belinda said.

Kosta rubbed his eyes. "Our website, it allows members to store diaries, planners, spreadsheets, and the like. Gus had a journal."

"How do you know?"

"Like Belinda said, he referred to it. Gus had a heavy childhood. He used his journal as a release. Jesus save me, why did he have to die?"

"The committee will have your balls for this," Stella said. She stalked from the room.

Kosta wheeled his chair to a computer and brought up a web page: Elysium in fancy letters, pompous fantasy crap below it. He typed and clicked. A box popped up asking for a password.

Kosta said in a near whisper, "He never told me his password."

"Me neither," said Belinda.

Tusk moved in next to Kosta and typed in "Belinda," pressed Return. A directory of documents came up, one of which was labeled "New Life Diary."

Belinda gasped.

Tusk nearly whooped. He imagined telling Gentle, this hacking is a piece of piss.

Sighing, Kosta slouched away down the hall. Tusk opened up the New Life Diary, went to the end. The final entry was for

Tuesday, three days ago. Painful stuff, Youde psyching himself up to pop the big question to Van Kressel. The last sentence was stark: "May the gods give me rare courage."

Belinda began to wail.

An earlier line caught Tusk's attention. The day before, Monday. Amidst a general whinge about his office day, one line seemed odd: "Why oh why can't Camilla stop bearing a grudge? Are all spurned women so bitter?"

Nothing else in the final ten days' entries had relevance. Tusk scrolled to the beginning of the huge document, which began in March 1999. He used the Find facility, typed in "Camilla."

The first twenty occurrences were banal. Then, breakthrough!

Stella was back in the room, glaring at Tusk and patting Belinda, now a weeping bowed figure. Tusk was thankful for Belinda's collapse, for on Tuesday 6th July, 1999, Youde described a seduction attempt by his coworker. A pathetic attempt, had to be said. Youde had invited Camilla Brown home to sit in on a late gaming session, an event she'd led him to believe she was interested in. But once through the front door, she flung herself at him. Youde had been shocked—probably missed all the signs, Tusk thought—and pushed her off. Tears, angry words, immediate guilt on Youde's part.

Christ, Tusk thought, a motive and a half.

He closed the document. "Belinda?"

Stella stiffened. Belinda raised swimming eyes.

"I have to go." Tusk touched her arm. "Ring me if you need anything from us. Anything at all."

***

Tusk drummed on the steering wheel, pretending at John Bonham's obligatory solo in Led Zeppelin concerts.

A student cycled past, his hair plastered down in the rain.

Before driving off, Tusk made two calls, the first a message for Gentle: "Listen, genius. Camilla Brown came on to the victim. Could still be carrying a torch. Tell Dee, send someone to Carlton to check out Youde's diary."

Second call to Unforgiven: "Just to let you know I'm heading to Box Hill. I'll ring when I'm at Lim's computer."

In the background, Tusk could hear clattering, voices. He'd imagined Unforgiven as an accountant somewhere, but this sounded more like a market.

Unforgiven said, "No, please. Me too. Wait for me."

***

Box Hill's Station Street, Melbourne's eastern Chinatown, all but deserted at 9:44. Through steady rain Tusk jogged across the road from the railway station parking lot. The address turned out to be a Chinese restaurant, Summer Palace. He peered in through the window. Mid-market place, patterned wallpaper, padded chairs, tapered black chopsticks. A young Chinese waitress, hair pinned back, serving two tables, maybe ten people in all.

A hundred meters down Station Street was a tiny church, a palm tree out front. Tusk remembered last May, how he'd stood nearby, waiting for Gentle to emerge from Dumpling King after his first date with Mandy. Not one mention of the woman this morning, didn't seem right.

His body was poised, all his muscles toned. Outer suburban

life was good for fitness. He strolled up and down the street, marveled at the wonders in the window of the adjacent Chinese grocery.

Five minutes later, Unforgiven turned up in a taxi. Rain streaks on his sunglasses, ponytail, daggy sweater. A reek of garlic and onions.

"A restaurant," Unforgiven said. "How odd. Sir, any guess which is our John Lim?"

"No. And the name's Mick."

"Oh, yes. Pray don't be offended, Mick, but you look so unlikely."

"You can talk."

Unforgiven shrugged. "Shall we pursue our enquiries inside?"

"Enquiries?" Tusk felt the long-neglected sensation of calm before action, the feeling he could never explain to Dana. "Results, U. That's what we're after."

He breasted the door, saw immediately that none of the patrons were Chinese. He weaved through the tables, Unforgiven close on his heels. The room fell quiet. The waitress, a pretty girl, came running behind. A Chinese woman in her forties, dressed immaculately in a multicolored jacket, emerged from a tiny hall at the back.

She gestured to the waitress, who stopped still. "May I help you, gentlemen?"

"John Lim," Tusk said. "We need to speak to him."

She could have been onstage. "Who is this John Lim?"

Before she could react, Tusk barged past her. A glance into the kitchen, just a wizened man washing dishes.

"I call the police," the woman shouted.

"Mama," said the waitress.

Up the narrow staircase, two stairs at a time. No one in the restrooms on a small landing. Up to the top floor: a storeroom, a minuscule room with a bed, a cramped office. No people.

Unforgiven emerged beside him, gasping for breath. "Methinks he's not here."

Tusk switched on the office light. Desk, computer, shelves, a tall filing cabinet. Piles of invoices and receipts on the desk. Shapes writhing on the computer screen. On the top shelf a dozen trophies of some kind. Hung on the back of the door, a framed photo, the woman from downstairs next to a smiling Chinese man of similar age, his arm around a youth in a graduation gown.

He knew time was limited. Outside, he handed Unforgiven a pair of latex gloves. "Slip these on and get to work. I'll mind the fort."

"I only came to watch. I prefer not to do physicals."

"Use your head. You want to keep Mrs. Lim at bay while I handle the computer shit?"

"You have a point."

Unforgiven's hands shook as he donned the gloves. He vanished into the office. In Tusk's head roared the triple-voiced "Coppers" song from Rancid. From '98, if his memory served him.

Barely a minute later the matriarch marched up the stairs, followed by a middle-aged man wearing a shopkeeper's apron.

"You are trespassing," the man said.

Tusk crossed his arms, issued his stoniest glower.

"We ring the police."

Tusk stayed immobile. The pair backed down the stairs. Tusk's heart beat righteously. Flaming sounded like the electronic equivalent of a hate letter campaign, nasty but not exactly evil, despite being thousands of emails. But flaming could have been just the beginning. If John Lim was the killer, Mick Tusk was on his trail.

Unforgiven burst from the office, his face shiny with sweat. "It's him all right. The tools, the emails, everything."

"The Diamond hacker?"

"I don't believe so. This guy is a klutz."

"Come on, U, you saw the architecture books?"

"A computer klutz, then."

"Hundred percent sure he's not Diamond?"

"No," Unforgiven said. "He could have a more sophisticated set-up at home. But trust me."

Tusk's mobile vibrated in his pocket. It was Gentle. Tusk held the phone out so Unforgiven could hear the breathless summary. "A dead end here, Mick. Adam's been detained and released. Tagliaferro confirms Phillips' computer was wiped as well. And Maguire's computer was sold at auction."

"Fuck." Tusk had a thought. "Look, Maguire is the key. That guy has left records somewhere. Truckloads of them."

"How do you know?"

Tusk flashed on his images of Maguire. "The kind of guy he was." He updated Gentle on the flamer. "He's not here now. Don't move on this until we're well clear. My turn to ring back."

Downstairs, voices argued in Chinese. The furious face of Mrs. Lim bobbed up to check them out, then disappeared.

"Listen, U." Tusk's lips were dry. "In case we need to hoof it.

I remember who Maguire's widow is staying with. Name's Hugh Long, her stepson's grandfather, somewhere on the peninsula. We'll need the address."

Unforgiven hugged himself. "This is clutching at straws."

"True, but unless this Lim is the hacker and killer, where else will we track down the Diamond connection?"

Unforgiven ran back into the office. Judging from the to-and-fro of guttural voices, a crowd had gathered below. Tusk breathed in the aromas of Asian spices, remembered how Gentle had once boasted he could identify the precise cuisine of a restaurant blindfolded.

"U," Tusk hissed. "Better scoot."

The ponytailed hacker emerged, eyes alight. "I found his electronic diary backup. And guess what? At this very moment, John Lim is playing table tennis in Albert Park."

Tusk's adrenaline stepped up one more notch. "Ripper."

He led the way down the stairs. A band of Chinese traders, huddled with Mrs. Lim, shrank back. Tusk felt sorry for her.

"You," someone shouted.

Tusk made for the back door.

CHAPTER 29

"So, is Adam the murderer?" Irene Skews' hands still trembled from her fright, but her eyes shone. "Is that it? Is he, dear?"

Blood pounded in Peter Gentle's head. He sat on the edge of Gus' desk, surrounded by day traders. Breakfast was forgotten. Oleg seemed especially excited, guzzling can after can of Coke. Even Phillips had lost his doleful expression. Finola had joined them and seemed to be trying to steer the discussion toward the upcoming market opening.

Inspector Conomy had quizzed Peter about Adam.

"He's hiding something," said Peter. "I'm just not sure what."

Conomy had smiled calmly. "I knew his karma was bad. Don't worry, mate, we'll get it out of him."

Now Peter longed to be free of gasbag Irene. His gaze drifted past the gathering to Brad Funder in his office. The accountant sat as if frozen. Their eyes connected. Peter experienced a momentary flashback of Mick, one of those explosive images that terrified him. He came to a decision.

"Irene, I'll be back."

In the action room, traders were arriving in strength, calling to each other, sipping takeaway coffee, limbering up for trading. Peter half-ran into Jim's office.

"I need your help," he said.

Jim, his expression moody, looked up from a file. "Anything."

"I just found out. Funder has been conspiring to set up in opposition to TPT. I think Gus may have stumbled onto it."

The transformation was frightening to behold. Red and purple flooded Jim's cheeks. His eyes bulged. "You're certain?"

"Actually, no. Underground whispers, that's all, Jim. So let's be careful. But he won't talk to me."

"The hell he won't."

Jim tore past Peter and down the aisle. His hip flaring with discomfort, Peter struggled to keep up. At least Jim's depression has gone, he thought, but what have I unleashed?

Oleg saw them coming. "Papa!"

Irene called to Peter, "Dear, you're back."

Jim ignored them. The TPT founder, Peter on his heels, burst in on Funder.

Funder rose. "What—"

"Shut up!" roared Jim.

Hairs stood up on Peter's neck. Outside Funder's office no one stirred.

Funder's face turned white.

The chief executive thrust his quivering face over Funder's desk. "You ungrateful dog. Tell me."

"Jim, Jim—"

"Who with, you mangy mongrel?"

"Business." Funder's glasses slid down his nose. The face that had so intimidated Peter now struck him as pitiful. "It was only business."

"The trouble I've gone to…"

Funder stumbled back into shelves. Books slipped to the floor. "You know I disagree with you on strategy, Jim. You're never going to make it like this… with this pint-sized mess. All I thought was… some venture capital. There were discussions with Carmody Peate. It was just talk, Jim, I swear."

Peter gulped. "How did Gus find out?"

Funder's gaze locked onto Peter as if he were a preacher offering salvation. "I wanted to tell you."

The accountant edged away from Jim, pushed the glasses back up his nose. "My father said every lie comes back to haunt you. Oh, God, he was right. Listen, I had nothing to do with Gus' death, I swear. It was just business."

A guttural sound issued from Jim. He scooped up a paperweight—Peter registered a craggy black stone, one of Adam's gifts no doubt—and advanced.

Peter lunged to grab the raised arm. Jim's skin was hot.

"Don't lose it," Peter said. "Irene's watching."

That worked. Jim smashed the paperweight on the desk. He stepped back to glower.

"What happened, Brad?" said Peter, employing his most reasonable voice.

"Oh, God." Funder's eyes ranged heavenward. "Sara will use this as the final excuse."

"Brad…"

"I know, I know. You don't realize how close I was to telling you the first time. Gus overheard me on the phone, hinted as much at lunch. I was consumed by worry, you've no idea… so I went to see him at home. Just after seven. I begged him to keep it quiet. He didn't promise, but I think he would have. I swear, I was there only ten minutes, fifteen minutes at the outside."

And Funder closed his eyes, stood with head bowed. His shoulders rose and fell.

Peter turned to take in the stunned group outside. His eyes met Finola's; she nodded. Irene's mouth hung open. Oleg looked gleeful.

At this transitory moment of triumph, Peter felt flat. Unless Funder was a consummate actor, he wasn't the answer. Just business, he'd said, and Peter believed him.

Jim had regained control. He mopped his brow with a handkerchief. "You're fired, Brad. Clear out your desk. The sight of you makes me puke."

***

When Peter returned from splashing his face with water, he found Robyn leading Nick Tagliaferro, a green tie clashing with his blue suit, to Camilla Brown's desk.

The traders had dispersed. Funder had gone. Stir the mix, Peter thought. He reached the systems gurus just as they shook hands. Worry filled Camilla's face.

Robyn was striking in black slacks and a black vest over a buttoned-up blouse. She eyed Peter curiously.

"What's to report?" Peter asked Tagliaferro.

Camilla's eyes widened. Robyn had turned to go.

"When I'm ready." The policeman's face was sallow.

Peter manufactured a grin. "I'll trade you."

"You've gotta be joking." Tagliaferro inspected Peter as if he were an insect. "If you know anything, Gentle, you'd better tell me. I gotta remind you, I'm the one can take you down to St Kilda Road."

"Try it." Peter smiled as sweetly as he could. "Come on, let's swap."

Tagliaferro considered for a moment, then shrugged. "Make it snappy."

Peter delighted in the rising envy on the swarthy face as he spelled out John Lim's real email address. In return, what the policeman told him was negative enough to be the truth. Maguire's possessions had been sold by an auction house. And Saul Phillips' computer had also been formatted clean of all data.

"He's escaped," Peter said.

"No way," Tagliaferro said. "That email address is my key. Haven't a clue how you got it, but we've got the power to find out his identity from the ISP. Then we've got him."

"No." Both men turned to Camilla. Today she'd swapped the professional look for a homely cardigan and a tartan skirt. "They're not the same person. The flamer and the hacker."

"Says who?" said Tagliaferro.

"I mean, I'm no pro." Camilla's hands were clasped together with nervousness. "But their English is different."

"I agree," Peter said.

The effect was delicious. Tagliaferro exploded.

"I've never heard such crap," he said. "Leave this to the experts."

"Experts shmexperts," said Peter.

"Break it up." Rich Conomy's relaxed frame appeared between them. He stared at Tagliaferro, then into Peter's eyes.

"Didn't I tell you boys to get along?"

"Get along?" Peter's good-humored needling switched to annoyance. Did he need to suffer fools all day? "I'm lucky if he tells me the time. Who's the one making progress here?"

He thought Tagliaferro would hit him then.

"You blokes remind me of little kids," Conomy said. "We've got a killer to catch, remember? Now, into Mr. Van Kressel's office, the pair of you."

Conomy, ambling with hands in pockets, took the lead. Immediately they rounded the corner, Peter sensed the jittery tension in the trading room. Backs faced the aisle, even Irene's. The television screens showed a commentator talking to a chart of the plunging Nasdaq. Over the intercom, Murray's voice announced, "Markets… open."

Conomy halted and the three of them watched the traders set to work. Backs grew hunched, heads craned at screens pulsing with action, fingers flew. Staccato clicking of keys filled the room. What a moment, Peter thought, the opening of trading, the unfurling of a nation's hopes for the day.

Conomy shook his head ruefully.

"Such a waste," Peter heard him say to no one in particular. "All these poor souls, kicking against fate."

Even Tagliaferro's face softened as he stared at the figures pouring down a screen.

"Go, go, go," one of the traders urged.

Peter walked along the aisle, observing the traders he knew. Saul Phillips' bottom lip jutted out in concentration. Irene fingered her necklaces, her lips moving soundlessly. Crazy Oleg kicked his chair back and stood over his keyboard, a hunchback with arms as kinetic extensions.

Awesome, Peter thought. Quite what he really concluded about these misfits, daring to compete against the professionals with their systems and years of experience, he couldn't say. Logic said they would fail. But at that moment he felt pride in Jim and Finola and their edifice to human endeavor. Go, go, go, he thought.

He sidled away to check his mobile messages. As soon as he'd retrieved Mick's damning news about Camilla, he rang Mick and whispered Tagliaferro's feedback. Mick's deep voice gave an update on John Lim. Peter's spirits soared.

Finola was already in Jim's office. Peter stood by the window, counting umbrellas below, while Conomy took charge. If the policeman had any theories on the killer, he certainly wasn't divulging them. The official autopsy report had been released—time of death was estimated at minutes before Peter's arrival at 8:05 PM. A gun had been found in Belinda's bedroom—it turned out she was an avid shooter—but it didn't match the murder weapon. Funder's statement reiterated his claim that he'd left Gus after fifteen minutes, at 7:30 PM; police were checking out his alibi, for he'd claimed to be in a nearby pub by 7:35. If all that wasn't discouraging enough, Conomy's initial interview with Adam had been a flop.

"Come on," Peter said. "You know Adam's lying."

Conomy's gaze turned to Finola, who had paled. "Of course he admits to a past relationship with Belinda. But he claims he has a new girlfriend and no interest in his ex. I confirmed with his father that he was at home on Wednesday night."

"Why did he react like the plague to my accounting investigations?"

"Said he doesn't like you, mate."

Peter snorted.

Conomy said, "We'll try again at HQ."

"Inspector." Jim was fully restored, somehow had changed his shirt and doused himself with that aftershave. "I don't mean to sound negative, but this all sounds fruitless. What about you, Constable? Have you anything to report?"

Tagliaferro flashed glances of loathing at Peter during his summary of the minimal progress on the hacking front. His grudging acknowledgment of Peter's assistance earned Peter a nod of approval from Conomy.

"I've got some news too." Peter paused for effect. "Camilla Brown made a pass at Gus last July. There's a diary at Gus' place. She may have a motive."

Jim passed a hand over his face.

"Oh, no," Finola said.

Conomy's eyes flashed. "Where does all this come from?" He turned to Jim. "You told me Gus was the universally loved Mister Nice Guy. Now literally everyone seems to have had reason to hate his guts. What's going on?"

Peter's mobile trilled. The room froze.

Peter couldn't resist. He turned into a corner and answered.

As usual Mick was blunt. "Reckon we've found the flamer. Albert Park. Table tennis courts."

Peter's heart took off. "I'll see you there."

He hung up and realized he had no choice but to inform the gathering. The reaction was immediate.

Tagliaferro pointed a finger at him. "Cowboy time is over. You'll ride with me, Gentle."

"Too right." Conomy's face had darkened. "You and me can have a natter on the way."

"No way," Peter said. The last thing he wanted was to ride in sourpuss' car or to bring the police to Unforgiven.

Jim's roar startled him. "God almighty, Pete, you're wasting time. Get the mongrel."

One look at his client sealed Peter's fate—he would ride with Tagliaferro.

Deirdre, her face tight with exhaustion, was waiting outside Jim's office. She smiled uncertainly at Peter. Conomy spoke into her ear. Camilla, Peter guessed.

Finola gave him a hesitant wave.

Tagliaferro hissed, "I'm onto you, Gentle."

CHAPTER 30

10:47. Surely Lim has a mobile, Mick Tusk thought, surely he's long gone.

Across the access road, Tusk saw the curved form of a swan floating on Albert Park Lake. Sunlight sparkled off the rain-soaked lawns outside the Melbourne Sports & Aquatic Centre. He'd often driven past the Centre's massive shape but had never entered. Racquet sports were for wankers.

Unforgiven was panting.

"Keep up," Tusk said.

He reached the automatic doors at a near-run.

Signs directed him through the huge entrance area to the Table Tennis Hall. High ceiling, three rows of tables separated by blue meter-high partitions. The reek of B.O., the surreal ambience of ping-pong balls, slapping feet, grunts. Figures lunged and darted at a dozen tables.

"Here, this may assist with identification." Unforgiven thrust a tiny framed photograph into his hands.

Tusk recognized John Lim from the graduation shot. In this photo, Lim was trim and handsome in a double-breasted suit.

Black stubble hair, grave features, the faintest of smiles.

"You graduating to physical theft now?" Tusk handed back the photo.

They skirted a coach feeding ball after ball to a teenager who slapped forehands with grooved efficiency.

Tusk recognized Lim on the next table just as Lim spotted him. The flamer wore black shorts, a hand towel tucked into the waistband, and a club T-shirt dappled with perspiration. He held a table tennis bat with the pencil grip Tusk had seen on television. At the other end of the table, a younger version of Lim gaped.

A mixture of resignation and defiance came over Lim's face. He dropped the paddle and ran.

Tusk took off after him. Lim was quick, damn quick, but ran the wrong way, toward the dead-end corner. When he changed direction to sprint for the exit, Tusk ducked around a table and managed to lay a hand on a slippery shoulder.

Lim went down, came up swinging.

The calm that held sway over Tusk felt like home. He batted away the flailing arms. With ease he twisted Lim onto the ground, onto his stomach, arm up behind his back. He held the writhing young man down hard.

"Why'd you do it?" he asked quietly.

"How did you find me?" grunted Lim. "You're from TPT, aren't you?"

"No. Tell me about it."

A trickle of sweat ran down Tusk's cheek. Lim settled, grew still. Tusk let him sit up and squatted next to the slumped figure. He rubbed his forearm, a sore spot where Lim had got lucky.

"They deserve it."

The hatred in Lim's face was so intense, it jogged Tusk's memory. Of course, he thought.

"Your father," he said. Lawrence Lim, Maguire's very first victim.

Tears flooded Lim's face. Tusk knew he'd hold back nothing.

"They killed him." Lim twisted his hand towel. "He used to bring me here. He loved his table tennis, we could play for hours. They gave that Maguire beast a margin facility, anyone could have seen it coming, but all they care about is money, money, money. He'd let me win, my dad, he'd let me win."

Tusk waited for another burst of weeping to wind down into snuffles. "Why attack Oleg Kilpatrick, Saul Phillips?"

"What?" Lim's expression was either Oscar material or utter incomprehension.

It was then that Tusk noticed Unforgiven was nowhere to be seen. And fifty meters off, four men were headed his way. He recognized Lim's teen brother, Boy Wonder's head, Conomy's gait.

"Where'd you get the gun, John?"

"Gun?" Lim shivered. "What are you talking about?"

Tusk rose to await the approaching group. So U was right, he thought, Lim's just a coincidental diversion.

In the distance, the players and coaches stood staring at the ruckus. Devoid of ping-pong sounds, the hall was eerie, seemed to stretch forever.

Gentle's gasps heralded his arrival. He stared at Lim.

"Waste of time," Tusk said quietly.

"You're joking."

Rich Conomy had this way of walking, loose yet surprisingly speedy, like a cat. He was next on the scene and Tusk saw his face alter with the shock of recognition. Hadn't Gentle told the good inspector about his partner?

John Lim's kid brother raced past, threw himself onto the figure on the ground. The fourth man in the party, the one Tusk had spied yesterday, peered at Tusk before moving to shake Lim's shoulder. Tagliaferro—this had to be the computer cop—had tight black curls like Dana's cousin Theo.

Gentle had finally cottoned onto Conomy's odd expression. "Inspector, meet—"

"What are you doing here, Ivory?" Conomy asked.

Tagliaferro began to read Lim his rights.

Did you fuck me over, Tusk wanted to ask. "Good to see you, Rich. I'm with him."

Gentle wore a confused smile. "You know each other?"

The hacker and his brother were up on their feet, Tagliaferro gripping Lim's elbow.

"Is that man a policeman too?" Lim asked loudly.

"Shut up," Tagliaferro said.

It was Cap who'd warned Tusk that there are none more furious than the righteous. What did Conomy's expression hold? Hesitation certainly, anger yes. Fear? Did he think Tusk would thump him? Tusk folded his arms and tried to dampen the body language.

"He attacked me," Lim said. "I'd like to make an official complaint."

"Shut your mouth," Tagliaferro said.

Gentle asked, "Inspector, can I have a minute?"

Tusk had always admired the speed of Conomy's decisions. The Inspector flicked a hand at Tagliaferro. "Okay Constable, let's head in."

"Inspector, what happens now?" Gentle said.

Conomy's squinty eyes rested on Tusk for a moment, then he grinned that grin of his at Gentle. "Ivory here can give you a lift."

You Buddhist-holier-than-thou arsehole, Tusk thought. "Catch you later, Rich."

Hands in pockets, Conomy strolled away in the wake of Tagliaferro and his party.

"What?" yelled Gentle. "At least can you explain why?"

Conomy stopped and turned. "Ivory there. Mate, you could have told me."

"You didn't ask," Gentle said.

"Ah well. Now I know. Say hi to your dad."

"But what's Mick got to do with this? My client wants me involved."

"Read the newspapers like everyone else." And Conomy, shaking his head, was off.

A silent tableau of gaping table tennis players across the hall. Gentle, mouth catching moths, stood rooted.

See that, Dana, Tusk thought, not a trace of temper. "Look at it this way, genius. We got twenty-four hours of cooperation."

By now three tables away, Tagliaferro turned for a final farewell to Gentle, a jab of his middle finger skyward.

"Fuck," Tusk said.

***

Flawless Feet Art Gallery, a stylish black-and-white building nestled between a design studio and a wholesale jeweler. Collingwood under a cloudy sky, puddles on the potholed road. Converted factories all around.

12:03. Tusk ran fingers through his stubbly hair. They came away damp. Sweat. Bloody temper, he thought.

On the short drive from Albert Park to Collingwood, Gentle had prattled on and on, a transparent attempt to wean Tusk's mind off the fury that had soared when the computer cop flung his insult.

"Shut the hell up," Tusk had snapped at one point.

"Conomy has nothing to do with you anymore."

"The bastard."

"Then hit him where it counts. Big guy, we have to solve this."

The fervor in the nerd's voice was the circuit-breaker. Gentle was right, of course. Another of Cap's maxims: words lie, actions speak.

Tusk followed Gentle into the gallery, a reception desk flanked by two narrow viewing rooms. Meaningless abstracts in black frames in one room, oil paintings of bush and sea in the other. It meant zip-all to Tusk. To him, beauty meant music; art signified upper-class snobbery.

Gentle, his face serious, jingled a bell on the desk. The first flush of working together had clearly been punched out of him by the Conomy episode. Buddhist bastard, Tusk thought, then started another round of relaxant breathing.

"Ah, Jim's private detective," mocked a cigarette-infused voice.

Alison Van Kressel, dressed in Armani trackpants and a halter-neck top, was sex on a stick. Bare feet. A hawkish face, powerful in effect and intent, with a huge schnoz. Her eyes were wired.

"Mrs. Van Kressel." Gentle offered his hand. "My partner Mick."

The woman ignored him. Tusk felt her eyes range over his body. "I bet they call you Donkey Dick."

It didn't make sense to Tusk. Gentle had described Alison's outbursts, her recent contriteness. Yet here she was, all razor blades.

Tusk decided to try friendliness. "If only."

"Are you two art aficionados by any chance?" Alison asked.

"A little," Gentle said.

Ha, thought Tusk. Until Mandy began dragging Gentle to galleries, Tusk doubted he'd ever been in one. Tusk elected to stay silent.

Gracefully, Alison swept into the room displaying the abstracts. "Aren't these evocative? Winston is attracting so much attention. Rather good for a year-old gallery, if I say so myself. Do you like the name?"

"It's unique," Gentle said.

"With compliments like that, who needs publicity? See these flawless feet?" And she pirouetted across the gleaming floorboards, finishing with a twirl on her toes.

"I was a ballet dancer." Her eyes glinted.

"Mrs. Van Kressel." Gentle's face was unsettled. "When did you first learn your daughter was planning to marry Gus Youde?"

That stopped her. "My daughter is marrying no one. Was

never marrying anyone. A mild fling, that's all, a taste of the exotic."

"When did you find out?"

She nibbled at the tip of a fingernail, her eyes smoldering at Gentle. "Jim told me on Tuesday night. I never met this boy Gus, but think about it, why don't you? It was never going to happen."

"Are you certain you never met Gus?"

"When would I, Mr. Private Dick?" she snapped. "I blame it all on that Vines bitch. You saw her last night. Boy, would she like to get her hands down Jim's pants."

Gentle's face wrinkled with distaste. "Gus' head was half shot off on Wednesday night, Mrs. Van Kressel."

"Oh, and I'm meant to feel compassion for the fortune hunter. The rest of the world may shed crocodile tears for him. Not me."

"Where were you on Wednesday night?"

"Ah, the ever diligent investigator. You've got cheek. Jim makes me sick, sending you to check up on me."

"Can you answer my question, Mrs. Van Kressel?"

Attaboy, Tusk thought.

Alison yawned theatrically. "Go back and tell him to do his own dirty work. You ask him, am I a murderess now?"

Tusk decided the woman's vitriol was chemically stimulated. Burning bridges, that was the only viable option for him.

He walked up close enough to catch Alison's fragrance, a tart fruity aroma.

"Alison," he said.

Alarm sparked in her eyes. "The muscle man, right? Good cop, bad cop?"

"Cooperation always makes a difference, Alison. Either that or I'll have Inspector Conomy come down on you like a ton of bricks."

"Boofhead," she spat. "Clear the hell out and take your freaky friend with you."

Christ, Tusk realized, she wants me to hit her.

In his experience spousal abuse was ninety-five percent males bashing females. But you did see the reverse. And he'd made up his mind long ago. Never give abusers a break.

And this one could easily be a killer.

He put menace in his face, his schoolyard face-em-down look, and pushed his chest out. "Alison, Alison. Easy to hit family, isn't it? But Homicide will make mincemeat of you."

"Jerk!"

He took another step, close enough to see the pulse flickering in her neck. Christ, she was potent. He felt disgust at her, at himself.

A harsh voice boomed, footsteps resounded. "Hands off, buster."

The man striding across the room was tall and wide, mid-thirties. Similar trackpants to Alison, tight blue T-shirt showing off gym muscles. Silver ear-studs, tanned face with flabby cheeks. Pinprick amphetamine pupils.

"Hey!" cried Gentle.

Alison commanded, "Phil!"

The man smacked Tusk on the chest with his palm. Fear sprang into his eyes when the hand jarred.

Alison was stumbling backward. "Stop it, Phil."

Tusk caught her dawning comprehension. He now knew what to do.

213

He turned away from the man, grinned at Alison. "Come on, Alison. You're joking, right? This hairball's your alibi?"

Out of the corner of an eye, he saw Phil the Dill swing a fist. He ducked, spun and clobbered Phil in the guts. The bozo fell with a gurgle.

Alison's teeth were bared with instant pleasure. Tusk felt revulsion, familiar revulsion. Blood roared. He leaned down to pluck Phil up by his T-shirt. His fist felt huge but feathery light.

"Mick." Gentle was at his side, urgently insinuating.

Tusk ground his teeth. Closed his eyes. Tried to count.

CHAPTER 31

Rory Menadue's office was in reality a single room, part of a suite of serviced offices in an old nondescript building near the Stock Exchange tower. Rory greeted them in a heavy green worsted suit with elbow pads, a white skivvy, and brown loafers.

"A pleasure to see you again," he said.

Every inch a professor, Peter Gentle thought, except he isn't even a real academic.

"Thanks for finding time for us, Rory," Peter said. "Mick Tusk, my partner."

Rory raised his nose to study Mick. "I thought we'd lunch at the club."

"Whoops, forgot my top hat," Mick said.

"Don't mind him," said Peter. "The club would be fine."

He'd known what to expect. Mick, still steaming after the explosion in the art gallery, had made his feelings clear: "If Adam's got one silver spoon up his arsehole, I bet his old man's rectum must be stuffed with them."

The reek of incense—had Rory lit the smoldering stick just as they knocked?—competed with the fusty odor of a collector's accumulations. Peter registered thick Asian rugs, an antique mahogany desk, a boxy computer, an oriental chest, a radiator under a small window with a gold-patterned curtain. Two jade door lions crowded the entranceway. Every inch of wall seemed to be covered with scrolls of Chinese calligraphy or sepia paintings of trees and valleys.

"I know what you're thinking," Rory said. "My wife is an electronic commerce guru, yet I steep myself in the ancient past."

"Study is study," Peter surprised himself by saying. "I've always loved to study. Anything almost."

"Yes, yes." Rory beamed. "If you don't invest in your intellect, what are you? Mick, are you involved in study?"

Mick's brow knitted. "I was gonna learn up on bloody psychopath profiling, once."

Rory didn't miss a beat. "Well, I think we'd better get moving."

On Collins Street, the drying footpath was lit by sunshine escaping through a cloud break. A woman strolled past carrying a bulging Schwob's Swiss sandwich. The square on the corner of William Street was dotted with workers perched on newspapers to avoid getting wet, tapping cigarette ash into drink cans or forking from plastic takeaway bowls. Peter breathed in the aromas of drying bitumen, cigarettes, and food. Was Mandy nibbling at a sandwich right now?

For some reason Harvey Jopling came to mind. An avowed anti-intellectual, Harvey nevertheless had a rare ability to package concepts memorably. Every few months the investment banker would arrange for Peter what he called a "pick-me-up booze-up," a long chatty dinner at an up-market restaurant new to both of them. The timing always seemed to coincide uncannily with the black periods when the world threatened to engulf Peter.

A few months back, in Ocha, a tiny but chic Japanese restaurant in Kew, Harvey had suddenly turned serious after having Peter in stitches with a tale about a botched cross-border merger.

"You know, Skull," Harvey said. "The key is to pile on the pressure. Without the props our old folks had, we need to pile it on. Whatever gives us a rush, pile it on, that's my philosophy."

Maybe that's it, Peter thought, as he followed Rory up the incline of Bank Place, the short alley off Collins Street dominated by the Mitre Tavern. Setbacks were nothing as long as data was pouring in or meaningful analysis needed doing. So what if Gus' killer mystified him more than ever? Pile it on, he thought.

Rory's club was in an unlabeled green building halfway up Bank Place. A flag flew above ostentatious external pillars. Peter's lips curled at the olde worlde paneling inside, the stuffed moose's head on a wall. While Rory signed them into a guest book, Peter remembered another of Harvey's remarks: "Everybody jeers at these relics of clubs until they're invited to join. In Melbourne you always join."

Up a flight of echoing wooden stairs, Rory ushered them into a large carpeted dining room overseen by silent waiters. The exclusively male patrons were mostly gray or graying, all in suits except for the two interlopers. Amongst tables of varying sizes, Rory chose an empty one with ten seats.

"Club rules, no booking," Rory explained. "Early arrivals get their own tables. We'll have to share."

Peter caught Mick's eye. Great, he thought, interviewing a suspect amongst geriatric businessmen.

"Mr. Menadue." The pimply waiter must have had a butler's training in obsequiousness. "What will it be today, sir? The salmon or the tournedos?"

"Craig." Rory put on a pair of spectacles. "Methinks the salmon. Gentlemen, what will be your pleasure?"

During his recent stint living at his parents' home, Peter's equivocal opinion of his childhood fare had turned to disdain. But the one thing his mother cooked with flair was the Wednesday evening steak and kidney pie.

"The pie," he said.

Mick regarded the menu in apparent confusion. "Bloody hell. Nothin' plainer?"

"Perhaps the steak, sir." Craig held back a smirk. "The Bearnaise sauce is a creamy one."

"Does it come with tomato sauce?" He took pity on the young man. "The pie also, thanks."

Rory paid no attention. After a fastidious examination of the wine menu, he ordered a bottle of Shiraz. At least, Peter thought, if Mick ruins the interview, I'll manage a drop of the good stuff.

"Now." Rory's smile was equable. "Before we're joined, let's deal with business. And"— he stared pointedly at Mick—"no more games, young man."

Mick shrugged.

"As you may have been informed, gentlemen," Rory said, "I held high hopes for my son and Belinda Van Kressel. A delightful young lady and a good match for Adam. But it was not to be, and I did not, repeat did not, sneak into the house of that young man and kill him. I can't conceive a more ridiculous notion. Adam and I spent an evening together, just watching television, something I treasure more and more as he inevitably expresses a young man's independence."

"Can you recall what you two watched?" Peter asked.

Rory pretended to dredge up a memory. "*The 7:30 Report* and *Blue Heelers*. Look, the person behind this heinous crime must be caught and I acknowledge you need to be methodical. But I never even met Mr. Youde."

Mick leaned forward. "Know him or not, Mr. Menadue, his fucking head was damn near blown off. An upstanding man like you, just you make sure you do what's right."

Peter sucked in a breath.

Rory smiled thinly but his eyes clouded. "Very impressive, Mr. Tusk. And my, hasn't your diction improved. Ah, Craig, thank goodness. My guests must be famished."

Touché, Peter thought. Rory had maintained his and Adam's alibis with complete aplomb.

While Craig, glancing with amusement at Mick, delivered their dishes, the table filled with an assortment of businessmen, all of whom greeted and chatted with Rory. Peter and Mick ate in silence. The steak and kidney pie was burnt.

Mick refused Rory's insistent offers of wine, so Peter compensated by loading up. A dead end, he thought, another one.

CHAPTER 32

Today's TPT announcer sounded like a cross between a DJ and a stationmaster apologizing for delays due to defective stock. Not that Mick Tusk could make out the man's words, for bedlam reigned. Traders ran to and from their cubicles. The TVs were up loud, computers pinged, people cheered and hooted. The huge room stank, a melange of machinery, sweat, and corn chips.

Tusk drew sidelong glances from passing traders. They can tell, he thought, this is one guy who never owned a share in his life, probably never will. Well, fuck 'em.

Oleg Kilpatrick rushed from his cubicle to embrace Gentle.

"Peter, Peter." Kilpatrick's fingers wove patterns in the air. "Get stuffed Nasdaq, eh?" He bounced on his toes, leered at Tusk. "Mick, Mick, Mick, a day for winners. I get lucky or you shoot me, right?"

He sprang back into his littered cubbyhole. Christ, Tusk thought, the Russian maniac clicks his bloody mouse, another bank branch shuts its doors.

A thirty-something brown-haired woman, her face troubled, trudged out of Van Kressel's office. Camilla Brown, Tusk guessed. She flung wounded looks at Gentle as she passed.

"You beauty," came a cry.

The DJ intoned, "Solution 6, up five cents to $8.35."

Tusk whispered, "What's going on?"

"Almost a miracle, if I believed in them," Gentle said. He'd been subdued since the humiliation in the Club. "The US markets fell overnight but Aussie shares have bounced. After three weeks of tracking the Nasdaq index up and down, this bear market's gone bullish."

"Bears, bulls. Any elephants?"

"No," said Gentle, "just one dumb ape."

Saul Phillips and Irene Skews were next to rush up.

Phillips was ranting. "Peter, I knew it, I knew it. Who says turbulence is doom and gloom? It was so easy!"

Skews, dressed oddly in lacy black, seemed thrilled to see Gentle. "Peter, dear, look. Look at the joy. Didn't I tell you?"

Deirdre materialized beside Tusk. "Mick, I'm surprised you'd risk it here."

The policewoman, once the resident of his dreams, wore a creased blue jacket. Despite her obvious fatigue, she looked pretty. It was the work that made her attractive, animated her plain face with purpose.

Tusk smiled. "What would he do? Arrest me? Dee, I had no idea he hates me like that."

"It's not hate, Mick. Just his black-and-white view of the world." She yawned. "Look, he's good to work for."

"After Vinci, anyone would be. Back scratch time?"

Tusk tried to tune out the clamor, the sound of slick money. What time did this frigging mayhem finish? He and Deirdre worked quickly. He told her everything—Alison the cuckold, the slippery Menadue alibis, Lim the flamer who wasn't Diamond—except for Unforgiven's presence. In turn Deirdre reported on the initial chat she'd just concluded with the Brown woman. Brown admitted to an old crush on the victim but claimed no involvement since the abortive seduction. Her alibi, at home with her children, wasn't watertight, but Deirdre reckoned her genuine. And Kilpatrick's alibi—his girlfriend—held up. Indeed they'd already checked most of the traders, for zero result.

"We're still interviewing anyone and everyone," she said. "Something will come up."

Conomy's philosophy, Tusk knew. Do the hard yakka and something will turn up. Tusk himself subscribed to it, partially at least.

Gentle's fan club had gone and Boy Wonder was talking with Van Kressel. Gentle still looked fresh enough, but for how long with all that grog in him? As a teen Gentle had been endlessly hyper. As an adult, Tusk observed swings up and down.

The tycoon slapped Tusk's arm. "The traders love you, Mick. A bit of positive drama you are, after all of the recent wrist slitting."

"You want me to shatter some bricks?"

Van Kressel roared with laughter, his fat quivering. He stank of wine and aftershave, but his energy was palpable.

Gentle was frowning.

Van Kressel said, "Funder's gone, Inspector Conomy carted him away. Robyn's packing up the snake's gear, good bloody riddance. And how's this, the inspector has excommunicated me."

Shit, Tusk thought. "Really? Rich has shut you out?"

"Totally. He claimed you were a rogue cop, Mick." Van Kressel's gaze was direct but not unfriendly. "I lost my cool. Told him TPT's reputation has been tarnished because the police haven't made any progress. Off he went."

"Sorry about that," said Tusk.

Van Kressel spread his arms wide, revealing stained armpits. "But hallelujah, it's a bumper trading day. Fi and I received twenty queries from potential clients just this morning. Some of them ghouls maybe, but we need bums on seats. Had a couple of contract terminations yesterday. But best of all, Pete, Belinda just rang to say sorry."

No mention of super bitch, Tusk noted.

"That's great, Jim," said Gentle.

"What's progress on the investigation front?" Van Kressel said.

Gentle shook his head.

A phone rang. Van Kressel ran into his office.

"I didn't tell him about Alison." Gentle led the way down the aisle. "Just that she's alibied."

"The alibi's not cast-iron," Tusk said.

"Ah, but in your professional judgment…"

"Yeah, it's good."

Around the corner the din fell away. Brown stood staring at them from the equipment room. Adam Menadue was at his desk. The family resemblance to the toff in the club adorned with a moose's head was obvious to Tusk now.

Menadue smiled triumphantly. "What's going down, fellers?"

"Just a matter of time," Tusk said.

"After all I've done for you guys," Menadue quipped.

In the bean counter's office, Robyn—was she anorexic?—was packing books into boxes. Her gazelle's eyes studied them both.

Tusk waved. She smiled fleetingly.

In the other office, Finola Vines beamed.

"What a difference a few hours make," she said. "Trading volumes were so positive this morning, I've dusted off the presentation I was preparing for a capital raising. How did it go with Rory?"

Her face turned somber at Gentle's summing up. Tusk guessed she'd shied from slapping down her stepson. Shit, he thought, families…

Unusual for a city office, a small stereo sat behind Vines' desk. A gig poster, a sweating face behind a microphone, caught his attention.

"Van Morrison?" he said.

That brought the smile back. "Do you like him?"

Tusk tried to recall the title of the one Van Morrison LP he'd bought back in the '80s, something about being inarticulate. "My tastes are rockier but he sure is a big figure."

"A big figure? Mick, he's the man. I'm webmaster of one of his biggest fan clubs."

Seeing for the first time a totally open smile, one prompted by a rock singer for Christ's sake, Tusk decided Vines had his seal of approval.

"But…" Gentle said.

Tusk and Vines turned to look at him.

In this mood, Gentle, slouched and weedy with downcast

eyes, could have been a rock star himself. Drug overdose material perhaps.

"It's all dead ends," he said. "No one hacked your traders, Finola. No one executed Gus."

"But they've caught this Chinese hacker," Vines said. "And Brad Funder was in Carlton."

Gentle shrugged. "Maybe. Maybe."

"You just need a shot of coffee," Tusk said. Hard to say, in front of Vines, that her stepson was a prime suspect. And what about Unforgiven? He pictured the long-haired hacker tunneling through electronic burrows. As if I have any idea what U does, he thought.

"It's true we need to stay determined," Vines said. "As Van Morrison put it, we can make dreams come true if we want them to."

Tusk was amazed. "As Tom Petty said, we won't back down."

He saw Gentle blink, had heard the unexpressed retort many times: rock lyrics, just vapid drivel.

Vines said, "In a few minutes a number of us are driving to Gus' funeral. Will you attend?"

Tusk had never met Youde but the idea struck a chord with him. He saw Gentle shudder.

"Come on, Gentle," Tusk said. "Day's agenda done, right?"

A trace of a smile, a sigh. "How can I argue with logic like that?"

CHAPTER 33

A rent in the polyurethane car seat dug into his lower back. Peter Gentle squirmed but could find no relief. Why hadn't he insisted on the yellow buggy, with its lingering new-car smell? But then he would have had to drive…

He watched the windscreen wipers at work. In truth his energy was faltering. His back ached, and a minute ago he'd brushed the skull lump painfully against the Peugeot's roof. A fog blanketed his brain, reminiscent of Friday afternoons during his Rock Mutual years, before downsizing frightened long lunches out of existence.

"You're right," Mick said over jarring guitars, a voice groaning something inane about putting your lights on.

"Hmm?"

"Adam bloody Menadue's the key."

Mick's fingers tapped the steering wheel in time with the music, turgid riff-rock of the type Peter experimented with for a while, back in his teens—hey, when he knew Mick—and then discarded as puerile.

"I'm not so sure," Peter said. "He's hiding something, but can you see him as hacker and killer?"

"Silver-spoon—"

"Yes, yes, yes. Half the boys we went to school with were like him."

"Spot on, genius."

Traffic was steady. Water sprayed off the Monash Freeway. Mick took the Wellington Road exit and pulled into a Shell service station. He jogged through the drizzle, returned with two bottles of blue Powerade. They drank in silence.

Mick flipped open his notebook, made a phone call.

"Thanks, U." Mick scribbled. "One more thing… no, no hurry, whenever. Adam Menadue has this mate called David O'Shaughnessy. Unclear on spelling. You track him down?"

At least someone's working, Peter thought. He guzzled the remnants of the welcome sweetness. "What was that all about?"

"You piss up like that," Mick said, "it makes me question why I bother."

"I haven't—"

"You fucking have. You're the one big-noting the importance of this case. Then you… I mean, take a look at yourself."

Peter did feel bedraggled, and he was slumped low in the car seat. He sat up, smoothed his hair, or at least tried to.

"Number one priority," he said. "A haircut."

"Christ." Mick grunted. "Here, you ring."

Peter accepted the notebook. The last entry was a name, Hugh Long, followed by a phone number and a Red Hill address.

"Who on earth is this?" he asked.

The rain had stopped. Mick accelerated out into Dandenong Road. "Maguire's first wife was murdered. Hugh Long was her father. He kicked up a big stink for years, claimed Maguire killed her. I read that Maguire's widow Edith has gone to live with him. Who knows if she's there now, but it's worth a try."

"And O'Shaughnessy?"

"You remember what Belinda said: 'that creep David.' Maybe we can hit silver-spoon arsehole from his flank."

Peter pictured O'Shaughnessy's clever face. It was definitely worth a look. His gloom lifted.

"That's slick stuff, big guy," he said. "Turn off that racket for a second."

He dialed the Red Hill number.

"Hello?" A reserved voice.

"Mr. Long?"

"Speaking."

"My name is Peter Gentle. I'm looking into a matter related to Len Maguire. I wonder, is Edith Maguire available?"

"And you are?"

"I'm a private investigator. My partner and I—"

"Mr. Gentle, when Len Maguire gunned down my Polly eleven years ago, I hired a series of investigators." Something in Long's diction made Peter wonder if he was drinking. "With one notable exception, they were worse than useless. In the process I developed a deep aversion to your profession. Good afternoon."

Peter pocketed the phone. "He hung up on me."

The Peugeot slowed past the shooting range, turned into the wide driveway of the Springvale Crematorium and Necropolis. Peter remembered Belinda, her rigid arm recoiling after firing. Jesus, he thought, was that twenty-four hours ago? Other images rose to his mind unbidden. Oh, Gus, he thought.

"Okay, it's Plan B then," announced Mick. Never mind that they were entering a place of mourning, he switched his noise back on.

CHAPTER 34

Back in February, Bob Cox, one of Arne's closest mates from his tramways days, had croaked, of what Mick Tusk was never informed. Coxy was a staple memory from Tusk's childhood, a sunken-faced pisspot regular at his father's card afternoons in front of the telly. Somehow Arne had persuaded Tusk to attend the funeral in Springvale.

Such a mistake. After a desultory sermon, a dozen men, no women of course, watched the coffin inch into the fire. The canned music made Tusk's skin crawl. He was first out the door.

Arne caught up with him unlocking the Peugeot. "Pissing off, eh?"

"I'm working."

"Coxy was a good bloke."

Tusk took in his father's taut, raised cheekbones, flamed by liquor. The wide-chested body, so like his own, stuffed into an ill-fitting suit. The muddy eyes.

The father-son past flooded back, an unwanted knife into Tusk's heart. A good bloke, he'd longed to say, but how would you know?

The incident came back to him as he drove past the ornamental waterfall inside the front gate of the cemetery.

What a great picture for a jigsaw puzzle, he thought. Rows of white headstones colored by crimson roses. Chirping birds hopping from lush grass to loamy flowerbeds carpeted with autumn leaves. Trees dripping. Ponds with fountains.

"Talk about middle class," he said.

"Crap." Gentle's face had tightened into gauntness. "A touch of beauty to help with mourning, and you call it middle class. And do we have to listen to that stuff here?"

Tusk turned Santana down to a rhythmic whisper. Marked blue lines snaked toward the chapels. The Renowden Chapel parking lot was packed.

Rain clouds again threatened. The wind whipped up flower scents mingled with a faint garbage dump odor. Steady tinkling and clanking noises told Tusk why—by coincidence this chapel overlooked the garbage recycling plant they'd stood outside of yesterday.

A sign—No Entry, Hearse/Mourning Coach Excepted— pointed down a long covered walkway. Tusk put himself on alert—not a likely spot for an attack, but it paid to be careful. As they walked through a stone archway, Gentle related Conomy's remark that so many people had reason to dislike Gus Youde.

"But none of those conflicts were Gus' fault," Gentle said. "I wish you'd met him, Mick. He was so… so meek."

Make that geeky ineffectual, Tusk thought. Like Unforgiven. Like Gentle himself.

He said, "Once a victim, always a victim."

Surprise, surprise, the chapel pews were three-quarters full.

The left side was crammed with an assortment of nattering people, young and old, most vaguely nerdy. The Elysium club, no doubt. Tusk spotted Stella in a flowery dress and red jacket. Kosta, dressed in the same suit as this morning, was further back, listening to a short priest with wispy sandy-colored hair.

On the right, contrastingly attired, sat a much smaller group, clearly Youde's estranged family. A poker-faced older man with a blotchy bald scalp, patting the hands of a freckly woman. Two overweight men with Gus Youde's features, talking solemnly. Three more rows of solid-looking men and women, bored kids.

Tusk and Gentle took a seat in the very back row. Just in time. The crowd hushed as the priest took the pulpit.

4:01. The ritual began and Tusk tuned out. He made out Belinda, angelic in a plain black dress, at the front of the Elysium faction. Next to her, the ample body of her old man. No Alison, of course. In the second row, pink hair drew Tusk's attention to the TPT-ers—jiggly Kilpatrick, the daffy Skews woman, horse-faced Phillips. Even from where he sat, Tusk could see tears streaming down Brown's face. He spotted the straight back of music fan Vines, noticeably absent any Menadues.

At the end of his sermon, the priest informed the mourners that he was a member of Elysium.

"The one person most beloved of us all," he said, struggling with emotion, "was our dear, compassionate Gus."

A wail sliced the air. Belinda collapsed against her father.

For some reason, the outburst made Tusk think of Dana. She'd be feeding the kids afternoon tea now, the house would be ringing with Nelson's high-pitched voice. In the backyard, Bully would be fetching tennis balls for Yolanda.

After the service, Tusk was yet again first to scarper. Gentle joined him by shrubs at the edge of the courtyard.

"I can't get rid of the memory." Gentle's face had paled. "That night in the kitchen."

"Don't try," Tusk said. "Those memories are for keeps. You just learn to hide from them."

Under the murky sky, Youde's friends and family filed out and split into two camps. The Elysium folk milled and laughed, the Youde clan fidgeted.

Tusk didn't believe in the power of funerals. He'd grown accustomed to coming across the dead much earlier, reckoned the real farewells were said at the time of discovery. But the outpourings of grief for Youde hadn't left him untouched. *Fuck you*, he aimed at a hazy image of Gus' killer, *I'm coming for you.*

In front of a curved wall covered with plaques, the Brown woman was talking to Kosta and Stella. Kosta, eyes red, nodded at Tusk. The other two turned and Stella glared. Brown's puffy face puckered up with venom. She headed across the courtyard.

"You're the one, aren't you," she said to Gentle. "How anyone could imagine…"

"Camilla," Gentle said.

"My life is an utter misery," she said.

Impatience seized Tusk. He saw them everywhere, these me-generation whiners.

"Camilla," Gentle said. "We're talking murder here. Why didn't you tell the police?"

Brown's cheeks were still wet with tears. "Have you any idea how hard you've made my life? All I ever wanted—"

Tusk interrupted. "Your life, your life."

He broke away, strode down the walkway, took a shortcut between low-hanging trees in plots. Hands on the Peugeot's roof, he listened to distant traffic, a crow cawing.

"Are you okay, Mick?" It was Gentle.

Why snap at someone he'd never spoken to before? "Fine. Let's go."

"We should never have come."

Mourners were climbing into cars. Tusk breathed in the sweet garbage odor from below. He saw that the bordering fence was dotted with plastic bags, windblown refugees.

He heard running footsteps and whirled. A trim man with gray-and-white hair and glasses jogged up. Gentle took a step back.

"I just wanted to say," the man directed at Gentle. His eyes were sunken, his cheeks spotted with flakes of skin.

Tusk stepped forward, hand out. "Guess you're Brad Funder."

The man had eyes only for Gentle. "I wish—" a burr entered his voice and he paused "—I wish I wasn't such a prick to him."

The angle-parked Peugeot faced the road. Tusk gazed at a white Fairmont, clearly the head of an entourage of Youdes, crawling past. The driver tipped his hat.

If Funder was the perp, he put on a good show. He raised his hands, let them flop down against his legs. "Business, that's all I thought it was."

CHAPTER 35

Strangled screeching over atonal guitars filled the Peugeot.

"Jesus, Mick," Peter Gentle snapped. "Enough is enough."

"You rang?" Mick's glance held either reproach or concern, both of which enraged Peter.

"Can't we have some peace?"

To his astonishment, Mick complied. Heavy silence suffused the car on the slow drive along the Monash Freeway and out through countryside to the Somerville turnoff. They cut across toward the bay highway.

The depth of Peter's sudden downer puzzled him. True, he was exhausted—anyone would be—after two nonstop days of confrontational data gathering. True, Mandy had abandoned him and he'd been attacked twice. And yes, he had to admit he'd imbibed a little too much.

But none of that explained this dark wretchedness.

After the dogleg over the railway line in sleepy Somerville, they drove through a stand of towering pines. Gloomy darkness blanketed the car.

"That bean counter," Mick said. "Reckon his performance

was genuine?"

"Yes." Peter pictured Funder's tormented face. "No. Who on earth knows."

"Everyone's an actor."

"So you keep telling me."

Mick's phone, perched on the dashboard next to his insufferable notebook, rang. Steering with one hand, the perennially alert and composed superhero answered, then passed the phone to Peter. "It's U. Take it, could you?"

Peter tersely acknowledged Unforgiven.

Unforgiven said, "Just so you know, Peter. I will not let Mick drag me into anything physical again. I'm still shaking. Physical is just not me."

"Nor me," said Peter.

"Anyway, the only address I can locate for David O'Shaughnessy is two years old. He was a director in a company called Magna Marketing. The principal shareholder was one Adam Menadue."

"Well, well."

"Magna Marketing went belly up on May 13th, 1998."

"It happens to the best of us." Without real enthusiasm, Peter recorded O'Shaughnessy's Fitzroy address in Mick's notebook. "Ciao, U."

By the time they reached the outskirts of beach town Dromana, shadows cloaked the features of the inland hills. Even this far out from the city, the homebound traffic was thick. Was the killer still stalking the night for him? Peter shivered.

Mick took the Arthur's Seat exit and they climbed the switchback to the chairlift. From there, Peter switched on the interior light to navigate with the help of Mick's tattered Melway street directory. He guided them on undulating roads across the plateau, to the green fields and vineyards of Red Hill.

Only then did comprehension surface.

He'd seen it in the consulting profession, partners who began to obsess over perfection at the expense of billable hours. Inevitably they departed a few years on, without fanfare but clearly disgraced. Peter could discern the same pattern in himself.

He remembered one drunken night, Harvey slurring, "Skull, Skull, Skull, a one-track mind like yours, what's there you can't do?" Everyone—Jim, Finola, Belinda, even the motley day trading crew—had expectations of him uncovering the truth. How pitiful that Camilla and even Funder had come to him for absolution!

A true professional would be pleased with all that he and Mick had achieved in the short space of two days, would be only too happy to report in to the client and accept fat daily fees. But no, his damned ego demanded a solution.

And he had nothing. Absolutely zero. After all the discoveries, what could he say?

Hacker: Funder—unlikely; Camilla—in theory yes, but also unlikely; Adam—unqualified; Lim—according to Unforgiven, no.

And murderer: Funder—maybe but why oh why; Camilla—again unlikely; Adam—maybe but what about the unshakable alibi; Rory—same alibi, no discernible motive; Alison—according to Mick, alibied by her affair.

Now here he was, heading into the hinterland on the most obscure lead of all.

Peter massaged his forehead.

A failure.

He was a bona fide, certified failure.

CHAPTER 36

Barking broke out the moment Mick Tusk swung in through the brick gateposts of Hugh Long's property. An overhanging sign, too dark to see. Paddocks, gum trees. A dirt driveway.

Gentle was silent, had sunk well into himself some time back.

Rows of vines were etched across the dusk sky. Two dogs, roaring in full throat, tore down the road to greet them. The loping animals accompanied the Peugeot into a clearing. Tusk stopped behind a muddy four-wheel drive.

Black sky overhead. A house, a small brick affair, dwarfed by a shed and two wine tanks. Tusk saw the city-boy hesitation on Gentle's face.

"Hang on a sec," Tusk said.

He left the parking lights on, stepped out onto sparse squelchy grass. Cool air, real country air, strong aromas of wetness and grapes.

The compact Bruce dogs, one spotted white on black, the other rusty brown, growled in a cautious circle. He squatted and extended a hand, curled-up fingers toward the ground.

"Jacko," called a man walking down from the house's small porch. "Chocko."

Tails wagging, the dogs ran to flank the man.

Something in the man's voice put Tusk on alert. He stood and extended a hand. "Mick Tusk."

Behind him he heard the passenger door open.

Arms crossed tightly, the man inspected him. Early fifties, a spare frame in a rainproof jacket. Graying brown hair swept sideways, thin pursed lips. His eyes careful slits nestled within crinkles.

"Are you the man who rang?" His accent a mix of Melbourne and somewhere offshore.

"That was me, Mr. Long," Gentle said. "Peter Gentle."

"I thought I made my feelings clear enough," Long said. "No offense, boys, but the investigators I had dealings with, they were just one evolutionary step up from the scum they investigated, and sometimes a mighty small step at that. I hope you haven't come far, boys, because you can head back now."

The brown dog came up to sniff Bully's scent on Tusk's jeans.

"It's important." Tusk rubbed Chocko's head without looking down. "Lives depend on it."

A tail thumped his leg.

"That's what I said back in 1990." Long turned and walked away. "And who listened then?"

The front door of the house opened and a short woman with slumped shoulders stood framed in light.

"Hugh?" Her accent was Scottish or Irish, Tusk could never tell the difference. "I'll see them."

"Are you sure, pumpkin?" Long said.

"Isn't it time?" she said.

Long turned back and came up close enough for Tusk to see the deep grooves in his forehead. He spoke quietly. "You heard Edith. You heard me. What she's been through is a hell and if you take advantage of her, you'll have me to answer to. Am I clear?"

"Perfectly," Gentle said. "Believe me, we have no intention of staying longer than five or ten minutes."

Long grunted and headed toward the house. Tusk switched off the car lights and followed, Chocko by his side.

On the porch Tusk paused to wipe his feet. Jacko growled. Tusk scratched Chocko's ear.

"Stay," he said.

The house was little more than a cottage, a tiny hall leading to the kitchen, three rooms off to the side. From one of the bedrooms, Tusk heard pop music—Matchbox Twenty?—then a radio announcer.

His face tense with suspicion, Long ushered them into a tiny living room. A two-seater couch, a rocking chair, a TV, room for no more. Edith Maguire, wearing a plain skirt and cream cardigan, sat on the rocker. She twisted and untwisted a handkerchief.

Tusk perched on the edge of the couch. Gentle sank in beside him. Long disappeared, came back with a wooden chair. He rolled up the sleeves of his old-fashioned striped shirt, sat with legs crossed. Tusk noticed his right middle finger was missing from the knuckle down.

"So what can I help you with, gentlemen?" Edith's voice was hesitant. "Excuse my nerves, but it's only the past few weeks I've felt like seeing people."

241

The Maguire widow was a decidedly plain, squat block of a woman. Early forties, Tusk knew, roughly the same age as Len, but in appearance older than Long. Lank hair, a mannish face, freckled skin running to mottled, no cheekbones to speak of.

Christ, what she's been through, Tusk thought. He caught Gentle's over-to-you look.

"Mrs. Maguire," he said. "We have reason to believe your husband was conned by someone sending fake emails to him. Guy by the name of Diamond."

"Emails." Confusion clouded Edith's face.

"Edith wouldn't know anything about emails," Long said. "Len kept her in the dark about everything. We only found out afterward he'd stolen all her money, blown it all at that sharemarket casino."

Tusk waited.

Edith blinked. "I'll tell you gentlemen something. What this is, it's not a question of knowledge. Maybe I did go into denial at first, but now I know what Len did. I know now he did kill Polly."

Polly was Len Maguire's first wife. She's a long way from email, Tusk thought.

Edith held up a shaking hand to halt Long, half out of his chair. "Hugh, I know it, though I never could bring myself to believe it then."

Tusk flashed on his image of Maguire. And his entwined image of Oldfield.

"I was a social worker," Edith said. "I am a social worker. So I can identify exactly what I am. I'm an abused wife coping with grief. But knowledge never helps to deal with problems. That's something else I know from my work."

Long sighed, a massive elongated breath. Gentle's eyes were wide.

"But I just can't get over my Timmy." Hoarseness took Edith's voice. "You know, I can picture it. Len would have said, Tim, lie in bed, shut your eyes, ignore this hammer in my hand. And Timmy would have done it. He was so trusting. Oh my God."

On the porch, one of the dogs, Tusk thought it was Chocko, barked then fell silent. Tusk's heart pounded. Christ, he thought, give me scumbags any day, just save me from the victims.

"Edith," he said, "did Len ever mention anyone called Diamond?"

She shook her head, angrily it seemed, and dabbed at her eyes.

"Did he keep a diary?"

Her hand froze.

There! He spotted the stilled handkerchief.

He leaned forward. "A man was murdered two days ago. A man at Tech Power Trading, where your husband... We believe your husband came across the killer. Edith, this person will kill again unless we stop him."

Her pained eyes engaged Tusk's. "I... I just don't know."

"There's no diary." Long came over to stand beside Edith. "I carted all of Edith's belongings in here. There is no diary."

"Did you know what was on Len's computer, Edith?"

A shake of the head. Tears on her cheeks.

"I told you," Long said. "He was a monster. God knows what he kept secret from everyone."

Suddenly Edith smiled and she was transformed into someone else, someone beautiful. Long gaped.

"Chocko knew," she said. "Do you believe dogs have wisdom—what was your name again?"

She hadn't asked. "Mick. And yes, my dog is the wisest member of our family."

"Ours too. Chocko is the one mending my Walter. And he came to you, Mick. He knows. Wait here."

Edith rose and left the room.

Long pointed at Tusk. "What the hell are you up to?"

Gentle made the mistake of responding. "Mr. Long, it's imperative—"

"Damn your imperative!" Long said. "Stirring her up like that, I won't have it."

"Shush, Hugh." It was Edith returning.

"You okay, mum?" A tall teenage boy, with Len Maguire's sloping forehead, his red hair. The boy's eyes, so like Edith's, glared at Tusk.

Edith said, "Hugh?"

Reluctantly Long ushered Walter away. As soon as they left the room, Edith lowered her voice.

"For your eyes only," she said. "Can you promise me that?"

Concealing evidence, it would be. Still, they'd already done that with Unforgiven. Tusk looked at Gentle for guidance. Gentle nodded.

From a cardigan pocket, Edith took a plain CD jewel case, handed it to Tusk. A CD? Music?

"A CD-Rom," Gentle breathed.

"Our thanks," Tusk said. "We'll return it."

"Ring first," she said. "Don't bother Hugh with this."

"Can I ask, why didn't you…"

"Give it to the police?" She sighed. "Would you, Mick? Spill that madness, all that badness, in public? But you know the real reason, Mick?"

He shook his head.

"That's the worst part. Remember, I'm a social worker. I know what I'm looking at here. But back then I couldn't see it, I was just... in it. You see, Len asked me to keep it secret. Mick, he ordered me to."

Fury welled up in Tusk's chest. Unable to come up with words, he nodded. He was stowing the CD-Rom in his jacket pocket when Long returned. Long clenched his teeth.

"Now you have work to do," Edith said. Her soft fingers squeezed Tusk's hand.

Long brooded all the way to the Peugeot. "What was that?"

"Who knows?" Gentle said. "Something the monster asked her to hide. We'll ensure it remains confidential."

The correct tactic. Long's shoulders relaxed. "Some things I'll never understand."

"Me neither," Tusk said.

Long's missing half finger was an odd absence during his handshake. "Maybe this session did help Edith. You boys excuse my temper. Since my wife died, the only thing that kept me going was this place. Maguire took my health, most of my heart too. Now I've got something worth fighting for, to get her back on her feet. And Walter, now there's a plucky kid. He deserves a supportive environment."

Tusk nodded into the cool blackness. "He couldn't find a sweeter place." He squatted. A wet tongue lapped his fingers. "Eh, Chocko?"

CHAPTER 37

"Wow," said Peter Gentle.

He marveled at the two rows of sexy gear. He counted eleven computers, networked with the aid of piled hubs, routers, firewalls, and other boxes he couldn't immediately identify. He admired the absence of dust, the lack of the junk typically strewn in techos' rooms. What a place to lose yourself in, he thought.

And the aromas! Peter identified garlic, fish, a mouth-watering brew of herbs.

The Red Hill trip had perked him up to no end. Quite ludicrous really, as no logic suggested the CD-Rom contained anything at all, let alone a connection with the baffling Diamond.

Mick sat beside him, unchanged, ever the unrelenting pro. He'd treated the drive back like a drag race, passing dangerously, running amber lights. A cassette of Cheap Trick, "chosen for those of us whose music education stopped twenty years ago," had accompanied the heart-stopping trip.

Unforgiven's terrace house was neat but cramped compared to Gus'. Peter wondered how Unforgiven managed to live in such a highly priced area—did he own or lease? Did he live with anyone?

Suppressed hunger surged. "A dinner party, U?"

The hacker, wearing a long-sleeved T-shirt captioned "Big Business Blows," shrugged. "Let me see that disc."

Mick handed over the jewel case. Unforgiven slipped the disc into a drive and they inspected the contents, Peter and Unforgiven up front, Mick craning his head from the back.

A directory of hundreds of files filled the screen.

"Look at that," Peter crowed.

Unforgiven laid down a flurry of keystrokes. "Gotcha." Up came a listing of emails. "All very standard. It looks like he routinely stored all his emails." He pointed. "Aha."

There it was, an email folder named "Diamond." In it were some eighty emails, with 1999 dates between 17th August and 22nd December, the day before the massacre.

Peter swiveled around to face Mick's faint smile. "You may be a moron but"—their palms smacked in a high five—"you're a stubborn moron."

"This is a gold mine," said Unforgiven. He brought up the very first email and together they began to read.

Unlike the reactions from Crazy Oleg and Phillips, the initial email from Kurt Diamond had seen an eager response from Len Maguire. Peter saw how quickly the pair achieved the oddly intimate rapport of email buddies. Using a mix of professional and awkwardly informal language, Diamond submitted stock recommendations to the hungry trader. In his third email, he told Maguire he was a contractor hired by TPT to provide independent advice. He urged Maguire to keep quiet in the office about his existence; incredibly, Maguire agreed.

Maguire apparently did well with Diamond's first few tips, for he began to refer effusively to "clever kurt," and to request all manner of trading information.

"You keep on with that," Unforgiven said. He wheeled his chair to an adjacent computer.

In September the character of the emails altered. "Christ," Peter heard Mick breathe. Now it was Maguire initiating dialogue, spewing forth diatribes against the other traders and his own bad luck. He implored Diamond for further tips, but Diamond had grown coy, often responding with terse statements like, "Sorry, have no solid advice to give."

Then in October, Diamond seemed to have gone off the air. Peter scanned a dozen Maguire emails, progressively shorter and shorter. One email ("kurt why won't you save me?") even sparked in Peter a momentary, unwanted feeling of sympathy.

Mick said, "He was screwing up badly then, was way in the red."

There were no November emails. In December, on the 20th, a Diamond email arrived out of the blue, this time with a tip for the HotCopper float.

The next day, Maguire sent back: "clever kurt you're my savior. more please more as these hook-nosed bastards plunder the ground from under my feet."

A final, twisted dialogue ensued. For the first time, Diamond's emails moved away from stocks to the grievances at the heart of Maguire's outpourings, namely Tech Power Trading itself.

A Maguire pronouncement, within a page of rants, went:

"That Jewboy sucks the life out of every decent god-fearing man around but he will surely meet his judgment." Diamond's direct riposte stunned Peter: "Ah, but how soon? You know how it goes. They evade, they slide."

On the 21st, Maguire: "the bitch said no. can you imagine it clever kurt? I could have ripped her eyes out. all I ask for is one chance one goddamn chance." Diamond: "The heart of darkness lives at TPT."

That day, again and again Maguire appealed for "scorcher tips," or asked for evaluations of his own irrational stock selections. Again and again Diamond held off, promising advice after "my next strategy evaluation." Peter's skin crawled as Maguire's tirades escalated.

"Diamond is as disturbed as Maguire," he said.

Mick nodded. "Only smarter. Look how he manipulates."

It was true. Diamond flattered, taunted, and prodded Maguire, all with one purpose. Peter's face drained of blood.

"Oh, no," he said. "Mick? Diamond pushed him into his rampage."

"Maguire would have flipped anyway. But this Diamond loony helped him over the edge."

The final entry was Diamond's, dated 22nd December, time-stamped 7:02 PM. Peter read: "No tips, Len. Time for you to go under."

What would Tagliaferro give for this, Peter thought. He slumped back in his seat.

"Whoever this Diamond is," Mick said, his jaw a rock, "he's got nine people's blood on his conscience."

"Not in a court of law. There's nothing explicit. No plot, no direct involvement."

"Let's not talk law, genius. Let's stick to morality."

Unforgiven had moved over to listen. "The good news is finding this disc. The bad news is that the emails are insufficient to help us locate Diamond. For that we require Maguire's computer."

"Why the hell not?" Tusk said. "You told us—"

"The email headers tell me they originated directly from TPT's server. No doubt about it. Yet the TPT logs don't show any such outgoing emails."

Peter smacked his hands together. "They're manufactured on-site."

Unforgiven gave his brief mini-smile. "Coe-rrect. We're talking a Trojan."

Peter's head spun. Why couldn't anything be straightforward?

"In simplistic terms," Unforgiven lectured, "Diamond took over Maguire's PC, maybe via an email attachment. It's not difficult when the user takes no precautions. We're talking a bit more study than script kiddie Lim's efforts, but believe me, you could do it with six months' practice. Then Diamond had this embedded Trojan program sitting hidden on Maguire's computer. Whenever he wanted to, he sent the Trojan some designated text, and it concocted a fake email for Maguire to quote unquote *receive*. Any outgoing emails would have been inspected by the Trojan, and if destined for Diamond, would have been secretly rerouted to our hacker. Tricky for the layman but not a high-grade exploit."

Peter said, "That's how the computers got wiped clean."

"Yes. The Trojan can destroy itself and all evidence."

"Then we're stuffed," Mick said.

"I'm afraid so."

Peter concentrated. "Did Maguire have any idea who Diamond was? Let's check the CD."

A dispiriting half-hour followed. The bulk of the CD-Rom was old files, diaries, and letters that Peter had no intention of opening. Only four files were created or modified from August 1999. Three of them, chilling although not new, were the letters Maguire wrote to Edith, Walter, and Tim, his intended victims.

Mick hissed.

The fourth file was Maguire's diary. Its size staggered Peter. He scrolled through pages and pages of mad rage, the worst eruptions of a demented mind.

"You were right, Mick," he said morosely.

"Unfortunately. These types have to record, to order."

Peter couldn't bring himself to read much of it. He did a search on "Diamond"—nothing.

Maguire's very last sentence, time-stamped 7:56 PM on the Thursday, at home after the spree killing, read: "Remember me oh world a righteous man ruined by the forces of evil."

They sat dazed.

Unforgiven said, "I have a suggestion."

On the opposite row of tables was a cleared space. Unforgiven reached behind a printer for placemats, cutlery, and napkins. He set three places.

"Do private detectives get hungry?" he said.

"Do hackers?" Peter was ravenous. "Let me buy this, U. What's the number for local takeaway food?"

"No, no." And Unforgiven rushed out.

"Sorry, Gentle," Mick said.

"For what?"

"Another no-go."

"No need to apologize. At least we know Diamond exists, that he's our man."

When Unforgiven returned, he juggled a bottle of red and three deep patterned bowls, filled with glistening butterfly pasta and a steaming sauce. A complex fishy smell seized Peter's senses. Glasses materialized.

"Bon appétit," this weirdest of hackers said shyly.

So the three of them sat in a row, diving into the most delicious meal Peter had experienced for days. He couldn't stop smiling.

"Clams," he said.

"Farfalle vongole." Unforgiven's eyes were averted. He only picked at his food.

"Divine," Peter said.

Mick said, "A packet mix."

Unforgiven's head jerked. Mick grinned and Unforgiven grunted. Peter guffawed.

The red wine was a prize-winning Jamieson's Run. Peter felt his insides unglue. He finished up his meal and let weariness wash over him. He stared at the hardware. An idea surfaced from his tired mind and he grabbed Mick's arm.

"Yeah, I know," Mick said, his meal only half-finished. "Edith, she's pretty courageous."

"No," Peter said. "Jesus, Mick, we're not thinking. Let's put up those last emails from Diamond."

He stepped through the final round of emails.

Mick ate while watching. "So what? This is Diamond venting."

"And he's clever. But suppose he wasn't clever enough?"

Peter absorbed the emails in a new light. He discerned how much Diamond hated TPT, how he echoed every one of Maguire's whines about Jim and Finola. Interestingly, Gus never received a mention. Perhaps Diamond took umbrage at him later, Peter thought.

"There." Mick pointed at a Diamond paragraph.

The paragraph read: "Too true, Len. But the root of it all is the uncaring heart, the blind eye. Why won't Van speak to me?"

"Shit a brick, we've got something," Peter said. "Come on, come on, come on. What does it mean? This feels personal to me. Does it to you guys?"

Unforgiven shrugged.

Mick expelled a garlicky breath. "Too right. Jim's the key, isn't he? Van is Van Kressel. Diamond hated Jim. Diamond still hates him."

"Yes!" Peter said.

"But why, I repeat," Unforgiven said, "did he target TPT traders then?"

"Unless he can't bring himself to attack Jim directly," Mick said.

Peter's mental excitement felt trapped in the equipment-filled room. His fingers tapped on his thighs, he rocked back and forth. "Yes, oh yes. I knew there was something missing."

"Mick, finish your farfalle, please," Unforgiven said. "Dessert is on its way."

"Mousse, I hope," Mick said.

"You didn't have to put on such a spread, U," Peter said.

"It's my relaxation," said Unforgiven.

He headed for the door but something on a screen brought him up short.

"Holy mackerel." The hacker was panting. "Whoever Diamond is, he's at work this very moment."

Peter's pulse raced. "What do you mean?"

Mick sprang to his feet.

Unforgiven's face was gray. "He's hacking right now. Your computer, Peter, yours."

CHAPTER 38

Mick Tusk leaned on his horn.

"Christ, quicker to bloody walk," he muttered.

Friday night in South Yarra. Time check: 10:20. The rich and poor spilled out onto the Chapel Street sidewalk tables. Young Turks cruised. Beautiful couples strutted. The traffic was immobile. The car in front of the Peugeot rocked with the force of its booming bass.

The Clash's "London Calling" thundered in Tusk's skull.

He honked again. The street erupted with swearing and angry tooting.

The whole hacker thing buggered understanding, although Gentle had pretended, had nodded. Apparently, just a couple of hours earlier, Unforgiven had installed one of those Trojan thingies on Gentle's home machine. This Trojan had detected an intruder. According to Unforgiven, Kurt Diamond had been in full control of Gentle's PC for nearly ten minutes. The gourmet hacker had been apoplectic: "If only someone had noticed the alert."

Unforgiven had launched into a flurry of keyboard activity,

simultaneously jabbering to Gentle. Two minutes it took the ponytailed freak before he bellowed, "An Internet cafe, Chapel Street. He's there now."

Screeching rubber, window down, had brought them here.

"What's the number again?" barked Tusk.

"202." Gentle's face was pinched, his hands wringing in perpetual motion.

Unforgiven, huddled in the back seat, looked even worse.

"Fuck. Another block." Tusk took a breath. "Hang on."

He zoomed out into the oncoming lane, cleared by a red traffic light ahead. Indignant horns on his left. He roared up to the intersection, glanced both ways, then zigzagged through the red lights and back into the correct lane. Three hoons on the footpath clapped and whistled.

"There." Unforgiven pointed.

De Grago's Cafe. In gold letters on the window: Internet Cafe.

Tusk yanked the Peugeot into a tram stop zone, tires scraping the curb. Out the door and into the cafe in a sprint.

A short-haired waitress in black and white: "Hey!"

He spotted computers at the back, three against the wall. Two occupied, one free.

He ran to the first machine. A young guy with backpack on the floor. Diamond? Tusk grabbed his shoulders, spun him around.

"What? What is this?" Thick German accent. The man shook free. A bloody tourist.

The frizzy-haired woman at the next computer rose to confront him with hands on hips.

"Here," Gentle called from the third, empty seat. Unforgiven was banging on the keyboard.

Tusk reached the screen, white writing on deep blue. He made out one word: Error.

"Too late," Unforgiven said. "It's gone."

Tusk touched the red vinyl chair. "Seat's still warm."

He scanned the cafe. Metal everywhere, all reds and blacks, the ultra-modern style he hated. A quarter full, all couples or groups, no obvious lone hacker blending in. He rushed to the restrooms. Nix. A fire exit door, empty lane outside. The stink of cat's piss.

Back at the stuffed computer, the pixie-faced waitress was swearing.

"It's ruined," she said. "He didn't even pay."

"What about my computer?" Gentle said to Unforgiven.

Unforgiven's hand went to his mouth. Gentle groaned.

Tusk commanded, "What did he look like?"

The waitress cringed from a hand Tusk hadn't realized he'd lifted. "Hey, man, cool it. He was… he was just a guy. Thin. Dark hair. Hey, do I look like I check out every guy comes walking in?"

CHAPTER 39

The Peugeot had reached the outskirts of Hicksville when Mick's mobile sounded. Peter Gentle grabbed it, answered before the second tone. "Mick's Mellow Massage."

Hope it's not Dana, he thought belatedly.

Senior Constable Lasker chuckled. "You're chirpy."

Peter debated filling Deirdre in on the night's extraordinary events, but obeyed Mick's shaking head. "A good meal makes all the difference. And you, Dee?"

"Struggling." She told him that a bartender had positively ID'd Brad Funder. The Chief Financial Officer was in the clear. Peter experienced a surge of relief.

Mick merely nodded when Peter passed on the news. The trip, first to drop Unforgiven off in St Kilda, now to Belgrave, had been another hour of Peter's life spent talking, over air-guitar rock, to a block of concrete.

When they arrived, a light came on outside Mick's front door. In the driveway, Peter listened to rustling leaves, smelled the tang of eucalyptus. The black sky was infinite, the quietness creepy. A cold drip of rainwater landed on his neck, startling him.

"Best behavior now," Mick said.

"I could take a taxi, find a hotel." After Diamond trashed his computer, Mick had recommended he skip going home. Peter had agreed with alacrity. A one-night stay out of the murderer-inhabited city had also appealed, until halfway to Belgrave, when the memory of his last conversation with Dana returned.

"Don't be stupid," said Mick.

Dana stood in the doorway, wearing slippers and a white bathrobe. One look at her face, her eyes narrowing at the sight of him, confirmed Peter's unease. He watched with a mixture of envy and embarrassment as the Tusks melted into an embrace.

"Was it okay, Mikey?" he heard Dana say.

"Piece of cake." There was something wonderful about the rare softness of Mick's face. "The kids asleep?"

Dana laughed. "It's 11:30, duffer."

Mick headed off to the children's bedrooms.

Dana finally deigned to acknowledge Peter with a nod. As always, he found himself thinking how powerful her looks were, every feature shouting for attention. The curls, the regal nose, the wide hips and large breasts, Dana was a cocktail that overwhelmed him.

"Look," he said. "I always seem to put my foot in it with you. I don't mean to."

He couldn't read her face, but for once she didn't seem hostile.

"Last time we put you in Nelson's room," she said, "but he kicks up a fuss now if he has to sleep with Yolanda. So if you don't mind, I'll set you up in the family room."

She led him down the hall. Peter blinked with exhaustion.

Outside the back door, the dog—what was its name?—whined. A Lion King video case lay open in front of the television. He rested against the edge of the table while Dana fetched linen and a thin mattress, efficiently making up a bed on the floor.

He was struck by the contrast between his orderly study-oriented apartment and the haphazard domesticity of the Tusk family room. Clumps of dog hair clung to the side of the couch and a half-eaten biscuit rested against the skirting board. Crumbs littered the carpet under a high chair. On the table was a crayon drawing of stick figures entitled "My Dad."

"Here's a towel and toothbrush," Dana said. "I've left you a pair of Mikey's PJs. Don't let Bully in, he's rolled in some mud."

"Thanks. Sorry to trouble you like this."

She tossed a Where's Wally book into a wicker basket full of kids' reading. "The children will be up early. Since summer they've been rising at the crack of dawn. You know where the bathroom is."

"Thank you."

"Mandy told me about the attack." A pause. "Sleep well."

Then she was gone.

Peter grimaced. He'd forgotten that Dana and Mandy had become friends. What had they discussed? The notion of Mandy telling Dana about the break-up seemed to grant Dana some power over him.

He pictured Mandy, in so many ways the antithesis to Dana's fulsomeness. At the thought of Mandy's lanky frame, her boniness, the square-jawed face, those wide eyes, her smile, an erection sprang up. Why hadn't he rung?

Ten minutes later, when he emerged fresh-mouthed from the

bathroom, Mick was in the family room, tidying up CDs. He looked as hardy as ever. The dog, not noticeably muddy, crouched by his feet, tennis ball in mouth.

"I'm rooted," Mick said. "You got everything?"

"Fine, Mick. Thanks for… for today."

"Like you said, at least the arsehole's real now."

"It feels like rape, Mick, Internet rape. He's violated me, Diamond has, may as well have destroyed all my business records. Lucky I made a backup last weekend, but still… Jesus, what could he have read?" Peter recalled the fake celluloid voice, shivered.

"Get some sleep. Tomorrow we'll crack this."

"Nothing surer. Good night, Mick."

Data, analysis, conclusions, ran the weary refrain in Peter's head after he changed and sank onto the mattress. The room smelled of milk, apples, and dog. The key was Jim Van Kressel. Who hated Jim enough to poison his traders' minds? What had Gus discovered?

Peter's bruises throbbed, the grazes stung, his eyes drooped. Analysis didn't help when data was missing. Should he ring Harvey? Jesus, the Diplomacy players would curse him for missing another overnight move. He sank into sleep.

CHAPTER 40

Halfway up Delma Street, a favorite steep stretch, the worry niggling at Mick Tusk crystallized. He halted.

"Fuck."

Bully trotted out from a garden, alarm in his raised ears.

Last night Tusk had slept, slept a full night. Five hours! Hypothesis: work satisfaction cures insomnia.

Time check: 5:48. Stopwatch: 0:31. Somnolent darkness broken by spaced streetlights. Not a single moving car the entire run, one cat fleeing Bully ten minutes ago. A chilly blanket over his second skin of sweat.

"Bully, come."

He headed homeward, urgency straining his hamstrings, his quads.

For ten minutes Kurt Diamond had roamed Gentle's computer. Internet rape, Gentle had called it. What if Diamond had come across the name Tusk? What if Diamond could track bodies half as effectively as Unforgiven? What if…?

The return trip took twenty-four minutes. When he finished, pain lanced his left heel—his bloody Achilles tendon! He dripped sweat. Bully collapsed on a side. Tusk eased the back door open. Gentle lay breathing noisily.

False alarm.

Careful not to wake him, Tusk made up a bowl of muesli with soy milk. He collected Saturday's *Age* from the front drive, settled down to breakfast on the back porch. TPT had moved to page six, Inspector Conomy refusing to comment.

Profound thought of the day: if only I'd got up a bit more speed last night.

***

Draconi's at 8:31, only half-full. White-collar slaves indulging in croissants, the new inner-city yuppies scanning auction notices over lattes. No Skulkers visible.

"Make it snappy," Tusk said to Gentle.

When Tusk had woken the geek at seven, Gentle had spent twenty minutes in the bathroom. He was neat and fresh-faced. And, judging from the patter, fresh-brained.

Anyone tells you a good night's sleep is a positive omen, Tusk thought, tell him to get stuffed. Count the missteps. The ridiculous predawn panic. The strained Achilles, making it hard even now to walk without a limp. Dana's shitty mood: "Mikey, he's emptying out our hot water supply."

"We've got plenty of time," Gentle said. "Jim won't be in the office until nine."

"The meals you order, we won't get there till ten."

Hector placed them midfield, fetched a newspaper. He winked at Tusk. "Grand to see you back on the job, m'boy."

"Just temporary," Tusk said.

"He says I don't pay him enough, Hec," Gentle said.

Tusk resisted even a cup of tea, headed for a piss. On the way back, he glimpsed a man's back disappearing into the kitchen. A ponytail?

Gentle was in full swing. "Hec, don't believe everything you read."

"Deutsche Bank's Tech Index was down twelve percent over the week." Hector tapped *The Age*, already a mess scattered in front of Gentle. "Are you claiming that's not Crash-dot-Com, to use the hip phrasing?"

"No, no. I'm not saying that at all. A bubble is a bubble, certainly. It's a question of timing. Listen, yesterday's rally felt very strong. I was there, Hec, I saw the traders."

Gentle's face was alive. Some people thrive on sleep, Tusk thought.

Hector tugged at a bulbous cheek. "That's not what Harvey says. He was in earlier, his advice was for me to sell all my shares first thing Monday."

"Hec, I tell you, I'd be tempted to buy."

Tusk cracked his knuckles. Today's the next day of my life, he thought.

"Borrow your organizer?" he asked Gentle.

He scrolled through the Palm Pilot's address list until he reached Fitzgibbon. Gentle was still rabbiting on. Tusk dialed his mobile. The instant a female voice answered, he jammed the phone to Gentle's ear.

Gentle gulped. "Uh, Mandy." He wrenched the phone from Tusk's hand, turned away in his chair. "Yep, it's… it's me… Fine, just fine… No, no, a good coward always escapes… Yes,

Mick's here… I'm glad too. What are you doing today?… That sounds great. Can I, may I, perhaps can I come too? Yes?… Okay, got it. See you then."

Gentle's eyes shone. "She's taking Elle to the museum. Me too, this afternoon. Isn't that great?"

"Hec," Tusk said. Gentle's crack about pay rates had spurred an idea, had reminded him of Unforgiven's gratis services. "This hacker you recommended…"

Hector's eyes swung to him, narrowed. "Aha. Hold on a moment, would you?"

The restaurateur hurried away.

Gentle slurped mouthfuls of bacon and eggs. "Don't tell me I got up his nose."

Tusk thought of Dana, wondered why those sweet times of unity never lasted two days in a row. "Stop yakking and keep eating."

Across the restaurant came Hector and a young man wearing a chef's apron. The young man had the mildest of eyes.

"U!" Gentle cried. "How did you know we'd be here?"

Unforgiven flushed.

Hector winked at Tusk. "Peter, Mick, let me introduce Vernon King."

"Don't tell me you work for this bastard," Tusk said.

Unforgiven defiantly raised his chin, as if his real name was a blight. "Indentured servitude would be a more apt description."

"U, why didn't you tell us?" Gentle pulled a chair over for the hacker.

"Vernon is apprenticing to replace Ricky, my chef, who heads off to Europe in June." Hector had his eyes firmly on

Unforgiven. "And you should be aware. Vernon is my grandson."

***

A pale sun caressed clear blue sky, a breeze swirled leaves in the gutters. A classic autumn day, wasted on the bloody city.

No eastbound tram on Collins. In spite of the tight Achilles, Tusk walked, Gentle alongside, carrying on about the case.

Skateboarders were already pouring into town. Business types carried Styrofoam coffee cups. A tramp hauled bulging plastic bags down the steps of the Town Hall restroom. A frizzy-haired woman with black tights wrapped around pudgy legs waddled down the hill.

The dream factory stalls were deserted. Van Kressel was unshaven, hung over.

"Don't get married, Pete," the tycoon said.

A burp from Boy Wonder. "Ha!"

Gentle perched on the desk. While he recounted the Maguire revelations, Tusk watched the exec's face. His mind drifted to Unforgiven's unmasking by grandfather Hector. Unforgiven had relaxed over a coffee, had enthused about his recently discovered passion for cooking. He hoped to quit hacking. All power to him, Tusk thought.

When Van Kressel heard about the wordfest between Maguire and Diamond, he grew agitated.

Eventually he slapped the desk. "I knew it. Didn't I tell you, Pete, I knew there was a connection. Len was mad but no idiot. Well done, you two."

Tusk pictured Conomy's sanctimonious face. Hey Rich, he thought, making progress?

Van Kressel's enthusiasm dried up when Gentle explained Diamond's role in inciting Maguire.

"Why?" Van Kressel said. "Why would anyone do this? What kind of deviant stirs up someone like Len?"

"Well, he's no member of your fan club." Tusk gazed out the window at the sooty roof of a tram. "This Diamond slagged off in the last few emails we found. Slagged off at you."

"Me?"

"Yeah, listen." Tusk read out the paragraph: "Too true, Len. But the root of it all is the uncaring heart, the blind eye. Why won't Van speak to me?"

"My God. And you thought…" Van Kressel pressed his eyes shut with his knuckles. "I'm afraid this is another wild goose chase like Brad Funder. I've never been called Van in my life. Van K at university, but never Van."

"Bugger," Tusk said. It was possible that Diamond had christened the TPT head as Van in his warped private world. Possible but only barely.

"Wait." Gentle had risen, mouth open, eyes wide. "Mick, I have it."

"Didn't you hear him?" said Tusk.

But Gentle was off, sprinting through the half-light of the trading area. Had he gone mad? Tusk followed him into Vines' office, where Vines was scribbling on the whiteboard. The room smelled of tangerines.

"There." Gentle shoved one hand through his hair.

His other hand pointed across the office.

"Christ," Tusk said. "That's it. Van the Man. Van Morrison."

Van Kressel arrived at the door, puffing.

"What on earth are you gabbling about?" Vines was as composed as Van Kressel was run down. She looked younger in jeans and a T-shirt, a 1998 Van Morrison tour T-shirt of all things.

Van Kressel said, "Fi, you won't believe what these superstars have managed to do."

Gentle was now feral, fingers twitching, feet tapping, as he recapped the Diamond material.

"I don't understand," Vines said when Gentle neared the end.

"This Diamond has some obsession," Tusk said. "Listen…"

He lifted his notebook to read, but Gentle jumped straight in from memory. "Finola, hear this, it's Kurt Diamond: 'Too true, Len. But the root of it all is the uncaring heart, the blind eye. Why won't Van speak to me?' "

Instant response. Vines' face paled.

"Jim," she exhaled.

She swayed. Jim rushed up. She clutched his arm.

"Oh, no," she said. Her head sagged.

Gentle looked like he'd just won the Nobel Prize. Tusk offered him a well-done nod. For the first time since he'd parked the Peugeot, a song took hold. "One," U2's bittersweet ode to love.

"There, there, Fi," Van Kressel said.

"Finola," Tusk said. In his head, the weeping guitar of The Edge meshed with the ache in Bono's voice. "You're Van. Am I right?"

Wretched gasps. "Oh, no. Oh, no."

CHAPTER 41

To Peter Gentle, the universe was orderly. Immeasurably complex, to be sure, but orderly nonetheless. Connections made sense of the most seemingly random of events. With sufficient data and a mind capable and wise enough, anything and everything could be explained.

His faith in this tenet soared at the sight of Finola's collapse.

"Fi?" Jim supported the bowed frame of Finola. "Fi? Come down to my office. I've got some donuts."

It sounded lame to Peter but Finola nodded. Peter's impatience grew as he trailed the TPT founders down the aisle. Breathing hard, Finola slumped into a chair. Jim pulled a chair up close and murmured to her.

Peter kept his voice restrained. "Finola?"

Finola waved a hand. "Go away."

By the window Mick whispered, "You reckon she'll tell us?"

Below, a van double-parked further up Collins Street. A whirring noise accompanied the lowering of a wheelchair on a hydraulic lift. A stoop-shouldered man pushed the wheelchair into a building. Peter looked out over the office skyline, resplendent below the most beautiful blue sky he'd ever seen. How blissful to be back in town, he thought.

"Why ever not?" he said.

"Why the hell should she tell us anything?"

Peter ground his teeth at the strength of Mick's logic. He suppressed mounting frustration by counting the taxis arriving at the Sofitel. He tried to picture Unforgiven—sorry, Vernon—working over a hot stove in a chef's hat, but failed.

Jim patted Finola's shoulder. He rose and walked over.

"Pete. Mick." Jim's voice was low. "You can see how much this has shaken Fi. I've been stressing how important it is to catch Kurt Diamond. But what we're going to hear stays in this room. Got that?"

Peter nodded.

"We're already in hot water for withholding," said Mick.

Jim's face tightened. "I'll factor that into your fee. Now let's expedite the situation." He turned to Finola. "Fi? Tell us where this Van business comes from."

Peter elbowed his partner. The cheeky bugger had just negotiated a fee increase! Mick's face stayed blank.

Finola raised her head. Peter was shocked at how bruised her eyes had become. "You don't know how hard this is." She stood to pace with hunched shoulders. "You hide something for twenty years and eventually it feels like a dream. It is a dream. But I think of what Van Morrison's songs said. He said every decision has a consequence and life consists of facing each one."

Her lips were bloodless, her face gaunt. For some reason she spoke to Mick. "In 1980 I… I walked out on my de facto and our five-year-old son. I had a breakdown. That was in Sydney. I ran to Melbourne and started over. That's the burden I've carried ever since."

Peter's legs vibrated with tension. He longed to yell, what does this have to do with Diamond?

"You two, you can't know what it was like in the '60s and early '70s. It felt as if the cosmos had opened up, like a new era. I left home early, lived on a commune for two years. It wasn't for me, so I skipped and took work as a secretary. That's when I met Stephen. He was five years younger, a musician and a hippie, and I fell for all the romanticism of music and the times. And he was a hunk, a counterculture sort of hunk."

She paused. Jim offered her a box with three remaining yellow-icing donuts. She shook her head. Mick also declined. Peter resisted, then smiled as Jim bit into one.

Finola continued. "Stephen moved in. A mistake. A big, big mistake. We had a child. Stephen's band broke up and he fancied working less and less. He took up drinking and other women. After five years I was at my wit's end, working all hours to support a child and a husband who treated me like dirt. One day I freaked out. I walked. No, no, I ran."

Her eyes filled with tears. "My mother died of lung cancer. Horrible. I made a fool of myself at the funeral. That's the day I broke down."

Seeing grief in such a headstrong person rattled Peter, but he could contain himself no longer. "And Stephen called you Van?"

She nodded. "From the first time we met."

His brow knitted, Jim sat down on the edge of his desk. "You just walked out?"

Finola looked at him, gave a bitter chuckle. "Oh yes, Jim.

That sits badly with you, doesn't it? Don't think it doesn't with me."

"Tell us about your son," Mick said.

"Yes," said Jim, his face growing ever graver. His donut sat half-eaten on the desk.

"Eric. That was his name. After Eric Clapton, see how we viewed the world then? My God, it feels foreign on my tongue, I've avoided even thinking it for so many years. Can anyone imagine what it's like to abandon an angel? Look."

She retrieved her handbag, rummaged through her purse. She handed Mick a creased photo. Mick inspected it without expression and passed it to Peter.

The photo must have been taken in a pub; in one corner Peter saw a round stool and a wooden bar. Finola's hair was then long braids of ringlets and her young face glowed with life. Her hands rested on the shoulders of a man behind a drum kit. The man wore a psychedelic-patterned dashiki, his black hair radiating outward in an afro. His long face was dominated by peaceful eyes and a smile. And on his knee sat a thin-armed boy with dark wavy hair, dressed in shorts and thongs. The boy's face was indistinct but Peter could almost feel his smile.

"Isn't he beautiful?" Finola's voice was husky.

Mick said, "Have you kept in touch with him?"

She rubbed her forehead. "No. It pains me to say this, but I've never made a single attempt at contact."

Jim asked, "Why not, Fi?"

Finola sighed. "Jim, Jim. Who knows why we do these things? I ran and ran and ran. You, you stay and stay and stay."

"For heaven's sake, Fi," Jim snapped. He heaved himself off

the desk and walked over to brood by his trophy shelves.

"Did Eric call you Van?" Mick was the unstoppable one.

"Yes," she whispered.

"Not Mum?"

"No, always Van."

"It's him, isn't it?"

Finola's eyes held untold misery. "How can it be?"

"Do you have any idea where he is?"

"I told you. No contact. Ever."

"And Eric? Did he ever write? Ring?"

"No, never." Her voice broke. "But he'd know where I am."

Mick's eyes narrowed. "How?"

"Stephen married. Moira, a hideous groupie who'd been chasing him before I came along. I know this because every Christmas I receive a blank card addressed from Moira Skellern. Skellern is Stephen's name. That's so Moira, she does it out of spite, just to keep reminding me that Stephen is hers now. The cards started about ten years ago, I'd say she spotted me in the press. And no, I don't have any of the cards. Straight into the bin."

"How do you know," Mick asked, "that it's not Stephen referring to you as Van in that email?"

"Ha! By the time I left him, Stephen was a pothead and an alcoholic."

Peter's mind churned. He burst out to Mick, "But why would Finola's son call himself Kurt Diamond and attack day traders? Or Gus?"

"Good question," Mick said. "Finola, do you know how we can find Eric? If not him, then Stephen or Moira?"

"I can't believe this," Jim said.

"Believe it, Jim," Finola said. "Believe it because it's true." She turned to Mick. "Last Christmas the envelope was postmarked Newtown."

Peter felt short of breath. Crikey, he thought, what can possibly beat the rush of discovery? He ran to Jim's desktop computer and brought up the White Pages website. The others watched mutely. He initiated a search for Skellern in Sydney. In a partially open drawer, he glimpsed a bottle of Dunhill cologne. So that's what Jim splashes around, he thought.

The search finished and he squealed in triumph—a match for S. Skellern in Newtown. No E's amongst the ten Skellerns. He wrote down Stephen's number and took it to Finola.

She stared at the paper.

Mick said, "Who will he kill next time?"

Finola's movements could have been arthritic. Peter held his breath as she tottered past Jim to the desk.

She dialed. Her voice shook. "Hello?"

Peter held his breath. He could make out a strident voice on the other end of the call. A ripple crossed Finola's face as if she'd been struck. She dropped the phone in its cradle with a thunk.

"God help me," she said, "that was Moira. I recognized her voice as if it was all yesterday. She knew me too. Called me a bitch and more. I'm so sorry, she hung up."

Her head slumped to the desk.

Jim was staring at the floor as if in a dream. A pall of horror hovered over the room.

Mick shrugged off his leather jacket and slung it over his shoulder. "Jim."

Peter's thoughts took off again. If Kurt Diamond was Eric Skellern, how the heck did he get close enough to hack the traders? What could his connection with Gus be? And always the question: why this course of action, why not simply knife Finola at home?

"Jim," Mick repeated.

The chief executive walked to the desk. His eyes were dull, he could have been somebody else. Ignoring the uneaten donut portion, he plucked up a fresh one and crammed it into his mouth.

Peter saw movement outside Jim's office. Crazy Oleg in a black T-shirt. What was he doing in on a Saturday?

"Reimbursement?" Mick asked.

Absentmindedly chewing, Jim nodded.

"Move it, Gentle," the leviathan ordered. "Airport time."

Too fast, Peter thought, you're moving too fast.

The phone rang. Dully, Finola raised her head and lifted the receiver. She stiffened.

"Stephen?" she croaked.

Peter's heartbeat accelerated.

Finola listened, then took part in a halting discussion that Peter found nigh impossible to follow. She explained who he and Mick were, said they needed to talk. Her face grew hard.

"You haven't changed," she said. "Right… right."

She lowered the handset, massaged her cheeks. She could have been seventy years old. "That was… He heard Moira and used Call Return. It's impossible, he doesn't sound any different. He says meet him in Newtown. A cafe, the Royal. Four o'clock."

Yes, yes, oh yes, Peter thought.

Mick glanced at his watch. "Why?"

"Why what?" Finola studied the troubled, averted face of Jim Van Kressel.

"Why's he seeing us?" Mick said.

"Oh, that's easy." Her wan smile held no hope. "Money. Bread, we used to call it. There was never anything else for Stephen."

CHAPTER 42

The big smoke of Sydney, expense-account style.

Big smoke, big deal, Mick Tusk thought. The suburbs flowing past the taxi window—Roseberry, Kensington, Redfern, Waterloo—meant little to him, although he knew they were skirting the southern border of the CBD. No megabuck harbor views on this route.

"Hey." He tapped the taxi driver on the shoulder, pointed to the radio. "Too bloody loud."

Their Indian driver scowled but lowered the volume of the Randwick race broadcast. Heavily marked-up betting form guides lay on the front passenger seat. Lucky we haven't crashed, Tusk thought.

It felt a few degrees warmer than the day they'd left in Melbourne. Sticky, of course. Blue sky, although blue didn't mean blue in Sydney. Tusk's sister Elizabeth had lived here for a few years during her married phase. In the early '90s, before the kids, he and Dana used to drive up occasionally and bunk with Elizabeth for a couple of days. Comparative verdict: bigger, prettier, smoggier, far more expensive, and full of rude city shits.

And don't mention the police force, he thought.

They'd whiled away a couple of hours at Tullamarine before their flight. Such a struggle to keep Gentle off the grog. The flight itself had been fun. Tusk hadn't flown for five years, had enjoyed the lift-off, the visual treats. How Yolanda would have loved looking down at the immense cotton clouds, he thought.

Even with all the hassle of travel, he felt powerful. Primed to move and move fast. This case had proven anything but regular. Hard to believe, he thought, we're chasing a ghost from twenty years ago. He recalled Van Kressel's lost expression—would the friendship with Vines ever recover?

As usual, Gentle was prattling on. A couple of years ago, after losing his cushy job, he'd spent two months in Sydney on some kind of contract, courtesy of his mate Fonti. He also claimed to dislike Sydney, not that you'd know it from the fulsome praise.

"This client—don't get me started about him, Mick—would take us down to Doyle's at Circular Quay. Can you imagine it? A working dinner, eating fish and chips, staring out at the Opera House, the Bridge. I was in heaven."

"What did Mandy say?"

"What?"

"Back in Melbourne. What did she say?" Tusk was remembering a phone call minutes before boarding. Gentle had almost forgotten his last-chance excursion with Mandy. The call had been short.

A sigh. "She hung up."

"Christ. Why don't you ring her now?"

"She'll already be at the museum."

"Her mobile?"

"Leave it, Mick."

In silence they listened to yet another Randwick betting plunge.

Newtown turned out to be a grungy inner-city suburb bordering the University of Sydney. Enmore Road, the main drag, looked like it was built in the nineteenth century. While Gentle paid the taxi driver, Tusk spotted a Thai restaurant, two pubs proclaiming live bands, a fancy boutique, a couple of bookshops separated by a two-dollar store, even an incense shop. A strolling gay couple in Goth outfits giggled at him.

The Royal Cafe was down-market but with its own charm. Loads of exposed timber, a scuffed floor, wide windows creating a sense of light. A few alternative types—students with studs in every orifice, writers discussing typed pages—sipped coffee.

Time check: 4:12. Bloody late.

He registered Stephen Skellern immediately, something in the stooped posture that gelled with the twenty-year-old photo. Skellern sat smoking at a window table. But it was a clearly drunken Moira Skellern who saw them first.

"Shit, look what the cat dragged in," she slurred at Gentle.

Gentle stuck out his hand. "Peter Gentle."

"Skin, check it out," she said over her shoulder. "Reckons he's Richard Ashcroft."

Skellern's placid eyes peered through smoke at the newcomers.

In other circumstances Tusk could have chuckled. Gentle did bear a passing resemblance to The Verve's singer.

Then Moira spotted Tusk. Her upper lip curled to almost swallow her tiny nose. "And an oink. Take a look, Skin."

Perhaps Moira possessed good looks once, the thin groupie sort, but time and substance abuse had ravaged her. Short, five-four maybe. Stringy blonde hair bound up in a glittering but scuffed headband. A pinched once-pretty face with pocked skin. Reddened eyes. A cheap floral dress, breasts partly exposed.

Gentle clearly didn't know where to head, so Tusk stepped past him. He caught the scent of pot.

"How much?" he asked Stephen Skellern.

Tusk was born in the year of flower power, 1967, but by the time the world's images impacted him, in his rebellious phase, hippie was a term of derision his father reserved for the peaceniks. So the era of peace, love, and understanding passed him by. But even as a police officer he never shared the general copper contempt for the radicals. They didn't beat their wives until ribs broke, they didn't butt their cigarettes on tots' chests, they didn't prey on the weak.

Stephen Skellern certainly fit the end-of-the-road hippie mold. Jeans, a grubby Velvet Underground tee, sneakers with a flapping sole. Tall, six-two. Hangdog features, sallow skin giving a first impression of someone considerably older than forty-five. Long black hair pulled back from a receding brow and tied in a ponytail.

Impossible to see him with Vines, Tusk thought. But maybe not. He remembered the easy charm of Skellern in the photo, saw in Skellern's limpid eyes how someone as intense as Vines might have fallen.

"Tell him to piss off," Moira said in a querulous voice. Tusk could smell her odor of beer, sweat, and herbal soap.

Skellern's blissed-out eyes watched his wife. "Babe—"

"Typical," she snapped. Tusk felt the spray. "Some pig comes nosing around and you're off with the fairies, crapping on about the glory days. It's pathetic, Skin. Who's the one put a roof over your head for year after bloody year, tell me that, you sleaze. It's the thought of that bitch, isn't it, her with her fake laugh and her flat chest, it's her, isn't it?"

A waiter watched the tirade from a safe distance. The Skellerns were regulars, Tusk guessed.

Skellern let Moira run out of breath. "Babe, that's no way to treat these guests. Why don't you cool it, take some fresh air?"

Moira glared at him, emotion working on her old-woman's face. She whirled and stormed away. Tusk was astonished to hear her singing, a pisspot rendition of Fleetwood Mac's "Go Your Own Way."

"Isn't she far out?" Skellern said.

"How much?" Tusk repeated.

"Lay it on me first." Was Skellern's hippie-speak an affectation or not? "What exactly are you dudes after?"

"Memory lane stuff." If there was any residual doubt that Stephen Skellern wasn't Kurt Diamond, Tusk settled his mind there and then. "You and Finola."

"Ah… Van." Skellern, eyes closed, dragged on his cigarette. Tusk saw his fingernails were cracked and stained brown. "Bro, I got nothing charitable to say about her, but she must want this in a powerful way. I'm down on rent. Let's say five hundred smackeroos."

"Okay," Gentle said.

Tusk glared at his partner. No clue, he wanted to shout, whatever happened to negotiation?

"No, no," Skellern said. "I'm ripping myself off here. Let's say a thousand, man."

"But you agreed," Tusk said.

"We'll take it," said Gentle.

Tusk almost kicked him but Gentle wasn't paying attention. He pulled a chair close to Skellern and counted out four yellow notes that disappeared the instant they hit Skellern's hands.

Tusk took a chair on the opposite side of the table.

"Stephen," Gentle said. "You and Finola…"

Gentle's acquiescence worked. Fueled by first one and then a second joint, and by sneering bitterness, Skellern opened up. He waxed on about his seventies band.

"The Cliffhangers had it all, man." Eyes momentarily sparkling. "Killer songs, heavy lyrics, vocalist cooler than Robert Plant, one mean ax man, and the best rhythm section around."

He claimed the marriage had been happy ("Van was a fox but I should have seen how uptight she got"). One day he arrived home to find son Eric weeping and untended.

"I thought we had something cosmic, me and Van. Man, when she did a runner, it freaked me out. I was between bands then. Between jobs, full stop. Stranded with a pup. Man, I don't reckon I've ever recovered."

"How old was Eric then?" Gentle asked.

"Five, five and a half." A look of disgust, mingled with guilt, crossed his face. "By the time Moira came along, a couple of years later, I was at the end of the line. Man, she's been good to me."

"Did you try to find Finola?"

"Van? Oh, yeah, man, did I ever try. Even tracked down her old man, some judge in Glebe. He'd never heard of me, claimed he had no idea where she was. I believed him. She vanished, man, left me high and dry."

"How did you cope with Eric?"

"He grew up fast, I tell you. The experience was good for him, I reckon. I was on the road, Moira's always worked. Eric became self-sufficient real quick smart."

Doesn't take a genius, Tusk thought, a case of neglect, neglect, neglect.

"What does Eric think of Van?" he asked.

"Man, the oink talks." A surprisingly engaging chuckle. "What do you reckon Eric thought? He hated the cow."

Tusk noted the past tense. "And he accepted Moira?"

Skellern's gaze slid toward the window. "Too right, man."

"Where's Eric now?"

"This is what it's all about, isn't it, man?" Skellern's brief charm vanished. "Super businesswoman with pangs of guilt. Restitution. Absolution. Man, that's a load of shit and you can tell her. We've never wanted anything to do with her and Eric wouldn't either."

"Wouldn't? You're not in contact with him?"

Skellern stubbed out his roach. "Come on, macho macho, you didn't run from your old man?"

Tusk nodded. Silence fell over the table. Gentle looked bewildered.

"He left." Skellern had turned sullen. "Just like his old lady. Disappeared one day, nine maybe ten years ago. No note, nothing. After all we'd done."

"Did you search for him?"

A shrug.

"Where is he now?"

Skellern fished in a pocket for a cigarette pack.

"Never rang, nothing," he said. "Like mother, like son, I reckon."

Bugger it, Tusk thought, the trail's nearly a decade cold. "Any recent photos of him?"

"Nope."

A father like this, Tusk thought, plus a mother who left him. He knew all too well how rage against parents fucked up a life.

He crashed a hand over Skellern's right forearm, forcing it to the table. The cigarette pack tumbled, spilling them. "If you were us, Skellern, where would you look?"

Skellern strained to lift his arm. His face grew red. "Pig."

"Let go of him," screeched Moira.

Tusk felt the lash of her handbag across his back. He released Skellern and rose. Moira's face was a livid sore.

"Nancy boy was her progeny," she snarled. "Her child. Nancy boy treated Skin like shit. The day he scarpered, I bought a bottle of bubbly."

"So did he, I bet," Tusk said. His chest felt tight.

If Eric Skellern was enraged, Tusk thought, why not take it out on this bitch? Or the scumbag father over there? Why track down the mother he'd have no memory of?

Suddenly he was sick of these joyless losers.

"Spend your money wisely," he said to Skellern.

Skellern's face, once again wreathed with smoke, held supreme indifference.

"Peace, brother," he said. "Tell Van, no one can forgive this one. Her aura's screwed for good."

"And yours isn't?"

"Hey, I'm cool."

Tusk's fury surged from nowhere. He kicked a chair and stalked off.

At the door, Gentle said, "Am I reading this right?"

"Hey!" They turned to see Moira cackling, middle finger stiff toward them. "Check the poofters."

"Shut your trap," Skellern said.

"You weak turd," she yelled at Skellern. Next to him she looked like a scungy pixie. "You didn't see him, sniffing me underwear." She smirked at Tusk. "The poofters, Oink, that's where you'll find nancy boy."

CHAPTER 43

Peter Gentle watched the night-lit towers of central Sydney, the Bridge, the black water swing past the airplane window. He could smell his own sourness, another day's effort translated into sweat. He needed a drink.

The man at the Qantas desk had told them they were lucky to squeeze onto the 7:15 flight, packed with Saturday-night commuters. In a hectic airport cafe, over a substandard coffee and a soggy hamburger, he'd listened to Mick curse the parental abuse of Eric Skellern.

"Of course," Mick had added, "that doesn't mean he's a killer now."

But Peter knew both of them were still clutching at this lead, now grown faint again.

The drinks trolley began its snail-paced journey down the aisle. He fidgeted.

In spite of Mick's urgings, Peter hadn't rung Jim or Finola from the airport. Until he'd reassessed the data in his mind, what was there to report? In any case, they would have to wait until Monday to begin the paper hunt for Mr. Eric Skellern.

The trolley finally arrived. He ordered a plastic cup of red, and only Mick's scolding eyes—the wowser went for soda water—prevented him from downing it in one gulp. Hunger gnawed despite the burger. He scoffed down his peanuts. Maybe he'd risk a flight meal.

He noticed the fingers of Mick's left hand rubbing together. No, they were rubbing an object.

"What's that?" he said.

Mick held up a streaked white stone.

"Since when do you take stones as souvenirs?" Peter asked.

"It's for Nelson. He's a bloody magpie. Loves his collection of shells and rocks."

Peter held out his hand. The angular pebble felt as slick as a beaded champagne bottle. A memory nudged.

"Sydney?" he said.

"No, Melbourne. Found it in a street."

Peter sighed, handed back the stone. He returned to his sour wine. The stale aromas from the approaching food trolley decided him—no meal tray. Perennial passenger Harvey had said it best: "My diet, Skull, abstaining from that thinly disguised cardboard."

"Actually," Mick said. "Some kid sold it to me. Outside Gus' place."

Peter almost spluttered wine across his tray. "Come again?"

Mick's eyes lost their dreaminess. "The other day. In the gutter."

"Big guy." Prickles surged up Peter's spine. "Adam. Adam Menadue. It's his."

"How—"

"Get this, that's his hobby, right? He collects them, polishes them. TPT is crawling with shiny stones. He was at the scene, Mick."

Mick peered at the stone. "Fuck."

But Peter's mind gave him no peace. His legs jiggled.

"Paper," he blurted. "Paper."

Mick handed over his notebook. Peter drew a large square, labeled it "TPT." Inside it, he wrote "Adam" over a solid dot. From the dot, he drew an arc to a small square, called it "Carlton."

"I thought no one believes he could be the hacker," Mick said.

Peter felt like shaking the moron. "Don't you get it?"

The seatbelt sign came on. A female voice began the descent announcement.

At the top of the page, Peter fashioned an amorphous blob he named "Sydney." From it he extended a solid line to a second solid dot, from which two arcs fanned, one a dashed line to the Adam dot, the other a solid line to the Carlton square.

His grin nearly split his cheeks. "This is the connection. This dot is O'Shaughnessy. David O'Shaughnessy is Eric Skellern."

He'd have swapped all the Grange Hermitage in the cellar of Draconi's for the sight of Mick's face.

***

The leadlight windows on the huge wooden door quivered with the pound of Mick's fist. Mick hadn't bothered with, or perhaps even noticed, the buzzer.

What do you call it, Peter thought, when someone switches

between two polar states, one glacially calm and efficient, the other rage-driven? The transformation in Mick, his sixth in two days, unnerved Peter.

"I don't get it," Mick had said on the plane. "This O'Shaughnessy makes friends with Silver Spoon, his mother's stepson, to stalk her?"

Peter had to admit the puzzle pieces failed to interlock completely. "Look, I know he's from Sydney. He said something about working in computers."

"Does he look like the Skellern kid?"

Peter had wished he'd brought Finola's photo. "I can't remember. He doesn't look vastly different."

"Okay, who attacked you, Menadue or O'Shaughnessy?"

Even that seemed uncertain. Nothing his senses remembered gave a positive match. Neither Adam's hearty voice nor David's quiet mellifluousness resembled the made-up voice that had terrorized him, but wasn't that the point of a manufactured voice? He had told Mick as much.

"Only one way," Mick had said, and the set of his jaw had alarmed Peter.

Now he stood and watched Arnold Schwarzenegger pummel wood.

Linda Crescent in Hawthorn was a borderline luxury street reached by turning off Glenferrie Road at the Coles supermarket, then driving past Glenferrie Oval, once home to the Hawks.

Not even the fact that Carlo Fonti lived nearby, in a spotless apartment down by the river, endeared Hawthorn to Peter. Of all the inner eastern suburbs, it seemed to him the most complacent and lacking in character. A precinct of trees, high fences, and mossy lawns, he found it cloying—although to be honest, he dated this disdain to his teen hatred of the rarefied dumbos of Scotch College.

Finola's two-story mini-mansion had a small front garden of roses and manicured shrubs, traversed by a curved brick path. The two private eyes stood inside a blue- and red-brick porch.

"Enough of that," Peter said. His hands were cold; while they'd been in Sydney the thermometer had plummeted.

Mick paused his hammering. "The fuck it is."

"Excuse me." It was Rory in a green velvet bathrobe and slippers.

"Rory—" Peter said, but Mick slammed the door back with a thud, grabbed a fistful of bathrobe. Peter heard a rip.

He experienced a pang of guilt. He'd known this would be the show, had done nothing to ameliorate it. My excuse, he thought, is this: we need to know.

"Hold on, this is simply—" Rory began.

Mick shoved Rory backward on unsteady legs. The hallway was as large as Peter's living room, with a marble floor and cream walls straddled by waist-high patterned wallpaper. A pastel-toned Chinese urn dominated a high decorative table. Peter could see his fearful face in a full-length mirror. A crowded coat stand stood next to gleaming mahogany stairs.

"You don't get it, cocksuck, do you?" Mick said. "You weren't listening, were you, when I asked you to do the right thing."

The coat stand toppled with a crash, coats sprawling across the marble. Mick had Rory against the banister. Rory grunted with pain.

Peter couldn't hear any other sounds in the house. Cowardly relief swept over him—Finola would be rocked by the O'Shaughnessy news. He laid a hand on Mick's hot arm and received a backward lash as thanks.

"Wednesday night," Mick spat.

"I told you."

"Christ, how thick can you get?" His left hand knotted hard into Rory's chest, Mick flailed with his right hand. The urn flew and smashed into fragments against the mirror. A diagonal fissure spread upward from the bottom of the mirror.

Rory whimpered. "All right, all right."

Mick released him. The heaving China scholar staggered away to slump against the mirror. Peter heard the crack a second before a pane of mirror glass shattered around Rory's feet.

The rampant Balt was also panting. How much is effect, Peter wondered, how much is madness? He felt frozen on the spot.

"In the name of heaven," Rory said. He straightened his clothes, attempted to restore his face to its practiced equanimity. But his eyes remained startled lamps.

Mick glowered.

Rory tried bluster one more time. "This is an outrage…"

Mick cocked his head. A fist rose.

Arms up, Rory quailed. "It's true. Adam was at a party. They will confirm it."

"He wasn't here then," Peter said.

"No. He was at a party. He asked me. He said it would be convenient if I vouched for him. Goddamn you, he's my son."

Mick expelled a breath and turned to the open front door. In the space of seconds, his face had spent all its emotions.

"Where is Adam?" Peter said.

"I don't know, I swear."

"He's with David, isn't he?"

Rory desperately shook his head but his body language could lie no longer.

CHAPTER 44

Fitzroy surveillance, 12:16 on a frigid Saturday night.

"Thought you said you were getting better at this," Mick Tusk said.

Through the slightly lowered car window, he could smell cooking, some curry.

Gentle jerked from near-sleep. "Am so."

Earlier Tusk had checked out Brunswick Street, alive as last night's Chapel Street but with a different clientèle. Trendy Northcote designers and media mavens strolled with slumming early retirees. Pseudo punks stared at dot-com slackers in jeans and corporate tees. A muted world, blacks and browns with splashes of aberrant yellow or red.

Their surveillance target: a hundred meters down a side street. Kellner Road, a mix of run-down and renovated terrace houses. Dark, largely silent. Every square meter of parking space taken.

Tusk had been lucky, had snared a spot three doors down from Number 47. He sat physically relaxed, controlling breathing and posture, eyes fixed on the terrace house with its blue picket fence and drawn curtains. The cold didn't bother him, helped stave off sleep.

They'd been here nearly two hours. No luck.

"Thank Christ I'm on the case," he said.

Gentle rubbed his eyes. "Says who?"

Tusk remembered a warmer Fitzroy night a year ago, maybe half a kilometer away. A restaurant, a battle, a blur, Gentle's matchstick arms hauling him off a pulped face.

Christ, he thought, save me from myself. Then he sneered at the piety of the thought. Next I'll convert to Buddhism, he scoffed.

At times like these, someone had to act. God knew he was keyed up enough. Rory Menadue's pale face, its blue-blood veneer shattered like the mirror, rose to Tusk's mind.

He hadn't bothered ringing Dana. They both knew the score with these sorts of jobs.

"Hey, Mick. Look."

Tusk's hands leaped. Christ, now he'd been the one dozing. Gentle pointed. A red coupe with protruding headlights had passed them, was slowing outside the target.

They hunched down.

The car halted outside Number 47. Tusk's pulse climbed. Five figures spilled out.

"That's him, David O," Gentle whispered, tugging at Tusk's jacket. "And Adam. And Adam's girlfriend, what's her name? That's a new girl with David. Who's he?"

"He's trouble."

"What?"

Tusk watched the final person stretch and survey his

surroundings. Based on looks and actions, classification: thug. The man was massively built across the chest. Buzz-cut white hair. Baby-fat face with close-set eyes. Tight black tee, arse-hugging white pants.

Tusk scanned Gentle's petrified face. "Stay here."

"No, I'm coming. Mick, you exercise control now, do you hear?"

Tusk nodded. Easier said than done. When they moved, rationality would be a luxury.

"I'm serious, Mick," Gentle whispered. "Everything depends on control. We're a team, we work together. Did you bring a... a gun?"

"Nup."

"Why on earth not?"

"Why didn't you, smart-arse?"

Truth was, Tusk had stuffed up. Had left his chosen weapon in a back drawer in his shed, had figured at worst this would be one-on-one fisticuffs.

No time to bandy regret. Menadue was kissing his girl. O'Shaughnessy had unlatched the gate. No mistake, white-haired Boofhead was some kind of bodyguard. Heaven help their chances if the party reached indoors.

He held a finger to his lips. Eased open the car door. Signaled for Gentle to do the same.

His life teetered on the edge of action. Always that, always that. Images: Nelson, Yolanda. Dana—sorry, love, he thought.

"Fuck it," he breathed.

And slid out, strode up to the revelers before they had time to react.

"Chat time," he said, voice as authoritative as he could make it.

All five whirled. Menadue's eyes wide. Menadue's girl swaying.

O'Shaughnessy was shorter than Tusk had anticipated. A tanned salesman type. Clearly, so clearly, in charge. A soft smile lit his face, his eyes. The tip of his tongue appeared. He shoved his blonde girl away.

Tusk stood, balanced on the balls of his feet, legs ever so slightly bent, arms light. Steaming breath drifted across his eyes. His senses took it all in: Gentle trembling by his side; troppo Boofhead held in check by O'Shaughnessy's raised hand; O'Shaughnessy poised; Menadue bewildered.

"What do you want?" said Menadue.

"Your alibi is all lies, Adam." Gentle's shaky voice. "We can place you in Carlton."

Adam gasped, looked to boss man O'Shaughnessy.

"You're the ones who attacked me," Gentle said. "Who killed Gus, you or him?"

Menadue shouted, "You're crazy!"

"Gus found out. Eh, Adam? And do you know your so-called friend's hidden agenda?"

For the first time O'Shaughnessy's face showed something less than confidence.

Adam: "David?"

Tusk smelled battle.

Panting Gentle: "That's right, David. We know who you are."

A knife appeared in O'Shaughnessy's hand. Boofhead roared and charged. Gentle cried out.

A voice: "David, no!"

O'Shaughnessy came fast, blade a twinkling blur. Tusk turned, felt its swoosh, chopped downward. A clatter as the knife flew.

He had O'Shaughnessy's arm, swung the bony body in the way of Boofhead.

Out of practice.

Slow.

A fist smashed his nose. Pain. A bellow, his bellow. Momentary blackout.

O'Shaughnessy slipped out of his arms.

CHAPTER 45

The instant he understood what O'Shaughnessy was thrusting at Mick, Peter Gentle rued each and every step taken since Wednesday.

His arms and legs shook. He felt raindrops on his face. Part of his mind imagined curling into a ball.

But he saw Mick knock the knife flying, saw him grab his attacker, saw white-haired Monster's rabid face as he swung his fist, saw blood spray when Mick took the blow on his nose, saw Mick stagger, saw O'Shaughnessy wriggle free, and he knew he had to act.

He circled behind Monster and round-armed him on the head, succeeding in catching an ear. Agonizing pain shot through his knuckles. Monster cried out, clutched his ear.

A shape bent to retrieve the knife from the road. With lithe ease, Adam jammed the knife point up to Peter's throat. Adam's face was wild.

"Don't," Peter said.

"Shut up," screeched Adam. He whipped around Peter to grip him in a stranglehold, the blade up under his chin.

Jesus Christ, Peter thought, help me, help me, help me.

Mick, doubled over, had a hand to his nose. The hand dripped. Monster rubbed his ear and grinned.

O'Shaughnessy stood on the other side of Mick and Monster. He shouted, "Do it, Adam, do it."

Adam's trembling arm pressed viciously into Peter's windpipe. Peter sucked in air, braced himself.

A sob. The arm relinquished Peter and he pitched to the ground. Pain seared his hip.

He gazed up into Adam's weeping face. Starless black sky high up, silver raindrops sliding through streetlight haze. The world so sweet.

He scrambled to his knees in time to see Monster's boot slam into Mick's side with a thud. Mick grunted, released his nose.

O'Shaughnessy, seemingly unhurried, had reached the gate to Number 47. He turned to smirk at Adam. He looked directly into Peter's eyes, lifted his eyebrows. Then Finola's son shouted, "Snowy, do him," and darted into the terrace house.

Peter rose onto unsteady legs. He heard voices, saw people running from the direction of Brunswick Street. Drizzle spattered his cheeks. Adam had made his way to slump in the gutter. The two girls were long gone.

Monster—Snowy was its name—howled and kicked Mick again. Peter shuddered at the sound of impact. Icy inertia gripped him.

Then Mick raised his head. Peter gasped. The face was blood, a volcano of blood, crimson swamping the cheeks, flooding the hair, splashing his T-shirt. Mick's eyes—boar's molten eyes—met Peter's without a flicker of recognition.

"Cunt," said Snowy, foot lifted back. He was huge, mythically huge.

"Do something, Lance," a woman cried.

Snowy kicked.

Mick simply straightened, absorbed the kick on his thigh, and burrowed into Snowy, his fists swinging. The two of them went down, a grunting, scrabbling bundle sliding across the wet bitumen.

"Kill, kill, kill," shouted a man clutching a stubby.

"A tenner on the big one," came a rasping voice.

Then Snowy screamed and Mick was on top. Blood flew.

Mick straddled Snowy like a surfer paddling on a board. His mouth was twisted. He rained down blow after blow, as if pounding a stake into the ground. Snowy's arms twitched by his sides.

Peter never could figure what roused him from his stupor, but he forced himself to the sodden pair. Through the mist of rain, steam rose off the straining back in front of him. He caught the metallic smell of blood. Around him, he could distinguish sounds, of people, of a siren in the distance, of his own panting, but what filled his ear was that inhuman smack of flesh on flesh.

"Mick," he said.

I've been here before, the awful thought came to him. A brainwave materialized.

"Mick," he croaked, up close. "Dana. Dana. Dana's here."

The fist stopped in midair. The body sagged into heaving equilibrium. Mick's head swung around. His face was inhuman.

Hazy eyes connected with Peter's. A groan issued from the wide-open mouth.

Peter's body burned with mad energy. He tenderly laid a hand on Mick's shoulder, then ran to Adam, disconsolate in the gutter.

"It's the end." Adam raised his head and Peter was struck by how, at the moment of capitulation, Adam looked exactly like his father had amidst the shards of his urn.

Adam intoned, "He said we'd just scare you away."

Peter squatted. "How did Gus discover it?"

"What's this crap?" Adam said. "It wasn't Gus, it was you, snooping, always snooping. Why the hell did David... why the knife?"

"You went to Carlton."

"I just wanted to tell him, that's why we went there. He shouldn't have competed with a Menadue. Not for someone like Belinda." Adam jammed knuckles up against his teeth. Rain glistened on his curls. "Ah, what's the use? It's gone, everything, it's all gone."

Peter stood, disgusted. Had Adam been the one who bashed him? Maybe, but he knew now that the Peter Lorre voice had belonged to O'Shaughnessy.

Sirens sounded close by. The pub yobboes huddled around Snowy's unmoving body. Where was Mick? Peter spotted him bent over a fence, spitting red.

Peter rushed through the ajar door of Number 47. Recklessness gripped him, though he knew O'Shaughnessy could be waiting, gun or knife in hand. Was this how Mick felt when he lost control? He plunged into room after room. Nothing. The back door gaped. He slapped the screen door open, kept going through the rear gate. A dark alley headed for the lights of Brunswick Street.

Too far gone now, he sprinted down the slippery lane, emerging to nearly collide with a middle-aged couple.

There! O'Shaughnessy stood in the street, carry bag slung over a shoulder. A tram whined to a stop. Peter ran. He reached the tram in time to slap its departing rear.

"Shit!" Suddenly he couldn't catch his breath.

"Follow that tram?" A toffee English accent.

A black convertible, top down despite the fine rain, pulled up beside him. Its occupant, a red-faced, red-haired man in a tuxedo, grinned as if this was a question he managed to pose every Saturday night.

Peter couldn't credit his luck. He launched himself over the passenger door, tripped and fell across the man. Pain stabbed his hip. The man stank of some kind of liquor. Peter struggled upright.

His chauffeur floored the accelerator. Traffic heading away from the city was nonexistent and the Englishman was insane. They passed the tram two or three stops along. The convertible skidded to a halt.

"Thanks." Peter scrambled out, pain confirming that he'd damaged the hip. He was soaked.

"My unreserved pleasure," came the slur.

Peter hammered on the tram doors. They folded inwards. He limped up the steps. The tram held a dozing Asian woman, a bearded drunk.

O'Shaughnessy had vanished.

CHAPTER 46

Superfreaky memories, superfreaky memories, superfreaky memories. Lyrics tumbling over and over, a narcotic riff fading whenever the pain lanced, the riff clear as a live gig when the drugs cut in.

Mick Tusk struggled to stay conscious.

It was a Luna song, he knew, another strange, dual-guitar trancy thing that he shouldn't like but loved. He fastened on to it, followed the rhythm.

Superfreaky memories, superfreaky memories. Aha, that was the name of the song, "Superfreaky Memories."

He unglued his eyes. A hospital bed surrounded by curtains. Accident & Emergency, must be. Which hospital? That shitty casualty ward smell, somehow piercing despite the nose damage, the sprays, the injections, the bandages.

"Bloody public hospital." A grumble from Gentle, his reedy body huddled on the edge of the bed. Disheveled, massaging his righthip.

Drifting.

Memories—pain, pain, a blinding red film, the molten band

inside his head, a faraway voice announcing Dana.

Drifting.

"Mikey!"

Open those eyes, arsehole.

Dana's hair on his chest, scratching under his chin. Her sobs.

It's okay, he wanted to say. Now that you're here, he wanted to say. Stay, he longed to say.

Drifting.

Banshee. His Dana, no one else could yell like that. "You did this. You always... I hate you!"

Wife tongue-lashes genius. It's okay, he wanted to say.

Wooziness.

Another voice, female, Mandy of course: "Grow up, Dana. Mick is doing what he wants to do. It's his life. Stop blaming Peter for something that's between you and Mick."

Dana: "But look at him!"

It's okay, he wanted to say. Peace is here, he wanted to say.

Tusk opened his eyes one millimeter. What he saw: Mandy's smile melting Gentle's superfreaky face.

Drifting.

Vitally important for some reason... what was the name of that Luna CD? Use that superfreaky memory, arsehole. 1999 release, was it?... *The Days of Our Nights*, that's what it was.

Dana's voice, other voices, no sense to any of it.

No wonder, arsehole, time to turn the days of our nights into the night of nights.

Oblivion.

CHAPTER 47

Tormented by the Alfred Hospital's reek of chemicals and sickly bodies, Peter Gentle clutched the lip of the restroom bowl. He retched until his ribs ached.

He flushed, lowered the restroom seat for his head to rest on. His eyes streamed.

Never again, he thought. He pictured the rust-smudged marble of the bandage-free regions of Mick's face. Sitting with poor Mick had brought his high crashing down; then Dana's insane outburst had acted as catalyst for his dash to the loo. His head pounded in waves, seemingly concentrated in that damned lump. Every bruise accumulated over the case had chosen this moment to ache. His hip pulsed—was it broken?

When Peter had limped back to Kellner Road, the men in blue were already in charge. Mick lay on a stretcher, his chest quivering in agony as an ambulance orderly bandaged up the nose. Snowy was nowhere to be seen. Adam glowered beside a tall policewoman.

Peter was frank with the fleshy policeman assigned to him. Apparently a witness had seen O'Shaughnessy draw the knife, so after a lengthy statement, he was permitted to ride in the ambulance with Mick.

Now he yawned and yawned. Let me feel happy, he thought. He should have been delirious with triumph. After all, he'd solved the case—the loose end of the flitting Skellern/O'Shaughnessy now a police manhunt responsibility. Belinda would see justice done for Gus' murder. Jim could get back to nurturing his second fortune. Finola would be in shock—her son was the maleficent leader behind the scenes, and Peter hadn't been able to honor his oath of confidentiality—but hopefully she'd perceive her fortune that son Eric had, for some reason, kept away from her.

But instead of joy, Peter felt only the scourge of despondency.

***

When he emerged from the restroom, he found Deirdre pacing the corridor in ambush. She wore jeans, a sloppy DKNY sweater, and short black boots, and for once looked nothing like a policewoman.

Her face battled fatigue. "I thought I was the driven one."

"Do you ever get that feeling, Dee?" Peter said. "It's what you want, it's working well, but it all feels too hard?"

"Nope." Deirdre smiled. "Or if I feel that way inclined, I book a skiing holiday. Peter, I'm here 'cos the boss hollered for you."

The prospect of seeing Inspector Conomy deflated Peter even further. "Come on, Dee, it's 2:15."

"No choice. Besides, you're in the box seat."

A nurse swept past without a sideways glance. Back in the casualty ward a baby wailed.

Peter sighed. He recalled how his heart had leaped at the sight of Mandy's smile. "Let me say goodbye to Mick."

"No, leave the maniac be. I'm told the nose isn't badly fractured. Peter, I really need you to come now. The Commissioner is on the boss' back. Anyway, this isn't the spot for you right now."

Peter could hear Dana's hysterical voice down the corridor. Deirdre's advice made sense.

Best of luck, Mick, he thought. Sorry, Mandy, sorry.

***

He almost dozed off in the police car. He remembered Unforgiven saying he didn't do "physicals." Well, I do physicals, U, he thought. In the Police Complex elevator, nausea forced him to rest his head against the wall.

The Homicide section was in darkness. Peter hadn't walked past these desks in nearly a year, but he shuddered at the memory.

Deirdre ushered him into a small, stale-smelling room. It looked through a one-way mirror into the very same despicable chamber in which, last May, Peter had suffered his interrogation. He suppressed a smirk at the sight of Adam, face drawn, slumped in the hot seat.

Slouched against a wall, Tagliaferro swore softly. The expert-at-nothing had grown half a beard, had obviously thrown his day clothes on again.

Conomy, dressed in an oriental-looking vest over a cotton top, was bounciest of all. The inspector's white hair looked recently washed and he was cleanshaven. And surely he should look pleased, Peter thought. His case was nearly finito, never mind that it took two renegade PIs to get him there.

"Well, mate," Conomy said. "You Gentles sure don't muck around." He paused to study Peter. "I've been through your scene statement, but let's hear it in your own words. Sit down."

Weariness a weight across his shoulders, Peter sat on a chair facing the three police officers and summarized everything he'd been through since the Friday morning rift, everything except Unforgiven's role. He was aware his version undeservedly cast himself as a hacking whiz, but he figured Tagliaferro deserved the humiliation. He handed over the CD-R, imagining Edith Maguire's face pained at his treachery, but what choice did he have? Conomy asked a handful of questions, Deirdre and Tagliaferro remained silent.

"Impressive." Conomy pointed to Adam, now dozing. "Adam Menadue admits to visiting the victim at about 7:35 PM on Wednesday, just minutes after Brad Funder left. He was inebriated. Claims he intended to scare the victim into ditching Belinda Van Kressel. He keeps insisting they left the house just before 8 PM. He also claims that as they were leaving, he and O'Shaughnessy spotted you arriving, and then assaulted you when you emerged. Again, he claims, to scare you. Here's the interesting part. He's confessed to faking an invoice at work, defrauding his own mother's company of $50,000, back in January. Says he thought you were onto him. He blames everything on O'Shaughnessy. I was especially fascinated to hear that O'Shaughnessy made an abortive attack upon you on Thursday, something you didn't bother to tell me."

I knew it, Peter thought, I knew there was something in the

accounts. "He's lying. Gus must have found out."

Conomy nodded. "As soon as we catch O'Shaughnessy or Skellern or whoever he is, they'll fall like a pack of cards. By the way, we've searched O'Shaughnessy's place. He'd packed to go, it was clean as a whistle. Our computer maestro here will analyze his computer."

The sarcasm didn't escape Tagliaferro. "I predict he wiped it like all the others."

"How convenient," said Conomy.

Tagliaferro's face clamped sourly shut.

Suffer, Peter thought. What did the inspector mean about "Gentles" not mucking about? Was that a dig at his father?

Peter asked, "Any sign of Skellern?"

"Patience, mate," Conomy said. "Now, let me be frank."

Peter saw Deirdre glance away.

Conomy rose to tower over him. "In the Force, we do not condone the use of violence. Repeat, do not."

Dull anger suffused Peter.

"Your partner's one sick man," preached Conomy. "You've done good work, I can't deny that. You've got nous, you're persistent. But I'm going to charge that animal Tusk with assault and battery, even if Taplin doesn't lay charges. You should see the man, he'll be in hospital for a month."

Tagliaferro was grinning.

How will Dana react, Peter thought. "I've told you. He attacked Mick. Kicked him. Self-defence. He was going to—"

"Right." Conomy sniffed. "Taplin's a low-grade thug, a menace to society." A finger jabbed the air above Peter's head. "And guess what? So is your partner."

"Look—"

"I've said my piece, mate." Conomy walked over to gaze through the one-way mirror. "For the rest of this case, I'm reverting to our initial arrangement. I'll keep you informed. I'll fully acknowledge your assistance. But afterward, next time we meet, if you haven't dissolved the relationship, I'll lock you up in the same cell as that psychopath."

Peter surged to his feet. His face flushed right up under his hair. He knew Conomy meant well and had in fact conceded much, but anger drove him on.

"Rich, can I call you that?" he said. "Rich, you informed me once that you divide the world into the good and the bad."

Deirdre blanched. Conomy's face darkened.

"Well, Rich," Peter said. "Would you say you're on the side of the good? Hah!" He mimicked Conomy's didactic finger. "Take a good look, Rich. A logical look. In practical terms, during this case you may as well have been the bad."

His pointing finger shook. "At least Mick did something."

***

Out in the piercing cold of St Kilda Road, Peter found he could barely function. A lone BMW passed, sending brown autumn leaf fragments swirling. Then the boulevard fell silent, devoid of cars and trams. Any chance of a lift back into town had been forfeited by his intemperate eruption.

If only savaging Conomy had buoyed his spirits…

He trudged toward the city glow.

When his mobile rang, his first thought was, it's Eric Skellern come to get me.

But it was Jim Van Kressel. "Sorry to ring at this crazy hour. Fi just rang, she's beside herself. Can't believe it myself. Adam is under arrest."

"I know." Peter pictured Jim in his hotel room. He caught a whiff of his rank odor. No Harvey to lean on tonight. Who knew where Skellern lurked? Fear prickled his nape. "Jim, you wouldn't by any chance have room for one more soul up there?"

CHAPTER 48

"I know. But that was then."

The Van Kressel I'm-a-CEO voice roused Peter Gentle from inchoate dreams. He clutched the blanket, opened his eyes to see cream-patterned hotel wallpaper a meter from his nose.

"Look, we have to move on," he heard Jim say.

Peter groaned. Thirst gripped his throat. He could smell the leftovers on Jim's supper tray, on the floor by the door. When he kicked off the blanket, his hip spasmed.

We did it, he thought, Tusk & Gentle achieved the impossible. Justice, thy will be done. The declarations banished his body's bleating complaints. He sat up.

Jim sat on the bed, looking like a teddy bear in a sloppy tracksuit combination. He spotted Peter and waved.

"Fi, I'm not perfect either," he said into the phone. He gestured to Peter, pointed to a coffee pot by the bed. "I mean, think about this. All my staff... Camilla fancied Gus, Adam robbed me, sorry to bring that up... and even Brad conspired against us. Hardly an honest person on the second floor... Really?... Yes, yes, ten o'clock. I'll bring our superhero detective."

The call finished, Jim rose and hoisted his trackpants. "I couldn't tell her."

The police had only informed Finola that Adam had confessed to fraud and was a murder suspect along with O'Shaughnessy. At 3 AM Peter had briefed Jim on Skellern/O'Shaughnessy as Kurt Diamond, to the chief executive's amazement.

"I don't blame you," Peter said.

"Let's break the news in the office. Pete, have a scrub, why don't you? I tell you, the Sheraton's showers would restore a corpse."

Jim was right. The needles of hot water sluiced Peter's physical imperfections away. His mood rocketed and his mind commenced cataloging data, delineating conclusions. How soon before the police caught up with deranged Eric Skellern? He wondered what a broken nose would mean to Mick.

By the time he finished drying his hair, he found himself singing tunelessly: "Data. Analysis. Conclusions."

In the hotel room, Jim was gathering up files from the tiny desk. "No hit record, that."

"You have to agree it works, Jim." Pride filled Peter's chest. Through the window he marveled at the cloudless sky, the office towers. "All along, we followed the gaps in the data. And then it just needed someone to fit it all together."

Jim chuckled. "Just kidding, Pete. Sing away."

The phone rang. Jim's voice progressively softened the longer he spoke. "Hi… Me too, me too… Look, it's not the best time to talk… No—" a huge, silent sigh, eyes shut "—no, of course it's not Fi… look, I can call her what I like… I am, I am… I am thinking… Alison, it's not the time… Me too, darl, me too. Yes, 12:30."

Peter kept his face composed. How could anyone be so impressive, he thought, yet so unraveled by a woman?

"That was Alison," Jim said needlessly.

"How is it going?"

Jim began to pack his briefcase. "Pete, thank your lucky stars you're not in deep. I'm… I'm contemplating going back. It's no life, vegetating in a bloody hotel. She's agreed to so many changes, I'd be a fool not to try one more time."

Peter yawned. He couldn't meet Jim's eyes.

Jim hefted his briefcase and faced the door, head up high. "That's what I've learned, Pete. The only way to make a marriage work is to work at it."

The lament of the abused, Peter was tempted to cry.

***

Their footsteps clomped on the Yarra footbridge. Melbourne's office spires rose like stalagmites into the pristine sky. Winter has come early, Peter thought. He pulled his crumpled jacket tight around his shivering frame. The river glistened, steam wafted from the strained mouths of rowers.

Peter's hip barely troubled him. Alone, he might have halted mid-bridge to spread arms and embrace the ice-laden air, the treasures of Melbourne along the riverbanks to his left and right, for he adored his city on these autumn days. But Jim waddled on, arms swinging, talking nonstop about TPT's plans.

Once they'd traversed the ancient tunnel through Flinders Street Station, Peter called a halt. He tried Deirdre's mobile number, without much hope.

But his police ally answered after three rings. "Peter, I cacked myself last night. The boss hardly said a word for the next hour. You okay? Death warmed up, you were."

"Brilliant, Dee, I'm just brilliant." Peter wondered if she'd slept at all. "Has Adam confessed?"

"No luck. He insists—"

"He's adamant?"

"What? Oh, boy. Gee, you are in a good mood. He insists on no knowledge of David O'Shaughnessy's real ID. We've already managed to track O'Shaughnessy back to 1992, when Adam claims he began university, down from Sydney as you said. The trail goes cold across the border. Early days, but. And the boss has flown to Sydney to interview the Skellerns."

Peter smiled, imagining Conomy dealing with Moira Skellern. "O'Shaughnessy?"

"Nope, not yet. But I'm hopeful. Apparently he's well known as a wheeler-dealer on the criminal periphery. Derek Taplin, aka Snowy, claims O'Shaughnessy hired him Friday night as a bodyguard. Taplin called him quote unquote bad news, ultra-smart. And get this, he isn't pressing charges against Mick."

Peter flashed on Mick's alien blood-soaked face. "Has Inspector Conomy?"

"Not yet. Interesting, huh?"

Peter thanked Deirdre and headed up Elizabeth Street with his client.

Sunday morning was the only downtime at Draconi's. Though all the bar stools, and a fair smattering of tables, were occupied, a rare languor rested over the skeleton staff. For patrons, mostly Postcode 3000s like himself, it was the day for flicking through catch-up piles of trade magazines, for mulling over PowerPoint slides, for revisiting that art book or biography. Peter beamed at the sight.

The moment they entered, Hector was all over him.

"M'boy, m'boy," Hector trumpeted. "Let's hear it. We deserve the grand saga."

Hector led them to Harvey at a window table overlooking drowsy Block Arcade. Unshaven Harvey poured on the congratulatory nonsense, pointed to an *Age* article. Above two photographs, one of the Kellner Road crime scene, the other a dignified portrait of Adam Menadue, Peter read the headline: "Society Heir Arrested."

Hector was flapping his arms. He rushed off.

"Harvey, see that?" Peter pointed after the restaurateur.

"Raise that at the next meeting, Skull," Harvey said. "A miracle. Hec runs!"

Jim smiled. "I'm famished."

Of course Harvey had *The Weekend Financial Review* and *The Australian* as well as *The Age*. After reading *The Age's* meaningless article on the arrest, Peter skimmed all three papers' financial sections.

"Hec tells me you're bullish," said Harvey.

"No, not bullish." Peter kept grinning for no reason at all. "Just not writing off the dot-com fever yet. I've seen it in action."

"At TPT?" Harvey's mischievous eyes turned to Jim. "Excuse me saying this, but the volume of TPT plus all the other online brokerages is only ten percent of the exchange's total volume. The Aussie market will be decided by the professionals, not the amateurs."

"My traders are professional," Jim said. "One of my boys

made half a mil last year."

"Sorry, Jim, no offense, but you know what I mean." Behind the jocularity, Harvey was serious, Peter realized, worried about his own money no doubt. "Last night I went to see the Kangaroos pip the Pies, and in our box there were guys from the big brokers. They're all bearish, Jim, Skull. Exceedingly bearish. I mean, Nasdaq nosedived on Friday."

Jim grimaced. Peter was saved from taking a stand by the return of Hector bearing coffees. And also carrying cups was the man with the ponytail, Vernon King.

"Where's Mick?" Unforgiven looked harassed.

Peter shook his head. "I can't… I just can't. U, can I keep calling you U?"

Hector chortled.

"Is it absolutely necessary?" said Unforgiven, but he smiled faintly.

The five of them squeezed in around Harvey's table. Peter's first sip of coffee affirmed the sweetness of the moment. He relished the prospect of recounting yesterday's dramas.

He said, "We did it, U."

"He sure did," Jim said. "Four days, that's all it took to crack a case the police barely dented."

"The black hat hacker," Unforgiven said. "You've apprehended him?"

"Just about," Peter said.

"This I must hear," said Unforgiven. "But first tell me, what about Mick?"

Harvey said, "Yep, where is our token hulk?"

Guilt seized Peter. How many times had he even thought of

Mick all morning? He was basking in glory while his friend suffered.

"It's not good news," he said. "Mick—"

"Mick what?" thundered a voice.

Peter didn't believe what he saw. Limping across the floorboards was Mick as horror-movie apparition. Bandages fanned out from his covered nose. Blackness rimmed both eyes. He wore yesterday's jeans, now filthy, and an outlandish olive jumper five sizes too small, from which sprouted the unmistakable collar of a hospital gown. And his feet were bare.

"Fuck a duck," said Harvey with a demented grin.

Peter knocked his chair over in haste. "Jesus, Mick, what have you done?"

A spasm wiped out Mick's attempted grin. All around them, Draconi's customers stared. Peter could smell his partner's hospital aroma. What's Dana going to do, he thought, when she finds Mick has escaped?

"Couldn't stand another bloody second," Mick said. "Break's clean, who needs bed rest?"

"But…" stammered Peter. He saw Hector's eyes soaking up another Tale Of Draconi's. Unforgiven looked baffled.

"No buts." Mick plucked a spare chair from under the nose of a man gaping from the adjacent table, and slapped it down next to Unforgiven. He planted his frame down in one swift motion and scanned them one by one.

"Work to do," he said to Peter. His voice was decibels too loud. "Trust me, that Skellern's one mean bastard. He's coming for us. For you."

"Pray tell," said Unforgiven. "Who is Skellern?"

Peter shivered. All his fears had faded away overnight. "But he's on the run."

"On the run," Mick said, again too loud. "I know the scumbag. He's never on the run. It's all grist to his mill, he thinks he's king of the fuckin' pigsty."

It's the medicine, Peter decided. "Mick, quiet. You're going for an Oscar here."

"Yes, m'boy," Hector said. "A bit of order, please."

Mick winced as he swung his head to see all the faces watching. "Bugger me, you're right." He lowered his voice to a strange near-whisper. "Hey, I came to grab genius here and get back on the job."

He gave the weirdest smarmy grin. "But one night in the sick house and I've worked up an appetite."

The thought of Eric Skellern's smile, his creepy fake voice, unnerved Peter.

"You had to have left in a hurry," he said, pointing to Mick's hideous jumper, straining at every seam.

"My oath," said Mick, scandalously loud again. "The nong in the next bed. Now, let's focus here, folks. Hec, cook me up the biggest, meanest mother of a breakfast in town."

CHAPTER 49

A tram up Collins, Gentle talking nonstop beside him, the rattle across each intersection painfully jolting the fucking nose. Mick Tusk issued the command: focus! Focus: find perp, catch perp, go home. Ignore the rest.

Hector's shirt billowed from Tusk's frame. The shoes lent by Unforgiven pinched his toes.

Off at Spring Street. Tycoon Van Kressel waved to the McDonald's staff, received waves back.

From the elevator into the TPT lobby. Robyn Fox the receptionist behind her desk, superwoman Vines handing over a sheaf of pages.

Vines, in a tan suit too formal for Sunday, was saying, "This is the press release, Robyn. Pay attention to spelling this time, will you?" A gasp when she saw Tusk's nose. "Oh, Lord, what happened?"

"Sharemarket accident," Tusk said. Volume control, he thought.

Van Kressel fake-grinned, as if sheer goodwill could reverse yesterday's flying shit. "These superstars, Fi... you won't believe what they've done. And they've uncovered more about your son." A pause. "Unfortunately."

Vines steadied herself with a hand on the high reception bench. She's aged decades, Tusk thought.

Fox wore a yellow top that left brown shoulders exposed. She seemed agitated, no doubt by Tusk's schnoz. Have to get used to people's reactions, Tusk thought. Trust me, the hospital doctor had crapped, it'll heal well, a minimal bump.

Pain. Focus.

A phone rang.

"Robyn, speaker please," Vines ordered.

The wide-eyed girl complied. A smooth-as-butter voice: "Finola, is that you?"

Vines' smile was grim. "It is."

"I've just come from seeing Adam, dearest."

Van Kressel made a move but Vines held up a hand: stay. "He stole from me, Rory."

"His lawyer is discussing bail. Dearest, I need to tell him we can raise it. The legal eagle says it could come to $50,000."

A vein throbbed on Vines' forehead. "Tell him what you like."

Tusk felt a wave of lightness. Focus.

Menadue Senior's voice took on an edge. "Dearest, I need your support. Tell me you'll pay it."

"No, Rory. We had this discussion two hours ago. You will pay any amount required."

"You know I can't. Not right now. For heaven's sake, Finola, he's your son."

"No, he's your son. I told you. No."

Petulance. "No?"

"No." Vines chopped the air.

Fox cut the connection. Silence.

Eyes narrowed, Vines studied her business partner. Van Kressel's face was as gripped by stress as hers.

"What?" Vines said.

Van Kressel looked away.

Tusk shifted off his left foot altogether. The left side, especially the thigh, was impossibly bruised. Focus.

"But you've done the same, Jim," Vines said. "For God's sake, you walked out first."

Van Kressel licked his lips.

Gentle was rubbing his fingers together, a sure sign he itched to butt in. Fox seemed fascinated equally with Tusk's nose and both her bosses.

"You didn't. Tell me you didn't." Vines' knuckles, gripping the bench, were white. "Oh, Lord, I can't take this. The rest, okay, yes, maybe, my past come to pay me back. I can cope. But Jim…"

"At least I'm trying," said Van Kressel.

"God help us, Jim." Wild eyes. "That's your trip, isn't it? You'll keep going back to her, again and again, until she buys a knife or an icepick or something." She turned to Fox. "Robyn, bring the letters down when you're done."

Wooziness. What could Tusk say? That you're stuffed if you stay, stuffed if you go? What he wanted to say: find a reason, find someone to share it with, bugger off everyone else.

"How can you talk to me like that?" Van Kressel whined.

Vines stormed off.

Tusk shook himself. Focus.

Just before Vines reached the door, he called, "Hang on."

She halted. In her eyes: sheer terror. Insight: she dreaded news about Eric.

"David O'Shaughnessy," Tusk said. "Adam ever tell you where he hangs out?"

"You! You broke my mirror."

And she was gone.

"She'll come around," Van Kressel said.

"Pigs'll fly," muttered Tusk. He gestured to Boy Wonder. "Move it."

Gentle had lost the pizzazz he'd shown in Draconi's. "Where?"

"Carlton."

Van Kressel's eyes sparked. "Belinda! Mick, you can't drive. Pete, I'll take you."

"No need, Jim," Gentle said. "This is our job."

Van Kressel picked up his briefcase, tossed it over the bench. Fox ducked. A crash.

"Sorry, Robyn, and thanks for coming in," Van Kressel said. "Pete, I have to tell you. For the first time since I inspected this office two years ago, right now this place gives me the shits."

Fox was trembling.

Amen, Tusk thought. Focus.

***

Carlton. People strolling. The sun's heat welcome on Tusk's cheeks. He imagined the sun in Belgrave. Focus.

Belinda answered the door. Hands to her cheeks at the

Elephant Man sight. Then she spotted her old man. Her face twisted.

"You!" she shouted.

"Belinda, darling," Van Kressel said.

"Ma rang me. How can you possibly go back?"

"Belinda—" Gentle tried.

She shoved Gentle aside, stabbed a finger in Van Kressel's chest. He tottered back in astonishment.

"It's true what Jim Junior says." Her face ugly. "You're a walking bag of wind. Nothing there, underneath all that talk, talk, talk."

"Please," said Van Kressel.

Tusk gripped the door frame. A fresh burst of hurts. Focus.

He grabbed Belinda's arm before the raised claws raked her father's eyes out. Her surprise was complete. She struggled, so he tightened. Her eyes met his and she sagged.

"What am I doing?" she said. "Did Adam do that?"

He released her. "David O'Shaughnessy." For some reason it hurt to speak. Focus. "You and Adam, where'd you hang out with David?"

"Belinda, if you can help—" Van Kressel began, a mistake.

"Piss off," she sprayed.

For the first time, Tusk saw self-pity cross Van Kressel's face. The bigwig raised both hands, backed up. The arms fell. He turned and walked through the gate.

"You're too hard on him," Gentle said.

"You too, dick-brain," she said.

"O'Shaughnessy," Tusk said.

"Swap meets." Belinda began to cry. "I'm sorry. Don't

families suck? Swap meets. David sells computer equipment on Sundays. Adam took me a few times."

"Where?"

"Malvern. Camberwell. Collingwood."

Tusk's words sounded mushy in his ears. "Gus was just in the wrong place at the wrong time."

She smiled through tears. How easy for Youde to fall in love, Tusk thought, as long as the poor bastard never saw her flip side.

Red-hot poker up his nose. Focus.

"Thanks," he said.

At the Rover, he paused. Blue sky over the horizon of terrace houses. Framed in Gus' doorway stood Belinda, as beautiful as when he'd first seen her, firing bullets of sorrow.

She waved.

CHAPTER 50

"Pete, Mick," said Jim Van Kressel, leaning on the steering wheel. "I can't tell you how much I owe you."

Peter Gentle squirmed with irritation. "Cash and referrals would help."

The Rover idled in traffic at the six-way nightmare of Camberwell Junction.

"No more hackers, no more headlines, no more disruptions, full stop," Jim said. "Business as usual, that's the ticket from now on. Get over these shocks we've all had."

Peter didn't bother responding. Most of Jim's garrulous stream had clearly been self-directed.

"Women." Jim's voice was bitter. "Who was it said, love 'em, hate 'em, you can't live without 'em. Belinda will come round. It's just a matter of time."

Scientists should study Jim's genome, Peter thought. I bet they'd discover an optimism gene.

He watched people filing into the Rivoli Cinema. Mandy had dragged him there days after the recent reopening, to check out what she'd called an attempted fusion of art deco style and functional multi-cinema layout. He'd yawned through some Vietnamese movie.

He nodded. "Women."

"Where is this market place again, Mick?" Jim said.

No reply. Peter turned to look into the back seat, at the stubborn ox's travesty of a bandaged face. Mick didn't seem to have heard Jim. Had the painkillers worn off?

"Mick," Peter said, "you need rest and recuperation. Use your noggin for once. Probability says he's already overseas, interstate, anywhere but here."

This trip—they'd checked the newspapers, Camberwell was the only one of the three suburbs holding a swap meet today—was nothing but a quixotic waste of time. Why would Skellern risk his neck to extract revenge? Peter's only contribution to the case had been an application of logic; he possessed no evidence or testimony that could harm the killer. The battle now joined was police versus criminal, exit Tusk & Gentle from scene.

Right now, all Peter desired was the haven of his apartment. A bath perhaps, then an hour or two, or even three, cogitating over the fate of Italy. He could join a second Diplomacy game, take on a fresh puzzle.

"Fuck probability," Mick said through clenched teeth.

"Yes, well," said Peter. "Typical."

It seemed everyone had mocked his principles at one point or another. But they worked, didn't they? Who else could have mentally juggled all that data, let alone combed through the permutations to find the connections? He pictured Gus' smile. Who else, eh Gus?

The Rover cruised across the Junction.

"You know, maybe Brad had a point," Jim said. "He kept saying that scale is the most critical variable for TPT. Me, I'm cautious, don't like aggressive gearing. But maybe now… Did I tell you? He's coming into the office tomorrow."

"Funder?" Peter said.

"Yes. When he read about Adam's arrest, he rang Fi, volunteered to hire a temp bookkeeper and train him up. He sounded so repentant, Fi said yes."

Mick grunted. "There."

Two hundred meters past the Junction, along Camberwell Road, a banner proclaimed "Computer Swap Meet." The Camberwell Hall of Commerce sat on a slope behind well-watered lawns and flowerbeds. The stench of freshly applied chicken manure swamped the air.

The three of them joined a queue and Jim paid their entry fees. Mick's limp had become pronounced.

"Maniac," Peter whispered.

"Get stuffed."

When they reached the high-ceilinged central hall, Peter's mood lifted. Dozens of tables, stacked with every known computer component or accessory, were arranged in tight snaking aisles over blue carpet. Peter registered CPU boxes, monitors, computer speakers, hard drives, video cards, rolls of cabling, DVDs of pop stars. The place even smelled of computers, that faint aroma redolent of wire and paper. Behind the stands, yawning or gesturing at prices punched into calculators, stood the vendors, many Asians but also Indians and Anglos. Techo shoppers, mainly men, milled patiently, their purchases loaded in thin white plastic bags. Everyone carried bottles of water or cans of soft drink. Peter saw dozens of sunglasses and baseball caps.

Jim's arms pumped as he led the way through the warren of aisles.

"You know," Peter said over his shoulder to Mick. "Maybe it's time you left the Stone Age and bought a computer."

A man in a cowboy hat was negotiating with a bored-looking Chinese woman behind a sea of componentry wrapped in tough plastic.

"How much for the Ricoh?" the man asked.

"Ricoh? $200."

No reply from Mick. Peter turned. The hospital escapee was nowhere to be seen in the crush.

"Hey, look out," said someone in a French accent.

Jim was fanning himself by a stall of empty computer cases, twin-tone winged affairs stacked eight feet high.

"Have you seen Mick?" Peter asked. He caught the faint sweet scent of laser printer toner.

"That's all I need." Jim's effervescence had deserted him.

Shit, Peter thought. He looked over Jim's shoulder, and that was when he spotted Eric Skellern, behind a table up on the stage, handing over a package.

"Jim, Jim," he said, pointing.

Jim looked toward the stage. His face bloomed with florid rage. Before Peter could react, Jim shook his fist into the air.

"You!" he shouted.

Heads turned. Silence descended around them.

Eric Skellern had heard. He looked in their direction. Even a hundred meters away, Peter could see, no, he could feel, the amused smile. Where was Mick?

"Stop that man," roared Jim. "He killed Gus!"

A white-faced man clutching a boy shrank away from Jim. A Chinese vendor was frantically dialing his mobile.

Up on the stage, Skellern seemed to have all the time in the world. His eyes met Peter's. Languidly, he saluted. Then he vanished from view.

"Come on," Peter shouted.

He barged through the crowd, desperately seeking some speed. His hand caught on a table corner, sending drives flying. He heard breath expel, someone stumbling behind him. Warned by the racket, people parted before him. But by the time he sprinted up the steps to the stage area, Skellern's stall—three tables stacked high with monitors, motherboards, and second-hand laptops, all bearing "Closing Down Sale" signs—was well and truly abandoned.

CHAPTER 51

The sound of running footsteps.

Instant recognition. Mick Tusk had never heard them before, but he knew the light, alert patter of these feet.

Blessed sunshine, by the stallholders' exit into the parking lot. His focus mantra now useless, he'd hung on by shifting foot to foot while constructing Top 20s.

Timing was everything.

Tusk stepped out into the doorway just as Skellern reached it.

Insufficient allowance for echo…

Skellern hit him hard in the chest. Tusk coughed. Pain from hip. Pain in nose.

Skellern fell back, righted himself. "Excuse me—"

A song for every moment: The Eurythmics' "Sweet Dreams Are Made of This." The look on Skellern's face!

A quicker recovery Tusk had never seen. Skellern skipped back.

"Yeah, yeah," Tusk said.

The mild eyes studied him for all of one second. Then

Skellern feinted to Tusk's right and plunged through the gap on his injured left side.

For the first time in this entire ball-breaking case, Tusk made the call.

He launched.

Not to his right.

To his left.

He slammed into the sack of shit. Agony! His bellowing, free-falling body mashed Skellern onto the concrete.

CHAPTER 52

"From Mandy with love," Peter Gentle read aloud.

He smiled. He was naked. He watched his cock stir in the full-length mirror. The right hip, although still tender, had traded black-and-blue for a more benign yellow-green. Red grazes covered his knees. But apart from these and his friendly head lump, that was it, folks. He was whole. A trifle out of condition, he had to admit, but whole.

Whole, but was he happy?

"You bet I am," he said, although in truth what he felt was more akin to relief than exhilaration.

He reread the spidery handwriting on the orange wrapper—she hated cards, Mandy did—of the bath bomb. A Christmas present. Hope it hasn't decayed, he thought.

The sizzling bath bomb functioned perfectly, foaming up the water, filling his bathroom with the smell of apricots. He lay in the scalding water.

In the end, he'd rung Dana himself, three hours ago, to ask her to come pick Mick up from the Police Complex. Mick kept insisting he'd catch a train. By that time the maniac was a stretcher candidate, but neither Peter nor Deirdre dared suggest he return to the hospital.

"This case will make us, big guy." Peter's voice boomed in the steaming bathroom.

Would Mick stay on as the other half of Tusk & Gentle? Not likely, if Dana's furious words were any guide.

Bubbles tickling his nose, Peter mentally assembled the case—he should accord it a name, maybe Day Trader Rampage—for the last time. A mandatory step, this.

The data—event by event, hour by hour, person by person— he already held exhaustively cataloged in his cranium.

Painstakingly he carried out the analysis, teased all the strands together. What were the critical factors? He stuck fingers into the air. One, access to names and email addresses since last August. Two, hacking ability. Three, investment knowledge. Four, a personal connection to Gus. Five, motive. Six, lack of alibi, call it opportunity.

The conclusions?

"Eric Skellern," he said in a mock judge's voice. "Also known as David O'Shaughnessy, thou art found guilty of being the only logical possibility."

But it was no laughing matter. He pictured Gus lying in the kitchen, Edith twisting her handkerchief, Belinda sobbing amidst the crack of shots at the shooting range.

He wondered whether Deirdre would wait for Inspector Conomy to return from Sydney before interrogating Eric Skellern. The quicker the better. Because one issue still niggled, something Conomy had said when they first met. Why, oh why, did Skellern shoot Gus, run out the back gate, circle the block, and then ambush Peter on his exit?

By the time he stepped out of the bath, the water was cool and the bubbles had dissolved into a scummy surface film. The undersides of his feet were wrinkly.

His mental roundup done, Peter felt light and free. On his way home, he'd indulged in a haircut and bought a white silk shirt. He dressed, brushed his hair until his scalp complained, then spent an hour rushing around the apartment, tidying, dusting, filing.

When the intercom sounded, his pulse raced.

"Hello?" he said.

The voice over the crackling intercom was hesitant. "Am I early?"

"Hours," he cried.

He released the lobby door and paced. As soon as the doorbell chimed, he flung the door open.

"Ta-da!"

Data: a shiny silver dress that hinted rather than revealed; black shoes; hair lustrous and swept back over the ears; that signature scent, from Body Shop, he recalled; red lipstick; a smile, though not *that* smile; quizzical eyes. Analysis: none needed. Conclusion?

"My, it is clean," Mandy said. She pecked him on a cheek on the way past. "Haven't you been home?"

"Actually, no." So this is heaven, he thought.

"Who is she?"

"Not she." Peter poured a champagne and offered it to her. "They."

"No thanks," she said. "Should I worry about them?"

Annoyance stabbed Peter; he'd made a special trip to Nick's in Swanston Street for the champagne. But if this case had taught him one thing, it was to hold on to opportunities.

"A taxi driver and a fifty-year-old movie buff," he said. "Look, I'm sorry you got involved with the Dana business. You liked her."

"I still do." She was assessing him, as if waiting for something. "I rang her this morning. She said she agrees with everything I said."

"No. Can't be."

"Oh, yes. She's not nearly as anti-you as you think. Peter, she gets worried. Can't you understand that?"

Peter gulped from the glass he'd poured Mandy. "Sure, sure, of course she does. Kids and all that. But Mick's got to have a life."

"A life like yours?" Mandy came up close. She gripped his arms. "Can't you see?"

See what? Peter longed to hold her face, to kiss her. His cheeks burned.

The doorbell pealed again.

Shit, he thought, it must be Topper. His next-door neighbor had borrowed his CD-burner a week ago.

Instead of Topper, Harvey and Unforgiven burst in. Unforgiven's collarless black jacket looked new. Harvey, hefting three black pizza carry bags, had dressed down, into jeans and a bright red jacket. A gold chain hung around his neck.

The apartment filled with a complex aroma of pizza, herbs, and seafood.

"How did you get in?" Peter asked.

Unforgiven cracked his knuckles. "The temptation proved too great."

"These pizzas are damned heavy," Harvey said. His bright eyes told Peter he'd already begun drinking.

Peter grinned. Of course the idea had been Harvey's, that Unforgiven use the Draconi's kitchen to bake "Super Sleuth" pizzas to a secret gourmet recipe. Carlo was to join them as well.

"Good evening, boss," Mandy called. She was looking through the bookcase, where Peter had strategically placed his unread Angela's Ashes, recommended by her.

"Fetch my whip, slave," Harvey said. He headed to the computer table, where the bottle and glasses awaited, and set down the pizza boxes.

Unforgiven asked, "Is Mick all right?"

Peter recalled Mick's grim departing smile, his words: "We fuckin' showed 'em."

"He's home," Peter said. "We'll ring him later."

"Ring?" Harvey lifted his champagne glass by the stem. "I'm calling a special meeting of the Skulk Club, just to raise money for his nose job."

Peter laughed. "Let's drink to Mick."

Their glasses clinked.

"You and your boys' club," Mandy said, but she was also laughing.

"Vernon," Harvey said. "I must get you a membership form. One of our guiding principles is to have a spread of occupations. Luckily we don't have a hacker yet."

Unforgiven looked uncertain. He removed the pizzas from the insulated bags. Steam rose from the inner cardboard boxes.

337

"I've hung up my hack belt."

"A minor detail," Harvey said. "The chef slot is also free. Look, there's one question I've been dying to ask. Where did that amazing nickname come from?"

Unforgiven gazed at the computer. "Remember Clint Eastwood? I loved that movie. Also, it aptly reflected my relationship with family, at least until Granddad took me in. These pizzas absolutely must be eaten hot."

Peter picked up the pizza boxes. They were heavy. "Grab a champagne, U."

The phone rang, his father no doubt. Peter balanced the three pizza boxes on his right arm, lifted the receiver with his left hand.

"Tusk & Gentle, Private Investigators," he said pompously.

"I thought you'd like to know." Senior Constable Lasker.

"Private?" Harvey said. "Who's the biggest gossip around?"

Peter waved for silence. "Know what?"

"I can't raise Mick," Deirdre said. "You can inform him."

"Mandy, meet Vernon," Harvey was saying.

"O'Shaughnessy finally cracked." Deirdre's voice was flat. "You were correct, it's a false name and he is from Sydney. But his real name is David Smith and he flitted after robbing his parents of Lotto winnings. Back to square one, Peter."

The pizza boxes slid from Peter's grip and crashed onto the champagne flutes. Glass shattered. A lid flew open and pizza slapped onto the carpet.

CHAPTER 53

Ah, heavenly pizza. Lashings of sausage and salami. Mick Tusk savored the fat-laden, body-destroying concoction.

Sunday night at La Bambina, the perfect family restaurant. Cheap, filling, a touch of class. Noisy, the nice noisy of a Draconi's.

No music inside him tonight, he wished he knew why. He'd put on a Springsteen earlier, had whipped it off right away.

"Daddy, you've got cheese hanging down your chin," Yolanda said.

Bouncing in his high chair, Nelson giggled. "Daddy got cheese, daddy got cheese." All evening he'd stared at Tusk's bandages.

"Have I, sweetie?" Tusk dragged Yolanda close. "Well, guess what. I like a cheesy chin."

Nelson grabbed a hunk of his pineapple-covered pizza and stuffed it into his mouth, letting it drape down over his lip.

"Oh, Mikey, stop teaching them bad habits," Dana said. But she was smiling.

Thank Christ for that, Tusk thought. He scraped strands of

cheese from his chin. He'd crashed to sleep on the drive home from the Complex, had napped on and off all afternoon, and in between had avoided Dana. She herself had been reserved. A good sign, he reckoned. Maybe, just maybe, she'd spent the anger and guilt he knew she was feeling.

A healthy body's a fast-healing body, he thought. For he was on the mend already, hardly felt the snout. Dana had insisted they make an appointment at the local clinic. The quack had freaked but eventually prescribed pills to be ignored.

A curse, this clamp across his mouth whenever he'd tried to talk to Dana, to deliver the spiel rehearsed during every waking moment: I'm okay. Yeah, it's not pretty but no real damage done. I enjoyed it, Dana. Felt alive. I was doing what I know best, making the world safe for Yolanda and Nelson. Not the peaceful life you long for, Dana, but it's peace to me. Tell me, what are we going to do?

What was Gentle up to tonight? Too much to hope that he'd rung Mandy, was taking her out, planned a healthy screw to patch up. Such a pity, Tusk hadn't even said a proper goodbye. Tusk & Gentle, he wanted to say, A-plus for effort, A-plus for result, let's do it again.

And Tusk was going to reward himself for A-plus. Coming out any day now, the amazing new retrospective box set *Songs of Yesterday*, covering the entire career of Free—Paul Rodgers' demos, a live version of "All Right Now"—he deserved it.

When Tusk ordered gelatos all around, Nelson clapped his hands.

"Bang your nose more often, Daddy," Yolanda said.

Dana chuckled. Tusk melted at the sight.

He took her hand while they stood at the counter to pay. Stroked her palm with a hidden finger. Her grip tightened. No limp, he promised himself.

Stars in the sky, winter in the air. Time check: 7:10.

"I'll drive," he said.

"You sure?" Dana said.

He did a U-turn and cruised around the bends of the Belgrave strip. After the soulless city, this sheer ordinariness thrilled him. He imagined the early walk—no running for another few days—tomorrow morning, in the peace and darkness, through dewy grass and a sea of yellow leaves, under rustling trees. With Bully, if the dog recovered from his fright at the bandages.

"This is the way to Katie's place," Yolanda said.

"Mikey, what are you doing?" Dana said.

Nelson said, "Mummy, Yolanda kicked me."

Tusk pulled up outside the rotting veggie patch.

"Guided By Voices," he said. He held up a CD. "Remember? I said I'd loan it to him."

"She wasn't at school on Friday," Yolanda said.

Tusk felt his heart drum a tattoo of uncertainty. But he hadn't expected Dana to jump from the car and unbuckle the children.

"Hey," he said. "I'll only be a minute."

"I don't want to," Yolanda said.

Dana's face warned Tusk not to argue, to hurry up the path fringed by ankle-high weeds. No SUV in the driveway, just the convertible, a kid's red rubber boot propped against a wheel.

The house was dark. No music, no sounds at all. The sound of his knock carried in the still air.

"They're not home," Dana said.

"Not ho," pipped Nelson.

The door opened a chink.

"Yeah." A sullen voice Tusk almost didn't recognize. A stink from inside.

"Gil," he said, a bright voice. "I've brought you that GBV, mate."

The door half-opened and Oldfield took a step out. Tusk heard Dana gasp. The same T-shirt, the same jeans, no shoes, no socks, a face ten meals lighter. Eyes from Mars.

"Never asked for any GB-whatsit, pal," Oldfield said.

Yolanda had backed away.

Tusk sighed, one of those sighs. What was the idea of coming here anyway? That he could say there was some evil behind Maguire, not just capricious madness? That evil had been vanquished?

Oldfield snatched the CD out of his fingers. "Thanks." He turned to shuffle indoors.

Tusk recalled Edith Maguire, her soft voice drawing courage from Christ knows where. Your wife and daughter might have left you, he wanted to say to the wreckage of Mr. Gilbert Oldfield, but Edith lost a lot more and she's battling on.

Instead he asked, "Been a good boy, Gil?"

Oldfield's shoulders shook.

Nelson said, "Mummy, why that man crying?"

Imagery careened in Tusk's mind. He grabbed Oldfield by a shoulder. No weight to him at all. Tusk spun him around. The CD clattered onto the porch.

Dana had her arms around his waist, pulling. "Mikey, Mikey."

Nelson wailed. Yolanda was running for the car. Tusk experienced all the conflicting, unresolved emotions—fury, pity, confusion, dread—that had sucked him into this whole thing.

"Go on," sobbed Oldfield. "Finish it!"

Tusk felt Guided By Voices underfoot, the crunch of splintering plastic drowned out by a sound swelling in his head. Guitars, guitars ascending heavenward, the sublime Page solo on "Stairway To Heaven." The most popular song ever and why not? Everybody longs to make a journey to heaven, Tusk thought, but what's my journey?

He released Oldfield.

Dana held on to him all the way to the Peugeot.

He knew precisely what was unsaid. Tusk: he'd have deserved it. Dana: look what your parasite friend has done to you.

But no one spoke a word on the short trip home. That fact kindled a smile inside him, a smile he offered with his kiss, after the kids were tucked in. Dana didn't smile back but her body spoke.

And his nose? Didn't ache one bit.

CHAPTER 54

Time for a constitutional, suggested Peter Gentle's dazed brain. Distracted into a zombie zone, he wandered from his apartment up to Parliament House. Clouds drifted to block the sun. He sat on the steps and watched a tour group in action. A pit of hopelessness gaped before him.

Last night Mandy had ushered the others out as soon as he broke the news. Unforgiven's Super Sleuth pizzas were unsalvageable. After another peck on the cheek, Mandy left also. All night long Peter lay on his bed or paced. No amount of analysis moved him any closer to a solution. If only Mick had been contactable...

The Monday morning commuters were no longer on the streets. His head throbbed. He found himself meandering down Spring Street. The Collins Street news kiosk, with its chocolate bars, beckoned. He fished in his pocket for change. The TPT banner fluttered fifty meters away.

He caught sight of *The Age's* headline. His heartbeat zoomed.

"Billion Dollar Share Losses Feared Today."

Of course! The two insights that flooded him seemed to gush from heaven.

"Everything starts and ends at TPT," he said. His eyes widened at the possibilities.

"You talkin' to me?" the kiosk man said.

"Everything starts and ends at TPT. And Maguire is the key."

"Tell it to the shrink, buddy."

What time was it? Peter's watch showed 10:20. Curses, he thought, trading has begun.

Cars honked as he sprinted across Collins Street.

"Come on, come on." He bit his nails, watched the elevator slowly descend from the top floor.

In the elevator, he breathed deeply, patted his hair. The silk shirt suddenly felt anomalous. On the second floor, Robyn sat at the reception desk, transfixed by her screen.

"Is Finola in?" Peter asked.

She nodded without turning her head.

As soon as Peter stepped into the trading room, he knew something was terribly awry. A panicky clamor filled the air, a medley of shouting and swearing and wailing. Fries and cups littered the aisle. Both television screens were off. One of Jim's garden bins lay on its side.

The PA was amped up, almost unbearably loud. Murray's voice shrilled: "Another 10, index at 2932."

Peter's scalp crawled. 2,932! The market was down five percent in half an hour.

"Meltdown," he breathed.

Murray: "Sausage Software $3.06, 31% down."

Jim's office was empty. Donut scraps lay scattered across the floor, orange icing was stuck to the whiteboard.

Peter could hear sobbing. He ran down the aisle, saw Saul

Phillips smash a fist onto his keyboard. A red-faced trader rushed past, clutching his stomach.

Around the corner, a small crowd was gathered around Gus' desk, fixated on the screen.

"God, God," Jim was saying.

This was a Jim Van Kressel Peter had never seen. The TPT founder's eyes were frantic, dangerously mottled cheeks sagged around his gaping mouth.

Next to him Finola hugged herself. Oleg, his mouth a circle of horror, clutched sweat-slicked pink hair. Only Irene, dressed in pastel blue, seemed calm.

"Jim, Jim, please," Peter said. He spotted Brad Funder waving from his office.

"God, another point," Jim said. "We're ruined."

"Shitting, shitting, shitting," raved Oleg.

"Jim, dear," Irene said. "Remember, there's no such thing as a bad trading day."

Chest heaving, Jim roared, "Get out of here, you loon!" He noticed Peter. "You see it? See it, Pete? It's the end."

Finola's voice was lifeless. "It was the end a long time ago."

"How dare you, Jim?" Irene said.

"Jim." Peter grabbed the chief executive's arm before he could turn back to the screen. He smelled Jim's reek. "I got it all wrong, Jim. If only I'd—"

A cry startled him into releasing Jim. He recoiled in horror.

A tall figure behind Finola gripped her tightly around the neck. A gray gun rested against her forehead. Finola struggled ineffectually.

"Robyn, what on earth are you doing?" Jim cried.

"Stay back." Robyn's voice had deepened, turned harsh. "If anyone moves, I'll shoot. Don't think I won't."

Ever since he'd realized, Peter had wondered why no one had noticed the obvious. He took in Robyn's well-defined thighs, the tight muscles around her shoulders.

"Are you mad, Robyn?" Jim said. "Put that thing down."

"Keep away."

Jim stepped forward. Robyn swiftly took aim and fired. Peter heard the muted shot—phut!—and his heart skipped a beat.

Jim fell. Cursing and moaning, he curled up against a leg of Gus' desk.

Irene gasped once, then collapsed like a pricked balloon. Her head struck the side of Adam's desk with a crack.

Robyn looked directly at Peter. "Oh, I wondered if you'd figure it out. Don't move now."

Finola whimpered. Robyn viciously pressed the gun into the side of her head. "Oh, Van, if only you knew what I've been through."

Finola turned rigid.

Robyn began to speak fast. "Becoming a woman, a real woman, can you even imagine how hard it was, with a shit for a father and no mother." The voice veered in and out of a mad whisper. "Where were you, Van, where were you during all those years of hell, oh my mother? Let me tell you, Van, where you were. You ran away, you abandoned me." Tears ran down her cheeks. "So tell me, Van, what should I do with you? Love you? Or kill you?"

"Eric?" Finola twisted, trying to see the face behind her. She cried out when Robyn wrenched her head back.

Peter trembled. He struggled to control himself, to stay still.

He could see the very tip of Funder's head above his desk. The accountant had to be on the ground, had to be ringing the police. Too late, Peter knew. Irene lay buckled and unmoving. Muttering with pain, Jim stirred on the carpet. Oleg was a pink-and-white mannequin.

"Every time you walked past me, Van," Robyn said, rubbing her face against Finola's ear, "I was dying to confront you. Can you imagine the pressure? Day after day, month after month. But I never could. Not bloody once. You know why, Van? Just that question: love or hate? Why couldn't I decide?"

Peter took a risk. "Those tally marks."

Robyn stared at Peter. Her face was twisted. "Oh, you smart bastard." She kissed Finola's cheek and resumed her litany. "Every time I had you alone, every time my nerve failed me, I kept count. Van, Van, do you know what those rows of marks felt like? Like lashes, lashes on my back."

Finola croaked, "But Maguire."

"I've been a hacker for years." Peter could see foam nestled in the corners of Robyn's mouth. "That's what outcasts become these days. All I wanted was to hurt you a bit. How was I to know Maguire would…"

"But Gus?" Finola said.

Peter heard Oleg gasp. Fortunately, Robyn didn't notice. For, incredibly, behind the interlocked heads of captor and captive, Peter saw Camilla inching forward. The computer room, he thought.

He forced his eyes back to Robyn, desperate not to give Camilla away. Would Oleg do the same? Mick, where are you, he cried mentally.

"During the massacre, down there, in that room, I said something." Robyn's voice shook. "Last week, Gus, he came calling at my flat, said this hacking thing had reminded him. Said I needed to do the honest thing. You'd know honest, wouldn't you, Van? I didn't even open my door, just followed him and… I mean, I couldn't just stop then." She stroked Finola's wet cheek with the gun muzzle. "This is what I've been dreaming about since the day you left. Oh, Van, time to decide, don't you think?"

Camilla's raised hand held something slim and metallic, a modem perhaps. She brought it down onto Robyn's head with a thud. Robyn jerked. Another phut!

Finola screamed and pitched forward, smack into Peter.

Peter heaved Finola out of his way but overbalanced and landed hard across Adam's desk. His arm knocked the monitor off which landed with a crash.

He looked up at a terrible sight. Blood streamed down the left side of Robyn's head. Her face was ablaze in a rictus of fury. With her right hand she pressed Camilla's squirming head onto the surface of Gus' desk. Camilla screamed. Robyn's left hand, waving the gun, was held aloft by the two clutching hands of Oleg.

Oleg grunted and strained.

Robyn was stronger. She wrenched free of Oleg and turned toward Camilla.

Peter's hand felt a hard, irregular, slick object. He leaped with it. Screeching, he rammed Adam's streaky-gray rock against Robyn's forehead.

"Oof!" Robyn—Eric—dropped.

***

During the chaos that ensued, amidst interviews with uniforms while the second floor emptied out, Peter held three final memorable conversations with TPT-ers.

Jim Van Kressel, his arm bandaged, lay on a stretcher. His face was wan. "Brad tells me the market's still in free fall. The bubble's burst. I've asked him to pay you before the vultures arrive."

"Vultures?" Peter said.

"You did such sterling work, Pete. All for nothing." Jim drew a deep sigh. "I gave Crazy Oleg a whopping margin on Saturday."

Peter thought, so that's why Oleg came in.

Oleg had left an hour ago; he'd raised a hand in farewell to Peter. Camilla, sobbing hysterically, her face bruised and scratched, had gone even earlier. Irene had come to, had been taken to the hospital with a suspected concussion.

Jim continued. "He's wiped himself out so many times over. He knew it, I knew it, in the first ten minutes." He smiled, the indefatigable Jim smile. "Oh, we could survive the crash, even cover Oleg's losses somehow. But another shooting on the premises… day trading is dead in Melbourne now."

Peter had the shakes. "Come on, Jim, the public always forgets."

Jim grabbed Peter's hand. The cold fingers squeezed. "C'est la vie. I always wanted to lose a fortune, did you know that, Pete? It's called having a go." He turned to shout at the paramedic. "Where's Alison? She said she'd come with me."

The swansong from Finola Vines proved briefer. She was lucky, her son's shots had missed altogether, although she was temporarily deaf in her right ear.

"I should have recognized him." Her mouth hung open, the effect of sedation. "My little boy."

Peter sighed.

"All of it," she said. "All of it, all that struggle to build a new life, it's all been a waste."

Peter said, "What would Van Morrison say?"

A tiny light sparked in her eyes. "Who cares?"

But as Senior Constable Lasker escorted her away, she turned and cried, "He'd say make a brand new start."

The third farewell took place when Peter finally broke free of Tech Power Trading. He felt ill. Phone calls—Mandy, Mick, Harvey—beckoned. At the elevator, Funder raced up, check in hand.

One look at the amount and Peter's mood picked up.

"Jim insisted," the accountant said.

"Hallelujah," Peter said. "This is what it's all about."

Brad's smile, the first Peter had seen, was a revelation. "You don't believe that."

CHAPTER 55

Trust King Kong to draw stares. As soon as Peter Gentle entered the ground floor bar of the Continental Cafe, he saw that the entire packed crowd kept glancing at the distinct figure of his sometime partner.

Peter was late. 8:45, Mick had said, "Come savor Melbourne's best music venue." But Peter got lost in the maze of Prahran streets behind Chapel Street, so he didn't reach funky Greville Street until almost nine.

Mick's freshly shorn hair shone in the muted light. The nose bandage had slimmed down into an efficient beak held in place by a couple of strips. He wore a black T-shirt with words Peter couldn't decipher, his trusty boots, and what had to be a brand new lime-green jacket. He sat erect, chest bashing against the world, clutching a half-full beer glass.

"Genius," Mick shouted. "What happened to the hair?"

"Annual cut, Mick, annual cut."

Peter felt so, so glad to see Mick. Over the week since the infamous Monday, they'd spoken daily on the phone, but events—the aftermath of the Day Trader Rampage case, Mick's broken nose, an urgent surveillance job for Peter—had kept them apart.

Both of them had been pursued by reporters. The media slobbered over the story, equating spree killer with transsexual killer with day trading. Jim Van Kressel had been correct—the scandal was too much for onsite day trading.

In any case, the sharemarket had killed TPT for good. The All Ords had recovered five percent, but Harvey kept warning Peter against what he called the "dead cat bounce," and tech stocks were still way down. The Skulkers were all telling Peter that investment money was fleeing from the "virtual rubbish," as Paddy O'Loughlin put it, into safe havens. The New EConomy of clicks was after all the Old Economy of bricks. The Dot-Com Boom was now the Tech Wreck.

Peter ordered a glass of Pinot. "How's the nose?"

What an awful place, he thought, too loud, not friendly-loud like Draconi's but intrusive. God-awful music boomed from the floor above. His stool was too small and the bar stank of smoke.

"What nose?" Mick said. "Dee tells me they're having trouble getting Finola Vines to the committal hearing. She flew to Port Douglas last Tuesday, refuses contact. Hubby followed, she gave him the finger. They'll have to subpoena her."

"Running again," Peter said. "When will the hearing be?"

"Not sure yet."

Peter thought he might attend the trial. The more he pondered, the more he found Eric Skellern interesting, maybe even tragic. A sexually mixed-up teenager when he ran away from home at age seventeen, he turned tricks as a transvestite in Kings Cross until he met transsexual Rachel. Rachel picked him up

ANDRES KABEL

from the gutter and mentored him to undergo sex reassignment surgery, a lengthy and costly process. Emerging as Robyn Fox in 1998, he/she came to Melbourne looking for mother. She found Finola and a job ad for a TPT receptionist…

Peter said, "We'll have to testify at the trials of Adam and Smith-cum-O'Shaughnessy."

"My pleasure. Hey, have you heard? U popped into our place yesterday. Dropped off this reject computer he's giving us. He's been approached by Papa Van Kressel, starting up some kind of computer security company."

Peter had heard as much from Jim, indeed Jim had offered him a job. Anti-hacking was the next big thing, according to Jim. The millionaire had already filed to liquidate TPT. Apparently the office had sat empty ever since Skellern's arrest, and Brad Funder was sorting out the financial mess.

"What was U's reaction?" he said.

"Told him to get nicked. Cooking's his bag, it seems."

Peter had visited Irene Skews, still suffering from dizzy spells, in Epworth Hospital. Irene had told him that Camilla, who'd taken in Irene's cats, was in financial trouble. Peter knew he probably owed Camilla his life, but as yet he'd shrunk from contacting her.

"Jim tells me Crazy Oleg will have to file for bankruptcy."

"You're way behind the eight ball, Gentle. I got Oleg started driving for my Uncle Mart. Last night. Thank Christ he didn't crash."

Peter was incredulous. "Oleg, driving cabs? But I thought you were going to get that job back."

Mick waved to the bartender. "A red? No, no, I'm buying. Tell me again about Oldfield."

"He was sitting on a fortune of shares but refused to sell them." Peter had been amazed when Mick informed him Gil Oldfield was a neighbor. "Most of them are just penny stocks now, barely worth anything."

"Unbelievable." Mick shook his head.

"I went out again with Mandy last night," Peter said.

Mick grabbed his arm. "And?"

"Good." Peter grinned. "Great, actually. I'm going to change my whole approach to life."

"Yeah, yeah." Mick laughed. "And you're sticking with this caper? Putting up with murder, bashings, stress, fear?"

"That's what Mandy asked. You know, I actually really enjoyed this case."

"Enjoyed?" Mick's expression was blank. "Faulty analysis, I reckon, to reach that conclusion."

"Justice is a worthwhile outcome, isn't it, big guy?"

"Maybe. I was a hundred percent sure at one time. And I must still believe it, 'coz I got you here to tell you something." Mick sculled his beer. "No more cabs for me, genius. It's Tusk & Gentle. Full-time. Teach you how to make real money."

Peter was thunderstruck. "Come again?"

"You got wax in your ears?"

Confused, Peter raised his glass in salute. "Magnificent. What about Dana?"

"As they say in the home loan ads, terms and conditions apply. I got lucky, received a check in the mail from Funder. You know, sometimes I wonder what keeps this marriage alive."

"You've got to be joking. I've never met two people more in love."

"It's me. Half the time I'm like a guitarist without his guitar. Lost."
Peter was seized by emotion.

Mick glanced at his watch. "Time to celebrate."

The walls of the Continental Cafe's stairs were papered with concert posters, some going back years. A waiter showed them to their tiny table next to the stage. Almost immediately crimson velvet curtains drew open.

Peter fingered the indistinct remnant of his head lump. He was filled with wild joy. The infinite vista of the future stretched before him.

But honestly, he thought, why couldn't Mick have told me over a quiet meal by the sea?

"Is the food any good?" he said.

"Food? Bloody hell. We're here for the music."

"Speak for yourself."

A short-haired man with a screen-handsome face, dressed in black pants and a sleek black-and-white shirt, strode onto stage. He talked agitatedly with his guitarist. Deafening cheers went up around Peter.

"Who the heck is James Reyne?" he asked.

"Where have you been? Lead singer for Australian Crawl. Remember?"

Peter's memory clicked when James Reyne began to sing, eyes shut and teeth bared, a harsh, indecipherable voice over a clashing riff. "The Boys Light Up"—the hit Peter had hated in his teens.

"Isn't he amazing?" Mick's smile almost compensated for the music.

My kingdom for earplugs, Peter thought.

Mick's head bobbed. "Fucking boomer, eh?"

MEET THE AUTHOR

Hi,

Andres Kabel here, hoping you enjoyed *Deadly Day Trading*, the second in the mystery series set in the wonderful Australian city of Melbourne, the metropolis in which Peter Gentle cogitates and Mick Tusk roams. I'm 63 years old and in a rush to write more installments in this series, as well as a substantive history. Find out more about me on my website.

Most importantly, you probably know that indie authors easily drown in the vast sea of ebooks and print books. Do me a favor and help me get noticed, could you please? Hop on your ebook retailer's website and leave a review. An honest rating and a few words will suffice. Do this even if *Deadly Day Trading* failed to meet your high standards.

Secondly, stay in touch by leaving your email address for my occasional newsletter. I won't spam you and I'll respect your privacy.

There's more to me than Melbourne crime fiction. I write history! I blog! Come see:

AndresKabel.com

Big Decade - my blog of a decade of aspirational obsessing.

Nuclear Power History - my blog of offcut snippets from my forthcoming history book.

Facebook (also on Facebook—Big Decade and Nuclear Power History).

Lastly, don't hesitate to drop me a line on Andres@AndresKabel.com.

MY THANKS

Over three quarters of this book passed through the tough-love mincer of the Inner City Writers critique group. A debt owed: Fiona Skepper, Rachel Martin, Jock Read-Hill, Jack Cassidy, Marina Dobbyn, Siobhan Argent, Eddie Brauer, Ruhi Yaman.

The next-to-last input of my beta readers group added improvements, and spotted bloopers and prose clunkers. A pasta night out: Marcus Foster, Pasquale Mammone, Margaret Bennett, Sharon Boffa, Pam Kabel, Frank Kennedy.

Quite why I've been fortunate enough to have such steadfast family supporters, I don't know. Gratitude: Donna and Pete, Daniel and Meg, and Ashley and Katie. Special hugs to Harry and Rosanna, both of whom don't know about writing yet but already love books.

Image for Pam: fist thumping heart.

www.ingramcontent.com/pod-product-compliance
Lightning Source LLC
Chambersburg PA
CBHW030347120726
47901CB00007B/1948

* 9 7 8 0 6 4 8 3 0 6 8 3 2 *